BLUE VOYAGE

BLUE VOYAGE

By
CONRAD AIKEN

AUTHOR OF "PUNCH: THE IMMORTAL LIAR,"
"PRIAPUS AND THE POOL," ETC.

NEW YORK
CHARLES SCRIBNER'S SONS
1927

TO
C. M. L.

E coelo descendit γνῶθι σεαυτὸν.

> Juvenal XI, 27.

What is there in thee, Man, that can be known?
Dark fluxion, all unfixable by thought,
A phantom dim of past and future wrought,
Vain sister of the worm——

> COLERIDGE: *Self-Knowledge.*

BLUE VOYAGE

I

'WILL you stop,' said William Demarest, leaning his head out of the taxi window, 'at that corner drug store?' Just like a cuckoo-clock, he thought.

It had suddenly occurred to him that he had forgotten his sea-sick pills—the little pink and green box was indispensable—oh, absolutely! A charm against sea-serpents. As he stood on the marble floor, amid the thousand bottles and vials and jars, in a heavy smell of soap and disinfectant, watching the clerk wrap up and seal the box, the sound of the approaching voyage came loudly about him. Waves crashing against black port-holes at midnight. Bugles blowing in sour corridors—red-carpeted corridors which suddenly, unaccountably, became hills to climb. O God, what a prospect! And the ship—what was the ship? A congregation of gigantic mushroom-like ventilators, red-throated, all belching a smell of hot oil and degenerate soup, with sounds of faint submarine clankings. Among them, a few pale stewards, faces like cauliflowers, carrying gladstone bags and hot-water bottles . . . He suddenly felt queasy. This would never do: it was all a matter of nerves. Day by day, and with every wave, the sea gets smoother and smoother. It might, in fact, be a regular yachting cruise—blue sky, blue sea, sunny decks, and a beautiful,

mysterious young lady to talk to. Why not? It
had happened before. 'Thanks!' he said . . .

In the taxi, as they passed through Twenty-third
Street, he lost fifteen years of his life, no less, and
caught sight of himself (a very pale, sober-looking
young man) mounting the stone steps of No. 421.
The shy young widow was sitting in the garden
watching her child. How had she managed to conceal so long from him, in their meetings in hall or on
stairs, that she had only one hand? . . . And
Stedman, the literary hack, came in at lunch-time
to say, 'Willst hog it with me over the way?'—his
reference being to the free lunch at the saloon
across the street. And the bed-bugs! Stedman
had left on his desk a small crystal phial, half full
of bed-bugs, alive, crawling, labelled, *'Take one
before retiring. Dr. Stedman.'*—A gay time, then!
Now those people were all gone. Stedman, in his
spare time (of which there was precious little),
made models of ships—exquisite little things. He
had gone into an insurance office. The old painter
was dead. What had become of the detective?
. . . and his thin submissive little wife, who never
lifted her eyes from her plate.

'Here you are, sir!' said the taxi driver, turning
his head.

And there he was. The wharf. An enormous,
depressing place, cavernous, engulfing bales and
trunks by the cartload, but with no sign of a ship
anywhere. Where should he enter? The usual
terror assailed him. Everywhere stood uncompro-
mising officials, emblems of stupidity. He carried
his bag into the great sounding gloom, which was
itself, with its smells of oakum and hemp and slimy

piles, like a vast ship; dodged his way among thumping trucks—trucks were everywhere, each pushed by a pirate; and at last, through a great sea-door, caught sight of the black iron side of the vessel, streaked with filth and rust. A qualm came over him. What disgusting animals ships were! always fouling their sides with garbage. However, perhaps the lavatory would smell of antiseptic . . . 'Second cabin? Next gangway' . . . He crawled up the next gangway, steep as a funicular, and stepped on to the resilient deck. O Thalassa! Thalassa! Unmerciful sea. He was already fairly launched into the infinite, the immense solitude, which seemed (to the steward who took his bag) to mean so little. Yes: alone. Alone with the sea for eight days: alone in a cage with a world of tigers roaring outside.

'Am I alone in this cabin?' he asked.

'I don't know, sir. You'll have to ask the cabin steward, after we start.'

Now, Demarest, survey this cabin which will be your cell for eight days. Running water? Yes. Four berths. Ring once for Mr. Tomkins, twice for Mrs. Atherton. No port-hole, of course. Red carpet, and the usual smell. He poured out a glass of water, and took two pills, as prescribed. The water was cloudy and tepid. Footsteps rang on the deck over his head . . . And suddenly a feeling of unutterable desolation came over him, a nostalgia made only the more poignant by the echoes it brought of other voyages. Ah, that incurable longing for escape, for a spider's cable by which he might swing himself abruptly into space or oblivion! But this time, was it an escape or a return? . . . And the voices of his former fellow-voyagers, fellow-crawlers toward the infinite, came round him in melancholy chorus. 'A safety razor? Just like a bally little lawn-mower. And a thundering hot towel on your face.' That was the 'pynter and gilder' on the *Empress*. And his poverty-stricken room-mate, who had got a Marconigram —for which he had to pay—saying, 'Have a Guinness on us, at your expense.' His comic fury, his bulging eyes! To make it worse, his only hat, left carelessly in a bunk, was a moment later sat upon and crushed beyond recognition . . . The German girl, with the long blue ribbons down the back of her skirt, deliciously fluttering as she walked, whom he had been too shy to speak to. She came and stood beside him while the stewards danced and sang below the hatch, stood very close to him, put her hands on the rope. 'Curiously melancholy,' he had thought of saying, 'all this folk music is! . . .' Melancholy it was. But his courage had failed him; and next day, as he passed her (she was walking—how buoyantly she walked! —with the Professor), he heard her saying, 'No, he vas afraid!' She laughed as she said it. And afterwards she had married the Professor. He had watched them pacing the deck, pacing the deck, looking more and more earnestly at each other. One time as he passed them the flying word was '*gymnasium*.' The next time it was 'But SHAW!' Were they falling in love? Yes,—as the voyage drew to its end they became inseparable; inseparable because they saw the inevitability of separation. They stood together at the railing, looking sadly at the grey waste of water. 'Oh,

how persuasive is the sound of the sea !' And he
had felt curiously sorry for them, somehow,—as if
they had become in a sense, the sea's victims:
nothing of them but doth change . . .

He edged his way along the corridor, past a con-
tinuous shuffling line of stewards carrying bags, and
up the brass-edged stairs. The sun had come out;
on the cool east wind sang the soft quarter-bells of
the Metropolitan; playing their melodious prelude
to the solemn striking of the hour. Three o'clock.
A few of his fellow-passengers idled about on the
deck, stood in groups talking, or watched the last
trunks being swung in a great net over the opened
hatch. A whistle blew, and the net, with its bulging catch of trunks, dropped soundlessly into the
hold, the donkey-engine emitting a rapid rattle.
Stevedores pushed boxes down the polished gangway, caught them with hooks, and pulled them into
the ship.

'Is this Mr. Demarest?' A young man stood
before him, earnest, a little shy, deferential.

'Yes?'

'My name's Roscoe—I'm on the *News*. Helen
Shafter told me you were on the ship, and I
thought I'd look you up.'

'How on earth did you know me?' (Demarest
felt flattered.)

'Oh, I've seen photos of you! . . . I've spoken
to the purser about you—hope he'll make you comfortable . . .'

'Helen Shafter? You know Helen Shafter?'

'Oh, I know Helen very well!'

One of Helen's mutton-chops? Had he been in
love with her? Well, he must be discreet himself:

it would never do to betray too great an intimacy
with Helen.

'I hope,' said the young man, offering a cigarette,
'you're not joining the expatriates over there. Are
you coming back?'

'Good Lord yes. I'm just going over for a——'
Demarest laughed.

'Drink?'

'Yes, a drink! put it that way . . . No, I'm
too old to transplant. Too many roots to be
broken, too much underground bleeding. Ten
years ago—well, that would have been a different
story.'

'I see . . . I'm glad to hear it. We don't like
to see our best men running away from us.'

'Oh! Best men!' Demarest felt a little idiotic.

'Your last book—I hope you don't mind my
saying so—I liked enormously.'

'I'm glad you liked it!'

'I certainly did . . . Hello! There's the bugle!'

The bright brass notes came from a steward,
who blew solemnly, facing the dock. The donkey-
engine had become silent. There was a rattle of
chains, an air of poised expectancy.

'Well, so long,' said the young man, putting out
his hand. 'I hope you'll have a good trip.'

'Thanks. So long!'

Roscoe disappeared down the deck-stairs. Well,
well—how remarkably pleasant. He was beginning to be a kind of celebrity. How fatuous it
was! Pursers would bow to him, stewards would
sing,—Captains and second mates dance in a ring!
. . . And all because he was slightly, but uncon-
trollably, mad. Damned decent of Helen, too.

He wished now that he hadn't parted with her at eight o'clock on the subway stairs, last night—or had arranged to meet her later, at the hotel . . . Would she have come? . . . Perhaps not. An unaccountable, brooding, witty, perverse creature. 'I'm becoming unduly agitated, Helen.' 'Very well, then!—I'll remove the immediate stimulus.' And she had withdrawn her hand, which, under the restaurant table, lay on his knee . . . Just like her!

A devastating roar came from the siren: it was prolonged, shook the ship, and he noticed that the dock had begun to glide away. They were being blasted away from America. Handkerchiefs were waved, then dashed at tears; there were calls and cries; children were held up, their puppet arms wagged by enthusiastic parents. Good-bye, New York, city of cigar shops and marble towers! The sight of the hysterical crowd was painful to him, and he walked to the other side of the deck.

They were not a very promising-looking lot of passengers. He might, after all, have to look up Dr. Purington in the first class,—a snob, but intelligent. Two solid prelates, with kind eyes and soft beards, stood talking to a girl, perhaps their niece. She, at any rate, was pleasant to look at—tall, straight, graceful, with innocent grey eyes and a mouth just amiably weak. Still, one couldn't have a flirtation with the niece of two Irish prelates. Or was she merely a comparative stranger,—travelling, by some remote arrangement, under their protection,—and anxious, for other purposes, to be dissociated from them?

'Well, what kind of voyage we going to have?'

The old-middle-aged man with the grey moustache and cigar: he leaned on the railing, gently revolving the cigar in his mouth with thumb and finger, staring exophthalmically at Staten Island.

'Looks all right now,' said Demarest, with a little laugh. 'Still, you never know.'

'No. You never know . . . Not very exciting, I guess—ship's half empty.'

'Is that so?'

'That's what they say. Off season . . . Can't go on too long for me though! Let her rip.'

'Good God, don't suggest it.'

'Don't you like a voyage? Nice ship, nice people?—just suits me. Yes, sir, it just suits me.'

'No. I'd like to be chloroformed, and called when we get to Liverpool . . . You heard about the man who said he wanted the easiest job on earth—calling the stations on an Atlantic liner?'

'Ha, ha. That's good . . . Yes, that'd be a nice job for me . . . just let it go on for ever.'

The old-middle-aged man turned a humorous beam on Demarest. An oblique purple scar cleft his moustache near the left nostril.

'Only one thing I regret,' he said.

'What's that?'

'Didn't get myself a cap. I meant to do it—remembered it, too, last night on the train, when I was taking off my shoes. "Frank," I said to myself, "don't forget that cap!" But I did. It went clean out of my head. I don't feel just right in this tweed hat. I hardly ever use it. Does it look all right?'

'Looks all right to me!'

'Well, guess it'll have to do . . . Been over before?'

'Yes. This is my tenth trip.'

'Tenth! My Lord. You're a fish.'

They both laughed lightly. A red ferry-boat passed them, crowded with faces, the waves swashing under its blunt bow; a golden eagle flashed on the pilot-house, where they could see the pilot shifting the easy wheel.

'Was that a reporter talking to you?'

'Yes.'

'I thought so. I heard him mention the *News* . . . Well, there goes the Statue of Liberty— what's she waving at, I wonder? Long may she wave. It's about all she does . . . Fine piece of work, all the same . . . I'd like to have had the time to go out and see it.'

A flock of gulls sailed in the blue high over the Goddess; the towers of Manhattan began to soften in the October haze. The ship throbbed more palpably, the wind freshened. How quickly one forgets the sound of sea, thought Demarest— the death of a wave, the melancholy chorus of subsiding drops when wave breaks against wave, flinging white water into the air! There was Midland Beach,—where he'd so often gone swimming, swimming among flotsam, old bottles and butter-boxes. Was that the island he had swum across to? . . . Not so much of a swim after all. There, for the last time, he had seen Alan—Alan carrying a soiled towel, and grinning. Inconceivable vitality and charm: dead now, turned to ashes, fit to scatter on an icy sidewalk. He saw

Alan leaning over the back of the sofa in the London boarding-house, smiling amorously, with all his freckles, at the Welsh manageress. 'What's your hurry, Bill? . . . Mrs. Porter wants to talk to me,—don't you, Mrs. Porter!' And in the Underground, smirking ridiculously at the Great Lady, who blushed and smiled in answer. And in Piccadilly Circus, while waiting for a bus, bowing so elaborately to the girl who stood in the doorway. 'Miss Simpkins, allow me to introduce my old friend Prince Schnitzkipopoff, sometime of Warsaw! . . .' Sometime of Warsaw! And where was Alan now, sometime of—life? Or was it Indiana?

'Have a cigar?' said Frank.

'Thanks! I don't mind if I do. Have you got plenty?'

'More than I can smoke. I bought two boxes myself, and then the Boss, Mr. Charlton, gave me another. Pretty decent of him, wasn't it? Havana too—expensive cigar. Well, it's only natural —I've been in his employ for thirty years: Yes, sir, thirty years. A long time.' The old man looked wistfully at the water. 'Yes, sir, thirty years. I felt bad about leaving—guess everybody felt bad about it. The Charltons gave a farewell party for me—I know them well, like one of the family. They know I'm crazy about cigars—and they had a little practical joke on me. You know those cigars that are loaded—explode? They gave me one after dinner.—*Bang!* Gee whillikins, I was startled. And you know, even Selina, the old nigger cook, had been tipped off. She came to the door to see me light it. You ought to have heard her laugh! . . . Well, you know, they're nice people, fine people, and New Orleans seems like home to me; but you can't go on for ever. I thought I'd like to see the Old Country again . . . There goes Coney Island.'

'You were born in England?'

'Devonshire. Left it thirty years ago; went straight to New Orleans; and been there ever since.'

'You'll find England changed.'

'You know, I'm sort of afraid, in a way—I don't believe I'll know a soul in my town.'

'No relatives?'

'All dead . . . Isn't it funny? And yet I've got this craving to go back and walk round there. That's what I'd like to do—walk over the country. I was a great walker then—knew every stick and stone. And I may hate it—be lonely—come running back inside a month.'

The wind whipped their coats about their knees. Green waves from the south-east, fluctuant pyramids of water tossing their points into the wind. The bow lifted gently, far ahead. The ship fell into a long leisurely swing, first greeting to the sea, the unvintagable sea . . . What was this strange passion for crucifixion that overcame the old man, as it overcame himself?

'You're like Ulysses, setting out at last to find the rim of the world, the Pillars of Hercules.'

'Not much! No exploring for me. I want to get back, that's all.'

The old man looked at him with brown eyes comically solemn, in which there was just a trace of something shy and fugitive. The arched grey

eyebrows gave his eyes an odd startled roundness
of appearance, childlike and charming.

'No, sir, I'm too old for any exploring!'

'But isn't that just what you're doing? You
don't know what you're going to . . . I don't
believe we're ever too old to explore—we're
always exploring something. There was an old
ex-Senator on a ship with me once—by George,
he was a wonder. Eighty years old, with gout
so bad that he could hardly walk, and had to keep
one leg up in a chair when he sat in the smoking-
room. He'd outlived all his relatives except one
son, who'd taken over his law practice—outlived
his friends, his own generation, every damned
one. He fought in the Civil War, was one of the
first Government surveyors of Arkansas—surveyed it when it was a wilderness, hostile Indians.
He knew Walt Whitman—Walt used to come and
see his aunt, he said. He didn't have much use
for Walt. "Well," he said, "why should I hang
around Washington? I can't live for ever.
There's nothing for me to do here. I might as
well die with my boots on. Besides," he said, "I
haven't seen Australia for thirty years, and I'd
like to see it again. I hear it's changed." So
off he was going alone, eighty years old. A
magnificent man, the kind we don't seem to produce any more: huge frame, head like a lion, face
like Gibraltar. He sat and listened to the argu-
ments in the smoking-room. When he said anything, it settled the discussion. We didn't exist
for him—we were just a lot of little yappers, still
damp from the womb. I felt a sort of affection
for him, and on the last morning as we were

tying up, I hunted him out, on deck, to say good-bye. "Oh, good-bye!" he said, sort of surprised, as if he'd never seen me before: and turned back to look at the landing-stage . . . And you know, I don't believe he ever *had* seen me—never bothered to focus his eyes on me, though we'd been talking together for a week.'

'Funny business,' said the old man. 'How soon do they open the bar, I wonder? I wouldn't mind a nice glass of Scotch.'

Demarest laughed. 'And let there be no moaning at the bar, when we put out to sea!'

'Too deep for sound or foam, eh? That's good —that's good!'

'Guess I'll go below and get a sweater. Maybe they'll be giving out the seats in the saloon. Shall I get you one?'

'Thanks! I wish you would. My name's Smith.'

In the smoking-room half a dozen men were sitting carefully apart; they smoked meditatively, eyeing one another askance. They were waiting for conversational openings, each of them eager to pour forth his story. When Demarest put his head in to look round, they all regarded him simultaneously with a mute interrogation, a dumb wistful invitation: perhaps he was the necessary solvent; and at any rate the feeling was manifest that acquaintance would become easier as the room became crowded. A steel-faced clock ticked briskly on the wall of fluted and varnished wood. The small windows, with screw fastenings, were of cheap stained glass, vicious mustard yellows and bilious greens hideously devised into marine

patterns.   Anæmic crabs, pale-ribbed scallop-
shells, star-fish, weeds, cornucopias.   The bar-
steward, tall and thin, leaning against a chair-
back, gave him an ironic smile, meant to be
friendly: Malvolio. 'Bar not open?' said Demarest. 'Not yet, sir: waiting for the keys.' *Tick-
tick-tick-tick;* and someone spat resonantly into
a brass spittoon . . . Six tables . . . this would
be his sitting-room for eight days.   The sound
of the sea came softly here, muted, like the hush
heard in a conch-shell: *Sh—sh—sh*. A loose
chair clicked gently as the floor inclined.

He descended the stairs into the main saloon,
a wide, pillared room, red-carpeted, with long
red-covered tables.   Here the sound of the sea
came fresher, through a long row of opened port-
holes.   A palm tree stood by the pale piano. its
branches faintly oscillating.   Two bored-looking
officers sat at the end of one of the tables with
ship's papers before them.   Demarest gave his
name, and Smith's, to one of these.   The other
leaned forward and said in a subdued voice, 'Oh
—the Purser's table.   Demarest.' . . . So this
is fame . . . A girl brushed his arm as he turned
away.   'Pardon ME!' she cried, drawling the 'r'
a little, and smiling.   Then, to the bored officers,
melodiously, extravagantly fluting—

'Are *you* giving out the seats? . . . 'Cause if
you are, I want one! . . . Pauline Faubion!'

Demarest was amused.   A wild little person,
he thought: a baggage.   Small, impertinent,
pretty, with large dark eyes far apart and challenging, and the full mouth a little sombre.   An
actress perhaps.   As he went out of the saloon

into the corridor he heard her laughing—a fine
bold trill, by George! She was losing no time
. . . Crucifixion. Why do we all want to be
crucified, to fling ourselves into the very heart of
the flame? Empedocles on Aetna. A moment
of incandescent suffering. To suffer intensely
is to live intensely, to be intensely conscious . . .
Passionate, perverse refusal to give up the unattainable—dashing ourselves blindly against the
immortal wall. 'I *will* be crucified! Here are
my hands! Drive nails through them—sharp
blows!' . . . He looked at his face in the cabin
mirror, under the caged electric light, and mar-
velled that such madness could go on behind so
impassive a forehead, eyes so profoundly serene.
He looked long into his own eyes, so unfathomable, as if in an effort to understand himself, and
—through his own transparent elusiveness—the
world. What was it he wanted? What was it
that was driving him back? What was this singular mechanism in him that wanted so deliberately,
so consciously, to break itself? A strange, a rich,
a deep personality he had—it baffled and fascinated him. Everybody of course, was like this,
—depth beyond depth, a universe chorally singing, incalculable, obeying tremendous laws, chem-
ical or divine, of which it was able to give its
own consciousness not the faintest inkling . . .
He brushed the dark hair of this universe. He
looked into its tranquil black-pooled eyes. Its
mouth was humorous and bitter. And this universe would go out and talk inanely to other
universes—talking only with some strange minute fraction of its identity, like a vast sea leaving

on the shore, for all mention of itself, a single white pebble, meaningless. A universe that contained everything—all things—yet said only one word: '*I.*' A music, an infinite symphony, beautifully and majestically conducting itself there in the darkness, but remaining for ever unread and unheard. 'Do you like cigarettes?' says one universe to another. 'No, I prefer a pipe,' says the second. 'And what is truth?' says one universe to another. 'Truth is pleasure,' answers the second. Silence. The two universes smoke cigarettes and pipes . . . And this universe sees another, far off, unattainable, and desires passionately to approach it, to crash into it—why? To be consumed in the conflagration, to lose its identity? . . . Ah,—thought Demarest, drawing on his sweater,—if we stopped to consider, before any individual, his infinite richness and complexity, could we be anything but idolatrous—even of a fool? He looked again into his reflected eyes, but now with a long melancholy, a mingling of pity and contempt. *Know thyself!* That was the best joke ever perpetrated. A steaming universe of germ-cells, a maelstrom of animal forces, of which he himself, his personality, was only the collective gleam. A hurricane of maggots which answered to the name of Demarest.

There was a knock at the door.

'Come in!'

'The bath-steward, sir. Do you wish a bath in the morning?'

'What time is breakfast?'

'Eight o'clock, sir.'

'Then let me have it at seven-thirty.'

'Hot or cold, sir.'

'Cold.'

The footsteps went along the alley, another knock, the voice again, farther off. 'The bath-steward, miss,' a girl's voice answering. A girl next door—that was good. Who was she? Another universe brushing its hair under an electric light, calmly, with vanity. And all of them crowded together in this small ship. What was it for? Everything seemed senseless. The ship throbbed, the bed-curtains vibrated on their rings. The woodwork creaked gently, slowly, as the long ship rose to the sea. Thalassa! Thalassa! The wine-dark sea.

As he went out of his room the girl next door came forth also—the Irish girl. Shutting her door she eyed him with a sort of tentative candour, a smile withheld. A brown woollen scarf, brown woollen stockings, nice ankles. He felt shy and turned stiffly away, his head lowered a little. He heard her steps behind him, apologetic, unobtrusive, oddly contriving to say, 'We're not following you,—no,—no;' and his own steps, becoming lighter, replied, 'We wouldn't *dream* of assuming it.' Curious how such relations can spring into being! . . . He went fugitively up the stairs and on to the deck.

It had grown cloudy and cold. The clouds were bringing an early dusk. White-caps, on a dark grey sea:—lines of white on a sullen sea. Should he look up Purington? He walked to the companion-way which led to the deck above, and there, of course, was the sign—'*Second Cabin Passengers Not Allowed on This Deck.*'

Perhaps he would see Purington go by.   He stood
by the railing and watched a straggling procession
of First Class Men striding round the corner
above.   Their collars were turned up, hands in
pockets.   They eyed the sea with hostility.   There
was Purington.   'Purington!' he called.   But
Purington didn't hear.   The words had been
blown overboard.   Two old ladies, passing, looked
at him curiously, looked up at the first cabin deck,
and smiled, as much as to say 'Harmless!' . . .
Disgusting old toads . . . Well, there was no
rush about seeing Purington: he could wait.   Besides, would Purington want to see him—a second
cabin passenger whom he didn't know particularly well? . . . Perhaps not.   He turned reso-
lutely away and started to walk.

When he went down to dinner, he found himself sitting on the left of the Assistant Purser,
who occupied the end seat.   Old Man Smith was
next to him, and opposite him were Mrs. Faubion
(how delightful!) and another girl.

'No, sir,' the old man was saying with bantering severity.   'I think you girls are too young
to be travelling alone like this.   It isn't right.'
He supped his soup loudly and intently.

'Too young!   Well, I don't know about Miss
Dacey.   But I'd like to tell you, Mr. Man, that
I'm married; and if a married lady can't travel
by herself I'd like to know who can!   And what
right have *you* got, anyway, to talk to us like that
—huh?'   She glared at him with a comic imitation of anger.

'Married, eh?   She says she's married.   I
don't believe she's out of school . . . Besides,

I'm old enough to be your father. I leave it to you, Mr. Captain, whether these girls aren't too young to be travelling alone like this.'

The Assistant Purser, Mr. Barnes, red-faced and grey-eyed (sea-gazing eyes, thought Demarest—but they gazed for the most part at ledgers and passenger-lists), was a little inclined to be stiff and pompous; reserved, perhaps. He laughed with uneasy amiability, looking from one face to another and crumbling his bread.

'But we mustn't have a quarrel, must we, on the very first night of the voyage,—what? Besides, where could Mrs. Faubion and Miss Dacey be safer than on a ship?'

'There!' cried Mrs. Faubion, triumphantly.

'I don't know about a *ship* being so awfully safe though,' said Miss Dacey, wriggling and grimacing in a manner intended to be arch. 'We know all about these sailors with a wife in every port—ha ha! Of course, I don't mean *you*, Mr. Barnes!'

Mr. Barnes opened his mouth, a little taken back.

'Oh, of course not, Miss Dacey! How could you dream of such a thing!' He looked at Demarest, laughing. 'The only "ports" I know are New York, Liverpool and Southampton. So I suppose you credit me with three.'

Miss Dacey blushed furiously and gave another desperate wriggle. She was blue-eyed, anæmic, with a long, thin mouth. She wore a bangle. Not more than twenty, thought Demarest.

'Now you know I didn't mean that . . . How *mean* of you. I didn't mean it at all. Though,

of course, these *handsome* men——!' She gave
a peculiarly vapid little laugh, and eyed Mr.
Barnes sidelong.

'Now! Now!' cried Mr. Smith. 'That's
enough! That'll do for you. We can't have our
officers demoralized like this!'

'This is becoming a little *personal*,' said Barnes.

'Highly,' said Demarest. 'You're elected.'

Mrs. Faubion laughed absent-mindedly, looking
rather hard at Demarest. She was handsome,
saturnine, though her features were not particularly good. There was something brooding and
dark about her which, combined with her extreme
youth and brilliant vulgarity, intrigued him enormously. She was extraordinarily alive. And
the fact that, although a mere girl, she was married, piqued him. What did she know? Certainly there was a good deal that was hard and
blatant about her,—and she had picked up, in
America, an astounding vaudeville sort of accent.
But at the same time there was something oddly
unsophisticated in her sombre eyes, a burning
simplicity and candour. She looked now at Smith
with amused suspiciousness, and asked him:

'Are you two travelling together?'

'Why, of course!' cried Demarest. 'We're
father and son.'

'What! With different names! You're kid-
ding me. Is *your* name Smith?'

'Well, now, father, that's a delicate question,
isn't it . . . Shall we tell the lady the truth?'

Smith laughed. 'Go on—go on!'

'Oh, don't be silly! I *know* you're not father
and son.'

She eyed him with a doubtful gleam, half smiling.

'Come now!' said Demarest, 'don't you observe the startling resemblance? . . . You see, it was like this.'

'*Yes*, it was!'

'Father, you see, had an unfortunate little affair some years ago—he has a peculiar psychological affliction—which caused him to spend two years in—er—jail. And when he came out, he changed his name.'

'*Really!*' cried Miss Dacey, leaning forward intensely. 'How exciting! And *what* is the affliction?'

'Are you sure we ought to know about this, Mr. Smith?' asked the Purser, with a fine, grave air of concern.

'Oh—among friends——!' laughed Smith, flourishing his fork.

'Yes, it's sad, it's sad,' said Demarest, shaking his head. 'No one knows what father has suffered—nor me either. You see, father is a kleptomaniac.'

A *what*?' Mrs. Faubion cried. '*What* did you say?'

'He has, every now and then, an uncontrollable impulse to steal. Spoons and forks are a great temptation to him. We can't let him go out to dinner alone—have to watch him every minute. And a restaurant or hotel! he goes simply cuckoo when he gets inside the door . . . It was a restaurant that undid him! A little restaurant on Sixth Avenue. And all for a couple of nickel-plated spoons!'

'Dear, dear,' murmured the Purser, 'a year for each spoon, too! How unfortunate!'

'Oh, but be serious! You *aren't* together, are you?'

She leaned back in the small swivel chair, and regarded him from an immense distance.

'Why, of course! . . . Don't you believe me?'

'No! I'm from *Missouri*,' she replied savagely. 'And I think you're real rude.'

Smith poked Demarest with his elbow, not spilling the potato from his fork.

'Now see what you've gone and done—made the little girl mad. Just when I was getting on so well, too.'

'*Who* was getting on so well!' . . . Mrs. Faubion glowered.

'Of all the *conceited* men——!' contributed Miss Dacey, bridling.

'Ah, father, you shouldn't blame *me* like this . . . Is it *my* fault? . . . Is the child father to the man? . . . No; if you'd only *resisted* those nickel spoons—sternly—walked out proudly with empty pockets and a pure heart——'

'Well, you don't have to *tell* everybody, do you? . . . You've spoiled my chances. What hope is there for me now?' He looked sadly at Mrs. Faubion. 'Me, an ex-convict, a klepto-maniac!'

'What a *lovely* word,' said Miss Dacey. 'Don't *you* think so, Mr. Barnes?'

Demarest thought she was about to lay her head on Mr. Barnes's plate,—so yearningly did she gush forward. Mr. Barnes leaned back a little.

'Oh, a lovely word!' he agreed. 'Still, as Purser of this ship, I suppose I ought to be careful—what? . . . I must warn you, Mr. Smith, that everything you say will be held against you. It's a beautiful word; but I'm a dutiful man.'

Miss Dacey clapped her hands, jingling the bangle.

'Oh, doesn't he talk nicely! Beautiful—dutiful! Just like poetry! Do you like poetry, Mr. Barnes? Do you like poetry, Mr. Kleptomaniac? Do *you* like poetry, Mr. I-don't-know-your-name'?

'Demarest? . . . Certainly. If I can have a little beer and cheese with it, or a game of billiards after it!'

'How vulgar of you! . . . And you, Mr. Barnes?'

'Oh yes, yes!' cried Mr. Barnes.

'*I* don't,' snapped Mrs. Faubion. 'I think it's all tosh. Me for a good dance, or a nice show, and plenty of jazz. On the beach at Wy-kee-kee!' She snapped her fingers lazily, dreamily, and gave a singular little 'H'm'm!' like the dying-fall, cloying, of a ukelele.

'Twangle, twangle, little guitar!' said Smith. 'I'm right with you, darling! Make it two!'

'Careful, father. Remember your years. Forgive him, Mrs. Faubion. He means well,—but you know—bubbles in the think-tank . . .'

'Yes, sir,' said Smith. 'I sure do like a little jazz. Give me a good nigger orchestra every time. I remember once, at the Starcroft Inn, a dance-hall—but no. No, I can't tell it here. Too many ladies here.'

'Well! If *that's* the way you feel about it!'
. . . Mrs. Faubion folded her napkin, thrust it
venomously into the ring, and rose. 'Good
night!' She walked away bristling. At the door
she turned and looked hard at Demarest, who
was watching her. Their eyes met, then wavered
apart. Smith laughed delightedly.

'That time, father, it was *you.*'

'*Don't* call me *father*!—makes me feel too old.
Brr! . . . On the beach at Wai-ki-ki . . . Some
girl! . . . Have a cigar, Mr. Purser? . . . Mr.
Demarest?' He beamed, offering cigars. Then
he walked solemnly away, pinching the end of a
cigar between finger and thumb.

'Jolly old boy that!' said Mr. Barnes. 'Have
you known him long?'

'Never saw him till to-day.'

'Jolly old boy! . . . Are you going, Miss
Dacey? Have we fed you well enough?'

'Oh, beautifully, thank you, Mr. Barnes! Do
you have to go and do that *awful* work now?'

'Yes, I'm afraid I do.'

'Good night, then!'

'Good night!'

'Daisy Dacey,' said Mr. Barnes to Demarest.
'How's that for a name, eh? And look at her
card, she gave it to me. "Miss Daisy Dacey.
England and the United States!" Isn't that a
scream?'

'The Western Hemisphere and Mars,' murmured Demarest.

Feeling suddenly that they had nothing more
to say to each other, they drifted shyly apart.
The orchestra, which had just come in from the

first cabin, finished arranging its music on tri-
pods, and struck loudly, coarsely into '*My Little
Grey Home in the West.*' Flute, violin, piano
and double-bass. The flute-player, a young man
with a pale, fine girlish face and a blonde cascade
of hair, hooked his lip earnestly over the flute:
uncous lip. How white his hands were, too, on
the black flute. *My lit-tle grey ho-ome in the
West.* A brick vault in the cemetery, overgrown,
oversnarled, with gaudy trumpet-vine, steaming
in the tropic sun. Bones in the tropic dust. My
little red house in the south. Bees and bones and
trumpet flowers: nostalgia, Gaugin, heart of darkness . . . Mrs. Faubion passed him, singing '*My
lit-tle grey ho-ome——*' her eyes wide and . . .
absorbent. Demarest felt like turning up his coat
collar against a draught. A tall dark romantic
young man came after her, carrying her coat and
a steamer rug. Victim No. 1. Daisy Dacey
stood at the corridor door, engaged in lively conversation with the Chief Steward. She pirou-
etted, slid, waved her arms, giggled, and the Chief
Steward looked down at her intently, preening
his little black moustache abstractedly, as if he
weren't so much listening as watching, waiting.
'Hello!' she cried to Demarest as he passed.
'Hello!' sang Demarest mockingly. After he had
passed, he heard her crying, amid the harsh music,
'Never—never—*never* !' At the same time, thin
and far away, he heard the ship's bell hurriedly
striking eight: *tin-tin, tin-tin, tin-tin, tin-tin.*
What watch was this—Dog Watch? No. The
Watch of the Great Bear. The Watch of the
Lion. The Watch of the Sphinx. The Queen

of Sheba would be sitting in his state-room, on
a small golden chair, clawing a pomegranate on
a golden dish. 'Naughty, naughty!' she cried to
her Sphinx-cub, wagging a finger. Then she
put down her locked hands, crying, 'Jump,
Sphinx!' and the little grey sphinx leapt, expres-
sionless, over the alabaster hoop. 'Mad, mad.
I'm completely mad.'

He walked twice round the deck in the wind
and dark. It was cold. The deck was dimly
lighted, and everything looked a little fantastic,
—enormous ventilators, mysterious people stepping out of mysterious doors, a submarine murmur of ragtime. A cluster of tiny lights far
away to port indicated Long Island. As he
crossed the shelter-deck behind the smoking-
room he saw Pauline Faubion, and the Romantic
Young Man, sitting, well-wrapped, in steamer
chairs. The Young Man was leaning his head
very close to her, talking in a low confidential
voice—she regarded him with solemn probing indifference. Why was it not himself who sat beside her, talking? Oh, he knew well enough why
—though he knew also, with conviction, that
Pauline would have preferred him to her present
company . . . The sea was black, with hints of
white, and the wind brought unceasingly from
it the fluctuatingly melancholy and savage sound
of charging waves.

The smoking-room had become noisy and
cheerful. Bottles stood on the table with half-
filled glasses, blue smoke drifted in long lazy-
swirling parallels, like isobars on a weather-chart.
Four men played whist at the table in the far

corner—*bang!* went down a card; *knock!* went
down another. Card games as a form of physical
exercise. In another corner, Smith sat back alone,
solemnly and appreciatively smoking. He tapped
indicatively the seat next to him, blowing a rich
plume of smoke. Demarest sat down, feeling
relaxed and melancholy.

'Well,' said Smith, after a pause. 'I've told
you what *I'm* going for—what are *you* going
for?'

Demarest laughed,—looking through Smith,
through the wall, through the sea, the night. He
waved his hand weakly.

'Me?' he answered. 'Oh, I'm going to see the
Chimæra. The Great Chimæra.'

'I didn't know it was in captivity.'

'It isn't.'

'A girl? I get you, Steve.'

'Yes.'

There was another pause, and Smith added
humorously:

'Well, I'm an old man, but I keep my eyes open
myself . . . Those girls at our table—they have
the stateroom opposite mine. There's something
funny about those girls—something queer.' He
eyed Demarest provocatively. 'Don't you
think——'

Demarest thought, but did not answer . . .
After a while they played chequers.

II

IT was manifest to Demarest that he had got
into the wrong place. It was totally unfamiliar. He walked quietly along the side of
the grape-arbour and then, cautiously, passed
under a fragrant trellis overgrown with roses.
He emerged upon a wide lawn enclosed with trees
and flowers, where a garden party was in progress. A score of glitteringly-dressed men and
women stood talking, sauntered here and there,
or set cups down on flower-decked tables. How
horrible! He felt out of place, furtive and shabby,
an intruder. But how was he to escape? He
couldn't recall where he had got in. Was it over
a wall? . . . He turned back through the trellis,
hearing behind him a mild laughter. He looked
down, and saw that his shoes were covered with
mud and that his trousers were torn. Passing this
time to the left of the grape-arbour, he hurried
along the narrow path of deep soft turf, and was
horrified to encounter a group of ladies coming in.
They looked at him with hard eyes. Perhaps they
thought he was some kind of a gardener? . . .
This, then, might be the way out? . . . A flunkey
in knee breeches eyed him suspiciously. Then
he saw a green wooden gate; but just as he was
about to open it, there came a loud knock at the
other side, which was at once terrifyingly repeated, repeated——

'Bath's ready, sir.'

He groaned with relief, waking . . . The

28

ship, of course! he was on a ship. He relaxed,
becoming conscious of the regular remote throbbing of the engines. His coat, hanging on the
stateroom door, sidled a little . . . That curious
dream! It was just a new version, nevertheless,
of the familiar theme—his absurd 'inferiority
complex.' Good God! Was he destined never to
escape it? Why was it that he never could be
at his ease with those who were socially his equals
—only at ease with his 'inferiors'? It was very
strange. Formal occasions, polite people, froze
him to the marrow: he couldn't remain himself
. . . It was not that he hadn't had every opportunity to become accustomed to them,—for all
the rest of his family were happily and intensely
social . . . Mary and Tom adored parties, and
so had his mother . . . But he had always been
instinctively hostile to such things; and while he
recognized in himself a passionate attachment
for the fine and rich—by way of environment—
he wanted the fine and rich freed from the
'social'; and moreover, every so often he wanted
a good deep foaming bath in the merely vulgar.
An occasional debauch was imperative,—whether
it was only a visit to a cheap vaudeville, with its
jazz, its spangles, its coarse jokes, its 'Chase me,
boys—I issue trading stamps,'—or a shabby little
clandestine adventure of his own, in which his
motive was largely, if not entirely, curiosity . . .
It was precisely this damned inferiority complex
that had put him at such an initial disadvantage
with Cynthia. By the time he had succeeded in
adjusting himself, psychologically, to her exquisite old-worldliness, the dim, deep constellations of

refinements and manners amid which she so statelily moved, and by the time he had put out of his
mind the feeling that he was a mere ugly duckling,
and had scraped from his shoes (metaphorically
speaking) the mud of the brief, violent, disgusting
Helen Shafter affair: by this time Cynthia had
left London and gone to the continent.   Gone!
and that was the end. . . .   He shut his eyes in
a spasm of pain. ·

Presently he put on his ancient slippers and
his raincoat and shuffled along the corridor, in-
haling a dreadful odour of coffee.   The bath was
green, deep, dazzling: electrically cold.   He was
inclined to yelp like a dog, as he emerged—or no
—to blaff like a seal.   Blaff!   Superb word.   It
suggested the blowing away of the water from
mouth and nostrils, and also a certain *joie de
vivre*.   Laughter.   He overheard, as he was dry-
ing himself, a fragment of conversation.

'. . . She says she's married to an American
naval M.D.'

'Oh, does she?   Well, maybe she is . . . She
looks to me like a wild one.   You'd better be careful.'

'Oh, I know the ropes . . . She told me last
night she was going back to visit her family.'

'She's English?'

'Yep . . . though you wouldn't guess it.   That
accent!   You could cut it with a knife.'

'I'd like to meet her—introduce me, will you?'

'Sure—if you like.'

One of the men, Demarest saw as he came out,
was the Romantic Young Man.   The other was
a short plump individual, swarthy and sleepy, with

a walrus moustache and small green cupidinous eyes . . . He gathered that they were merely ship-acquaintances.

'The Lord's Day,' murmured the plump one through his lather. 'Guess I'll go to church. They saw there's a good stewards' choirquartette. Anything to pass the time.'

'Well, put sixpence in the plate for me. I'll be among the missing.'

'I'll pray for you—for those lost at sea.'

'Do.'

Demarest shaved, glancing now and then at the smoke-blue Atlantic framed in an open porthole. A glittering day. A pleasant soft surfy sound came through the port and filled the white-floored bathroom, giving it oddly the air of an aquarium. Pale water-lights danced on the ceiling.

'And who's that other one—the girl with her?'

'Dacey, her name is. I haven't talked with her.'

'A silly-looking cat of a girl.'

'By Jove, she is.'

Rasp, rasp—the bally little lawn-mower. *'A pynter an' gilder, I am, an' I've been to Vancouver.'* . . .

*　　　*　　　*　　　*

Walking the deck after his breakfast—at which he had sat alone—Demarest gave himself up, for the first time, to the enjoyment of the full salt flavour of sea-voyage. The sun was hot, the breeze was cold, the sea was an immense disc of blue light, just sufficiently rough to escape monotony; and the bright ship burned and sparkled in the

midst of the infinite, swaying its high yellow
masts ever so slightly against a witch's finger-nail
of white moon, lifting and declining its bows
against the cloudless horizon. The long white
deck, polished like bone, rose and fell just per-
ceptibly, and with immense leisure, to the soft irregular accompaniment of waves broken and falling; and with it rose and fell the promenading
passengers. The sense of the infinite, and of
being isolated in its garish and terrifying pro-
fundity, was beginning to work upon them. Delighted with the ship and the sea, inquisitive and
explorative, nevertheless they were restless; they
paced the deck, climbed the companion-way,
walked through the smoking-room and out at the
other side, as if driven by a secret feeling of
being caged. It amused Demarest to watch them.
It amused him to see them, like imprisoned
animals, furtively try a bar, when none was looking, elaborately pretending all the while that no
bars were there, that all was peace and freedom.
They had put on their 'old' clothes,—supplemented
here and there with grotesque white yachting caps,
which the wind ballooned on their heads. Tweed
suits were strangely accompanied by glaring white
canvas shoes; and binoculars, obviously new,
were extracted from strapped cases and levelled,
with knit brows and a heavily professional air,
at remote plumes of smoke which lay faint and
supine along the horizon. Every slightest action
betrayed their inordinate consciousness of one
another. Those who walked, walked either more
emphatically than was their wont, or more sheep-
ishly, aware of the scrutiny, more or less veiled,

of the row of sitters. Those who sat in deck-
chairs were conscious of their extended feet, their
plaid rugs and shawls, and the slight physical and
moral discomfort of having to look 'up' at the
walkers. The extraordinary feeling of kinship,
of unity, of a solidarity far closer and more bind-
ing than that of nations or cities or villages, was
swiftly uniting them; the ship was making them
a community. How often Demarest had observed
this process! He now felt, with almost physical
vividness, its powerful, secret, and rapid operation. He felt it turning the head of one passenger
to another, he felt the yearning confusion of
friendliness, curiosity, loneliness, and love, which
made them all puppets and set them bowing and
nodding at one another; smiling mechanical
smiles which concealed outrageous happiness;
laughing a little too loudly or a little too politely;
all like automatic performants of a queer primitive
ritual. Every one of them wanted to be overheard or seen, wanted to be exposed, wanted even
—it seemed to Demarest—to be stripped. Those
who already knew each other, or were relatives,
talked to each other in a tacit mutual conspiracy
of unaccustomed emphasis, loudness, and good-
nature, made humorous remarks, delivered themselves of aphorisms or scraps of knowledge, with
the one aim of making, in all directions, a favourable impression. It was a grotesque sort of love-
dance. The young women flaunted and fluttered
their ribbons, loitered in the sunlight consciously
and gracefully, leaned on the railing with a melancholy abstraction which was deliberately and
beautifully an invitation. The young men, be-

ginning to talk with one another, but as yet timid
about extending their adventures to the realm of
the other sex, tramped the deck, a little flustered
and unsteady when they passed the young women.
They all desired keenly to talk with the latter,
but none wanted to be the first, fearing the eyes
and laughter of the community. Only the ship's
officers, coolly sauntering and smoking, were free
from this singular spell. Demarest watched their
adroit manœuvres, admiring their skill, and their
deep social wisdom. He observed the doctor and
the young wireless operator strolling appraisingly
back and forth; imperturbably selecting, as they
did so, the most promising fields for exploits.
They were in no hurry—they felt no pressure.
They were artists; and having selected their ma-
terial with care, would manipulate it with the
finest of tact and discretion. Ah! how admirable!
They had stopped beside an old married couple
and were lightly bantering with them. The wireless operator tucked up the old woman's feet, and
the old woman laughed, delighted and flattered,
at something he had said. An exquisite approach!
They were now in touch with the new cargo of
passengers, and in the best possible way,—the
way which would give them, later on, the greatest
possible freedom. The pause was only for a
second, the merest skimming of the water with
swallow-wings, but much had been set in motion:
eyes had seen them, ears had heard, they were
marked and sealed now as 'such nice young fellows.' The young men among the passengers,
who beheld this little manœuvre, were frankly
scornful and hostile, without knowing why; the

young women were envious and reproachful, looking after the retreating officers with a faint momentary pang, soon forgotten, as of sorrow . . .
Ah, these sea-dogs, thought Demarest, what cunning devils they are! How well they know human
nature! How he envied them their aplomb and
cool sophistication, the effrontery with which they
accomplished, in such fine publicity, the right
thing! Why could he not do likewise, instead of
slinking furtively along red-carpeted corridors,
avoiding the too-crowded decks, or sitting for
whole days at a time in the stuffy smoking-room
at games of chess or bridge, or vainly endeavouring to read? Why? Why? . . . Walking towards the smoking-room, which was well aft, he
passed the Irish girl, who stood with the two bear-
ish prelates. Her eyes turned friendlily toward
him, but he averted his face, pretending a dis-
traction. Then he cursed himself. Nothing
could have been simpler than to have smiled. Nor
could anything, for that matter, have been easier!
Her grey eyes, of an innocence not without daring, her kind mouth amiable and a little weak, her
tall easy figure, the brown woollen scarf and rough
brown stockings to match—he noticed sharply all
these things—and noticed also the slight stiffen-
ing of shyness with which she observed his approach. Unconsciously, she had contrived to
admit the fact that she was aware of him and liked
him. The way in which she shifted her balance,
at the same time lifting a little before her one of
her brown slippers, and frowning at the bright
buckle, and the way in which she broke rather
emphatically into the middle of something that

the older prelate was saying—ah! She would be friendly, she was prepared to like and be liked, and to make confessions by moonlight.

It was the brown woollen muffler and grey eyes which most disturbed him. Grey eyes, and brown muffler, on a ship's deck, in sunlight, at sea—this meant one thing to him: Cynthia. Cynthia, on the *Silurian,* had worn such a muffler: throwing it languidly over one shoulder and round her throat as she started forward, with that odd look of distance and sombre detachment in her grey eyes, sea-gazing and imperious. Good God, what an absurd pang the mere visual thought of her still gave him after a year! A disgraceful weakness. He sank into the corner seat nearest the door of the smoking-room, dropping his book on the table. The pianist of the ship orchestra sat next to him, a small golden harp embroidered on the sleeve of his soiled and stained blue coat. He was a pale, ill-shaven young man, with reddish hair slicked back from his clammy forehead and watery blue eyes behind thick spectacles. His mouth was small, curled and petulant, and his voice had a complaining quality. He was leaning forward on the table, talking to an extraordinary-looking young woman whom Demarest had not noticed before.

'You're Welsh aren't you?'

The young woman looked at him sidelong in a manner intended to be vampirine. Her green eyes were by nature narrow and gleaming under long black lashes, and she deliberately over-exaggerated this effect. An extraordinarily lascivious face, thought Demarest—the eyes cunning and

treacherous, and the mouth, which might have
been beautiful had it been more moderate, extravagantly red and rich and extravagantly and cruelly
curved downward at the corners. A vampire,
a serpent, a lamia, a carrion-flower,—yes, a
mouth like a carrion-flower, and giving out
poisonous juices; for as she laughed, Demarest noticed that the lower lip, which was undershot, was wet with saliva. She lifted her strange
face to laugh, giving only two short musical
sounds, then lowered her face again and wiped her
mouth with a crumpled handkerchief.

'Welsh? Why do you think I'm Welsh? . . .
You ought to be Welsh, with a harp on your
sleeve!'

She gave another laugh, eyeing Demarest; and
Demarest noticed, as she again lifted and dropped
her head, that her throat was singularly beautiful.
The pianist turned to look at Demarest, smiled,
and went on:

'Well, I don't know if you *look* Welsh: except
that you're dark. But you asked if I had any
Welsh songs, so what could be simpler? Eh?
. . . What could be simpler? . . .' The pianist
smiled oilily, showing three gold teeth. He
knitted his white plump fingers together before
him on the table. 'What's your name?' he then
went on.

The young woman assumed an air at the same
time injured and arch. She drew back a little,
narrowed her eyes at the pianist's thick spectacles,
then directed suddenly at Demarest a serpentine
smile, at the same time giving him a gleaming
wink quick as the eye of a kodak.

'Isn't he smart? . . . And personal! . . . sweet hour.'

Demarest smiled, lighting his pipe. He was taken aback, but somewhat excited. The creature was so obviously—— What? While she turned, half rising, to look out of a port-hole at the sea (again wiping her juicy mouth) he tried to analyse the effect she had on him. Tropical. He had never encountered at such close quarters so scarlet-flowering and rank a growth. The invitation, certainly, was tremendous. Here, close at hand, was the rich jungle,—poisonous and naïve, treacherous and rich, with its tenacious creepers, its bright voracious birds, and its flesh-like fruit. Should he enter? He recognized, also, the pressure exerted upon him to do so by the mere fact of the pianist's presence, the pianist's prior pursuit and inquisitiveness. His impulse was to compete with the pianist: to be at the same time more tactful, more humorous, and more charming: to snatch the scarlet flower from under his very nose.

Against all this—ah! the manifold complications! For it was easy to foresee that this girl would be swarmed about by the men on the ship; swarmed about as by flies; would be talked about by every one, sniggeringly— 'Yes, sir, she's a warm baby!'—and would be signally avoided by the women. To attach one's self to her too publicly—and *any* attachment would inevitably involve a publicity sufficiently rank—would be to make one's self conspicuous and a little ridiculous . . . Smiling, he picked up his book and opened it. He would neither refuse nor accept.

'Oh well,' he murmured, more to the pianist than to the girl. 'We're all personal on a ship! What else is there to do?'

'Right!' beamed the pianist. 'What the devil can we do if we don't talk?'

'Talk!' sneered the vampire. 'A lot of good talking does.'

'What's wrong with it? There are worse things than talking.'

'Ha—ha!' She laughed, lifting her throat. This amused her intensely, and she contrived without much subtlety to suggest that it was a little wicked of her to be amused. Her chief means to this end was another rapid green wink at Demarest. 'Worse things—I should hope so!'

The pianist grinned sharply, eager to take her up on this.

'What do you mean?' he said, leaning toward her.

'Mean?' She drew back, her face becoming hard and distant. She was rebuking him. The rebuke, however, seemed to grow with difficulty in her mind, and before it had flowered into speech (as for a moment Demarest thought it would) she relented, changed her purpose, and again gave her short empty musical laugh.

'What's he talking about?' she said to Demarest. 'I mean worse things, that's all! . . .'

'He's got an evil mind,' said Demarest. 'He thought you meant a particular kind of worseness.'

The girl's undershot jaw dropped. This was too deep for her.

'Are you talking English, or am I crazy?'

'He's talking Welsh,' the pianist went on . . . 'You haven't told me your name. I'll bet it's Evans or Jones.'

'No, Davis, Peggy. You can call me Peggy, as we're old friends.'

'Help! I'm married already.'

'*You* married?' she cried. 'Well, you do look sort of married, come to think of it.'

'Oh, I say!'

'Don't you think so? He has that look—you know, sort of meek.' She gave a hoot behind her handkerchief, gleaming at him askance. 'I'll bet he washes the dishes.' She hooted again.

The pianist flushed, grinning. 'What about you? Are you married too? I'll bet you're married to a dozen!'

'No, I'm a widow. My husband died last month, in Providence—that's where we lived.'

'A widow! . . . You're a widow?' The pianist was unembarrassed.

'Yes. I had a good job too, but my brother thought I'd better come back.'

'A brother in Wales?'

'Mm! A miner. Oo such a fine, big boy. He's going to meet me at Liverpool.'

. . . Abstracting himself from the persistent dialogue, Demarest tried to read. A phrase,— a sentence,—but the dull dialogue which kept intruding, mingled with shouts and laughter blowing through the open port-hole, and the softened *sh sh* of the sea, prevented him from much concentration. Malvolio, the bar-steward, smirking, made a pretence of wiping the table and chairs; opened another port, smirked again at the girl;

rearranged the brass spittoons, pushing them with his foot; then came and leaned his long black-haired hands (the wrists bony) on the table, the dusting cloth under one palm. He addressed Demarest ingratiatingly.

'Your friend was looking for you.'

'My friend?'

'The old man,' said Malvolio confidentially. 'The one you played draughts with. He said he had something particular to say to you.'

'Oh, did he!'

'Yes. Something about those two young ladies, I think he said it was.'

Demarest felt himself blushing. Malvolio, still leaning his long wrists on the table, turned slow, greedy eyes toward Peggy Davis, who returned the look haughtily.

'Those two young ladies, eh!' pursued the pianist. 'Seems to be a lot of young ladies on this ship!'

The bar-steward smiled, gave one formal wipe at the table, and withdrew lightly.

'Why all the mystery?' inquired Peggy.

'No mystery. They sit opposite me at meals. Amusing kids—nothing but kids.'

'Oh yes—these kids! Travelling alone, I'll bet —under the chief steward's protection! Ha ha!' Peggy hooted unctuously,—dabbed her mouth, —gleamed lasciviously.

'You seem to know all about it,' said the pianist.

'Ho! That'll do for you. You don't have to do it yourself to know about it.'

'No?'

'No . . . Say, aren't you impertinent! . . .'
Looking at his opened book, Demarest wondered about the old man and the two girls. What was up? Smith had been frank about his interest in them—franker than he himself had been. He found the thought vaguely exciting. Had Smith made advances, taking advantage of the proximity of his cabin to theirs? He hoped Pauline—no . . . How perfectly ridiculous . . . Here he was, setting out three thousand miles to see Cynthia, and almost immediately allowing himself to be attracted by the small, impudent, brazen baggage of a vaudeville queen—good God, how disgusting! He flushed, thinking of it. 'Off to my love with a boxing glove ten thousand miles away.' Disgusting? No. A pluralistic universe —as plural of morals as of worlds. The magnificent 'thickness' of things . . . A bugle blew just outside the port-hole. 'Church!' cried Peggy, jumping up. 'Don't go!' the pianist replied holding her hand. She slapped him playfully and departed . . . Men began coming into the smoking-room, evidently from a desire not to be seen on deck during the services. He rose, intending to go out and taste the Sabbath stillness and desertion which he knew would possess the ship at this hour, but as he rose a voice shouted 'Who plays bridge?' and he found himself automatically replying, 'I do!' 'What's your name, Mr.——?' 'Demarest.' 'Mr. Demarest'—the Jew waved a thick hand which hooked a cigar—'Meet Major Kendall, Mr. Hay-Lawrence and myself,—Solomon Moses David Menelik Silberstein.' There was a laugh, slightly uneasy, while Silberstein

placidly and heavily but with dexterous hands shuffled the cards. 'I'm not one of those Jews,' he went on, 'who think it's a disgrace to be a Jew. And I always think it a good plan to be explicit on that point—if you'll forgive my little idiosyncrasy, gentlemen—at the beginning of an acquaintance. It helps to avoid mistakes.'

'Hear, hear,' said Hay-Lawrence faintly, unfrowning his monocle, which fell on its black cord.

'I've got time for just one rubber—or two fast ones . . . I'm glad I found this nice corner with you gentlemen,'—Silberstein pursued—'cut, please Major,—because anything more like a mausoleum than the first cabin is, on this trip, I've never even considered possible. Thirteen passengers altogether, of whom half are octogenarians. One old man in a wheel-chair sitting in the smoking-room being uproariously rowdy all by himself, and half a dozen female century-plants sitting as far from each other as they can in the drawing-room. They look to me like Boston's best . . . I perceived that if I was to live for another twenty-four hours I would have to seek life down here with you fellows . . . My God, the meals up there! It's like a funeral . . . Your bid, Mr. Demarest . . . You come from New York?'

'Yes . . . One spade.'

'One spade he says. My partner's going to say something—I can see it in his eye. It's all right so long as I don't see it in his hand . . . Sometimes the eye is quicker than the hand, on these boats. No reflections, gentlemen.'

'Double one spade,' said Hay-Lawrence, frowning his monocle into place.

'Now that's a new one on me,' said the bald-headed Major, flushing. It was explained by Silberstein, and the game proceeded. The Major polished his pince-nez, endeavouring to look firm.

'Observe,' murmured Silberstein placidly, 'the game in the opposite corner. Particularly observe the gent sitting with his face towards us. You notice that his left eye is glass—a little too far to starboard—the man, I mean, who strikes you as skull-faced. He was on the same ship with me two months ago. A professional card-player, addicted to poker. Notice also the rabbit-faced timid little gent who sits two places to his left. Partners, though they pretend not to know each other. They never meet on deck, you'll find, and they probably don't eat at the same table.'

'Poker, what?' said Hay-Lawrence, grimacing as he peered over his shoulder. 'I'd like to have a go at him. I've got a score to wipe out against poker. I had a little experience in my hotel the night before we sailed.'

Silberstein lifted a slow finger, diamonded, thickly reprehensive.

'Never play poker with strangers . . . Or bridge either. Not for high stakes.'

'Of course. I'm not a fool, man! In this case, I was bored and I took him on for pure love of adventure. I knew quite well he was some kind of sharper, but I wanted to see how he would do it.'

'Well, how *did* he do it?'

'That's the joke! *I* don't know. For the life of me I couldn't see anything wrong with it. He sauntered up to me while I was reading in the

lounge, and asked if I'd like to play. I bought
a pack of cards, and we went up to my room.
Then we sat down and drew cold hands for a
dollar a hand. In an hour and a half I'd lost a
hundred dollars. Then I quit. He thanked me
politely, put on his hat and departed . . . I
watched him like a hawk—mind—and I couldn't
see a *damned* thing that looked wrong.'

'No. You never do. Those men are artists.
They wouldn't do it if they weren't.'

'Three men asked me to play bridge with them
on the train from Buffalo,' said the Major, blushing. 'I refused at first, but then as they said
they'd been unable to get a fourth anywhere, I
joined them, stipulating that there should be no
money in it. After three hands, they said there
was no fun in it without a small stake—say fifty
cents a hundred. "Good-bye, gentlemen!" I said
and cleared out.' The Major giggled, blushing;
then frowned severely, looking at his cards. Silberstein, with green eyes far apart, glanced at him
casually and massively. The Frog Prince.

'The Major takes no chances,' he said. 'Even
in the Army, discretion is the better part of valour
. . . How do you know, Major, that Mr. Demarest and I aren't conspiring together to defraud
you? . . . Consider the circumstances. We
three meet, and look for a fourth . . . I sing out
here in this crowded smoking-room in my un-
abashed Jewish way, and out of all those present,
and endowed with bridge talent, *Mr. Demarest,*
total stranger, steps forward . . . Think it over!
Looks sort of bad, doesn't it?'

'You alarm me,' breathed the Major.

'And me too,' said Demarest. 'What am I up against?'

'And as for the Duke of Clarence, my partner,' Silberstein placidly pursued, while he arranged his cards and Buddha-like serenely surveyed them with slow slant eyes from end to end of the firmly-held fan, 'just take a good look at him, gentlemen. I ask you, was there ever a more perfect specimen of the gentleman villain? One look is enough. Monocle and all. Raffles isn't in it, nor Dracula, nor Heliogabalus. That bored Oxford manner, the *hauteur*—you know, those English go in for a *hauteur*—correct me, partner, if my French pronunciation isn't all it should be—and the skilfully introduced little story of the hundred dollars lost to a New York con man—— Well, I say no more.'

'Oh, dry up, Silberstein,' said Hay-Lawrence, grinning uncomfortably.

'See the guilty look? . . . That's the only weakness of these English sharpers. They're too proud and sensitive. Make personal remarks about them, and they'll betray themselves every time . . . Now, Mr. *Demarest* here, has the cold, unmoving New England face, the sacred cod; he conceals his feelings better even than the Englishman, simply because he hasn't got any. Am I right, Mr. Demarest?'

'Perfectly,' Demarest laughed. 'As for *you*——!'

'Well?'—calmly staring. 'What about me?'

'The Sphinx, beside you, has as mobile a face as an *ingénue*!'

Silberstein played a card, reached his hand

(cigar-holding) for the trick, then drew back as if stung.

'Ouch. He fooled me. He saved that up.'

'Yes. I saved it up,' said Demarest, tapping the trick on the edge.

'Now that we're so well acquainted, Mr. Demarest, I should like to ask you about that young lady—the term may be taken to have some latitude—to whom you were talking just now. I wouldn't call her a beauty, exactly—but I think it could be said with some justice that her appearance is very remarkable.'

'The Welsh Rarebit?'

'Ha!' cried Silberstein, rolling his large head back and half-closing his eyes appreciatively. 'Ha! is that what you call her? Welsh Rarebit is good, is very, very good. Welsh Rarebit she is . . . And what about her, if I may ask without seeming to be too impertinent?'

'Peggy Davis. A widow of one month—so she says. Returning from Providence, where her husband died, to Wales. Her handsome brother —a miner—will meet her at the dock.'

'Yes? . . . It sounds fairly circumstantial? . . . It convinces you?'

'The damndest face I ever saw,' said Hay-Lawrence. 'It makes me ill to look at her.'

'You mean'—the Major lifted off his pince-nez and endeavoured to look fiercely out of gentle brown eyes, under a brow beetling but more academic than military—'the queer-looking girl who sat over there talking with the musician? . . . She looked to me like hot stuff! . . . *He he.*' He put on his pince-nez, bridling and blushing,

looking naughtily from one to the other of the
bridge-players.

'Go to it, Major,' breathed Silberstein smokily.
'We give you a free hand—go as far as you like.
Only I feel it's my duty, as one hideously experienced, to warn you that she will probably see you
coming . . . Ha!' He took a puff at his cigar,
shut narrow eyes ecstatically, and then, while the
others laughed, gave another 'Ha!'

'I'm no chicken myself,' said the Major. 'I
haven't spent two years in Constantinople for
nothing.'

'Have you got any photos of your harem?'
asked Demarest.

The Major quivered with delight at so much
attention. 'No,' he giggled, 'not this year's.'

'I suppose,' said Silberstein, 'you Orientals
change the houris in your harems—(By Godfrey
doesn't that run off nicely?—houris in your
harems! Have you a little houri in your harem?)
—as often as we poor stick-in-the-muds change
the goldfish in our finger-bowls. What's a houri
more or less? And you must develop a very fine,
a very subtle taste in those matters.'

'Smubtle,' suggested Demarest.

'Score two for Mr. Demarest. Yes, you
Oriental potentates must be full of smubtleties.
Thank you for that word, Mr. Demarest—a permanent addition to my vocabulary . . . A smubtle allusion! Good.'

'The poker-player is mad about something,'
said Hay-Lawrence, turning.

'Is it true that glass-eyes sometimes explode?'
Demarest leaned to look at the angry face. 'I've

heard somewhere that they do. Here's hoping.'

'This is nothing to what will go on, on the last night, when they'll propose a no-limit game. That will be the time to get your money back, Duke.'

'For God's sake, don't call me *Dook*.'

Smith's cherub face appeared at a window, looking in. He waved his cigar, disappeared, and then came in through the door, soft-stepping and sedate.

'Playing bridge, I see,' he said perching temporarily on a chair arm. 'I've been looking for you.'

'Where were you at breakfast?' said Demarest. 'It looked bad.'

'Sea-sick? Oh, no. I'm never sea-sick. Never . . . Oh, I see, I see what you mean! . . . Ha ha . . . No—but I'll tell you something later. Come out and walk when you've finished. Beautiful air this morning—beautiful.' He rose absent-mindedly, stared wistfully out through the window, which careened against the smooth blue sea, then softly departed. His cherub face passed the port-window outside, in profile, evenly gliding.

'He was clever,' murmured Silberstein. 'He knew we were playing bridge.'

'A nice old bird,' said Demarest. 'Spent his life —thirty years of it—selling sheet-music and opera-tickets in New Orleans. Knows every nigger song and jazz tune from the time of the flood. He'll make life miserable for the ship's orchestra.'

'Made a large fortune at it, I don't doubt!'

'Enough to go back to England on. It's really rather pathetic . . . He's going back to see his

childhood place, where he hasn't got a living relative and won't know a soul . . . Why does he
do it?'

'Nostalgia,' blew Silberstein. 'He's looking for
his mother. He wants to die, and doesn't know it.'

'Good God,' cried Hay-Lawrence. 'I believe
that's what's wrong with me.'

'And me!' said Demarest.

The whistle blew, vibrating the table. 'Twelve
o'clock,' said the Major and they all set their
watches. Ten minutes later, the Third Officer
came in, swiftly stepping over the brass door-sill,
a notice in his hand. He affixed this to the green
baize bulletin board. The day's run. Three hundred and one miles, fine light W.S.W. breeze, smooth
sea . . . 'One day gone, gentlemen,' said Silberstein. 'The game is adjourned till later . . . Some
time this afternoon?' . . . Demarest, loitering a
moment to look at the chart, saw the glass-eyed
poker player slam down his cards, face upwards.
'*Jesus Christ!* I never saw such a lot of pikers!
. . . What's the matter, you afraid to bet? *That's*
what I've got—a pair of deuces!' He drew the
piled chips toward him. 'Come on, ante. And
put some ginger into it.' He turned dissociated
eyes arrogantly about the room, seeking approval.

Released from church, the passengers were pacing the deck briskly, in couples, or composing
themselves complicatedly in chairs, entangled with
rugs, cushions, mufflers and gaudy magazines.
Smith, at the forward end of the second-class deck,
leaned on a stanchion, watching a sailor chalk on
the polished deck the squares for shovel-board.
Demarest, his back against the broad railing, hear-

ing behind him and below him the laughter of
steerage passengers and the whine of a concertina,
watched the figure of Smith, small, immaculate
and pathetic, cigar in hand, rising slowly against
the wide arc of sea and sky, and again as slowly,
with a slight swerve, descending. He stood there
immovable, heroic and tragic, describing unconscious patterns against the infinite, watching the
stooped sailor. Was it only the imminence of sea
and sky, the immense solitude, that gave poor
Smith a sort of grandeur? No. These factors did
not so much confer as reveal it. Selling sheet-
music in New Orleans ('*Cuddle up a Little Closer,*'
or '*Every Little Movement has a Meaning All Its
Own*') or speculating in opera-tickets during the
opera's annual visit, or swinging like a tiny pendulum here between water and space—Smith was
equally portentous. He epitomized superbly the
tragic helplessness of the human . . . Better than
himself for example,—or Hay-Lawrence, or Silberstein? Yes, somehow better,—better perhaps because he was less conscious of hostile destiny than
these, and therefore gave the effect of being more
impotent. He had also the air, somehow, of being
extraordinarily complete. There were no loose
ends . . . An ant in the grass, crawling up a dry
twig, waving stupid antennæ at the void; descending patiently again; exploring an enormous pebble
all the way to its barren top,—descending once
more; and so on, and so on, one vast obstacle
after another patiently and stubbornly encountered; an oak-tree climbed, right out into the infinite, suspended in the blue; a stone wall, vast
labyrinth of monoliths, stout-heartedly and mi-

nutely overcome. *Smith!* . . . Who the devil was
Smith? . . . Demarest watched him rising and
falling there against the ultramarine abyss; unconscious and infinitesimal; smoking the 'expensive'
cigar which Mr. Charlton had given him. His
whole career was poised there,—hung in the blue,
—twinkled,—and disappeared. There he was, to
begin with, in the stationer's shop in Bideford,
rosy-cheeked and amiable, handing down boxes of
blue envelopes for a customer, checking off returned books of fiction in the Circulating Library
(two hundred volumes) and reading them all himself, particularly the works of Thackeray; on Sunday afternoons, trudging in the rain over the red
fields to Hartland Point. Then the scar on his
upper lip,—some sort of row,—over a girl perhaps?
Disgrace, discouragement, love of adventure?
Adventure! Straight from the stationer's shop
in Bideford, to a music shop in New Orleans, there
piling and turning music for thirty years! The
opera tickets. He got a corner in them once—and
sold them for five dollars each. Even to angry
old Mrs. Schneider! (whoever *she* was). That was
adventure. And now his second great adventure
—the return! No doubt Silberstein was right—
it was an unconscious desire for death, for the
mother . . . The sailor was pointing at the shovel-
board pattern. Smith leaned, goggling, and suddenly took a couple of quick unpremeditated tripping steps, irresistibly suggested by the sea. Re-
covering, he pointed along the deck, nodding his
head. Then gave the sailor a cigar . . . Yes, one
saw the whole of Smith's career transacted there
on the swaying deck in sunlight, poised between

sea and sky. It was amusing to run it off, like
a cinema film, at terrific speed, so that the whole
life-story unfolded itself like one of those flowers
which the cinema permits one to see in the act
of blooming: the calyx breaking, the pointed petals
whitely springing apart and curling back, and then
in a little while the rapid shrivelling . . . The
sailor climbed the companion-way; and Smith,
turning, stared exophthalmically at the sea.

'Ah, there you are! . . . I was just wondering,
because I saw that slimy Jew go up the stairs . . .
Jews! deliver me. I don't like them. What you
want to play with him for?'

'Oh, he's harmless. As a matter of fact, he's
an extremely interesting fellow.'

'May be, may be . . . Come down to my room.
I'll show you something. Something that'll make
your hair stand on end. Yes, siree! It'll make
your hair stand on end.' Smith revolved his cigar
softly between thumb and finger, his brown eyes
solemn and comic under the arched grey eyebrows.

'Lead on, father!'

'Don't call me father. Brr. Makes me shiver.
I feel my coffin . . . Look! There she goes now!'

He nudged Demarest violently. Mrs. Faubion
came running up the companion-way from the
steerage-deck,—sea-blown, wild-haired, impetuous,
—and flashed saucily round the corner and out of
sight. Daisy Dacey, grinning fatuously, and picking her pink muslin skirt up a little too high (consciously) came after her. She too disappeared.

'Come along,' said Smith. He walked rapidly
after the two girls, turned the corner, entered the
main door aft, and descended the red plush stairs,

Demarest following him a little embarrassed. No
sign of them in the dining-room. The rows of
white tables were set for dinner. Stewards went
to and fro with napkins, turned the revolving
chairs into position, put down forks or linen-cov-
ered dishes of bread. Smith passed into the corridor beyond the kitchen, the same corridor off
which Demarest lived; but went to the alley beyond. Down this he turned and proceeded to
the end, his room being at the left. The door opposite his, which had been ajar, was shut sharply
just before they reached it. Smith, beaming,
tapped it with white knuckles. 'Coo hoo!' he cried.

'Who is it?' The voice was Pauline Faubion's,
stridently challenging.

'The dressmaker. Any orders for lunch?'

'No. Go way! Don't be silly!' A trilled giggle from Daisy Dacey.

'Oh, very well, very well.' He winked at Demarest, opening his own door. 'Look!' he said,
dramatically waving his cigar at the back of the
door, which he had shut. Half a dozen dresses
hung on it, suspended on hangers—black, scarlet,
white, green, and two flowered muslins.

'What's the idea?' said Demarest.

'Dresses.' Smith goggled mournfully.

'So I see! I know a dress when I see it . . . I
didn't know you were travelling in dresses, as the
saying is!'

'I don't as a rule. But I'm always willing to
oblige.' He smiled mysteriously, cunningly.

'Well, what's the idea?'

'Ha! I wish I knew . . . She knocked at the
door this morning when I was shaving. She had
on one of those pink things that you can't quite see

through. Good morning darling, says I!—Good
morning grandpa, says she!—What can I do for
you darling, says I?—Have you got room for some
dresses, says she?—Sure, says I!—Well, here they
are, says she!—And she gave me an armful of
them, and helped me to hang them up. Not hooks
enough in their cabins, and they were afraid the
dresses would get wrinkled staying in the trunk. . .
What do you think of it?'

'Think of it!'

'Mm . . . Funny idea.' The old man gleamed
cherubically. 'You've got to hand it to father. I
guess I made a good impression. What do you
think?'

'Looks like it. Or maybe they think they can
trust you!'

'Ha! . . . May be—may be! . . . Nice dresses
anyway.' He ran his fingers down a fold of scarlet
satin. 'Look at the beads on this . . . Cost a lot
of money, that dress, I'll bet . . . A party dress—
cut kind of low. Soft, eh? Feel it. And there
are the little straps that go over the shoulders.'
He took the frock down on its hanger, and turned
it slowly, appreciatively about. 'Velvet, too.
Must feel nice to have velvet next to the skin.'

'I wonder if she's been on the stage,' said Demarest. 'They almost look like stage frocks.'

'Don't think so. She got married to this chap
when he was stationed in Dover during the war.
After the war she went out west with him . . .'
He hung the scarlet satin up again, then lifted a
fold of flowered blue muslin against his face.

'Mm!' he bumbled. 'Smells nice . . . Heliotrope . . . Smell it!'

Demarest, agitated and embarrassed, pleasantly

shocked by the old man's candour, lifted the blue muslin.

'Heliotrope . . . Yes! . . . I congratulate you.' He solemnly shook Smith's hand. Smith smiled, but with something mournful and questioning in his puzzled brown eyes.

'Seriously,' he said, pausing to fling his chewed cigar through the open port, 'what do you make of them?'

'Make of them? How do you mean?'

Meditative but twinkling, they looked deep into each other's eyes. Why was it that Demarest felt an obscure impulse to discourage the old man? . . . Jealousy? . . . Pauline was, of course, attractive to him: and he resented the fact that her frocks hung here in the old man's cabin. But this was superficial. Wasn't it, more profoundly, that he enormously liked old Smith, and wanted to keep him out of trouble? Wasn't it also that he resented, savagely resented, this evidence of the un-waning magic of sex? He pitied him. The old ox being led to the slaughter. Did he also, pity-ing poor old Smith, pity himself,—foreseeing, with dreadful certainty, himself grown old to no greater wisdom? . . .

'I mean,' said Smith, rocking gently backwards with the ship, 'do you think they're straight?'

'Straight! . . .' Demarest gave a short laugh. 'God knows . . . My guess would be that they are. Faubion is, I should think anyway—I'm not so sure about Dacey . . . I saw her flirting with the Chief Steward last night.'

'Oh! You think Faubion's straight? . . . I wonder! . . .' He ruminated sadly. He sat down on the edge of his bunk, drawing himself up like a jackknife so as not to bump his tweed hat, still ruminating. He tucked his plump hairless hands under his knees. 'What makes you think so? Sit down. We've got a few minutes before dinner . . . Nice sound the sea makes through a port-hole—wish they wouldn't clamp it shut at night.'

'I wish I had a port-hole at all . . . I don't know, she strikes me as straight—that's all. Straight but fidgety.'

'Straight but fidgety! No siree, Bob. I'm an old fool, and never knew a woman, if that girl isn't——!' He lifted a twinkle, sidelong, toward Demarest. Demarest sat down on the red plush divan. A sour smell came up from it; and the clicking of the water bottle in its wooden socket, and then the loosely delayed return click, hollow and slack, made him slightly giddy. He lifted his nose toward the pure stream of air from the port. Porpoises. Flying fish. Icebergs. Cobalt and snow . . . A slice of porpoise, Mr. Smith? Thank you no, Mr. Demarest . . . Wing of Faubion, Mr. Smith? A little off the breast, please, Mr. Demarest . . . Faubion gazed at him, morose and sombre, reserved but yielding, implacable but affectionate. Poising the bread knife, with waved edge damascene, he prepared to make Faubion an Amazon. One-breasted. Tell me when it hurts, Faubion. Does it hurt? . . . A-a-ah-mmm—you're hurting—*now*! . . . Still hurting? . . . *Phhh*—not so —much. . . . She turned her head far to one side, closing her eyes . . . This was the moment—this was always the moment; that delicious moment of utter anguished surrender: the flushed face turned extravagantly aside, eyelids shut, mouth relaxed with pleasure but curved with apprehension and rigid with pain . . . The dew on the forehead . . . Singular, that we should so desire this of all possible moments, a moment the essentially fleetingest of moments, that one must dedicate one's life to its pursuit. A half-dozen such moments in a lifetime—moments which yield the full goblet, the nymph-cry in the blood, the whizzing off into space of the body . . . Helen Shafter, lying face downwards on the beach, crying, while it began slowly to rain . . . Eunice, suddenly letting her arm fall over the frayed edge of the couch, nerveless and abandoned, while with her other hand she covered her eyes, murmuring . . . Mary, on the hill near Banstead, looking at him through her fingers, frightened, while a little way off they heard the mowing-machine clattering and slaughtering among tall grass and poppies . . . What is man that thou art mindful of him? Melancholy. Men, in a smoking-room, recounting their conquests to one another. Was it, as always assumed, a mere boastfulness, a mere rooster-crow from the dunghill? No . . . It was the passionate desire to recreate, to live over again those inestimable instants of life, so tragically few, so irrecoverably lost. *'That reminds me of one time when I was staying——'* Yes, you can see the wretched man trying to summon them back, those few paltry episodes, and make of them, for his solace, a tiny immortal bouquet.

'She's damned attractive,' he said.

'Attractive!' moaned Smith. 'She's a ring-tailed screecher. She's got me going—yes, sir, she's got me going. She can put her slippers——'

He broke off, pondering. Click, and then cluck, went the water-bottle, while he ponderously pondered. The throb of the ship's engines was the throb of Smith, pondering the imponderable. One could see him in the act of evoking Faubion; an old wizard, toothless and long-bearded, putting one claw out of his coffin to make the last sign, then hooking his nail over the coffin's edge, bat-like. What, to him, was Faubion? *'Faubion!'* cried the withered brain; and saw flames dancing scarf-like in a jungle of lewd sounds and sights. Faubion, flame-bodied, wavered toward the coffin, bearing a slipper in each hand. Zebra-striped were the slippers, white and green, ophidian, with ruby eyes; and a fount of ostrich plumes jetted from each. She placed these adoringly beside the coffin, kneeling, and the bat-claw was drawn in, drawing with it flames and plumes . . . Are you warm enough, Mr. Smith? . . . Quite warm enough, thank you, Mr. Demarest! . . . And what is the flavour of Faubion, Mr. Smith? . . . Flamingo, hibiscus, and guava, Mr. Demarest! . . . Take then—eat, drink, live! . . . And lo, Smith lived; the coffin glowed about him, an incandescent chrysalis, burning translucently, within which lay Smith, gleaming and waxing; the fiery chrysalis flaked away, in small dissolving flakes of flame; and Smith, luminously waxing, with fiery veins and god-like nimbus, sprang up rejoicing, naked and blazing, a leafy vine of gold rapidly growing all over his body and burning off as it grew. To right and left of him jetted the ostrich plumes, spouted higher, arched flashing, and crashed upon him foaming. Caligula. King Caligula and the immortal daughter. *King Caligula setting forth:*

after a seven days' meditation : marched huge armies
a day to the north : and in the evening took his station :
on a green hill-top : peaked and——

'I wouldn't like to make a mistake though.   No,
sir.   Not much . . . Barnes—that officer—is supposed to be looking after her.   Suppose my foot
slipped?—Mmmm.   No.'

'You'd be shot at sunrise.   Walk the plank.'

'All the same—with care.   And the circumstances are favourable.   These dresses,—and their
cabin being just opposite,—don't you think——?'

'Take my advice and go slow.'

Smith blinked brown eyes under his tweed hat.

'You know—it's bad when you get to my age.
Bad.'

'When *isn't* it bad?'

'You wait . . . Specially if you're sort of a
timid fellow like me.   I never was much good at
love affairs.   Guess they don't like the timid fellows.   That's where I always made my mistake
. . .'

'Well, I don't think there's any golden rule for
success.   I'm no Don Juan myself.'

'No?   You look like the sort they throw themselves at.   I've only had one what you'd call "affair" in my life—yes, sir, just one.   And *that* was
my wife.'

'Oh . . . Is your wife dead?'   Demarest
smoothed his voice—discreetly, hypocritically.

'I don't know, and I don't care much.   She ran
away from me after six months.   Flew the coop.
With a little shrimp of a one-lunged candy salesman—married man, too.   Sixteen years ago—all
but three weeks.   She wrote me a couple of years

afterwards and wanted to come back . . . Not
much! No siree, Bob. She had another "think"
coming.'

'Was she young?'

'Young? Yes—too young. Twenty-one, and
I was thirty-five. She came to work in the piano
department, played the piano too, good little
pianist . . . Last I heard of her she was playing
the piano in a movie in St. Louis . . . Good riddance, I guess . . . Of course I've had a little
fling now and then—you know—but never what
you'd call a nice girl . . . That's what I'd like,
to settle down for good with a nice girl.'

'Marry again?'

'Oh, well, I'm not so particular about marriage
—besides, I've never got a divorce . . . But
some nice young girl to wash the dishes, and
look after me, and get my money when I die. I've
got a tidy little sum saved up and nobody to leave
it to.'

> . . . *I'm tired of living alone.*
> *I'd like some young wife of my own.*
> *Some bow-legged Venus,*
> *To call me Silenus*——

Smith had bored his young Venus? Too at-
tentive and exacting, too worshipping. Pawing
her all the time, probably. 'Now darling! I don't
want you tiring yourself out. You stay home and
rest this afternoon, and I'll come home early . . .'
Mrs. Smith sat down at the piano when she heard
the front door shut. *The Holy City. Ho-sanna-
i-in the high-est, ho-sann-a-a-for-evAH mooore*
. . . Singing captivatingly, eyes on the ceiling,

nevertheless she revolved on her stool now and then to see if anyone was coming. Nope!—not yet. *Flutter—flutter.—Waltz me around again Will-ee; a-round—around—around.* A footstep on the 'stoop'? Mrs. Smith turned sharply her eager white chin and oystery blue eyes. There he was. He had a newspaper in one hand and a box of candy in the other. He tapped with the folded newspaper on the window. She rose and opened it. 'Did you meet him?' 'Yes, but he didn't notice me. I've got tickets to Nashville. Four o'clock.' 'I told you not to.' 'Hurry up and pack your things.' 'Don't stand *there*!—wait for me at the station. I haven't got a cent.' 'Here . . . if you leave a note for him, *don't* tell him where you've gone.' 'Darling! Do you think I'm such a fool? I may be *crazy*——!' She took the five-dollar bill and the box of chocolates. Huylers: with pistachio acorns. Smiling, she put her forefinger to her lip, transferred the kiss to the back of his right hand, drawing it softly the whole length of his yellow-haired little finger, then shut the window and ran to pack . . . *Waltz me around again Will-ee . . . around—around* . . . At four-twenty Smith came in, beaming. 'Coo-hoo!' he fluted, and then again softly stepping toward the kitchen, 'Coo-hoo!' . . . No answer. 'Waltz Me Around Again Willie' on the piano, and still hanging in the air. An opened box of chocolates, with only the pistachio acorns gone. A note on the dining-room table. '*Frank —I've gone away. Try to forgive me. I couldn't have stood it. I don't love you and wouldn't have made you a good wife. Terribly sorry. Will write you sometime. Miss Dillingham will be glad to take the cat. Try not to think too badly of me. I'm not good enough for you, and that's a fact. Maydie . . .'* Poor old Smith. Incredulous, he cried 'Coo-hoo' again; then again. All a joke. He flapped his wings, goggled, and turned into a cuckoo, flying from top to bottom of the house, dashing against walls, looking repeatedly and dementedly in the cellar, the kitchen, the bathroom, the attic. 'Coo-hoo!' he cried, and even put his absurd head out of the cupola window and coo-hooed at the roof, thinking she might be there. No answer. Not a sound. He returned to the kitchen, where he met Nicodemus, the cat. 'Ptrnyow!' said Nicodemus. His saucer was empty, and Smith filled it. Tears came into his eyes. 'Poor old Nik,' he said, 'was a nice old nickums . . .' Gone. Gone. Gone. Gone . . . He had a sense of having been excavated—a hollow, aching shell. He sat and thought. At eight o'clock, getting hungry, he opened the ice-chest. And at the sight of the butter dish he burst into tears. Coo-hoo: boo-hoo. Tohu-bohu.

III

HAY-LAWRENCE frowned his monocle into his left eye-socket, stretching the left corner of his refined cruel mouth. A point of green handkerchief protruded from the checked breast pocket. The offensive plushy shoes—brown suède?—were neatly crossed under the table. Blue cuff-edges showed, starched and sharp, at the sleeves, as he held out his brown lean hands.

'Which?' he said.

'Right,' said Demarest, touching the right with light fore-finger, refined and arch.

'Right is white,' said Hay-Lawrence, replacing the white pawn and then the black. He turned the chess-board. Pawn to king four—Pawn to king four—Knight to king's bishop three— Knight to queen's bishop three. Bishop to knight five—Pawn to queen's rook three. Bishop to rook four . . .

'Ruy Lopez,' murmured Hay-Lawrence haughtily.

'Ruy Lopez.'

The Major, self-conscious, smiling, blushing, stepped over the sill with the Welsh Rarebit, one hand under her arm, his tweed cap and book in the other. The grey flat sea washed in with the opening door, was shut out hissing.

'*There's* a corner,' he said, consciously a man of the world, conscious because from Murryville, Ohio.

'Where?' The Welsh Rarebit wiped her mouth. She peered cupidinously into the smoke.

64

'There.' He lifted his book and cap. 'Hello! The intelligentsia are exercising their brains.'

'You flatter us,' said Demarest. 'Do you play?'

'Not often. I used to play a good deal in Constantinople—I knew an old Turk general who played a most awfully good game. He'd have been too good for me,—if he hadn't constantly made howlers!' He twinkled, apologetic and vain.

'What is it?' said Peggy Davis, smiling with moist affection at Demarest and then with fleeting slyness at Hay-Lawrence. 'Halma?'

'The Royal Game of Chess, Mrs. Davis! Shame on you. He he!' The Major giggled, wriggling.

'Royal crumbs!' croaked Peggy. 'Let's sit down.' They moved to the next corner, stiff-kneeing past the table-edge, the Major putting his book down, then his cap on the book, then his pince-nez on his cap. Leaning his neat striped arms on the table he turned and inclined his flushed academic brow toward the Welsh Rarebit, pinkly and intimately. He began speaking in low tones. Malvolio smirked at them through the smoke, corkscrew in hand.

'God,' swore Hay-Lawrence, 'that woman gives me the pip . . . Did you ever see such a face in your life?'

Knight to bishop three he curved with lean fist.

'Is this the face that scuttled a thousand ships? Opened the sea-cocks. It's that undershot wet lower lip that gets me,' said Demarest, castling. 'Can you imagine kissing it? Holy Smackerel! It glistens!'

'Good God! Don't suggest it: *cloaca maxima*.

Accidental death by drowning would be the verdict at the inquest.'

'No . . . suicide whilst of unsound mind.'

Hay-Lawrence, smiling retrospectively, with slow-consuming satisfaction, lifted the king's bishop. To king-two. A careful player, orthodox and gingerly. Rook to king-square, Demarest moved delicately, conscious of Hay-Lawrence's sharp refinement and expensive dress. He must be, in England, well connected. Latent arrogance, and rudeness overlaid by good manners. Sloane Square—or a Sloane Square Mews? . . . Cheyne Walk? . . . Perhaps he had met Cynthia. There was something a little flashy about him, however. And the sort of refinement that invites coarseness in the beholder.

'She reminds me,' Demarest refinedly grinned with one side of his mouth, 'of the little song about the spittoon.'

Out came the monocle.

'The spittoon? No! What is it?' The pawn in his paw went to queen's knight four. Back, bishop. Draw in your mitre! To knight three.

'Say not spittoon . . . Nor cuspidor . . . Spit not too soon . . . Nor yet too far . . . Spit on the floor . . . Not on the wall . . . Or better yet . . . Spit not at all! . . .'

"Ha!' cried Hay-Lawrence. 'Jolly good! Ha! Ha! Jolly good, that.' He grinned the monocle back into his left eye. 'Nor cuspidor!'

'It's very nice sung, but I can't sing . . . A doleful hymn-tune.'

The half-opened windows opposite, rising, scooped a rapid green evening sky; then slowly, forwardly, swooped again, scooping a nacreous cloud touched with flamingo. The evening would be cold and clear. Stars indistinguishable from mast-lights. Seal up the ship-boy's eyes. Imperious surge. One of the poker players began humming the tune of *My Little Grey Home in the West,* then all began singing, furtively, fruitily sentimental. 'Ante, boys,' said the glass-eyed gambler evenly in the midst of it. The words dissolved, lowering, into an ululating hum, richly harmonized. *Ho-ome in the We-est.* Faubion. She came out of the West, flamingo-winged, with eyes far apart, sombre and absorbent. 'Hello, you!' she cried, provocatively brushing past him with saucily jerked shoulders. The opera-cape, flamingo-lined, streamed after her, billowing. *'Faubion!'* sang all the evening stars together. 'Oh, Faubion!' they sang, strumming their psalteries of gold and chrysolite. Faubion, coming out of the West, unperturbed, darkly walked eastward on the dark waters, Napoleonic, sardonic, ironic, Byronic. And what of Cynthia, sleeping in the east, deep sleep of the undefiled? *'Cynthia!'* trilled the morning stars with diamond voices . . . And Smith, little grey homunculus, came out of the sunset, paddling furiously in his coracle, dipping now to left and now to right, bird-like nodding his cuckoo-head as he paddled in the infinite. *'Faubion!'* he carolled—*'Coo-hoo Faubion! O Faubion!'* The paddled foam burst into trident flames to right and left as he coracled from wave to wave of the abyss. Phosphorescent foam dripped chrysolite from the paddles, from his fingers, from his drooped moustache; phosphor

glowed on his arched eyebrows, outlining fierily
his serio-comic eyes. *'Coo-hoo Faubion!'* he sang
in tiny tenor, while behind him the evening stars
drew together, blue cloak to cloak, psaltery against
psaltery, their mountain shoulders touching, their
eyes earnest and fiery. 'Deep Faubion!' they
diapasoned. *'Faubion in the lowest!'* . . .

'Say not spittoon,' murmured Hay-Lawrence,
and pushed the queen's pawn to queen three with
three tiny pushes of a clean finger-nail. Again
orthodox and safe. The queen's knight unde-
fended—but mobile. Queen Faubion,—the black
queen; Queen Cynthia,—white as the moon; and
King Caligula, corrupt and lecherous monarch,
ripe Camembert of kings. 'I would that all the
Roman people had but one neck.' Was that a
castration complex? . . . Ah—that dream this
afternoon during his nap. The asphyxiated baby
in the railroad station. Horrible and strange; for
as he worked over it (the Schafer method) pressing with merciful palms the small back to induce
breathing, regarding the small blue neck and wondering at the parents who had so casually abandoned it on a railway platform, he suddenly noticed that the head was not a head but a—— A
spasm of disgust . . . Sleepless Caligula, much
troubled by dreams, dreamed nightly that a figure,
—a form,—a shape,—vague and terrifying and
representing the ocean,—came to him speaking.
This was why he had bidden his army to collect
sea-shells, as trophies of his victory over the sea.
Pawn to queen bishop three was the move. His
horse, Incitatus, he had intended to make consul.
What form to represent the sea? Seaweed-

bearded, arms of green water and fingers of
foam; coral-branching; eyes wide, hollow, glau-
cous, where phosphor bubbled slow-winking, blue
and lemon-yellow, vitreous, moon-mocking. And
the voice? The dithering crack of two boulders
smitten together under the sea? The short cruel
resonance of submarine bells? The skirling lollop
of a wave running vortical into a dripping cavern,
weed-hung, wagging anguishedly like a tongue
against the horny barnacled palate, and then out
again, inarticulately noisy? *'Oo-wash-oo-wallop-
are-you-awake-King Buskin?'* . . . 'Attendants!
What ho! Attendants—lights!' . . . Sweating,
staring, Caligula started up. Two frightened attendants, with torches, ran in, kneeling. 'Is Pyrallis the prostitute there? Sleeping? Wake her
and bring her in! Wake also Valerius.' . . . 'My
lord?' said Pyrallis . . . 'Ah, Pyrallis, such a
nightmare I have had!—you would not believe it.
That wave again, with eyes, but no face. What
can it signify?' . . . 'Wine for supper, my lord.'
. . . 'Ah, Pyrallis—a throat so lovely,—to cut
when I like! Shall I cut it, to discover the secret
of its loveliness? I have told Caesonia that I will
vivisect her, so as to find out why I love her' . . .
Pyrallis cringed, frightened, at the look in the
goat's eyes. If she said, 'Yes, vivisect her,' might
he not—cruel madman and pervert—vivisect herself? . . . 'Let me soothe you, my lord,' said
Pyrallis . . . Black slaves hoisted a canopy of
purple. And Valerius, running out to weep in
the street—listen, good Romans and you shall
hear of the midnight ride of poor Valere!—that
mysterious Catullus Valerius rag.

'The climate?' said the Major, in a pause during which the poker players arranged and examined their cards. 'Delightful. Hot in the middle of the day, but you retire for a nap . . . There! those are the stone stairs I told you about. Look at the size of them. Each step two feet high. It's a humorous custom there to take ladies to see them. You let the lady go first, and if you loiter a step or two below—*he he!* That's Mrs. Grant, wife of one of the officials. A jolly good sport. *She* didn't give a damn—and didn't wear any petticoat either! . . . I stayed behind, admiring the view . . .' He laughed at the Welsh Rarebit with scarlet forehead; his face, flushed with invitation, moving jerkily upwards and downwards. The Welsh Rarebit, holding the photograph in one hand, regarded the invitation snakily; with an air of stupid appraisal. Then she squeezed his wrist.

'Naughty man!' she crooned.

'Well, boys,' sang the glass-eyed poker player. 'I think I'll have a look at this. There's fifty, and I'll raise it ten. It's a great life if you don't weaken.'

Hay-Lawrence brooded downward with cheeks sunk upon fists. Thought was moving in his brain. Like a train in a dark subway. A red spark coming nearer through the darkness, gliding round curves. Other thoughts too, going in other directions—he was listening to the voices in the room, listening to the half-excluded sound of sea, the thrum of the engines which vibrated his English body. What else? A brass telescope at Cowes; three pairs of white flannels; four pairs

of white shoes; tea on the lawn with Lady Daphne
Twinkleplume (slightly literary) followed by a
week on his little shoot in Wales. At home, his
neurotic wife, Gladys, sitting by the fire, looking
out of the darkening window on which long
bright gashes of rain began to glisten, looking
into the gloom of a London dusk, then again sitting by the fire, shivering. Tea at five. Vivien
had sailed from Cartagena. He had sailed from
Rio. He had sailed (a postcard said) from
Panama. He was sailing (a cable said) from
New York. The maid was taking Ching (the
Pekingese) for a walk round Sloane Square and
perhaps as far as Harrods. She ought to have
known it would rain. 'Vivien, tell me, why is it
you go away so much? Why are you always
going away to sea? leaving me alone?' 'Are we
going to discuss that again?' 'I can't stand it,
Vivien—I can't stand it . . . and all my friends
saying——' 'Let them talk. Tell them it's doctor's orders. Always tell them that. It's doctor's
orders that I should go to sea, and go to sea alone.
Would you like me to go mad?'

Knight to queen's rook four, the black horse
taken firmly by the ears.

'This is the part of the game where I always
go wrong,' said Hay-Lawrence.

Exchange the bishop for the knight? No. Concentrate on the centre—then the queen's pawn
forward. Bishop back, out of reach, to bishop
two.

'The part where I invariably go wrong,' murmured Hay-Lawrence lifting his queen's bishop's
pawn to bishop four. Pawn attack on the queen's

side—not too difficult to dispose of. Hay-Lawrence was human, after all—began shrinking to
commensurable proportions. Refinement without taste, intelligence without originality. From
either vantage point, one could probably intimi-
date him; for he was intelligent enough to know
his weaknesses and weak enough to be snobbish,
to want to make a good impression. Silberstein,
for all his vulgarity, had ruffled him and put him
at a disadvantage. 'Why shouldn't *I?*' thought
Demarest, secretly smiling. *'The Duke of Clarence, my partner.'* Pawn to queen four. Moses
Caligula Silberstein. Solomon Caligula. Did
Jael: with a nail: pierce the *viscera*: of Sisera?
No, his head! He is dead ... Caligula in Italian
sunset under a purple canopy, on which flashed
the eagle: Veronese, crouching in the dark fore-
ground, saw the scene. The wide eye of Veronese
saw the royal canopy, saw the black hand that
drew the curtain, watched the distance brightening among the hills. The cold, precise, lavish
hand of Veronese took possession of these things;
but it lacked madness . . . Again: *King Caligula,
setting forth; after a seven days' meditation;
marched his army a parasang north; and in the
evening took his station: on a green hilltop peaked
and gleaming: in the last slant of Alban sun.
Black slaves hoisted a canopy of purple—to hue
the vision of the god-like one* . . . The movement too jaunty altogether—but no matter.
Let it go—let it come—let it blossom and
die. Why did it blossom, though, out of the
massive face, dead white brow, and cruel eyes
of Silberstein? . . . *There, as he slept, he had*

his vision: but what was the vision? Elysian, fountain, mountain—threadbare rhymes, but let them serve. *There as he slept he had his vision: candles burned by the sacred fountain; sadly he walked, through a twilight Elysian, and came to the wall of the laureate mountain.* (Why laureate?) *Bathe your heart in the lustral water* (a voice, this was—a voice on the air, out of a grotto, out of a tree) *until like silver it burns and shines* (pleonastic), *and lo from the sky comes heaven's tall daughter—down from a star—by a stair of vines. Seven ripe peaches, from the walls of heaven*—not six, not eight, but seven. The Pleiades. Mystical seven. The seven moles on Juno's back. The seven stages in the life of man. The dance of the seven veils. Come seven—come eleven; everything at sixes and sevens. SEVEN. The word was extraordinarily beautiful, had a balance analogous to the balanced rhythm of the number itself—seven digits, of which the second was the s and the sixth the N. NEVES: Eno, owt, eerht, ruof, evif, xis, neves. A less emphatic series, but decidedly more interesting as sound, more varied. Queen to bishop two. Yes. He might have withdrawn the knight, however—to knight two. No—a pawn given up. The king's knight to queen two, then? That might have been better? . . .

'Oo, no—certn'y *not!*' cried the Welsh Rarebit with all-embracing archness, loudly and proudly.

'Why not?' The Major leaned forward over clasped fingers. His eyes, without the pince-nez, were beginning to look strained—but he liked his brown eyes to be seen. He had probably been told that their effect was fatal.   They twinkled, small, dark and bright, shy yet challenging, attractive in spite of (perhaps partly because of) their boyish vanity.

Peggy lifted her black-and-white striped coat-collar against the side of her face as if she were taking the veil.   Over this she swerved green eyes at him, upward.   Then lowered the long lashes and looked away.   An expression of practised fright—yet perhaps there was some faint survival of genuine feeling in it.   The Major, still gazing at her, as she did not reply, gave the little crisp musical giggle (very appealing) with which he was accustomed to fill in awkward pauses; and cast a quick glance over the small room to see if he were being observed.   When his eye met Demarest's, he looked sharply away, preened his moustache briskly with thumb and finger, then leaned, flagrantly confidential, towards the Welsh Rarebit and said something inaudible, gravely. Peggy ululated, lifting her throat.   The crumpled handkerchief was pressed against her lamia mouth.

'She drinks blood, that trollop,' said Demarest.

'Who? Oh . . . Can I look?'

'No.   The Major has his eye on us . . . The Major's a fast worker, as the saying is.'

As the saying is.   He had added this phrase for fear Hay-Lawrence might suppose him to use slang unconsciously—a disgusting cowardice! 'Yet I feel, somehow, that the Major will play safe, oh, very, very safe.'   Queen's knight to queen two.   'With masks and buttons—a friendly bout, no injuries, and a sweet heartache, not too severe, at farewell.'

'He's welcome,' muttered Hay-Lawrence, not looking up; unexpectedly severe. Something unconquerable in him after all. He scowled at the chess-board. Knight to queen's bishop three—retreat, confound him—he must be beaten; beaten thoroughly, but with inexpressive modesty, not to say apathy.

'I wouldn't touch her with a tent-pole,' Hay-Lawrence added. Hay-Lawrence with a tent-pole, walked sedately, haughtily. The Welsh Rarebit darted before him, twittering. Spare me, Clarence! . . . Damn silly . . . Pawn to queen five: *Now*—move your blasted knight again—move it, damn you! And hurry up.

'Damn it, why don't they open the bar?' Hay-Lawrence was angry. 'Absurd to keep us waiting like this. Steward?' A commanding finger.

Malvolio, languidly smiling, took four steps; steadying himself *en route* against a chair-back.

'Yes, sir.'

'When does the bar open?'

'Seven o'clock. Not till seven on Sunday. Ten minutes yet, sir.'

'What's yours, Demarest?'

'Mine? Oh—double Scotch.'

'Bring us a double Scotch and a port flip, as soon as you open.'

'Double Scotch and a port flip.'

'Utterly absurd on a ship . . . Absurd enough on land.' Scowling he lifted the knight, held it a moment in air, choosing a landing-place, then deposited it on the queen's knight's square. Home again. Black was beginning to be bottled up uncomfortably. Malvolio tapped at the bar window, which was opened an inch.

'A port flip, to come at seven.'

'What's that to me? I can't do anything without the keys, can I?'

'The gentleman wants it as soon as you open . . .'

Seven again—the mystic number. S for seven and Silberstein—Silverstone. Good morning, Silverstone! . . . Now to break open that queen's side—a Cæsarean operation—Cæsarean tactics. Very simple. Pawn to queen's rook four—that was it—that would do it. Afterwards the knight could get through. That is, if Hay-Lawrence, as he expected, moved the knight's pawn . . . Those fingers of his, so damnably refined, poised, clustered, above the pawn—like Cynthia's. Not really like Cynthia's; but they belonged, somehow, to the same constellation. Cynthia, pondering over the chess-board, frowning, poising her fingers thus—stately, reserved, leaning forward for a moment out of a world so remote from his own, stepping down for a moment from her heavenly treasure-house, with a star on her finger, to move the king on the board and then re-ascend—yes, *heaven's tall daughter . . . Seven ripe peaches from the walls of heaven, she holds in her hands. Bright, in her hair, the Pleiades glow: the Fire-flies seven, shine above her eyes and her forehead is fair . . . Angels follow her; gravely, slowly; with silver and vermilion and rainbow wings . . . One, more luminous—lost in his own light—sits on a cherry-tree bough, and sings: Blest be the marriage betwixt earth and heaven!* Cynthia's

fingers moved the knight's pawn to knight five.
Ah! Cynthia—not so skilful as usual! You will
be checkmated, Cynthia,—or else you'll resign
. . . That first game they had had on the *Silurian*
—when he had fetched the board from the smoking-room. She had received it with delighted
surprise—with what a lighting up of her face!
'Why, where did you get this? Is it yours?' . . .
And the book. He had been carrying the book
under his arm when Billington stopped him and
introduced him to her. 'I've found a chess-player
for you!' he had cried, fatuously. 'Miss Battiloro,
may I introduce Mr. Demarest? Mr. Demarest
has been looking everywhere for a chess-player
. . .' Then Billington had disappeared . . . The
astonishment, the incredulity, on finding himself
thus introduced to *her,* whom he had been avoiding for three days! He had been excited, frightfully excited. What was it, about her, that had
so agitated him from the outset, when he had
seen her climb up the gangway, slowly, then turn
about on the deck,—flinging the brown scarf-end
over her shoulder,—to wait for her companion?
The obscure shock had gone through him at once,
as he watched her from the deck above,—gone
through him like a tidal wave of the blood . . .
She, then—he had said to himself—is the one I
must escape! I must keep away from her . . .
This had not been difficult; for the simple reason
that she had, from the beginning, produced a
peculiar change in him: She had made him shy,
she had stripped him of his defences, she had
taken ten years from his age and made him again
a callow and awkward youth of seventeen. The

thought of talking with her simply terrified him.
And then, from the blue, the introduction! . . .
And regarding the title of the book, when he had
put it down on the deck beside her, she had said—
'That's *lovely,* isn't it! Don't you like it?' . . .
The effect of this commonplace remark had been
overwhelming. Its nature, the nature of the
magic, was dual; for first it was the slender
beauty of her voice, which everywhere broke
through and into him; and then it was the swift
revelation, no less intoxicating, that she had a
'mind.'—The two perceptions came upon him together, came like the opening of the sky for a
bewilderingly beautiful confusion of music. He
was done for; and he knew it instantly . . . Pawn
to rook five . . . Hay-Lawrence castled, not
pausing to think. Now, then—knight to bishop
four! *This* would make him think . . . Six bells
from the brass clock on the fluted wall—*tan-tan;
tan-tan; tan-tan.* The bar-window opened with a
bang, the bar-tender withdrawing a white linen
arm. Malvolio stepped nimbly, ingratiatingly,
with the tray.

'Double Scotch and a port flip,' he smirked.

'Oporto fleep,' grimaced Hay-Lawrence.

'To fornication,' said Demarest.

'To crime,' said Hay-Lawrence.

'No, sir,' nasally boomed the glass-eyed poker
player. 'This is on me. Waiter! One minute.
Now, gentlemen, give it a name and let it rest.
You, what'll it be? Bass? Guinness? Double
Scotch? . . . Well, then, three Basses, two double
Scotches, and a Guinness . . . God, I'm as
thirsty as a camel . . . If you'd 'a' come in, my

boy, with that pair of tens, you'd have been sunk
so deep they'd never have found you . . . that's
the time I *wasn't* bluffing.'

'There's much to be said for strong drink,'
murmured Demarest, filling his glass. 'Aha! The
Major is giving a little party . . .'

'Two Martinis,' Malvolio was saying, while he
regarded the Welsh Rarebit with a loitering eye.
He clearly felt that he had more right to her than
the Major had—he knew her level. This made
the Welsh Rarebit uneasy. She was uncertain
whether to be friendly or rude. Consequently she
was both, alternately. Queen's knight to queen
two . . . Hm . . . not so bad. Better threaten
the queen's rook pawn? Queen to king two . . .
For goodness' sake don't hold the door open like
that! Someone outside was holding it open, and
the night air, cold and full of sea-sound, galloped
round the smoky room. Silberstein stepped over
the brass, cigar in hand, and lazily, leisurely,
serenely, greenly, surveyed the lighted roomful of
people. Oh! Silberstein. Sorry, Silberstein,
didn't know . . . Annoyed with me, are you, for
keeping the door open? Run home and tell your
mother. Tell her a boy bigger than you hit you.
Bury your blubbering whelp's face in her apron
and bawl. I know you, you damned little coward
and sneak and tattle-tale . . . Silberstein saw
them and came toward them slowly, with un-
changing expression. Something flippant must be
prepared for him. Something smubtle . . .

'Well, Dook, is he trimming you? I'll bet you
two drinks New England will beat you.'

'Don't call me *Dook!*'

'Oh, all right, all right, Clarence—keep your
shirt on . . . Ha! This was a Ruy Lopez . . .
And Black, as they say in the books, has a seriously compromised position.'

'He's clever,' murmured Demarest. 'He knows
we're playing chess.'

'Chest,' corrected Silberstein. 'In the army
they call it chest.'

'What army?' Hay-Lawrence scowled.

'The grand army of the republic.'

'I'm surprised they ever heard of it,' said Hay-
Lawrence.

'That's all you know, is it . . .' Silberstein
leaned backward against the settee-back, half
standing, half sitting. He expanded his chest,
lazily, narrowing his eyes. 'My boy, the best
chequer players in the world are in the American
army. They know all the numbers.'

'Chequers! What the devil is chequers?'

'Never heard of chequers? No?'

'The same as draughts,' simpered Malvolio;
'they often ask me for chequers . . . You wanted
something, sir?'

'Yes, will you repeat, gentlemen?'

'Not I, thanks,' said Hay-Lawrence.

'Two double Scotches, then . . . You don't
mind if I watch, do you? Of course not. Everybody likes an audience.'

Hay-Lawrence pondered, brown right forefinger lying on ruddy right cheek. With the
other hand he revolved his *oporto fleep*. He was
annoyed. Liberties were being taken with him by
one who was not a gentleman. A frosty silence.
A pity to have the game spoiled, nevertheless. If

one could only keep separate the things one liked! Bawdy conversation with Silberstein—chess or literary conversation with Hay-Lawrence. Philately with the Major. With Smith—what with Smith? Poor old Smith. I wonder who's kissing him now? Where is our wandering Smith to-night? Pawing her dresses in his stateroom: like the fawn. M-m-m-heliotrope!

'Go away, man! How can I think with you sitting there, a mass of expert knowledge?'

'Go away? Not by a damn sight. I came here to drink.'

Rook to knight square. So: Hay-Lawrence would fight for command of this file. Bishop to queen three. Attack the rook's pawn. Can he save it?

'How!' said Demarest.

'*Gesundheit*,' said Silberstein. 'While he's thinking how to save his little goy—christians, that's what they call them on the east side, where they used to play you for a nickel a game,—I rise to remark that there's a clairvoyant on this ship . . . A full-fledged clairvoyant. I dug him out from under a palm tree in the second-class dining-saloon, where he was deep in the *Occult Weekly* or the *Mystic Monthly*, or some such thing—horoscopes on every page and ectoplasms running all over the place. Clairvoyant *and* clairaudient,—he's a wizard! You've got to take your hat off to him. A most peculiar specimen. And full of bright little predictions. "You," he said to me, after one look at my hand, and a glance at my left eye—"are hoping to sell chewing gum in England." How did he guess it?'

'Too easy,' said Demarest. 'Probably your bed-room steward.'

'You may be right, you may be right; the usual method—find out in advance. And easy enough on a ship. He also observed, sadly, that there would be a death on this ship. Not so cheerful, that. Who's elected? A chance for a pool. The dead man wins.'

'Well—does he say how he'll die?'

'Murder.' Silberstein was placid, but stared a little.

'Murder? On this ship? He's off his head.' Hay-Lawrence sipped his flip. A signet ring on the fourth finger.

'This grows interesting,' said Demarest. 'Also of personal concern.'

'It does . . . He felt something wrong with the ship when he got in—something wrong with the ship's aura.'

'I noticed that myself. Especially in that cor-ridor beside the kitchen!'

'Then last night he had a nightmare. He woke up thinking someone was in his room, turned on the light—no one. Looked out in the hall—not a soul. Everybody asleep. Then he remembered his dream. An old man with a hole in his head, walking toward him, stretching out his hands—in his pyjamas, he was—as if asking for some-thing.'

'An old man? That lets *me* out,' said Demarest.

'And me,' Hay-Lawrence sighed. Rook to king square . . . Bishop to queen two, Demarest moved smiling. All as anticipated.

'An interesting question. He says he's sure to

recognize the victim—hasn't seen him yet. When he *does* see him, ought he to tell him? If so, what?'

'He's cuckoo,' said Demarest. 'No harm if he *did*.'

'Would *you* like to be told?'

Silberstein stared with lazy penetration, his eyes cruel, at Demarest. A shiver went up Demarest's backbone and coldly, slowly, flowered phosphorescent in his skull. Singular! No, he wouldn't. Not by a damn sight. Another shiver, more fleeting, followed the first. He felt it also down the front of his arms. Death. Murdered at sea. Demarest dead, with a hole in his head. A murder at sea—why was the idea so peculiarly exciting and mysterious? *Blood—blood—blood—* throbbed the ship's engines. A pale steward creeping along the corridor. Two bells. The steward threw something white over the side. His white linen jacket—bloodstained. An inspection next day—'Tompkins, where's your jacket?' . . . 'Burned, sir.' 'Burned? How was it burned?' 'Well you see, sir, I was smoking, and . . .' The knife discovered; a cook's knife from the kitchen. Usually a belaying pin. Or one of those red axes hanging in the corridors *For Use in Case of Fire*.

'Gives me the creeps,' said Demarest. 'What else did Jeremiah say?'

'Jeremiah, as a matter of fact, is a fatalist— that's funny, isn't it? Says he never interferes, even when he knows, because it's sure to happen anyway, and the knowledge merely adds to the victim's misery. Nice, isn't it? . . . It occurred to me that it might be me. Why not? I'm not

young. Maybe somebody has discovered that I've
got a trunkful of chewing gum under my bed.
Maybe it's Jeremiah himself who'll be the murderer.'

'Nothing more probable,' said Hay-Lawrence.
'If you don't shut up and let me think, I'll murder
you myself.'

'Don't be snotty, Clarence. Remember the
freedom of the seas.'

He took the pawn. Demarest retaliated. Bishop
to bishop square moved Hay-Lawrence—to free
the rook.—Was Silberstein making up all this
yarn of the clairvoyant? *Well? It convinces
you? It sounds fairly circumstantial?'* Yes—it
was circumstantial.

'Who is this bird?' he said, lifting the king's
rook to the knight square.

'Clark, Seward Trewlove Clark, from Califor-
nia. Unitarian minister, clairvoyant and clairaudient. Smokes a kind of herb tobacco which
looks like confetti and smells like hell. Turns in
his toes when he walks, and is only four feet
high.'

'You've made a careful study of him. Does he
wear B.V.D.'s? Boston garters?'

'A hair shirt, probably . . . Are you castin'
asparagus on my story? Are you—as they say—
questioning my veracity, Mr. Demarest? Have a
cigar.'

'Not in the least . . . Thanks; I'll smoke it
after dinner . . .'

'Oh, he's full of it. Astrology, mediums,
trances, crystals, table rappings, and the cold and
slimy ectoplasm. Who knows? It may be an

ectoplastic murder . . . Hello! Is that our friend the Major? Getting his hand in already, is he? Fie.'

'Easy money,' murmured Hay-Lawrence.

Silberstein, turtle-faced, impassive, watched the Major with reptile eyes.

'Check!' said Hay-Lawrence, taking the rook.

'Check, says he.' Demarest recaptured the queen's rook. How much of the game was Silberstein taking in? A good deal probably. He had seen that Hay-Lawrence was uncomfortably placed, and that his vanity was suffering. This 'check' too—no doubt Silberstein saw it to be partly histrionic. Hay-Lawrence stared, flushed, at the pieces, fists on cheeks. Then, frowning, he moved the bishop to knight two. The conception of defeat. *Blood—blood—blood*—throbbed the engines, impersonating the furies. How delightful, this discovery of Caligula's about the clairvoyant! Just the sort of thing he *would* unearth. One could see him coldly and implacably questioning the little fool—taking off his very B.V.D.'s. 'You believe in these things, do you, Mr. Clark?' 'Yes.' 'Well, I don't: but I shall be interested to hear any evidence you have to offer. Speak up— don't be frightened—I'm listening!' . . . 'We must go forward with caution, reverence and hope,' replied the clairvoyant . . . Now, then, knight to knight six—and the crisis arises. My horse for a kingdom. Hay-Lawrence stared, immobile, an expression of stupor, or perhaps terror, in the fixed unseeing eyes: loss of psychic distance. One could almost hear the blood hammering at his temples—gush, clang, throb, thrum,

pound, pulse, boom. *Blood—blood—blood*—sang
the furies, Hay-Lawrence is doomed. Hay-
Lawrence is being done to death. Demarest is
murdering him, murdering him in little on a chess-
board. There lies Hay-Lawrence, disguised as
fourteen pieces (still living) and two pieces
(dead) dispersed on a chequered board, fighting
for his life. There Demarest, disguised as fourteen pieces, articulated like the adder, coils, hisses
and straightly strikes. Death in miniature. Death
in a cobweb. Was there a tear in Vivian's left
eye? No,—the reflection of a light in the rondure
of the monocle. A tear falling in Vivian's heart,
like the reflection of a moving light, tiny, down
a lacquered edge—the cold secret tear of a noble-
man, falling remotely and soundlessly. Miss
Gadsby, of Andover. 'Why do people come to
me in their trouble? It is strange. They come—
they come. There was the case of Henry Major-
ibanks, only last month. He telegraphed from
Chicago—or was it St. Louis?—to say that he
was coming. When he came he walked straight
into the drawing-room, where I was sitting, knelt
before me without a word, and buried his face in
my lap. I put my hands on his head. "What is
it, Henry?" I said. He wept—for five minutes
he wept, shaken by sobs. Then, without a word,
he rose and went away—went back to Chicago, or
St. Louis . . . Why? . . . What is it in me that
is so unconsciously beneficent, so comforting, so
healing? I am only an ordinary woman. Why
should Henry—whom I have never known very
intimately—come all the way from Little Rock—
to weep in my lap? Tears from the depths of

some divine despair! . . . Yet I am grateful for
this gift which God has given me, even though I
cannot wholly understand it . . . They come to
me for solace . . .' Knight to knight square,
moved Hay-Lawrence, the murdered man.

'You're sunk,' sighed Silberstein. 'See you
later, gentlemen. I now struggle into a stiff shirt.'

'Good riddance,' said Hay-Lawrence. 'He's an
interesting chap but he *can* be a damned nuisance.'

'He has a strange effect on me,' said Demarest,
moving the bishop to knight five. 'What is it, in
such a man, that disturbs one's balance so extraordinarily?'

'Thick-skinnedness.'

'Partly, perhaps. But something more. Is it
his massive confidence, rock-like integrity? I lose,
in his presence, my own integrity entirely. I
feel as if I have no personality at all. Or rather,
I feel that my own personality is only a comple-
ment of his—and I catch myself actually trying
to demonstrate this to him—trying to be as like
him as possible. Such occurrences make one wonder whether one has any more personality than a
chameleon . . . I have, afterwards, a weary and
disgusted sensation—as of having wagged too
much an ingratiating tail.'

Hay-Lawrence gleamed. He placed the king's
bishop at king two.

'By Jove, that's perfectly true. I know people
who affect me like that . . . My father always
did . . . So does my doctor.'

'Well, boys, later on,' sang the glass-eyed poker
player. He pocketed two packs of cards. They
trooped out, whistling and singing. Cold air from

the sea-door. Bishop takes knight? No—next time. Queen to knight two.

'It doesn't seem to make much difference,' Hay-Lawrence resignedly murmured. 'Suppose I advance the rook's pawn.' Pawn to rook three. Now—bishop takes knight! Hay-Lawrence dies slowly. A caterpillar attacked by ants. Then bishop takes bishop. A piece will be gained? Knight back to bishop four—the bishop twice attacked. Ten to one he advances the rook to king two—he does. Queen to knight six: the *coup de grace* . . .

'Oh—well! I'll hide the bishop in the rook's corner . . . No—*that's* no good . . .Suppose I exchange queens?'

'Queen takes queen and rook takes queen,' said Demarest, suiting the action to the word.

'Absolutely nothing I can do—I surrender.'

'I'm afraid you've lost a piece—whatever you do . . .'

'Yes. Thanks very much. We'll have another some time . . . Has the bugle blown?'

'I think so.'

Why 'think so'? He knew it had. They descended the red stairs to the dining saloon. The orchestra was beginning the *Blue Danube:* and the music rose to meet them, mixed with a confused sound of voices and dishes. The palm trees trembled, swayed slowly trembling, in the bright light from pearly ceiling lights. Pink curtains were drawn over all the port-holes save one, which yawned black, night-engulfing. A hundred faces feeding as one. Stewards running soft footed on the stinking carpets, dishes clattering, dishes chir-

ruping, trays clanging—all interwoven, pouring,
with the *Blue Danube*. The pale pianist, with
frayed and spotted sleeves, smiled wearily at the
score, *tum-tum:* the girl-faced flute player hooked
his lip, uncous lip, over the flute, and eyed Demarest mournfully, *tootle-too. Blaue Donau.* Should
he tell Hay-Lawrence Wagner's remark? . . .
'My God, what a melody! . . . But—*Jesus Christ!*
what orchestration . . .' No, too noisy, not the
right moment for it. Save it up. *Da,* die, dee,
dum :—die—*dum*: die *dee* . . . Anita. He always, when a kid, at dances, danced the *Blue
Danube* with Anita. Her odd, delicious laugh,
which ended in an inbreathing bubble, like the
bubbling of a starling! Darling starling. Darling,
hoydenish, long-legged Anita. *Down from a star
by a stairway of vines.* That Sunday in the rain
by the pond. 'But *William,* you don't seem to
think anything about *marriage!* Do you?' Then
the street-car in the rain, the rain-soaked curtain
blowing against their backs; flap, flap. Rejected.
Was he heartbroken? Surprised at being able to
eat a good dinner at Memorial Hall. 'Where are
my waffles, Sam Childers?' 'On de fire, suh—
waffles on de fire.'

'Good evening, Mr. Barnes—Good evening,
Miss Dacey—Good evening, Mrs. Faubion—
Good evening, father.'

'All right for *you,* Mr. Demarest!' Mrs. Faubion, mournful and reproachful, mock-angry.

'For me? What have *I* done?'

He dived, laughing into the sombre eyes, which
darkened maliciously to receive him . . . Swimming. I swim, you swim, he or she swims. We

swim, you swim—the rich sardonic mouth tearing bread.

'Oh, I know what you've done.   And *you* know *too.*'

'Cross my heart and hope I die . . . Not guilty. I appeal.'

She cut her meat savagely.   Roast beef *au jus,* underdone, in watery gules.   Green and celluloid cabbage. Barnes was drinking black stout. Jingle, went Daisy's bangle.

'The little girl's in a bad temper, to-night,' said Smith, lowering his voice.   'I wouldn't let her have the dress she wanted . . .'   Then louder— 'Who's your dressmaker, Madam?'

'*You* be *careful!*'

'Careful!   Reckless is my middle name.'

'Water, Miss Dacey?'

'Oo thank you Mr. Barnes.'   Titter, titter.

'Walking right by me like that!'

'Never!'

'You did!   On the deck this afternoon.   And I was alone.'

'You don't ask me to believe *that,* do you? Alone!'

'Where was Australia?' said Smith.   'How come?'

'I'm not talking to *you,* Mr. Smith.   I'm talking to your *son.*'

'Oh! . . . God.'

'Sixpenny fine, Mr. Smith.   Swearing at meals.' Mr. Barnes serenely peeped over the tilted stout.

Da dee die *dum*—die *dum*: die *dee.*—Anita looked over the silver-spangled white fan, long-leggedly, gracefully gliding, the green irises of her

eyes irregularly flecked, gold-flecked, the pupils
dark and—witty. 'I thought you were *afraid* of
dances! . . . I believe it's all a pretence!' . . .
That lesson in the dining-room. 'You don't hold
me *tightly* enough—that's the trouble!' And the
peal of laughter, bubbling, inbreathing. Her *Em-
pire* gown—high-waisted, white, like the Empress
what's-her-name, standing at the top of the stairs
—stairs of alabaster. Sorosis; Sesostris. 'But
she's *nervous*—very highly strung,' Anita's
mother had said. 'Ever since her operation' . . .
Well, what of it? Why did she eye him (knit-
ting) so meaningfully? Ah—! she had meant to
warn him off. Die *dum*—die *dee* . . . *Da* dee die
dum—Faubion was looking at him rather hard—
but as if she were not quite focusing her attention
—no, she was beginning to smile, but obviously
the sort of smile which is an answer to a smile—
it must be for someone behind him. He turned
his head—it was Australia, the Romantic Young
Man, who was now in the act of passing the
water-bottle. A well-dressed, vapid young man
with a high collar and a high colour; he was a
little too self-conscious, elaborately polite, a shade
too much of the travelling salesman's genuflectory
manner. 'Swipey—I don't like this cat—he's too
swipey.' O God that word—how fond of it Aunt
Maud had been, and how terribly her choice of it
lighted that part of her vulgarity which he had
always hated. There must be the same stratum
buried somewhere in himself, of course,—or his
disgust would not have been so intemperate.
Where had he got it? No,—he was damned if
he had it! It must have been a natural dislike—

that element in Aunt Maud's sensibility (or lack
of it) had done him a violence from the beginning. What could so have poisoned her? Her
mind, her character, her outlook blackly poisoned:
—a savage coprophily, a necessity for dwelling
on the foulness of things. Well—he did this himself! but not surely in the same unclean way. Aunt
Maud's perceptions were somehow septic. A
septic sceptic. Himself, an aseptic sceptic. Tut
tut . . . This was probably completely wrong.
More likely it was simply Aunt Maud's lack of
sensibility—a failure to perceive things clearly, to
make fine distinctions? A bitter and unbridled
woman.

'Penny for your thoughts,' said Faubion.

'The fleshpots of Egypt,' said Demarest swiftly.
Why? Faubion=fleshpot.

'What! . . .'

Smith shook sadly his close-cropped grey head.

'Eating *this* dinner, he thinks of fleshpots! . . .
No. Give me a Creole chicken dinner. Okra
soup.'

'Would to God we had died by the hand of the
Lord in the land of Egypt, where we sat by the
fleshpots . . . For we, alas, the Fleshpots love
. . . Man cannot live by bread alone.'

'Shame!' cried Fleshpot. A flaming shame.

'It's all the bible I know.'

'Did you go to church this morning?' A finger
uplifted, school-teacherly.

'Certainly not. I played bridge.'

'Bridge! Oo aren't we swell,' Daisy derisively
carolled.

'He's got too much brains,' said Smith. 'He

plays chess, too . . . But I beat him at draughts just the same, didn't I?'

'You did.'

'Got to hand it to the old man! . . . Chess is an old lady's game. I don't like chess. Let the old ladies play it. But I'll beat you at chequers any time. Yes, sir, I'm all right at chequers.'

'And what do *you* play, Mr. Barnes?' Daisy Dacey wriggled, jingled, slanted her long white face, and wide blue eyes, leaning against the table-cloth with phthisic breast. Mr. Barnes, tolerant, slow-smiling, with slow-burning eyes of amusement, looked down at the proffered head. Herod and Salome.

'Golf,' he said.

Daisy was disconcerted. Golf! What the devil was golf? She smiled a weak smile, too elastic, and looked sadly forgetful,—Ophelia straying by the stream. Let me Ophelia pulse! There's rosemary—that's for remembrance. Wan, and oh so wistful. Weak, and oh so helpless. But no pansies—ah no: for never a thought had she. Straying with little white feet among the lilies. Oh, pity me, a shopworn Ophelia! Come and find me where I wander at twilight, sadly singing, or perchance weeping, among the cowslips! Put your strong arm around me, and hold me, hold me! Don't let me remember—O God, don't let me remember! . . . When I was thirteen. It was dreadful! . . . and I trusted him . . . Have you read the Rosary? . . . Where the cowslips, there slip I.

'. . . a clairvoyant,' Faubion was soberly saying.

'You don't say,' said Smith. 'Where?'

'Under the middle window, at the end of the table.' Window equals port-hole.

A little mournful sallow face, dark-eyed and shy. A hurt and frightened little victim, eating stiffly.

'Yes,' said Demarest. 'Silberstein was telling me about him.'

'What did he say? Is he a real one?'

'Don't ask me! He told Silberstein that he's going to England to sell chewing gum—which was correct. He's also a clairaudient.'

'Clairaudient! What's that?' Her dark eyes are wide and serious. Melodiously fluting.

'He hears things—at a distance. Voices. Probably hears what we're saying about him.'

'Don't be silly! . . . I think they're all fakes.' She looked witheringly toward the meek little clairvoyant.

'You can't fool *her*,' said Smith. 'She's from Missouri.'

'He predicts,' said Demarest, a murder, on this ship.'

Daisy Dacey gave a little screech, pressing her hands together. A crumb of gorgonzola shot from her mouth into Mr. Barnes's tumbler. She slapped a hand against her mouth, too late.

'Oh!' she cried, blushing. 'Mr. Barnes! I'm so sorry!'

'Quite natural, I'm sure,' said Mr. Barnes. 'Worse things might have happened, under the circumstances! A little upsetting to hear a murder predicted, what? . . .' He lowered his left lid at Demarest. Poor Pol.

'An old man came to him in a dream—an old
man, pardon me—wearing pyjamas; he had a hole
in his head. He stretched out his hands to the
clairvoyant, as if beseeching . . . The clairvoyant
jumped out of his bunk—and probably bumped
his head—thinking there was someone in the
room. He turned on the light, and of course
there was no one. But he says he'll recognize the
man when he sees him . . . Father!'

'*Don't* call me father! . . . What.'

'. . . . Nothing . . . A goose walked over my
grave. I think it must be *me* . . .'

Why conceal it? He had suddenly thought—
and thought vividly, with absurd apprehension—
that it was *Smith!* Ridiculous, both to entertain
the thought and to suppress it . . . Nevertheless,
he had seen Smith, with shattered forehead, blun-
dering into the dark stateroom. Plenty other old
men on the boat. Poor old Smith. What if it
were true? There was nothing in such predictions, of course,—if it proved true, it was simply
a coincidence.

'I dream things myself,' he said. 'I once
dreamed three times in succession that a certain
ship—the *Polynesian*—had sunk. I was shortly
going to sail on her. The dream was confused,
and it seemed to me in each case that she sank
somehow in the dock—collided with it, or something . . A few days after the third dream I was
walking in London, and saw a headline (one of
those posters the newsboys wear, like aprons)
saying: *Atlantic Liner Sunk.* I *knew,* absolutely
knew, it was my ship; and it was.'

'You're making it up,' said Faubion.

'You *never* take my word, Mrs. Faubion!
Why?'

She relented, smiling; but smiled coolly.

'When you dream about *me*, I'll believe you,'
she said, rising.

'I'll have something for you at breakfast!'

She turned her dark head away. The cold
shoulder. Humming, she walked slowly, with
abstracted thought, lifting her cape to her round
neck. A coarse lace blouse, slightly cheap, well
filled, through which one saw bits of blue ribbon.
Ah Faubion! Ah, Fleshpot! How attractive,
how vulgar, how downright, and yet how mysterious you are! *'O Faubion,'* sang the evening
stars . . . *'deep, deep Faubion!'*

'Coming for a walk?' said Smith. 'Beautiful
air to-night—beautiful.'

'I'll join you in fifteen minutes. In the smoking-room?'

'All right. I'll wait for you' . . . Smith departed sedately, brown eyes among the palm trees.

. . . A curious remark, that of Faubion's—
'When you dream about *me*——' Extraordinary,
her instinctive directness; this observation of hers,
and his reply (of which she had dictated the key)
left their relationship changed and deepened. To
sleep, perchance to dream;—one dreamt only of
those for whom one had profound feelings?
'When I walk, I *walk* with Willy——' He had
never dreamt of Anita—not once. But on several
occasions he had dreamt, erotically, of women for
whom he had never consciously felt any desire;
and had found them, when next encountered,
magically changed; they belonged thereafter to the

race of salamanders, opalescent and fiery. But
Faubion had now, in a sense, saved him the
trouble of dreaming—the suggestion of the dream
was sufficient. It was a tremendous step towards
intimacy—intimacy of that sort . . . But a step
(alas!) which perhaps meant, for her, little or
nothing. She would say the same thing to everybody—to any male who was reasonably attractive? Was she, perhaps (as the Welsh Rarebit
had suggested), under the 'protection' of Barnes,
and being handed about from one member of the
crew to another? Such things, of course, were
common enough. A special technique was always
employed in such cases. The girl avoided the
officers in the daytime—consorted only with the
passengers; but after the lights were out,—the
dark ship sleeping, sleep-walking on the dark sea,
—then it was her footstep which one heard,
furtive and soft and quick, passing one's door, or
treading nocturnally over one's head. Was Faubion leading this kind of double life? Time
enough to find out. Meanwhile—

Tin-tin: *tin-tin*: *tin-tin*: *tin-tin*: eight o'clock.
The flute player folded his tripod, the pianist
closed the yellow-toothed piano. The *Blue
Danube,* miles behind, sank into the Atlantic, was
caught by mewing gulls.

'Good-night, Mr. Demarest . . . Are you comfortable in your stateroom?'

'Quite, thanks.'

'That's good . . . Good night.'

'Good night . . .'

'G'night, sir,' said the table steward, flicking
crumbs.

. . . Smith's alley: but Smith was not there,
and neither of the girls . . . The long red carpet
abruptly declined before him.   The wind had
freshened.   The sea was getting rougher.   142-
156.   Home.   A light in the room beyond his
own—the Irish girl moved about, there, with door
half-opened.   *Snap,* went a suitcase lock.   A tumbler clinked.   The bed-curtains were harshly slid
along, brass rings on brass rod—ZRING . . . An
electric bell buzzed remotely, twice: a voice, remote, called 'Mrs. Atherton! . . . *Mrs. Atherton!*
. . . One sixty-eight . . .' 'Coming!' cried Mrs.
Atherton . . . Mrs. Atherton could be heard pelt-
ing down the corridor, a whirlwind, and laughing,
then a male voice, laughing, and Mrs. Atherton
gave a squeal, and 'Don't!' she cried.   'Get out of
my way!' she cried, then both laughs sliding down
the scale, *diminuendo* . . . A mad-house.   I am
in a mad-house, thought Demarest . . . Figures
given for the year 1920 show a considerable in-
crease in the number of cases admitted to institu-
tions in the United Kingdom.   Of these 56 per
cent were female, 44 per cent male . . . It is
noted with interest that few insane people die of
cancer . . . General paralysis of the insane . . .
Certified as insane . . . All is insanity . . .
Whoso among you that is without insanity, let
him think the first think . . . Shall we read, to-
night?   A nuisance carrying a book . . . The
amusements provided for the insane show a grati-
fying variety . . . Croquet, phonographs, picture-
puzzles in great numbers . . . We are happy to
report that the Society for the Encouragement of
Vocal Therapy has co-operated with us now for

six months with . . . Music and hot baths . . .
Therapeutic value of jazz . . . Even staid old
country preachers are engaging tango teachers
. . . You can't get away from it—can't get away
from it—you can't get away from it at all . . .
If one could only establish a direct mode of communion with another being, instead of undergoing
this pitiful struggle of conversation? Extraordinary, the way conversation, even the most intimate
(not at present *apropos*) concealed or *refracted*
the two personalities engaged. Impossible to present, all at once, in a phrase, a sentence, a careful
paragraph—even in a book, copious and di-
shevelled—all that one meant or all that one was.
To speak is to simplify, to simplify is to change,
to change is to falsify. And not only this—there
were also the special demons who inhabit language; and again, the demons who make a
perpetual comedy, or tragedy, of all human
intercourse, the comedies and tragedies of the misunderstood. These were the same thing,—or
aspects of the same thing? The experience of an
individual is co-extensive with the world and
therefore infinite?—he is, in epitome, the history
of the world, a history still being lived. But this
'language'—by which one such epitome seeks to
make himself understood or felt by another (felt,
rather than understood!)—this meagre affair of
signs and sounds, this tiny boxful of shabby,
worn trinkets, few in number, dim in colour and
crude of shape—how much, of one's infinitude,
could one express by an earnest stringing together
of these? Little or nothing. And these demons of
language,—they invited one, how tiresomely often,

to disregard the reference of the trinkets, and
to play a *game* with them, to toss and catch them,
to match their colours and shapes, to demonstrate
one's *skill:* turning human intercourse into a game
of anagrams.   Ah, the disgusting way in which
one is always trying to 'make an impression!'
and the even stranger way in which casual groups
of people actually co-operate to make a *collective*
impression, a mutual deception of smartness,
gaiety, good humour, good breeding, vulgarity,
or wit!   Their dinner table, for example—all of
them unnatural.   Bridge with Silberstein and the
others—unnatural.   Chess with Hay-Lawrence—
unnatural . . . Smith?   Ah—this seemed closer
to the real . . . Faubion?   Relations with her,
too, would be real or nothing.   And what a profoundly interesting experience!   A marriage with
earth . . . With reversed meanings :—*Blest be
the marriage betwixt earth and heaven!   Now, in
the round blue noon of space* (round blue noon
was delicious) *the mortal son, and the daughter
immortal* (immoral!) *make of the world their
resting-place* . . . Not so bad : the colours a little
aniline, perhaps, as in a flower piece by Hiroshige
Third . . . Curious that Silberstein—Caligula
(who seemed so almost identically one person!.
should have started this train of feeling and pre-
cipitated a poem involving (so transparently!)
Cynthia and himself.   But of course, the Caligula
strain in himself was familiar enough,—from the
age of ten (that vacant lot, with ruined cellar
walls, grass-grown, secret) all through the horrible furtive years of adolescence.   Little Caligula
ran on the sidewalk, pulling after him a toy fire-
engine, from which poured the thick smoke of

burning excelsior. Little Caligula invited Gladys
Dyson to come to the vacant lot. Little Caligula
was kissed unexpectedly in the tailor's shop by the
Italian tailor's black-eyed daughter. Walking
through a slum alley, little Caligula heard voices,
peeped in through the wet green shutters, saw a
negro and negress embracing, heard the negress
moan. He had wanted to remain and watch, but
hadn't dared. The vocabulary of little Caligula—
the profane vocabulary—increased rapidly. The
cook made startling contributions to it, screeching
with laughter as she did so. Then there was that
Swedish sailor, caught in the same doorway during a shower, who on seeing the two dogs had
cried *'Jesus!'* Why Jesus? What connection?
Little Caligula looked from dogs to Axel, from
Axel to dogs, and sought a clue. Jesus, then, was
not merely a god who had suffered crucifixion,
but could be mentioned, laughingly, on such occasions as this? . . . There were also the singular
totems carved out of wood by the 'gang' to which
he had once or twice been admitted. And there,
too, strange words had been pronounced, which
had rendered him more than ever a little Caligula
—a Caligula with strange festered recesses in his
mind, with wounds in his body. Love (he had
been taught) was sensuality, sensuality was evil,
evil was prohibited but delicious: the catechism of
the vacant lot. But how, then, had beauty come
in? How had it so managed to complicate itself
with evil and sensuality and the danks and darks
of sex?—It had come in with the trumpet vine.
It had come in with the seven-year locust and the
china-berry tree. It had come in with the sten-
cilled shadows, on a tropic moonlight night—

shadows, on the walls and floors, which suddenly
galloped. It had come in with the song of the
negress who walked in the sun with the basket
swaying on her head and sang 'Ay-y-y-y prawns
—ay-y-y-y-y prawns . . .' No—the tissue was
too complex;—it was impossible to say where
beauty had come from, or even to predicate that
there had ever been a beginning; to be born, to
become conscious, was to be, and at the same time
to face, pain and beauty . . . 'All this, Faubion,
is what I am trying to say to you when I make a
vulgar joke and laugh at you! . . . It is Caligula,
who nevertheless has the rainbow wings of a
seraph; Caligula, corrupt and yet devout, who be-
seeches you to be kind to him. And yet it is not
entirely Caligula—it is something less than Caligula, and also something more; it is a life small
and innocent, inconceivably naïve and at every
instant new, a life infantine and guileless; but
unhappily this ethereal waif harbours in his
heaven-born mind a little black seed, the gift of
Tellus. This little black seed is the yearning to be
Caligula. I MUST be Caligula. And is it not you
who provide me with the opportunity to achieve
my destiny—you and your sisters? It is in your
presence that the black seed begins to grow.
Eunice warmed it, smiling upon it. Helen Shafter wept upon it, watering its terrible roots. Mary
gave her body to be devoured by the terrible roots.
Anita, fleeing, tempted it to grow like a vine . . .
And here are you, Faubion,—vigorous synthesis
of all these; the familiar theme repeated, but repeated more emphatically than ever . . .' O God,
if he could only escape! But did he really desire

to? . . . The Irish girl in the next room again
moved the bed-curtains, brass rings on brass rod
—ZRING. The light, which had shone through the
reticulated grill at the top of the wall, above the
upper berth, suddenly went out. She was going
forth—he could meet her. It was time to meet
Smith. And the five minutes of solitude, of
morose reflection, had been (as he had foreseen)
just what was needed to restore him to himself.
His periodic need of escape. To re-establish his
boundaries—to re-establish his awareness of his
own periphery. Now he could go forth calmly—
to face the Irish girl calmly, to face Smith calmly,
to face the sea with joy.

To have collided with the Irish girl would have
been simple and agreeable; but in the very act of
willing it he also inhibited the length of his stride
over the brass sill.

'Oh!' she said, smiling.

'I'm so sorry!' said Demarest, drawing back.
He regarded her with friendly inquisition.

Lowering her soft flushed face, she passed him,
close against the white wooden panelling, the
smile gently dying. Innocent grey eyes: not without humour and boldness. My wild Oirish Rose.
When I look into your eyes—Then I think of
Irish skies . . . Anita's favourite song—he used
to sing it in the shower-bath. Sure as you're born,
top of the morn . . .! 'Come—come—come—'
said her slippers on the red carpet, as she turned
away to the right. 'No—too—shy,—' his own
feet whispered, stammering and inarticulate, as
he turned away to the left.

The cloud of smoke in the smoking-room was

dense and turbulent. The poker game had been resumed, bottles and glasses assisting. The glass-eyed gambler sang loudly: '*Some* girls live in the country:—and *some* girls live in town:—but MY girl can't keep her reputation up, 'cause she *can't* keep her petticoat down:—By! God! she! is!—a lulu:—yes, b'God, a lulu:—a lulu is that little girrrrrrrl of mine . . .' All the players broke loudly into the chorus, 'By! God! she! IS—a lulu,' to the grave delight of Malvolio.

'There you are,' said Smith. 'Come on. I've got an idea.'

"What?'

'Wait, I'll tell you outside.' The brown eyes were solemnly mischievous. 'Somebody might hear us.'

The night had become cloudy, and a cold wind came in damp gusts from the northwest. A drop or two of rain—or was it spray? No—it was rain. The deck was nearly deserted. Patches of white light fell over the polished planks and tarred seams. A feeling of storm. At the forward end of the covered deck, beyond the first-class barrier, two sailors were moving to and fro under a ceiling light, stretching a canvas screen.

'Well,' said Demarest, 'what's this brainwave?'

'Why shouldn't we sneak up to the First Class deck—the upper one—and have a good walk? Eh? I don't know about *you*, but I'd like some exercise . . . Down here you can't get started before you have to turn around.'

'No sooner said than done.'

'The question is—how do we go? Straight up the companion-way? with the light shining on it?

Sort of public . . . The only other way is to go
through the barrier, and then up a companion-way
further forward . . . It has the advantage of
being darker.'

'With so few people aboard, I don't believe
they'll give a damn anyway. Let's go straight up
. . . They can't do any more than kick us out.
We'll do a dignified retreat, with profuse apolo-
gies . . . When I was on the *Empress of Ireland,*
in the steerage, I used to go up and drink beef tea
with the first-class passengers every morning: and
tea every afternoon.'

'It's easy if the ship's crowded.'

'Come on! there's nobody looking.'

Smith climbed the iron stairs warily and softly,
and swung the iron gate at the top. It squeaked
and clanked.

'Nobody in sight,' he said, *sotto voce:* 'not a
soul . . . This is something like! A crime not
to allow us up here—yes, sir, it's a crime. Absolutely wasted.'

The long white deck, exquisitely sloping and
curved, stretched away through alternating light
and shadow. High as a cliff. Yes! This was
something like. One felt at once like a first-class
passenger, and subtly changed one's bearing. If
they met Purington—well, so much the better.
They would be under his protection. Purington
meeting Smith—ha, ha! One could see his discomfort—one look at Smith's tweed hat (absurdly
big for him) would be enough, and all of Purington's heavy snobbishness would begin creakily
operating. It would be rather a joke. They
turned the forward corner, walking through a

crescendo of wind. Sparks blew from Smith's
cigar. *Ooo—wash—oo—wallop,* went the waves
against the unseen bow; the ship lifted slightly, he
careened against Smith's arm,—and then drew
back in the deep shadow at the corner to let three
women pass. Confound. It wouldn't be so comfortable, this being inspected twice on each circuit
of the deck.

'Yes, sir—this is something like. This is what
you come to sea for . . . Now, if we only had
those little girls—but no. No. They'd give the
show away. Nothing first class about them! Ha,
ha!'

'I suppose you'd let me walk with Faubion?'

'Not much, I wouldn't! She's the little girl for
me . . . I dropped a hint to her to-night. Sort
of risky, I guess, but I got the feeling that I
couldn't help it . . . Hm.'

'What . . . For the love of mud don't ruin
yourself, father!'

Smith meditated, his cigar in his mouth, his
cheeks pursed a little, right forefinger curved
round cigar. He stared along the long deck.

'Oh, it wasn't very much—nothing at all, . . .
It was when she came to get a dress before dinner
—I said, "You know that song, don't you?" "No,
what song?" says she. "What's the use of all
these things without the girl inside?" I said. "You
naughty old thing!" she said—that's what she
said. "You naughty old thing!" . . . She looked
sort of mad—but then she always does, half the
time, anyway, so you can't tell . . . What do you
think?"

'That's harmless enough—but I'd go slow if I
were you.'

'Damn it, life's too short—*my* life is! Time I had a little fun.'

'Do we walk right round at the back, where the Second Class can see us?'

'Sure, they won't recognize us—too dark.'

Turning the corner, they again met the three women. Tall women, easily striding, keeping step. Demarest averted his eyes again, shy and conscious. 'No,' one of them was saying—'I don't think——' A cultured voice, and English. The rest of her sentence was blown overboard. Getting back to England and Cynthia. Would he ever see Cynthia again? Would he dare to go and see her? She had never answered his two letters—not a word, not a sign. She had never acknowledged the book. She had thus rebuked him, of course—he had not asked permission to write; and to do so, and particularly to send the book, had been after so slight (!) an acquaintance a callow presumption. A warm wave of shame and misery came over him. That had been exactly characteristic of the state of mind she had induced in him—clumsy adolescence, shyness, awkwardness, misplaced audacities, occasional funks (as when he had allowed her to pay his fare on the bus!) and a mixture of abruptness and preciousness in talk . . . As for the two letters— again that wave of shame and misery came hotly over him. The letters had been in his very worst vein—the sort of disingenuous, hinting thing, self-conscious and literary, which he always achieved (how revolting) when the occasion was emotionally important. Was it impossible to fall in love without loss of balance? No loss of balance with Eunice or with Mary—but both were of humble birth. Helen Shafter? Well, perhaps, a trace. Yes. But no more than that. That first night in the house by the bay. Helen's aunt's house, when Helen's aunt had been called away, and they had been left alone—had there been, then, a loss of balance such as he had experienced with Cynthia?

'You never can tell, in these cases,' he said. 'Never . . . Once I was spending the week-end with a respectable middle-aged lady and her niece. I'd known them all my life. There was no thought of anything between me and the niece—well, nothing to speak of: a mild intermittent interest, perhaps a little more physical than intellectual. The aunt got a telegram and went away for two nights, leaving us alone. Well, it was extraordinary the way a kind of tension grew between us! We couldn't talk naturally, we began to look at each other, our voices seemed to change in key— we finally said good night to each other in a panic. That was the first night. The second night was worse. We were seized with a terror lest the conversation should come to an end—we talked frantically, incessantly, and as impersonally as we could. Absolutely nothing personal was said: and yet the personal tension was every second becoming more unbearable. I was aware, of course, that she agitated me—but I couldn't make out whether *she* was agitated; and I was determined to avoid a false step, which for various reasons would have been fatal. What really happened was that we were both in that state, but neither wanted to take the responsibility of declaring it: the ghost of respectability, perhaps, but also the fear of rebuff

and of making fools of ourselves. So we just sat
and talked, and it got later and later, and first one
lamp went out, and then the other, and then the
fire began to die and the room to get cold. Should
I put coal on the fire? It would seem to suggest
too coarsely that I took it for granted we were
going to continue sitting there in the dark, talking inanely, at one-thirty in the morning. So I
didn't. We sat, finally, for ten minutes in silence,
at the end of which she suddenly said, "Oh! I
feel as if the top of my head would blow off!"
... That seemed, in a way, clear enough! and yet,
could I be sure? I thought for a minute, and then
I said, "Why?" to which, after a long and desperate pause, she replied, "You ought to know, I
think." So it was she, really, who took the final
step . . . As soon as she had said that, we rose
from our chairs as if hypnotized, and moved together . . . Unfortunately in the dark, I got one
foot into the coal-scuttle, and our first embrace
looked more like a wrestling match—we staggered
and fell.'

'You fell,' said Smith.

'We fell.'

'I wish things like that would happen to me.
Yes, siree. But they don't. And never did.'

'It's luck simply. A friend of mine in a train,
once——'

They again faced the three tall women, drawing
modestly aside to let them pass. They had the
light at their backs, and their faces were in darkness. The outermost girl was wearing a knitted
jersey—remarkably like—he turned to look, his
heart beating in his throat.—But the gloom had

swallowed them up.   Impossible!   Impossible!
Impossible!

'—was practically proposed to by a young
woman who sat beside him . . . Total stranger
. . . She gave him, as the saying is, the glad knee.
He was getting off at Philadelphia—she was going to—I forget where—Atlanta.   She implored
him to come along with her—absolutely implored
him.   Offered to pay his fare and all his expenses
for a week's trip . . . '

He felt out of breath—excitement.   Dyspnœa.
His voice had shaken absurdly (and a little high)
on the second 'absolutely.'   He cleared his throat.
He must time the approach, so as to meet them
under a light.

'Good God,' said Smith.   'And did he?'

'No.   He was on his way to visit his fiancée
. . . Poor devil!'

'Oh, don't spoil the story!   My God . . . He just
let her go like that?   What sort of woman was
she?'

'Beautiful, he said—about twenty-six.   A buyer
for one of the big stores—Gimbel's or Wana-
maker's.'

Smith groaned.   He took half a dozen quick
puffs at his short cigar, holding it between thumb
and finger, then flung it over the railing.   The red
spark described a swift parabola in the dark, and
Demarest imagined—in the midst of all that thresh
and welter—its infinitesimal hiss.   Suppose they
shouldn't come round again?. . . .

'To think,' said Smith, 'of losing a chance like
that! . . . Oh, *boy!*'

'She gave him her name and address—and he lost it.'

'I don't believe it.'

'Yes—and all he remembered about her name was that it was Mabel Tupper something . . . '

'He ought to be shot at sunrise,' said Smith. 'Yes, sir, he ought to be shot down like a dog. And she made love to him, did she?'

Smith turned an eager round eye under the tweed rim. An eye like a well.

'*Did* she! He said he was embarrassed to death—and afraid somebody he knew might see him. She simply wrapped herself round him—stem to stern. He put his overcoat across his lap so that the confusion of legs wouldn't be too obvious.'

There they came, round the corner. He paused, feeling his pockets.

'Damn,' he said. 'I forgot my pipe . . . No matter.' He continued feeling his pockets.

The jersey—yes. Tall, too. Being on the outside, her face was in shadow. No. Too slender, too girlish. Something queer!

'Don't tell me any more stories like that,' said Smith. 'Makes me too sad.'

She came swiftly, gracefully—touched a palm on the rail, turning her face down toward the black water. Light fell on her lifting face—it was she. She looked, for some reason, slighter and younger—his recollection of her had not been exact . . . She had not seen him yet—they came nearer. Her mother—the one in the middle. She looked at him, but unrecognizing—no—yes . . . Suddenly her eyes took fire and she smiled, stop-

ping. He moved toward her, slowly, putting out
his hand, his awkward hand. The two other
women, turning their heads, walked on. Smith
drifted gloomily toward the companion-way.

'How simply extraordinary!' said Demarest.
He was aware that the speech was resonant with
too much feeling, too many references.

'Isn't it? . . . I've been in America again!' The
exquisite light voice was breaking through him:
oddly childish, subtly simple.

They drifted slowly, and leaned against the
railing, under a light; as they had leaned the year
before; as it seemed natural for them to lean.

'In New York?' said Demarest.

'Yes . . . And Philadelphia!'

'For long?'

'Three months . . . I'm glad to go back.'

She had been in New York and Philadelphia
—without letting him know! Good God. At any
time during the last three months he might have
——— She hadn't let him know.

'I'm going to be married!' she then gaily added.
She laughed delightedly, girlishly, leaning backward on the rail with lifted elbows—the striped
and diamonded jersey of richly mingled Hindu
colours.

. .'*Really!*' he cried. 'How *delightful!* . . . May
I ask——'

'And have *you* made up your mind,' she inter-
rupted, 'where to live?'

'It's been made up *for* me, for the moment . . .
I'm having—possibly—a show in London. So I
shall stay a year or two—perhaps settle.' He

frowned, confused. Things were confused, distressing, ecstatic.

'Oh! . . . My mother always says it's a mistake for Americans to expatriate themselves.'

'Yes . . . I remember she said so to *me,* last year . . . I'm not so sure! . . . It's an awful problem! Simply awful. If, when one's young enough, one develops a taste for Europe—I'm afraid it's incurable.'

'I think I'd stay in New York if I were you—you have there such a priceless sense of freedom ——'

She turned, sombre, and looked down at the black and white of water. She had used that phrase in a letter.

'I hate it,' Demarest said with surprising bitterness.

'Do you?'

Cynthia smiled at him amusedly. He must, somehow, mention that he was not in the first cabin—that he was a sneaking interloper; just what he had always been *afraid* of seeming! It was a perfect nemesis; caught red-handed. How surprisingly tall she was: how transparently young and beautiful. He remembered Wetherall's remark, 'too innocent.' Also Wetherall's comment on the ugly way her skirt hung, creased, at the back: that brown tweed skirt, with a small rip in the hem at one side. Blue woollen stockings. The rip stretching against her knee as she sat opposite him—sitting on the deck itself—playing chess, one hand supporting her (the long arched fingers crossing a tarred seam), the other touching her cheek. Sea-gulls. And now, everything so com·

plicated and difficult—her mother with her (who
had disliked him)—and someone else.

'Yes, I really like London much better.'

'It is lovely, isn't it! I can hardly *wait* for
London in the winter!'

As usual, when they talked, he had the sense
of their partaking of a secret communion, exquisite and profound : a communion in which their
idle talk, fragmentary and superficial, and even
their physical identities, had the remoteness and
smallness of the trivial and accidental. It seemed
merely to be necessary that they should be together : that they should stand together for a moment, saying nothing, looking at the same falling
wave or the same white sea-gull; or talk a little,
lightly; or loiter a little, with lazy bodies. This
had been true from the beginning—it was still
true. And yet—was it? There was this other
man. The communion could hardly, therefore, be
as perfect as he supposed. And indeed, had it
ever been? Was it conceivable that already, when
he had met her a year ago, she had been in love?
Was it possible that her luminousness, her lightness of heart and body, her delightful, delighted
swiftness in meeting him, had been simply the
euphoria consequent upon that :—and might it not
have been precisely her love (for this other man)
that he had fallen in love with? . . . On the other
hand, there had been something—well, just lightly
destructive, the loosing of a gay arrow, explana-
tory but not apologetic, in the quick laughing
announcement *'I'm going to be married!'* This
seemed to refer to a marked consciousness of former communion : to refer to it and to end it. As

if she said, 'I liked you—but how much better I like *him!*'

'It is astounding that we should meet again like this!'

It was a mistake—but Cynthia met it lightly.

'Isn't it? It makes one feel——' She hesitated, and gave a little laugh in which there was no tension, but rather an assumption of security and distance, the perfection and inviolability of her personal view, which she need not, if she did not wish, bother to communicate to him.

'How small the world is?' laughed Demarest.

'Oh, that! if you like . . . I was thinking rather, that it made one feel like Buddhists, or some such thing—meeting, reincarnated, every thousand years or so; and always in the same way; and always inconsequentially; and always with tremendous surprise.'

She smiled at him delightfully, again rocking back with Hindu-bright elbows, on the railing, which burned vivid and real against the darkness of the sea. The familiar shape of her arms, the familiar gesture and attitude, the colours, the youthful frankness, all these, together, suddenly released in him a torrent of remembered feelings.

'Pilgrims,' he said,—falling in with her image, in which she had so candidly delighted,—'who meet once in every cycle for the exchange of a remark on the weather? If they *have* anything so mundane as weather in their purgatories and paradises!'

'*And* infernos.'

'Yes!'

The two women approached, slowing their steps a little.

'Mother—you remember Mr. Demarest?'

'How do you do.'

'How do you do.'

To the pale girl, who stood under the light, waiting cynically, he was not introduced. Flight, prearranged, was in the air.

'I'll let you rejoin your friend,' said Cynthia, moving off slowly. Smith! His friend Smith!

She smiled: Demarest smiled and nodded: and the three women walked swiftly away. Good God —Good God—said the blood beating in his brain. He moved blindly toward the companion-way. He must rejoin his friend—by all means. Yes. And he must take his friend down to the other deck— he suddenly felt that he didn't want to face them again, particularly with old Smith by his side; Smith and his comic-opera tweed hat. Nothing first class about Smith! Ha ha. Nor about himself either. He hadn't had time, worse luck, for the necessary light touch on that point. How awful. She would look for him in the passenger list, and not find him, and laugh. How much it would explain to her! 'Mother—how very funny. Mr. Demarest must be in the second cabin!' 'Funny? It doesn't especially surprise me—I always felt there was something——' Etcetera. Then that pale girl, cynical—she would laugh, too. They would all laugh merrily together, with heads thrown back. What the Spanish call *car-cajada*—loud laughter, boisterous and derisive. Sexual laughter, the ringing scorn of the female for the defeated or cowardly male, the skulker

. . . He rounded the corner, but there was no Smith. Instead, at the far end, he saw the three women coming toward him. Cynthia appeared to be talking, the others turning their heads toward her. He must escape. Irresolute, he began pretending (absurd) that he was looking for a lost friend. What—he isn't here? Then I'd better turn. He turned, went briskly round the corner again, then rattled down the companion-way.

In the smoking-room, as he paid for his glass of port, Smith reappeared.

'Well, who's your swell friend?' he said, composing himself in the corner.

'Ah, that's the great chimæra I was telling you about.'

'What! The one you were going to see? How come?'

'The chimæra—more so than ever, murmured Demarest. 'Have a game?'

'Sure, I don't mind.'

IV

ZRING, went the Irish girl's bed-curtains
again, and *tschunk* went the electric switch
on the wall, leaving dark the reticulated grill over
the upper berth; and then the bunk creaked, and
creaked sea-sawingly, as the Irish girl got into it,
and creaked as she corkscrewed her Irish body
down the ship-folded bedclothes; and an elbow
thumped the matchboard partition close to Demarest's ear, and then grazingly bruised it again,
and then a padded round knee bumped, and the
elbow again more softly knocked . . . Who's there,
i' the name of the devil? . . . Is it you, strumpet?
Knock again. Knock at the door, or come in
without knocking. Is it you, darling? In the
dark? where? Listen to the wind moaning, humming through the ventilators. Listen to the sea,
the vast sound of sea, pouring down into the infinite, cataract of the world. What are we? We
are silences drowned in an abyss of sound. The
ship is sinking. The world is sinking. God is
sinking. What difference, therefore, does it make
who you are? Don't pause to knock, but approach swiftly through the night of sound and
water, step serenely from thrum to thrum of the
ship's engines, from heartbeat to heartbeat of the
terraqueous god. Is it you, with the candle in
your hand, you in a nightgown? Ah Psyche
from the regions which! You with a pocket flashlight? In, in brief candle! We'll fear not for
scandal. But diddle and dandle. And fondle and

fry.   Seven bells; the ship, sleepwalking, tintin-
nabulates like a gipsy.   The shipboy, hearing bells
below him, looking down at the dark ship, and
dark decks, and dark sea, and the dark bow lowering into a wide dim wash of white, and the dark
waves coming white-maned and flattening in
white—the shipboy sleepily strikes once the small
sea-bell, and the bird of sad sound flies on short
quick wings into the infinite misery . . . MISERY
. . . Misery is consciousness.   Misery is death.
Misery is birth.   Misery is creation.   Rain is falling in Portobello Road, the evening is winter, the
cobbled mud is inferno, and the cold rain slowly
falls in large, fat flakes, *larghe falde*, snowflakes
falling into slime and grease.   The man, shuffling,
undersized, leans pushing the barrow, on which
lies the two-year-old boy under rags of sacking,
unmoving, turning only his large eyes full of pain.
The woman hobbles beside the barrow, weeping,
pressing the back of a blue hand against her cheek,
turning her shrunken face to one side and downward as she whines.   The man is silent, pushing
the barrow rapidly; the woman trots.   Rain falls
into the boy's eyes.   They are hurrying home . . .
The man is thinking, while the dirty water runs
under his cap and down his face, he is used to
it, he doesn't mind the cold trickle among his hair
and down his neck,—but this other thing he is not
used to, he wants to shout out something horrible
about it, shaking his fist, except that he is too tired
and can't find the words.   Let me dictate for you
a course of action which will satisfy this longing.
Begin by shouting at your woman—'For Christ's
sake shut your jaw and stop your bloody whin-

ing. Stop it, or I'll knock your damn teeth out.'
Continue by striking her once in the back of the
neck, so that she stumbles and falls into a puddle,
moaning, and kneels there, moaning, as if unable
to move. Grab her arm, twist it, and wrench the
slattern to her feet. Hit her again, this time in
the face, your fingers open—the slap .will warm
your hand. Shout at her, so that all the people in
Portobello Road will hear. 'What's the matter—
are you drunk? I'll black your eye for you if you
don't get a move on you.' Think again. Think
of nothing but misery, of Portobello Road end-
less and eternal, of yourself and your slut and
your paralysed boy walking there in the winter
rain forever. Do you require speech? Would it
do you good to abuse her, to call her a draggle-
tailed, snaggle-toothed, swaggle-bellied, broken-
gaited ronyon? Enumerate her physical defects.
A wart over her left eye; a wart on her right eye-
lid; a wart (with hairs on it) on the chin; a pendulous wart, like a little pink cauliflower, coral-
hued and corrupt, between the lean breasts; and
a sore on the right thigh. Scars on the legs, blu-
ish or coppery. Puncture-wounds on the inner
surface of the left arm, below the joint: five, and
red. Five corresponding puncture wounds on your
own left arm. Blest be the marriage betwixt
earth and heaven! Now,—in the open sore of
space,—the mortal son and the daughter immoral,
make of the world their trysting-place. Ten posi-
tives in succession, the hollow steel needle prick-
ing and sliding under the taut skin, and into the
swollen vein, the glass tube steadily filling with
poisoned blood as the little steel piston withdraws.

The blessed spirochæte. Swarms. The blood boiling with hook-nosed spirochætes. MISERY. Horror, the maggot, hatches and quarries in the very pulse of love. Rain is falling in Portobello Road, hissing in the paraffin flares that light the barrows and crowds, illuminating the bestial faces and dirty hands. Barrows heaped with kippers. Rotten cabbages, rainsoaked. Collar buttons and woollen stockings. Terracotta Venuses. Winkles. Toy balloons. Detumescent pigs singing like cicadas on a hot night in New Jersey. The man, undersized, leans pushing the barrow on which the boy lies unmoving, turning an apathetic eye toward the smoky flares. The woman trots, moaning. Announce your grief. Stand at the corner where the crowd is densest, and shout it to them pitilessly—'You think you are miserable, do you! Well, look at me, look at us! Syphilis, that's what we got, syphilis!' . . . This was where Goya lived: in Portobello Road. The man pushing the barrow was Goya. The woman, trotting and whining, with averted eyes, was Goya. Goya was the paralysed boy lying numb and cold under wet-glazed rags. Goya sold maggoty kippers from a torchlit barrow: he inflated the singing pig, over and over again. *Nga-a-a-a,* sang the pig, Goya holding it up by the spigot in its back before the circle of dirty-faced children . . . *Goya drew a pig on a wall . . . The five-year-old hairdresser's son . . . saw, graved on a silver tray . . . the lion: and sunsets were begun . . . Goya smelt the bull-fight blood: The pupil of the Carmelite . . . Gave his hands to a goldsmith, learned: to gild an aureole aright . . . Goya saw the Puzzel's eyes: . . .*

sang in the street: (with a guitar) and climbed the
balcony; but Keats (under the halyards) wrote
'Bright star' ... Goya saw the Great Slut pick The
chirping human puppets up.   And laugh, with
pendulous mountain lip, And drown them in a coffee cup; Or squeeze their little juices out In arid
hands, insensitive, To make them gibber ... Goya
went Among the catacombs to live ... He saw
gross Ronyons of the air, harelipped and goitered,
raped in flight By hairless pimps, umbrella-
winged: Tumult above Madrid at night . . . He
HEARD the SECONDS IN his CLOCK CRACK like
SEEDS, DIVULGE and POUR ABYSmal FILTH of
NOthingNESS BETWEEN the PENdulum AND the
FLOOR: Torrents of dead veins, rotted cells, Ton-
sils decayed, and fingernails: Dead hair, dead fur,
dead claws, dead skin. Nostrils and lids; and
cauls and veils; And EYES that still, in death, remained (Unlidded and unlashed) AWARE of the
foul CORE, and, fouler yet, The REGION WORM
that RAVINS There ... STENCH flowed out of the
second's TICK. And Goya swam with it through
SPACE, Sweating the fetor from his limbs. And
stared upon the UNFEATURED FACE That did not
see, and sheltered NAUGHT, but WAS and IS. The
second gone, Goya returned, and drew the FACE;
And scrawled beneath it, 'This I have known' ...
And drew four slatterns, in an attic, Heavy, with
heads on arms, asleep: And underscribed it. 'Let
them slumber! Who, if they woke, could only
weep' . . . MISERY. Say it savagely, biting the
paltry and feeble words, and overaccenting the
metronomic rhythm, the same flaccid-syllabled
rhythm as that of King Caligula. Say it savagely,

with eyes closed, lying rigid in the berth, the right
foot crossed over the left, flexing and reflexing
against the coarse sheet. Explore the first cabin in
your pyjamas, find the passenger-list and the number of Cynthia's cabin, and putting your absurd
chin (in which the bones are slowly being rotted by
pyorrhea) over the window sill, recite in the darkness . . . not this, not this, but something exquisite, something young. *Awakening up he took her
hollow lute, tumultous; and in chords that tender-
est be He played an ancient ditty, long since mute,
in Provence called* 'LA BELLE DAME SANS
MERCI.' The boy stood on the burning deck.
Eating peanuts by the peck . . . Cynthia! are you
awake? . . . Yes! Who is it? . . . Saint William
of Yonkers. Listen! I will tell you all about my
childhood—everything. You will see how pathetic
it was. You will see what long, lonely, lugubrious
life I have led. The Irish girl, separated from me
by one inch of painted wood, is trying to attract
my attention, knocking with her sweet little elbow
against the wall. Last night I replied, tentatively.
To-night, so great is your heavenly influence upon
me, so permeated is my gross body by your beauty,
that I pay no attention. Are you listening? . . .
Yes, darling . . . I am a man full of pity and gentleness! My face is the face of one grown gently
wise with suffering—ah, with what years of un-
told suffering! I have been misunderstood,—
I have blundered,—I have sinned,—Oh, I have
sinned; but I have paid the price. My father was
cruel. When I was five, he burnt off my left
hand because I had been striking matches . . . I
begged in the streets, having no money to buy

the necessary books; for even as a little child I had a passion for knowledge and beauty. A Chinaman gave me a quarter, and I bought . . . what was it I bought? *Nick Carter in Colorado. The Arabian Nights. Almost Fourteen.* Fiske's *Cosmic Philosophy.* Nietzsche's *Beyond Good and Evil.* Espronceda's *El Diablo Mundo.* The Icelandic *Voluspa. An Essay on the Trallian School.* A Variorum edition of *Twinkle Twinkle Little Star,* in eighteen volumes. A Variorum edition of *Thank You Kindly Sir She Said,* in two hundred volumes. Are you still listening, Cynthia? . . . Yes, beloved . . . I adore you, Cynthia. I have been a fool—I have lost you—but I adore you, and I will adore you for ever. Your physical defects—do I not know them? A nostril just a suspicion too "painfle." A voice exquisite, light, Shelleyan—but lacking in those deep-throated qualities, voluptuous and resonant, with which I love a woman, now and again, to turn challengingly upon me. Breasts a little too low and large; a gait a shade too self-conscious; a bearing rather too much in the tradition of the 'expensive slouch.' But these are immaterial—forgive me for mentioning them. I adore them, I do not desire to touch them, nor to touch you. My feeling for you is wholly sublimated: I can trace in it no physical desire. I should fear and distrust any impulse to bring your tall body into contact with mine. I should like only to live with you in some strange, rarefied world,—cold, clear, translunar and spacious; a world of which you know the secret, and I do not; a world of the subtle and the fragile, of the crepuscular and the vitreous, of suggestions

dim but precise, of love inexpressive and thought
unconcealed. An imparadised Amalfi, marble ter-
races of orange groves and camellias, rising out
of the violet of the sea and ascending into the violet of the empyrean? No? Too much like mar-
zipan? Let us, then, leave the world as it is; but
make of it, by knowing all its secrets, our terres-
trial heaven . . . Are you listening, Cynthia? . . .
Listening, *smutsfink* . . . To-morrow I will write
out for you the history of my childhood. All sorts
of exquisite things will be in it—delicate perceptions, gentlenesses of feeling, of which you would
not have supposed a mere male to be capable. I
have always been kind to birds, dogs, children,
cats and mice. Particularly mice. Once I found
a swift, imprisoned in a house. I saw it flapping
against the window as I passed, flapping against
the curtains. The house was empty, deserted. I
walked miles to get the key, wondering how I
would capture the poor thing when I returned.
It wasn't necessary—I opened the window and he
flew out. He had fallen down the chimney. . . .
This, and many others . . . I would narrate them
humorously, of course—but you would detect the
gentleness and pity . . . A kitten—I climbed a telegraph pole, when I was eight, to rescue a kitten,
which had got all the way to the top and was
afraid to come down. I had stationed my brother
and another boy on the roof of the chicken-coop
—they were to hold out a towel between them,
into which I was to drop the kitten. Unfortunately, Tom (he's a darling, Tom—you'd like
him!) let go of his end. Still, the kitten wasn't
hurt . . . A dog, I saved once from drowning at

Keswick . . . Blind men I have led across the street
. . . Old women I have helped in and out of trains
—several thousand . . . The woman who fainted
in the Grand Central Station—I helped to carry
her into the waiting-room—how extraordinarily
white she was. Beggars. Hurdy-gurdy men. The
tramp in the ditch, who said, 'You might as well
be cheerful, especially if you're miserable!'—and
went on singing . . . Yes. All the unhappy world
—the overworked, the starving, the starved for
love, the deserted and lonely—MISERY . . . Like
the vampire I have been dead many times, and
learned the secrets of the grave; like the lobster,
I do not bark, and know the secrets of the sea.   I
am shy, I am sensitive, I am impressionable. How
many lovely things, how many horrible things, I
remember! This you would love in me if you
loved nothing else : this treasure house, this gold-
en thesaurus, of my memory.   If only I had succeeded in showing this to you before you fell in
love! You would have been astonished—perhaps
. . . Perhaps perhaps perhaps perhaps . . . On the
other hand, you might have thought me not sufficiently masculine? . . . A sentimental intro-
verted weakling, with that tendency to sudden
cruelty which all the injured manifest.   But my
trick of unexpected reticence, my impassivity of
appearance, my proneness to fatigue and indifference, the rapidity with which I tire of people—no
matter whether they be angels or devils—these
characteristics give an air of masculinity which
might have deceived you?   Are you listening,
Cynthia? . . . Listening, mud-puppy . . . My absurd chin is on your window-sill in the dark, but

I am like Fama, and my feet are not at all on this
deck, as you might imagine, but way down upon
the Sewanee River, far, far away. I am like
Daisy Dacey,—England and the United States
rolled into one. To see all is to be all. But it is
above all my childhood that I should like to put into
your lap—my romantic and beautiful childhood,
my suffering and pitiful childhood. I was disliked
and distrusted. I was cruelly beaten. I was hu-
miliated. My pride and will were broken before
I had come to my seventh year. I was in a state
of continual terror. I sneaked in and out of the
house, mouselike and secretive, my only purpose
to attract as little attention as possible. My favourite story—would you believe it?—this is very
touching—was the story of the ugly duckling.
This held out a ray of hope for me—I would revenge myself,—some day,—some day,—by turning into a swan. I read this story over and over,
memorizing every detail, and as I read it I search-
ed in my soul for signs of the wonder that was
to come. How was this to be? What gifts had
the good fairies given me, that I might some day
astonish and confound my cruel father, my forgetful mother? It could not be strength, for I
was weak, and I was constantly ill. It could not
be courage, for I hardly ever forgot what it was
to be afraid. It could not be beauty, for beauty
was not a prerogative of boys. Could it, perhaps,
be wisdom? This was conceivable—it was only
by my teachers that I was ever given encouragement. I remember how I was overcome, how I
blushed, when one day Miss Baring said aloud in
the classroom (there was a drawing of Julius Cæ-

sar on the blackboard behind her head), 'William will some day be successful. He is intelligent, and he works.' Successful! What a blaze of glory, what a bursting of stars of light, was in that word! Like sky-rockets on Christmas Eve! Like Roman candles vomiting their coloured balls of fire and slow streams of fading sparks! So perhaps it was in this way that I began to associate knowledge with success; or mental skill of some kind. I began by copying the drawing of Julius Cæsar—I showed my drawing to Miss Baring, and this too she praised . . . Eight bells . . . Changing the watch. With heavy boots, with oilskins, with a black oilskin hat, he climbs the ladder to the crow's nest. A fine rain falling on his face and hands. All clear, Bill? . . . A light two points off the port bow . . . Right. Getting a little sea up. Thickening a bit too . . . Smith is in bed at sea. Faubion, the Fleshpot, is in bed. The Welsh Rarebit is in bed—whose? Vivien Hay-Lawrence is in bed. The Major is in bed. Solomon Moses Caligula Silberstein is in bed. Cynthia is in bed. Mrs. Battiloro is in bed. The pianist lies awake, thinking of his wife and daughter in Blackpool. The Chief Steward is having a game of bridge in his stateroom, whisky is on the table. All the others lie horizontal, above and below the water-line, like chrysalids, like corpses in coffins. The clairvoyant? He too; but his sleep is troubled by vatic dreams. He sees each chrysalid being secretly attacked by ants, the larva detroyed, the psyche released. Ah psyche from the regions which. MISERY. Last night as I lay on my pillow—last night as I lay on my bed—last night as I lay on my pillow—I dreamed that my bonnie was dead . . . You know the story of Strindberg and the mouse? He was terrified by an electric influence, an evil stream, which everywhere pursued and persecuted him. It came through walls, aiming at his heart. He hid his head in the pillow, but the malevolent stream came up through the bed. He ran out into the hall and lay down by the banisters—but a mouse trotted up close to him and looked into his face: and he fled screaming. I am Strindberg. I look at his photograph and a feeling of self-love and self-pity, a profound narcissistic compassion and tenderness, comes over me. Those harassed and noble temples, the tortured deep-seeing eyes, the magnificent head, the small mouth, which is the mouth of the child and of the adder! . . . I am wise, I am weak, I am persecuted; I am unlucky, I am beautiful, I am strong. *Der Gekreuzigte.* I love my own body. When I was a youth, I used to stand naked before a tall glass, or walk gracefully toward it, transported by the beauty I saw, the exquisitely flexing muscles of abdomen and calf and thigh, the suave Greek brow, the candid eyes. Ah, the profile of the body, with the ribs arched, the lean hollow curve of the belly! The lightly hung and powerful arms, the hands large, fair and strong as those of the David! This is what is now rejected and despised. Therefore it is not beautiful. It is obscene, gross, despicable. It is a whited sepulchre; a mass of secret corruption, of filthy juices and clots of half-destroyed food; an infirmary sicklied o'er with the pale cast of consciousness. I have always been one in whose conscious-

ness illusion and disillusion flashed simultaneously.
My hand remains still, because it releases even
before it has grasped. Are you listening, Moon?
Are you listening, chaste Nymph? I am on the
First Class deck beside you, wearing pearl-grey
spats, carrying gloves and a silver-topped cane of
malacca, a gardenia in my buttonhole. There is
no obstacle between us, you are not in love with
another man, you have all this time been secretly
in love with me. I am your social equal (indeed
your superior) and my stick is really the wand of
Trismagistus. *How pleasant! Oh, how exquisite! Thy beauty framed for sweet delight!
Thy stature like an upright palm! Thy breasts
like clusters dropping balm!* ... *I my Belov'd first
raisèd thee From under the pomecitron tree; Thy
careful mother in that shade With anguish her
fair belly laid* . . . Queen and huntress, are you
listening? . . . Listening, but bored, woodlouse . . .
I was in a hurry—I hadn't time to explain to you
—I would like to explain to you—explain everything. I had no right on the First Cabin deck,
of course—I am in the Second Cabin. Poverty.
Poor but proud. I have often, for that matter,
travelled in the steerage. I believe in being dem-
ocratic, don't you? I remember you said your
brother William . . . always got along well with
people of humble origin . . . Yes . . . So do I . . .
I like them. Queer creatures, often, aren't they?
I really like them better than most people of my
own class. Why then, apologize for liking them
—or why claim it as a virtue? *Tee hee*—nervous
giggle. I believe you are a snob, Cynthia. I remember my friend Giles, who met you at a dance

in Oyster Bay—Oyster Bay!—said 'Battiloro?
Oh yes. I remember. An awful snob—looked
down her nose at everybody! . . . One of those
damned English snobs.' Ha ha! Apparently you
had been rather cool to poor good-natured Giles,
Giles with his loud bark and perpetually wagging
tail, Giles who at college was known as 'Susie.'
Poor Giles, a failure at everything, but so disarm-
ing, so ingenuous, so eager to please, so nice! How
had you the heart to be cruel to him? Are you
cruel, Cynthia? Or was it that you thought *him*
a snob? Well—perhaps a little. He probably
tried a little too hard to show you how much he
knew about England, and how many 'fish-heads'
he knew there . . . Lady Rustlebottom of the
Mount, Torquay. Etcetera . . . He bought a
blazer especially for the purpose and spent a week-
end there . . . I was in a hurry—I hadn't time to
explain — I must explain — all — everything —
Smith, for example. You probably noticed at
once that Smith is not a 'gentleman'—in the accepted sense. The way he cocks that absurd great
tweed hat! His dingy clerical-looking clothes,
and his shoes humped at the toes! A mere ship's
acquaintance, a rather interesting little character.
You wouldn't like him—he would bore you—but
you would like to hear about him, the salient features of his career brightly related by Demarest.
Of course, you aren't a very good judge of character! You remember Wetherall? You said, 'What
a really charming face he has. I'm sure he's awfully nice!' Ah! The joke was on you. Wetherall was at that moment seducing a little trained
nurse who was on board—he told me at every

meal of his progress, and dear Billington was so
shocked that he could hardly eat . . . One of their
difficulties was that she had two room-mates . . .
But the weather, you remember, was warm, they
stayed late on deck, and there was no moon.
Also, they did not attend the ship's concert. Wetherall described it all to me—every detail, his kind
brown eyes humorously bright, his Bradford accent at its very best.   What a curious pleasure it
gave me to share in that secret conquest, so passionate, so frankly carnal, so frankly obscene, and
so laconically casual, while at the same moment I
was conscious of falling in love with you, and
falling in love in a sense so antithetical, so ethereal!   While Wetherall was turning wine into
blood, I was turning blood into wine.   Yes.   It
was magnificent.   A slow and beautiful counterpoint.   Wetherall the bass and you the treble.
You remember that afternoon when I encountered you at the foot of the companion-way?—
you were carrying a book—it was a book of negro
spirituals—and you smiled, and then immediately
looked away, frowning, at the sea.   You hesitated
as if—you were perhaps really going somewhere,
you had an errand, you didn't want me to suppose
that . . . you in any way sought my company.   I,
too, hesitated,—as if I knew that my company
could not be of much interest to you, and yet—
might we not pause together for a moment, touch
our wings together in the air?   And besides I—
and perhaps you too (we discussed this problem—
so peculiar to ships—a few days later in the train
to London, in the light of the queer implicit intimacy which by then had sprung up between us)

feared that you might think me trying to avoid
you—it is so difficult, on a ship, to avoid the appearance of persecution, or, on the other hand, of
avoidance! . . . 'Have you been reading?' I said,
and you answered, 'I've been trying to—but it's
so extraordinarily difficult, on a ship, to *concentrate!* . . . I've had to give it up' . . . I too had
found it difficult—even with *The Spoils of Poynton*. I told you of this, and we discussed Henry
James, standing there, as we did so, a little uneasy with each other, or, as Mandeville (is it Mandeville?) puts it, in a mammering and at a stay.
And then, taking my flimsy life in my hands, I
said, 'Shall we go up on the boat-deck and concentrate *together?* It's rather nice forward of the
bridge . . .' Singular and daring remark! You
half smiled and turned, we ascended the companion-way; and at the forward end of the deck, leaning our backs against the old plates of the *Silurian,*
which we could feel buckling as the ship plunged,
we talked deliciously for an hour, for two hours.
And do you know what gave, for me, a special
exquisiteness to that talk? It was my fresh sharp
recollection of my conversation at lunch with
Wetherall. Behind that forward life-boat, on the
starboard side,—where later we played a game of
chess, the young student of architecture watching
us,—behind that lifeboat, the evening before,
Wetherall and Miss Kirkpatrick had lain together
till one o'clock. They had been discovered and
reprimanded. Of all this, naturally, you knew
nothing; and still less could you conceive the nature of Wetherall's confidences to me. You
would be astounded,—horrified! The grossness

of the human being! And the vulgar candour
with which one man to another confesses it!
Wetherall informed me that Miss Kirkpatrick
was, up till then, 'inexperienced.' But, setting out
for a two months' holiday in Scotland and Bel-
fast, she had in advance made up her mind that,
should a sufficiently attractive man be available,
she would give herself to him. Wetherall—a married man, with a daughter of eight—had been
the lucky man. He had noticed from the outset
that she smiled at him a good deal, and somewhat
intensely. On the second evening he kissed her
—and as he remarked, 'Didn't she come up to
it? . . . O *Boy!* . . .' But I give you the impression,—are you listening, Cynthia? . . . Still listening, earthworm . . . I give you the impression—
partly a wrong impression—that this organ-point,
supplied for our intercourse by Wetherall, was un-
alloyedly pleasant. No no no no no. Good God.
This is precisely what I don't want you to think.
It reminded me, certainly, of my own obscenity;
but it also served to show me already the immense
altitude of my—flight! Wetherall was precisely
what I was proposing, with your support, to leave
behind. More precisely still, what I was leaving
behind was Helen Shafter: coarse, voluptuous,
conscious, witty Helen, who had so ungovernable
an appetite for the farcical, and who had so skilfully and swiftly and horribly exposed the essen-
tial fleshliness of 'love between the sexes!' Yes.
The experience was horrible. And how even more
horrible was it to come thus to you, before whom
I so passionately longed to stand with something
of Parsifal's mindless innocence, bearing on brow

and palms the stigmata of that crucifixion! . . .
MISERY . . . And what intricacy of fate brings it
about that again it is from a meeting with Helen
that I come to you, and that as I passed you twice
on the deck this evening it was of our so miserable
affair—Helen's and mine—that I was foolishly
boasting to a total stranger? Is it possible that
you overheard it? . . . Well, that is what I am . . .
Even supposing that we could have . . . even supposing that you could have . . . *loved* me, it is impossible that I should always have been able to
deceive you—sooner or later I should have had to
drop the pretence (so skilful) of refinement and
idealism and innocence; you would have seen me
for the Caligula that I am . . . Somebody out in
the corridor—a stewardess giggling. And a steward. Mrs. Atherton. 'No—NO!' and then a little
appealing laugh, ending abruptly in '*M-m-m*,' and
then the stifled laugh again. Tompkins is kissing
Mrs. Atherton. Intervene, Cynthia! This sort of
thing shouldn't be permitted on shipboard. Now
it is Tompkins—I know his voice. 'What did he
say, eh? What did he say? . . .' 'None of your
business . . .' 'Well, I don't give a damn *what* he
said—he can stick it up—the flue' . . . '*Sh!*'
'What's the matter with you? This ain't inspection time' . . . 'No, but somebody might hear you
. . .' *Murmur murmur murmur* . . . For God's
sake speak up! I'd like to get to the bottom of
this . . . 'and said I wasn't going to have anything
to do with him any more . . .' '. . . drunk the first
twenty-four hours anyway—lying like a log in his
bunk with a wet towel . . .' 'It isn't the first time
either. Voyage before last they had to fetch him

. . . Carter and St. Clair it was . . . wife . . . she
was standing outside there looking . . .' *Murmur
murmur murmur*. Pause. Have they gone, or is
he kissing her again? Have to do it like this, poor
devils—on the q.t., late at night. Snatches between watches under hatches . . . 'Good night,
then.' 'Good night, sweet dreams.' 'Cheerio.'
Gone: a rustle of starched calico, muffled footsteps, and gone. The Irish girl is breathing heavily and slowly—asleep. What is she dreaming of?
Pittsburgh. She is in uncle William's house in
Pittsburgh. Uncle William has grown a black
beard, horrible, too long, obscenely alive. His
mouth, seen through it, is unfamiliarly round and
red, like a great red rose, but too opulent and
fleshly, almost mucous. He sits and looks at her.
Then he begins speaking harshly and says over
and over again, 'Thy belly is as an heap of wheat'
. . . Yes. Everywhere this motif—everywhere.
You too, Cynthia—who knows? What concupis-
cent pre-occupations, only fleetingly conscious and
perhaps obscure, do you perpetually conceal? Eunice—until once I laughed—used to tell me her
dreams. She dreamed one night that she was a
nun, in a convent. A fire broke out. The nuns
ran into the corridors, looking for the fire, but
only finding dense clouds of smoke pouring up the
stairs. They ran down the stairs, and coming at
length to the cellar, could see through the smoke
every now and then a fitful glare of flame in what
appeared to be a deep hole, or arched cave, at one
side of the cellar, a sort of underground entrance.
The nuns dragged a garden hose down the stairs,
thrust the brass nozzle into the cavern, and the

fire began to go out . . . Darling Eunice . . . I wish
she hadn't got married . . . disappeared. 'Don't
look at me like that!' she said—that was one night
when we had dinner on the Roof Garden.   We
were falling in love.   Blue taffeta.   Those sleeves
of a sort of gauze.   That night she was suddenly
sick in the street, and closing her eyes said, *'Oh,* I
can't even love you a *little* bit . . . so . . .sorry!'
. . . Then the time we were standing at midnight
in the dark Portico of the church—the church with
the angels blowing trumpets from the tower . . .
We thought we were concealed . . . but Eunice
murmured too much when I put my hand . . . and
the policeman . . . Good God what a fright he gave
us . . . 'Move on, now! haven't you got any better
place than that? . . .'   How delightful to remember it.   I wonder if Eunice, married, lying beside
her husband, thinks about me sometimes?   She
liked me, we were happy.   But I couldn't see her
often enough.   'No—' she said, 'this time you
mustn't kiss me . . . I'm going to be married!' . . .
MISERY.   Absurd, if I could face Eunice's departure with so much equanimity, that this about Cynthia . . . Different . . . Not much intellectual or
æsthetic   companionship   with   Eunice — well-
matched emotionally and physically (and her sense
of humour—delicious! and her courage!), but not
otherwise.   My longing to see her now is largely
nostalgic.   Still—I was frightfully fond of her
. . . With Cynthia—so extraordinarily at one in all
things—a kind of shorthand of understanding at
the very beginning . . . *Tschunk.*   The lights in
the corridor are off.   Dark.   The engines throbbing; late; the night shift of stokers; sweating

like a lot of firelit demons. The shaft, all the
way through the ship, gleaming, revolving—ectoplasm. Somebody coming. Faubion? Light!
Must be the watchman with a flashlight. At his
priestlike task—of bold intrusion . . . Ship, I am
on a ship. Cynthia is on board, but in the First
Cabin. Shall I transfer to the First Cabin?
Money enough; just barely. But nothing left for
tips and drinks and the train to London. It would
look too pointed. Cynthia is on board. Incredible! Anticlimax! . . . How am I going to see
her? Walk boldly into the First Cabin looking
for her? Besides, under the circumstances, do I
want to see her? It would be useless. It would
be 'pleasant'? Good God . . . After all these
dreams of ships, too! Always looking for Cynthia on ships . . . When I get to London, I won't
dare to go and see her. No point in it. Spoiled.
The whole thing spoiled. The world pulled down
and wrecked. Better be like Smith and gather my
rosebuds while I may . . . Poor old Smith! The
cherub, in pink pyjamas, sleeps surrounded by
Faubion's heliotrope-smelling dresses, and dreams
he is dancing with chorus girls. Lottie, Flo, Hyacintha, Vyolette, Dol, Maybelle, Parthenia. They
all dance frou-frouishly around him, squealing,
ring around a rosy, joining hands, and Cherub
Smith stands in the middle, in the grass, with his
finger in his mouth, looking coy. *Coo-hoo,* Parthenia! I see you, Maybelle! I know it was you
who slapped me, Nottie Lottie! . . . There's a corporal in the grass . . . Smith, impersonating a
satyr, runs with a resinous torch and thrusts it
under a translucent chlamys, igniting it. Parthe-

nia is burned. Goes off flaming. Ha ha! . . .
Splendid old Smith . . . This is what it is to be
homo sapiens, the laughing animal, the animal
who remembers and foresees . . . Smith and the
clairvoyant—the clairvoyant corporal springs out
of the deep grass, skull-faced and hideous, and
grimly pursues poor old Smith, who screams
among the tombstones—Flottie, Hyacintha, Par-
tha, Flow, Boybell, Dole, Violent. He is felled
like an ox. To what green altar, oh mysterious
priest? And all his crispy flanks in garlic drest.
The uses of assonance. Gloom and gleam. Birth
and death. Love and live. Mingle and mangle.
Fix and flux. Prick and puck. Pop and pap.
Twit and tot. Point and punt. Dram and dream.
So near and yet so far . . . What if it were at last
possible to talk of *everything* with a woman? To
keep no secrets, no dark recesses of the mind, no
dolours and danks, which could not be shared with
her? But then she would have ceased to be attractive. Is it simply because we have to *pose* before her . . . to pretend to be angels . . . the angel
with the sword? . . . *Ah, the awful fixed curve of
determinism!* MISERY . . . You overhear all these
reflections, Cynthia? . . . All, maggot . . . Forgive
me forgive me forgive me forgive me. I am horrible but I am penitent. I will crawl on my knees
to the Bilbao canal and drink of its filthy waters.
I will bathe in slime. I will fill my belly with
ashes. I will go naked, and show the corns on my
feet, the mole on my right fess. I will work for
ninety-nine years in a Chinese rice-field, sleeping
in the mud. I will pray to Kwannon to purify
my heart. I will hop on one foot all the way from

Sofia to Jerusalem, speaking to no one, and die at
the foot of the cross: the weeping-cross.   You
have seen, in Mount Auburn cemetery (beautiful
isn't it), that tombstone of white marble . . . with
a marble lamb . . . upon which, annually on a certain day, two drops of blood are found?   Those
drops of blood are mine.   Expiation.   On the
twenty-eighth of February each year, in the evening, I go there and cut my left wrist, letting two
drops fall on the stone.   Twenty-eight is my fatal
number.   The moon is shining when I arrive.
Snow is on the ground and on the graves.   Snow
covers the obscene vaults.   Crows are asleep in
pine trees.   The snow-plough moans along Mt.
Auburn Street . . . And I, solitary, grieving, expiate the sin and horror of the world,—its grossness,
its cruelty, its ugliness; its triviality, its vileness,
its deceit.   Bowed with sorrow, I ascend the little
snow-covered hill by the tower, pass over it westward, and come to the Lamb.   Then I take from
my pocket-book a razor blade (Gillette) and gash
slightly the left wrist . . . In heaven, those two
drops of blood fall like thunderclaps.   The angels
fly up like doves.   God, asleep, has a dream.   He
dreams: 'The infinite darkness is gashed redly
with a sword, and from the gash pours a torrent
of blood.   I am no longer unconscious suffering,
—I become an awareness and a shape.   I am the
region worm,—the undying and infinite and eternal caterpillar; and I am the host of red-eyed ants
who attack him in every part and devour him forever.   The infliction and reception of pain comes
to me from every particle of the caterpillar world.
And the particles become more conscious.   The

chorus of suffering swells unceasingly: it is the sound of the world—the sound of sorrow. Who will teach me how I may again return into the darkness of nescience? What Siegfried will ring his ram's horn and destroy both Fafnar and himself? What messianic atom among my wailing myriads will so crucify himself and die that his death will carry in its train ALL DEATH? . . . I writhe with all my length . . . Oh, man, save me! . . . But all I hear is the sound of gnawing and moaning, the sound as of the ten million silkworms which in China, at night, keep travellers awake with their champing of mulberry leaves . . . CLAP! CLAP! . . . What is that? Two drops of blood! Man begins to destroy himself: out of horror for his own nature, at the nature of Me. It is the beginning of the end! Ah! peace will return to me! I will return at last into the womb of nothing!' . . . *Tin-tin*. Two bells. One o'clock. I ought to be asleep. One three five seven nine eleven thirteen fifteen. Two four six eight ten twelve . . . One four seven ten thirteen sixteen nineteen twenty-two twenty-five . . . I'm on my belly with my palms crossed under my chest, right cheek on pillow. But the right nostril obstructs. On my back again, carefully, these damned ship-folded bedclothes come apart so easily. The cat's prayer. Give us this day our daily mouse. And forgive us our trespusses as we forgive those who trespuss against us . . . I really ought to give up this awful habit of punning. Just the same, I always regretted not saying, when her knitted sleeve caught in the log and stopped its ticking (reducing the day's run), 'A miss is as good as

a mile!' That was when we were discussing
Brooke's poetry. And I quoted—'*And suddenly
there's no meaning in our kiss . . . And your lit,
upward face grows, where we lie, Lonelier and
dreadfuller than sunlight is, and dumb and mad
and eyeless, like the sky . . .*' I told her also of
the Catholic poetess (so tiresomely self-conscious
and exquisite) who remarked about his poem
'*Heaven*'—'So stupid, don't you think? So very
stupid!' Squamous, omnipotent, and kind. Mrs.
Battiloro frightens and annoys me in the same
way. What was her phrase about Moore, when
I repeated his comment on Yeats? Something
deliciously Victorian. Hm. Offensive . . . No.
Noisome. No.—What the devil! Lie in wait for
it. How exasperating, especially when sleepless.
ODIOUS! Yes. An odious person! I laughed,
and she was annoyed. She didn't invite me to
come again—I said good-bye to her in the dining-
room, where she was giving instructions to the
maid for the dinner party. Who was coming to
that dinner party? How I longed to know! Good-
bye, she said, and turned back to her silver and
her refectory table (which I had been brought to
see!). Refractory table. That's what old man
Tucker always called it—frosty-faced old fool.
Table tipping. Ectoplasm. That reminds me of
old Duggan in his shirt-sleeves behind the coun-
ter, taking his false teeth out of the cigar-box on
the window-sill. I ought to have told Cynthia
about him. When his wife died! 'I miss her terribly, the lovely little dear . . . I was looking at her
grave . . . It looks sort of bare. I ought to set
out some flowers there. I thought maybe some

Christian anthems would look nice?' Chrysanthe-
mums. When I took M. there, hoping to get Duggan to repeat it (how heartless), it all went off
like clockwork, even to the furtive tear on his
cheek. Poor old Duggan. His wife was like the
sheep-knitter in '*Alice.*' Cancer of the liver. Dying in that shabby little shop, selling tins of tobacco, ten cents' worth of stale peppermints, sar-
dines, glue, shoe-strings. Patient and kind. I was
his only friend,—almost impossible to get away
from him some evenings—he followed me to the
door, talking, reluctant to have me go . . . Breaking out violently about some of his neighbours—
particularly the O'Briens, whom he hated. Their
hens getting into his yard, 'smelling up' the place,
waking his wife in the morning. A God-damned
nuisance. I've complained, and I'll keep right on
complaining. Yes, by God, I will. Think they
own the place by God . . . The shop shut, and
cheap crêpe hanging from the latch. The curtains drawn. Afterwards he had a fox-terrier pup
to keep him company—it was run over and killed.
Then a timid little mongrel, sleeping in a box by
the stove. 'Yes, you know, she keeps me company—and you'll be surprised how much she un-
derstands' . . . He got his own meals—bacon and
fried potatoes. Moonshine whisky—a fine plume
he used to breathe out sometimes in the evening!
'These travellers you know—*they* know where to
get it' . . . The Greens were nice to him when his
wife died—but nobody else was. Not a soul. Poor
old man. MISERY. Ashes to ashes and dust to
dust. Would you like to kiss your father? No.
The others were lifted up and kissed the dead face,

surprised. Why did I refuse? Shyness and horror. The people sitting there, after the service,
staring and weeping. The parson wearing a queer
thing with white sleeves and the bible with a pale
purple ribbon, and the parson's mouth getting
moist at the corners when he talked. Then we sat
in the carriage . . . feeling that we oughtn't to
talk or look out . . . Trot trot. Clop clop. The
palmettos swayed and flashed. The moss was hanging in long grey streamers. The shell road glared in
the sunlight. Too hot to walk barefooted. What
flower had that been that smelled so sweet? . . .
Tuberoses . . . The mortuary tuberose. Tomb-
smelling tuberose. Trot trot. The sidewalks
lined with crowds of staring niggers, niggers
smelling blood and death. That murder I saw
from the front 'stoop'—*bang bang bang bang
bang,* and the man's felt hat falling off, and his
head sinking down on his breast, and the niggers
flocking like ravens, flocking and cawing, while
the murderer (a fireman whom I knew, who
owned a pet monkey) stood there in his shirt-
sleeves, unmoving, as if surprised at what he'd
done . . . *Was* it he who walked past the porch, a
year later, in shirt-sleeves, carrying an empty coal-
scuttle? Back from the penitentiary, or the chain-
gang? . . . Disappointed at not seeing the mark on
his face. If I had kissed him—or perhaps it
didn't show anyway. Somebody said—Harry it
was—that one of his eyes had come out and rolled
across the floor. The bloodstained mattress had
been put in the outhouse—I and Harry went and
looked at it, pretending that we were looking for
the kittens. *Felo de se.* Being pushed forward,

in the crowd at the cemetery, to the edge of the grave. Sandy soil. An arrangement of pulleys and bands of canvas. Ashes to ashes. A little dust taken in the same parson's clean fingers. And dust to dust. Then the shovels, more businesslike.—My father. My father which art in earth. It was just over there he took my picture once, on the bluff by the river. In the white duck sailor suit. Hollow be thy name. . . . Julian, who said that it was always in the presence of death, or in the thought of it, that life, and therefore love (reproductive) most astonishingly asserted itself. He meant the merely physical. Quite understandable. Ain't Nature horrible? Love and Death. In Latin almost the same—ditto Italian. Death sacred and love profane. Eunice telling me of her friend the trained nurse, Miss Paine. Miss Paine was fond of poetry, she read Keats and Shelley. Periodically, she developed a taste for lubricious fiction. Presbyterian. Strong self-control,—but also strong passions. On that case in East Orange, on the night when the father died, the son, aged eighteen, through whose room she had to pass, put out his hand to her. She said afterwards she couldn't understand it—it had seemed so right. So absolutely right. The strain, the exhaustion, the grief, all breaking down into this other, this divine ecstasy, in which suffering has supremely its place. Her only experience of passion. Age: thirty. For a month afterwards she did nothing but pray: the whole of Sunday spent at church. Forgive us, for we know not what we do. MISERY. A child crying somewhere. The most desolating of all sounds

is the sound of a child crying. Harrowing—
makes you feel helpless. Might as well run, but
then you can't forget it. The echo rings in your
ear. *Ahhhhhhhhhhhh* . . . *oo-oo-oo* . . . *ah-h-h-h*
. . . *oo-oo-oo-oo* . . . the first thing we do when
born is cry. All language therefore must develop
out of the sound of crying—it is probably most
affecting when *plangent* for that reason. Make a
note of that—and remember it. Spring it on
somebody as if I'd always known it. There, there
darling, don't cry. There, there, darling, don't
cry. By baby bunting. When the bough bends
the cradle will fall. Lullaby. *Traumerei.* My
father whistled the *Lorelei* to the cat—he had a
theory that the *Lorelei,* whistled slowly, was in-
furiating to cats. But the cat seemed to be delighted. He would now be—let me see. He was
thirty-seven. From nought is 8. Fifty-five. What
would he think of me, I wonder. Would I be
afraid of him still? I am taller than you are. I
am more intelligent than you are. Freer from fetiches than you are . . . Look! You see that scar?
You gave that to me, holding my hand in the gas-
jet . . . You see these plays? they come from the
deep wound you inflicted on my soul . . . You see
the unhappy restlessness with which I wander
from continent to continent, this horrified and
lack-lustre restlessness which prevents me from
loving one person or place for more than a season,
driving me on, aimless and soulless? This is what
you did to me by depriving me of my mother . . .
Think of Silberstein saying that he wants to find
his mother. He wants to die. O God—O God.
To die,—to die in the middle of a deep sleep, to

sink deeper and deeper into the darkness... That's
of course, what *he* wanted—that poem he left on
the table—the darkness—'*closer, closer all about,
Blotting all the light of living out.*' Intra-uterine
reversion. Perhaps the fact that *he*—will prevent
me. Explode it. It was a sort of exhibitionism,
leaving a poem on the table like that—defeated
ego. Vanity. See what a great spirit has left
you. Mighty, I spread my wings and left you...
I suppose I liked him when I was very small, before the other kids were born—before I can remember. He must then have fascinated me and
drawn me out powerfully and skilfully. Yes, I
can feel that he did. There was something angelic
about him—later it became diabolic. The angel
that revolted. My God, what basilisk eyes, eyes
that shot through you, tearing out thoughts, blood,
and vertebræ. 'Where is that other letter?' 'There
wasn't any other letter.' 'Look at me. Where is
that other letter?' 'But there wasn't any other
letter.' 'You brought back three letters. Do you
deny that you gave one of them to your mother?'
'There were only two letters!' 'Why did you sneak
in by the back door?' 'It was because there were
some boys I didn't want to meet——' 'Don't lie
to me!... Why did you come in by the back
door?' 'It was because I saw "Butch" Gleason.'
... O God have mercy upon us. Pity us and have
mercy upon us. Shine down upon us, star of the
sea, and guide us gently to the haven of Heaven.
Manumit us from slavery to our passions; deliver
us from the tyranny of all-too-human reason. Take
from us that part which makes us to suffer, and
at whose bidding we bring suffering to others.

And lead us down into darkness forever. MISERY
. . . *Can never change the swan's black legs to
white*. Curious I should have opened to that line
when I tried the *sortes Shakespeareanae*. The
devilish *double entendre*. Swan—ugly duckling—
playwright=compensation. Black legs=black leg
=rotter=inferiority. My abiding sense of sin.
The feeling of being dishonest and filthy. This is
probably the cause of my curious failure in all
human relationships. This is why I try to write
plays. This is why, when I feel a friendship failing, feel myself failing to attract or hold by means
of personal charm (a fake), I begin trying to
impress—let my plays fight my personal battles
for me. Take my new play MS. to Cynthia to-
morrow. Yes—the impulse is perfectly clear.
This is what I can do—*this* is the angelic sort of
being I am! Read and admire! Sound me and
wonder! I sit near you with eyes modestly down-
cast while you read. You wouldn't think, to look
at me, that this rather harmless nice creature har-
boured in his soul such a shattering power . . .
How disgusting! . . . Never, never again will I
show my work *personally* to a living soul. Pub-
lish it, get it performed—yes, since that seems to
be the mechanism by which I preserve my sanity.
But employ it as a secondary sexual characteristic
—a bloodshot erect crest—a rainbow-eyed tail—a
mating-call! . . . The Bulgarian weasel. That
hideous tramp on the stage who said he would
now give an imitation of the cry of the young
Bulgarian weasel to its mother. 'Mommer! . . .'
in a quiet restrained voice. 'Mommer!' . . . It was
during the same performance that the Russian

girl, playing the xylophone, looked at me so fixed-
ly and invitingly. Did I go round by the stage
door? Can't remember. Probably not . . . Perhaps it's because I fear my rainbow tail won't be
liked, won't make a sufficient impression——?
That would simply add, of course, to my ruling
sense of inferiority . . . I wonder what it was
about me that always made people laugh. In
streets . . . On street-cars . . . How I hated to get
into street-cars or trains, facing all the staring
people! Probably only my self-consciousness and
sheepishness and furtiveness that attracted attention? Then I would blush. Always blushing—
with a sense of guilt, of having been found out
. . . Does your mother know you're out? That
was when I had on that grey Norfolk suit. It
probably *did* make me look absurd—with my pale
little chinquapin of a face, and sorrowful baby
eyes . . . I went home and looked at myself in
the glass, trying to discover what was wrong. As
usual, I looked admiringly, lovingly, into my deep
deep violet orbs. The eyes of a great man. All-
seeing and all-knowing. All-suffering and all-
saying . . . She returned the fifth act without comment—except that she didn't understand it. 'I'm
like the servant-girl,' she said, 'who remarked,
when . . . "I don't *presume* to understand" . . .'
On board,—Cynthia on board, stretched out in a
sea-berth. Like a dead fish. 'Its rather nice,—'
she was saying to Billington as I approached—'to
be seasick, and just lie there feeling like a dead
fish!' . . . 'But I don't *like* to feel like a dead fish!'
I cried, and she gave her exquisite swift laugh,
gay and understanding. Ah Psyche from the re-

gions which. *And turn, and toss her brown delightful head.* The conspiracy against poor Billington, to preserve her from his boring attentions.
'You owe me a vote of thanks . . . I sidetracked
—took him firmly by the arm just as he was
starting toward you . . . and walked him round
the upper deck for over an hour . . .' She was
grateful . . . She rewarded me later by telling me
of poor Billington's desperate efforts to get himself invited to come and see her aunt in London
—he tried in various ways to find out where she
lived. Cynthia, leaning over the Irish sea, laughed
lightly, slightly—in the act of gently deriding Billington, she contrived to say, 'You see—I take *you*
for granted—that *you* should come to see us is
admitted! Isn't it?' Yes. And this paved the
way. 'Shall I encounter you in London, I wonder?' Off Holyhead; the pilot putting out; his
sail tossing in the white south-west sea. 'Well—
if you should go to Battersea Bridge—and turn to
the left—and see a shabby little house with that
number on it—and ring the bell——!' 'I shall do
all as instructed' . . . That afternoon—I saw her
sitting in her deck-chair, wrapped in the brown
steamer rug, a book opened on her lap. Billington
—hm—yes—was *kneeling* on the deck beside her,
talking, oh so very earnestly, with all of his little
academic intellect. What about?—poetry? He
had been writing a sonnet series, *'Sonnets to Beatrice.'* As he talked, wagging a finger, he occasionally emphasized the point by touching, with
that forefinger, her rug-covered knee. A damned
outrage. I was furious. Cynthia—how saturnine,
how sombrely and unutterably scornful and bored

she looked. Twice, when I passed, I saw him do
it. Odd that it should have so sickened me. I
sat in the smoking-room, absolutely trembling with
rage and disgust. Partly jealousy? I would have
liked to be able to do it myself? . . . No no no no
no. Yes yes yes yes yes . . . It's true—forgive me
. . . but only partly true. I would have liked to be
able to do it, but *not* to do it—to be sufficiently
free from self-consciousness, that is. To touch
Cynthia's knee! Good God. Playing chess, I
used to forget everything, as we sat cross-legged
on the stone-scrubbed deck, and watch her hands.
How fearfully beautiful they were, how intelligent, as they lay at rest or moved meditatively to
king or queen. The gentle frown—the dark absorption. Her Italian blood. Italian nobility, I
wonder? Italian+American=English. She introduced me to her father there on the station platform at Euston. 'Father, this is Mr. Demarest—
who played chess with me . . .' The delightful
broken accent, the kind and wise face, the greeting at once intimate—'And dances? You had lots
of dances on board?' 'No—no dances!' 'You
see, there wasn't any orchestra!' 'Ah! Oh!
What a pity!' . . . It was after that that I went and
sat all afternoon in Hyde Park, unhappy. By the
waters of Serpentine I sat down and wept.
The separation: it was as if half of me had been
cut away. How soon could I decently go to see
her? Not before a week or two. No. She would
be busy—busy seeing all the rich and rare people
whom she knew so much better than she knew me.
Distinguished people, people of social brilliance,
wits, artists, men famous all over the world,—

how indeed could she allow herself to be bothered
by me? I would never dare to go . . . But after
her invitation—I couldn't dare not to go. I would
tremble on the doorstep—tremble and stammer.
And what, I wondered was the English formula—
'Is Miss Battiloro at home?' 'Is Miss Battiloro
in?' And suppose a lot of others were there, or a
tea-party! It would be frightful—I would make
an idiot of myself, I would be alternately dumb
and silly: just as when I used to call on Anita.
The whole day beforehand I was in anguish, wondering whether I would go, whether I would tele-
phone. That time when Anita's mother answered,
and I suddenly, from acute shyness, hung up the
receiver in the middle of a conversation! . . . But
of course I *must* go and see Cynthia—otherwise
it would be—impossible to live. I gave her *The
Nation* as I passed her compartment in the train
at Lime Street—'Why, where did you get this?'
Delight and surprise. Then later, an hour out of
Liverpool, she brought it back—as a suggestion
that I might talk to her? 'May I?' 'Rather!'
Her aunt, sleeping opposite, with crumbs on her
outspread silken lap, opening her eyes a moment,
smiling, and sleepily proffering the folded chess-
board, which we declined, looking at each other
gaily. Then—no, it was before—we were standing in the corridor, watching the English fields
rush by—daisies, buttercups, campion. The
hedges in bloom. 'I think,' she said, 'heaven will
be that—a green bank covered with buttercups!'
. . . 'Well—heaven might be *worse* than that!'
MISERY . . . And then I went after three days!
That was my first mistake . . . Or no . . . The

first mistake was my going there the day before,
in the morning, *just to see her house!* Incredible
mawkish folly! Suppose she had seen me? Perhaps she did. Well—there it was. Which window was hers? At the top? A young man coming out, and I crossed to the other side with face
averted. Brother, perhaps. Or someone she
knew, had known for years. A friend of her
brother's. A cousin. A cousin from Italy. That
young artist she had talked about—Rooker . . .
The child crying again—*A a a a h h h . . . oo . . .
oo . . . ooo . . . aaaahhhh—oo—oo—oo—oo*. .A
child crying at sea, crying in the infinite, *noia im-
mortale,* cosmic grief. Grief is my predominant
feeling—why, then, in talk, am I so persistently
frivolous? flippant? Probably for that very reason. 'Demarest has the "crying face" '—it was
Weng, the Chinese student, who said that. The
eyelids are a trifle weary. I wonder why it is. It
had never occurred to me before that—it shows
how little one is able to see the character of one's
own face. And that day when I said something,
jokingly, to M. about 'my mild and innocent blue
eye,' he replied quite savagely and unexpectedly,
'Your eye is blue, but it is neither *mild* nor *innocent!* Astounding! My eye was not the timid
little thing I had always supposed? And good
heavens—not innocent! I didn't know whether to
be pleased or not. But it radically altered my conception of myself, and helped me in my painful
effort to acquire assurance . . . *Aaaahhhh . . . oo
. . . oo . . . oo . . . oo* . . . Poor thing—everything
horribly unfamiliar. It's probably crying because
it misses one familiar trifle—the light in the wrong

place, or the wrong colour; the bed too dark; the
smell; the humming in the ventilators; the throb,
so menacingly regular, of the ship's engines. Or a
shawl, which was perhaps left behind. Everything
combining to produce a feeling of frightful home-
sickness and lostness. The way that kitten must
have felt, when we told Martha to 'get rid of it'—
instead of having it killed she put it down in the
street and left it. Poor little creature . . . It was
used to us . . . Its funny long-legged way of
walking, the hind legs still a little uncertain! It
liked to catapult back and forth in the hall after
dusk; or catching moths. And that night, when it
rained and blew all night, shaking the house—
where was it? Mewing somewhere to be let in.
Lost. How much did it remember, I wonder—
how much did it *consciously* remember? A lot,
probably. A warm and happy place with kind
people whom it trusted—irrecoverably lost. Paradise lost. *Where are they—where is that wonderful house?* Ask the policeman. Good God
it was a cruel thing to do—to take it in for a few
weeks and then put it out in the streets like that.
How horrible the suffering of any young thing
can be. Speechless suffering, suffering that does
not understand—the child punished by the parent
whose nerves are on edge. Struck for reasons
which it cannot conceive—dogs and cats the same
way. Man's inhumanity to dogs and cats. Cattle
too, driven into the abattoir—no wonder there are
complaints by the S. P. C. A. 'Those who eat
meat do not realize that it is not invariably at the
first blow of the pole-axe——' etc. Falling down
on their knees and bleeding, looking at man with

surprise—that look ought to be enough to destroy
the human race. *Lex talionis*. Cruelty is inevitable—all that one can possibly do is to minimize
it. We could live on nuts and vegetables—but I
go right on eating beefsteaks just the same . . .
The consciousness, though, of a lost kitten—what
an extraordinary thing it must be. I suppose it's
exactly like ours, except that it can't be partly linguistic—probably almost wholly visual, a kaleido-
scopic series of pictures. Memory? Hm. Not
so easy. Perhaps in that case all it really felt was
the terrifying unfamiliarity, strangeness, and of
course the discomfort. It would be sentimental
to ascribe any more than that—to think of it as
being as aware as *I* was, thinking in bed about it,
of the wildness of the night, the wind, the strange
shutters banging on strange walls of strange
houses, the torn puddles under lamplight, the
deluge of driven rain rattling against windows,
solid water sousing down from eaves. Yes, I
remember how sharply and dreadfully I visual-
ized it—seeing the black street blattering with
water, a green shutter hanging from one hinge—
and refusing (shutting my eyes) to visualize the
kitten as somewhere *out in it*—damned cowardice, sentimental cowardice! . . . I remember
getting out of bed early in the morning and tip-
toeing down to the back door to let in the maltese.
The time my father scolded me for it. 'Don't ever
do it again, understand! . . . I thought it was
someone who had broken into the house—a thief
—and I very nearly shot you . . . Next time, I
will shoot you!' . . . Perhaps *that's* the source
—that extraordinary cruelty both to the kitten and

to me. I can't remember what I felt about it at
the time—but it must have been appalling. That's
the sort of thing, in one's childhood, that's 'part
of one's experience of the world'—the discovery
of the sort of nightmare into which we are born.
MISERY. A voice cried sleep no more. There's
one did swear in his sleep, and one cried Murder.
Murder equals *redrum*. That's poetic justice. I
waste a lot of time in logolatry. I am a verbalist,
Cynthia—a tinkling symbolist. I am the founder
and leader of the new school of literature—The
Emblemists. I wear a wide black hat, a dirty
shirt, boots with spurs, and shave once a month.
Traces of egg can be seen at the corners of my
mouth. I am hollow-cheeked, exophthalmic, prog-
nathous: I express my views at any and all times,
savagely, and with a conscious minimum of tact.
I glory in my dirtiness—I am a Buddhist—I look
at you with sleepy cynicism to prove it—utterly
indifferent to the needs of the body. Nevertheless, I eat heartily, and I make no bones about the
tiresome necessities of sex. I am, into the bargain,
slightly mad. I have persecution mania. They
try to ignore me—they slander me—they suppress
mention of me—they whisper about me and laugh.
Insults are heaped upon me, but I stride on, magnificent, a genius manifest; the winds of my
poems whirl them about and make them whimper.
Ha ha! That last phrase, Cynthia—would you
believe it?—was actually used about me by a
famous poet in an interview—something I had
said annoyed him. 'The winds of my poems . . .
make him whimper,'—that's what he said. That
reminds me of an article I saw once—in the New

York *Nation,* was it?—called *'Wind in Tenny-son.'* Perfectly serious! Isn't it incredible, the singular things people will do . . . I do them myself . . . Yes . . . From time to time . . . I am a poet of the Greenwich Village School—slightly eccentric, but really quite commonplace. I make a point of never sleeping more than once with the same woman. Hilda J—? Yes. Sophie S—? Yes. Irma R—? Yes. Madeline T—? Yes. And Irma's sister too. And her seven cousins from Utica. And every actress in the Jack-in-the-box Theatre. Typists, poetesses, dancers, reciters, fiddlers, and organists. I have a particular passion for organists. You can see me any noontime at that charming little café in Sixth Avenue —you know the one. I look pale and bored. I carry yellow gloves and a stick, and my utter indifference to everything around me convinces you that I am distinguished. I can tell you all the secrets of all these people. That girl in the corner? Takes morphia. For ten years has been writing a novel, which nobody has seen. Smokes, drinks, swears, twice attempted suicide. M—, the dancer, gave her 'an unmentionable disease' . . . That other little girl, dark and pale, with one eye higher than the other? A hanger-on—the hetaira type. A nice girl, nevertheless, and once or twice has really fallen in love. No moral sense whatever,—a rotten family in Flatbush. She is hard up most of the time—on the one occasion when I slept with her I found it necessary (or charitable) to give her a pair of my B.V.D.'s . . . I am an unsuccessful artist, wandering from one city to another: New York, Chicago, Boston.

Everywhere I carry with me a portfolio of my sketches, drawings, etchings, colour washes, pastels. I show them to people on trains. I show them to people in restaurants, or on park benches. I have a large pale head with shiny sleek yellow hair and the yellow stubble on my cheeks and chin glistens in the sunlight. Once I grew a beard—but although I adopt the pose of indifference to public opinion, I must admit that the jokes of small boys, and the more violent comments of roughs, finally led me to shave it off. 'Look at the Bowery Jesus!' they cried: 'Pipe the Christ!' . . . One critic referred to me as 'that immoral and hypocritical *fin de siécle* Jesus' . . . In Chicago, I ran a private dance hall. In Boston, I conducted a tea-shop and edited a little magazine. In New York, I have sold cigars, dictionaries, soap and fountain pens. In St. Louis, I nearly died of flu. When Hurwitz, the poet, came to see me I was lying under a sheet, like a corpse. 'Why don't you take your shoes off?' he said, seeing my feet which protruded. 'They *are* off,' I said. It was only that I hadn't washed them for some time. I practise a saintly contempt for the physical . . . Yes . . . I am all these. A little flower of the slime . . . For a time, I was X, the novelist, the dabbler in black arts, alchemy, hasheesh, and all known perversions. How fearfully wicked I was! Women shuddered when I was pointed out to them: when I touched them, they fainted. I collected slippers—a hundred and sixty-three. The fifty-seven varieties were child's play to me, and the sixty-nine, and the one thousand. You know that poem of Whitman's—something about 'bussing my body all over with soft balsamic busses'? That's me—the omnibus. In my rooms, with a few expensively dressed women who considered themselves New York's most refined, I celebrated The Black Mass. One of these women, I discovered, was a cynomaniac . . . Several women have supported me . . . While the stenographer was paying my bills, I was absorbed in a passion for an Italian *castrato* . . . You hear me, Cynthia? . . . Darling William! You do not deceive me for a minute—not for a minute. I see through all this absurd pretence of naughtiness!—I see the dear frightened, fugitive little saint you are!—Ah, Cynthia, I knew I could trust you to understand me! I knew it, I knew it!— Come, William, it is spring in New England, and we will wander through fields of Quaker Ladies. Don't you adore the pale-blue Quaker Ladies?— Yes, yes, Cynthia! Four petals they have, and sometimes they are blue, but sometimes ash- colour!—Come, darling William, and we will romp among them joyfully. We will climb birches. We will discover the purple-banded Jack-in-the-pulpit, hiding in the snakey swamp. We will tease the painted turtle, and give flies to the high-backed wood-tortoise.—Yes yes yes. They sun themselves on stones. Plop, and they are gone into the water.—And the tree-toads, William! Their ethereal jingling at twilight in the water-meadows! Their exquisite little whis- per-bells!—Ah! the tintinnabulation of the toads! Poe wrote a poem about them.—How melancholy your New England is, William! One misses the hand of man. Deserted, forlorn, shapeless,—but

beautiful, wildly beautiful. I could cry when I
see it. It fills me with nostalgia . . . A poor
thing but mine own, Cynthia. These grey-lich-
ened pasture rocks—I created them out of my
tears. Out of my bitter heart grew these sumachs
with blood-coloured bloom. Out of my afflicted
flesh came these white, white birches. Nothing
of me but doth change into something rich and
strange.—And those huge desolate frost-scarred
mountains, the white and the green, lightning-
riven, scree-stripped, ravaged by hail and fire—
ah, William, my dearest, what a terrible weight
upon the soul are they! . . . *My* burden, Cynthia—the burden of my thought . . . *Aaaaahhh-
oo-oo-oo . . . aaaahhh-oo-oo-oo-oooo* . . . MISERY
. . . Damn that child, why doesn't it go to sleep.
Or damn its mother, anyway. Women are so
extraordinarily unperceptive. All nonsense, this
theory that the perceptions of women are acuter
than men's—or intuitions. No. I've never met
one with perceptions as quick as mine—I can
skate rings around them. You hear me, vain,
intellectual, snobbish Cynthia?—To me, William,
you would yield in this—to me alone. So sensitive am I to impressions, that . . . that . . .
that . . . that . . . *Quack . . . quack* . . . And
you beside me, quacking in the wood. For God's
sake, hold your tongue and let me love . . . The
sagacious eye of the duck—something of that in
Helen. And how she loved to quack. And how
she loved to sprawl ungainly and kick her heels
in the air and laugh and fling her slippers about
and make absurd, hideous faces! Too young—
it was merely the joy of release, rebellion, that

she was experiencing—she was, at the moment, incapable of love. Listen, chaste Cynthia! And I will tell you . . . tell you . . . Speak fearlessly, William, as you always do—I am looking at you with wide deep eyes of understanding. I see the pebbles at the bottom of your soul.—Yes, Pyrrha's pebbles. Arranged in pairs. Rose-quartz, white-quartz, gneiss. Rose-quartz, white-quartz, gneiss. And did you see that little trout hiding among them? That was my very me. My little trout-soul . . . But I was going to tell you, Cynthia—tell you——Wait, dearest—first let us find some quiet little backwater of the Cher. There! the very thing. Under that low-hanging willow, to which we can fasten our punt. Now we cannot be seen or heard. Oxford two miles away—Lady Tirrell, my dear, dear friend, unsuspecting. Arrange the cushion under my head. Is my dress pulled down properly? Put the bottles in the shade to keep cool, or hang them in the water. I bought this dress especially for the occasion, so that none of my friends on the river would recognize me. All the castles of England, Scotland, Ireland and Wales in the pattern. Here is Dover. Here is Harlech. Bodiam there, and there, on my left knee, Kenilworth. Why *will* these stupid people bring their wretched phonographs? So vulgar, so very vulgar . . . *Aaaaah-hhh-oo-oo-oo-ooo* . . . I was going to tell you Cynthia, of one night with Helen Shafter. Would you like to hear it?—Is it something I *ought* to hear?—Certainly. Why not? I believe in absolute frankness between the sexes—don't you? Tooth-brushes, sponges, cascara—everything.

Our comings in and our goings forth. Our sittings down and our standings up. One egg or two. Linen changed once a week—twice a week —four times a week—daily. The matutinal dose of salts. The nocturnal suppository. The application of lip-salves, clouds of powder, rouge, and deodorizers. The tweezers for extracting superfluous eyebrows—henna and orange-sticks for the nails. The stale sweetness of the clothes cupboard. All . . . Then, William, it is my painful duty to inform the police that you are a *voyeur*. Need I remind you of certain episodes of this character in your childhood—adolescence—youth —and early manhood? There was that time in . . . . But this, Cynthia, has a kind of beauty!— Beauty, smutbird? Beauty? Beauty in that lascivious life of yours? No—it's quite impossible. Quite.—But I assure you! I go down on my knees! I swear to God! I kiss the Bible, the Koran, and the Wisdom of Lao Tzü. This experience, although sensual and sexual in origin and fundamentals, nevertheless had a certain beauty. I swear it had, Cynthia! Listen, and you will see! You will be moved by it, I'm sure! —Poor Little William—I recognize in you this imperative impulse to confess—it is not for nothing that I go to confession myself and tell the holy father of my little white sins. But are you sure I am the proper repository for this secret? —Cynthia! Orbèd maiden with white fire laden! Moon-daughter, snow-cold and pure, but fiery at heart! It is from you alone that my absolution can come. I will tell you—But not so fast, William! This is Sunday, and I have tickets for the

Zoo. Don't you adore the Zoo—simply adore it?
The toucans. The pelicans. The ring-tailed tal-
lula-bird. The whiffenpoof. The tigers, miaow-
ing, and the lions reverberating, rimbombinando.
The polar bear,—trying to lift from the wintry
water, with hooked claws, a pane of ice. The
elephants, swaying from one rubber foot to the
other, swinging their trunks, and lifting their
tea-kettle spouts for peanuts. And the little
baboons and monkeys, so ingeniously and ingen-
uously obscene!—te hee!—Oh yes yes yes, Cynthia! I saw a madonna and child, once, swinging
in a little trapeze! The mother was searching
intensely . . . *Aaaahhhh* . . . *oo-oo-oo-oo-oo* . . .
This is really passing endurance. It shouldn't be
allowed on a ship. Steward, take this child and
throw it overboard. Push it head first through a
port-hole. Weight it with lead, or tie the anchor
to it. Drape it with the star-strangled banner.
Taps. The time the men in Company K, 4th
Illinois, lent me a bugle and four bayonets—we
paraded three times around the square. It was
magnificent. The hot tropical sun on the asphalt.
The trumpet flowers bugling on the graves, and
Dr. Scott's terrapins scrambling in the tubs and
bins. Then there was that terrifying green sea-
turtle with soft flat flappers flapping softly in a
separate tub. The cook said they would have
to build a fire behind it to make it put its head
out for the axe. Turtle's eggs—soft, tough, puck-
ered. They find them by thrusting a sharp stick
into the hot sand—if it comes up stained, they
dig . . . It must be the law of tetrahedral col-
lapse that gives them that peculiar shape . . .

Oh, that cartridge! I blush. I stole it—stole it from Private Davis's tent—after he had been so nice to me, too. Good God, how awful it was. It was Butch Gleason who suggested it—he said he always took money out of a cash register in his father's store. It must have been arranged. Sergeant Williams went out, and in a minute came back. I was leaning against the tent-pole at the door. As he came in again, brushing against me, his large hand fell naturally (so I thought!) against my jacket, and he closed it on my pocket. Why, what's this? he said. O God, O God. Then they were all silent and ashamed— they wouldn't look at me. Why didn't you say you wanted one, Billy? That's no way to go about it, stealing from your best friends! . . . Here, take it! You can have it . . . I didn't want it, but I took it. I wanted to give it back to them—I wanted to explain everything—I wanted to cry, to wash the episode out of history with a vast torrent of tears. But I could say nothing. I crept home and put it on the mantle- piece in my room, above the toy battleship, and never touched it again . . . By George, how nice they were to me: that first day it was,—I took them a big paper bag full of animal crackers, when they were just off the train, hungry. I believed them when they said they'd been living for months on nothing but tinned mule. After- wards I used to march into mess with them in the penitentiary yard—under a long wooden shed which had been built there, with long tables un- der it, tables of new pine. A tin cup, a tin plate, tin fork and spoon. *Soupy, soupy, soupy, with-*

out a single bean. That heavenly melancholy
nostalgic tune the bugler played when they
marched along the shell road into the country
—over and over . . . I was again given a bayo-
net and marched at the side, giving orders. Close
up the ranks there! . . . Get me a coupla chin-
quapins, willya, Billy? . . . Then they were singing. *Good-bye Dolly, I must leave you . . .
Just tell her that I love her* . . . I wonder what
place that was where they had their new camp.
I got lost that time coming back from it—the conductor gave us transfers, but we didn't know what
to do with them, when to transfer, and finally got
off and walked. We walked miles through the
negro quarters in the dark. Mysterious lights.
Noisy slatternly houses. Smells. That might be
where the gang we were always fighting came
from. Gang-fights with stones. Sling-shots.
Pluffers, pluffing chinaberries. I cut down an
elderbush in the park to make one . . . Sneaky
Williams it was who saw me cutting down a
young cedar to make a bow and arrow and took
me home by my sleeve, my feet barely touching
the ground . . . I thought I was being arrested . . .
Ah, that delicious dense little grove of sap-
lings with a hut in the middle! What was it
that made it seem so wonderful? It was dark,
gloomy, little leaf-mould paths wound here and
there intersecting, twigs snapped. There was
something Virgilian—I remember thinking about
it four years later when I began reading Virgil.
Et vox in faucibus haesit. It must have been the
sacred terror. I can remember the time when I
hadn't yet been into it. That day, when, after

being ill for two months, I went out for the first
time—my mother sat on the bench near it, and I
made little houses out of dry twigs in the grass.
The only moment at which I can *see* her—she sits
there, absent-minded in the sun, smiling a little,
not seeing the path and the cactus bed at which
she appears to be looking. The penitentiary walls
were behind us—the tall barred windows, behind
one of which I saw a man looking down at us.
He was moving his arms up along the bars high
above his head. And the Sacred Grove was near
us, and the red brick vaults, and the table-tombs
of white stone . . . Are you watching me, Cynthia? Surely I was harmless enough on that day?
Surely you like my mother sitting there with her
parasol? And isn't it nice of me to remember it
all so clearly, after a quarter of a century? . . .
O God, that swooning sensation, anguish that
contracts the belly and travels slowly down the
body . . . MISERY . . . This is what it is to be
in love. Unmitigated suffering. The most all-
poisoning of all illnesses. And nevertheless, it's
the chief motive of all art—we return to our
vomit. No, no, that's not fair. It has beauty!
. . . Think of the extraordinary way in which
it changes, suddenly, the whole coarse texture of
the universe!—I remember, when I first fell in
love, how I used to want to touch everything with
my hands. Stone walls. Bark of trees. Bits of
metal. Glass. Woollen clothes. All of them had
suddenly become exquisite, all of them responded.
And when I met you, Cynthia . . . But there's
no concealing the suffering it has brought, that
frightful and inescapable and unwearying con-

sciousness of the unattainable. The soul aching
every moment, every hour, with sharp brief par-
oxysms of intenser pain: the eyes closing in vain,
sleep vainly invited, dreams that concentrate into
their fantastic and feverish turmoil all the griefs
of the whole life; and the eyes opening again to
the blindingly unforgotten sorrow—this is what
it is, this is what now returns to me in even
greater virulence. The intolerable suffering en-
tailed in trying to remember a half-recalled face!
That night at the Northwestern Hotel, when I
had one nightmare after another all night long,
trying to find her . . . And then, when I went
down to breakfast in the morning, exhausted, and
still in a kind of dream, all unsuspecting that she
too had slept at the Northwestern, I found her,
with her aunt, alone in the breakfast room! What
an extraordinary discovery that was! She was
lost, and she was found. The light, laughing
'Good morning!' The eggs being eaten in English egg-cups! . . . And it still goes on. Her
face escapes me. Why should this be? It isn't
really, of course, that it escapes me any more
than any other recollected sense-impression. No.
Probably less. The trouble is precisely in the
fact that one wants too much of it,—wants it too
often, wears it out with staring, and not only that,
but one is also, in a way, trying to *revenge* one's
self upon it. One seeks to *possess* it—with a
violence not thrust upon one's ordinary recollections—simply because one has not been able to
possess the reality. One evening it is absurdly
easy—I can 'turn it on' at any moment and luxuriate in it. But the next morning it is gone;

and no sleight of mind will give it back to me.
I try the chin, the mouth, the profile of the cheek,
the eyes—all in vain.   The face is a complete
blank.   Perhaps one trace alone will be discover-
able—I can see how, at that particular instant,
when she found me staring at her, she looked
slowly down, lowering her eyelids, and with what
an extraordinary and baffling intensity of expression!   There was pain in it, there was annoyance,
but there was also, from the dark of her uncon-
sciousness—could I be wrong in thus analysing
it?—a frightful unhappiness and desire, a relaxed
and heartbroken desire, desire of the flesh, as old
as the world.   This alone I can remember, often,
when all other aspects of her face have dislimned
. . . Creek, creeky-creek, creeky . . . The Irish
girl moves from her left side to her right.   Easy
enough to remember *her* face—because I don't
feel any tension about it . . . Smith too.   Or
Silberstein—that massive stone face!   Bastile
façade!   Or Faubion.   Ah! a pang.   You see
that gleaming pang, Cynthia?—I see it, unfaithful
one!—No, not unfaithful!   Not unfaithful!   I
swear to God . . . Is fidelity an affair only of the
flesh?   No—that's not what I meant to say.   Not
at all.   It's very very complicated.   It's absurd,
this fetish of fidelity.   Absurd and chimerical.   It
leads to the worst hypocrisy in the world.   It
involves a lie about the nature of the world, of
God, of the human being; a misconception or
falsification of the mind and psyche.   Ah, psyche
from the regions which.   I am not faithful—and
I am faithful.   My feeling for Eunice will never
change.   Nor my feeling for Helen.   Nor my

feeling for you. Nor my feeling for Fleshpot Faubion. Why should it be considered an unfaithfulness, a betrayal, to love more than one woman or more than one man? Nothing sillier could be conceived. It's preposterous. We love constantly, love everywhere. We love in all sorts of degrees and ways. Can any one person or thing or place or belief possess one's soul utterly? Impossible. It is true that when we 'fall in love,' experiencing that intense burning up of the entire being which now and then some unforeseen explosion of the unconscious brings to us, our one desire is to possess and be possessed by the one object. But this is largely, or to some extent, an illusion—it's an illusion, I mean, to suppose that this will completely satisfy. An illusion, Cynthia! Even had I been destined—had we been destined —had I succeeded—had I not too horribly blundered—had I not lost every brief and paralysing opporunty and at every such turn shown myself to be a fool and a coward—even so, even had I possessed you as madly as in imagination I have possessed you—you would not wholly have absorbed me. No. There would have been tracts of my soul which would never have owned your sovereignty—Saharas and Gobis of rebellious waste; swarming Yucatans from whose poisonous rank depths derision would be screamed at you and fragrances poured at you in a profusion of insult, flagrant and drunken; Arctics of inenarrable ice; and the sea everywhere, the unvintagable sea, many-laughing. Do you listen, Moonwhite? —I hate you and despise you, lizard!—I am walking in Kensington Gardens, Moonwhite, telling

you of these things.   The man wades into the
Round Pond with a net to catch his toy steam-
yacht.   Nursemaids pullulate.   Would it shock
you to know that I could love even a nursemaid?
Is there anything strange or reprehensible in that?
For that matter, I did, once, fall in love (mildly)
with a lady's maid.   Her name?   Mary Kim-
berlin.   Age?   Twenty-four.   Where did we
meet?   In Hyde Park, where she was taking the
Pom for a walk . . . Afterwards she married.   I
liked her, and I still like her . . . Did Helen
Shafter interfere with my fondness for Eunice?
Not in the slightest!—You felt guilty about it,
William!   You felt guilty, you were furtive, you
concealed it, and you were in constant terror that
you would be discovered.   You never met her
without experiencing a sense of wrong-doing,
you never returned from a meeting with her to
your Eunice without a sense of sin, a sadness, a
burden of duplicity, that you found intolerable
and crippling.   Isn't that true? . . . That is true,
Cynthia.   True.   True.   Oh, so frightfully true.
And yet it ought not to be true . . . MISERY
. . . I admit the sense of evil which permeates
that sort of adventure, the sense of treason and
infidelity; but I affirm again that it is a sin
against the holy ghost to bring up humans in
such a way that they will inevitably feel it.   It's
hideously wrong!   It's criminal!   It is *not* an
infidelity for me to love Eunice and Helen at the
same time!   It is not! . . . No man can serve
both God and Mammon, William.—The distinc-
tion is utterly false!   If I find something precious
in Helen to adore, and at the same moment find

something equally precious in Eunice to love, and
if both of them love me—then what academic
puritanism or pedantic pietistic folly can that be
which would pronounce it wrong? NO! It is
not wrong. It is only that we are taught to
believe it so that makes it appear so. It is true
that I was furtive, that I concealed from Eunice
my knowledge of Helen—but why? Only because I wanted to spare Eunice,—who perhaps
believed (though I never tried to make her do
so) that she possessed me wholly,—the pain of
disillusionment, the pain of jealousy. Good God,
how much I would have preferred to be frank!
I hated the necessity for concealment . . . It is
only the necessity for concealment which intro-
duces ugliness; the thing itself is no less, and
often more, beautiful than the rest of daily life.
Honi soit qui mal y pense . . . No, William!
You are not being honest with me. You admit
that as things *are* constituted, as society *does*
view it, these furtive and clandestine love-affairs
are ugly. What defence have you, then, for deliberately seeking the ugly? I can see to the bottom
of your soul, William, I know everything in your
past, and knowing that, I see everything that
will be in your future. All. I can see the way,
whenever you go out into the streets, or ride in
busses or trains, or go to a concert,—in fact
everywhere and at all times,—you look greedily
about you for a pretty woman, you devour them
with your eyes, you move closer to them in order
to touch them as if accidentally, you lean backward to touch them, you luxuriate in every curve
of mouth and throat and shoulder, you step back

(as if politely) to permit them to get into the
bus first in order that you may see their legs as
far as the knee or even a little farther. You note,
as you walk behind them in a crowd, the way
their shoulders move as they walk, the curved
forward thrust of the thigh, the slight subtle
oscillation of the hips, the strength of the gait,
and the sweet straightness and resilience of the
leg-stroke as observed from behind. You gauge,
through their clothes, the proportion of torso to
legs, the breadth of waist. You never tire of
speculation as to the precise position and dimen-
sions of the breasts; watching a woman's every
slightest motion in the hope that by leaning this
way or that, drawing closer her jacket against
her body or relaxing it, she will betray to you
the secrets of her body. Confess! Kiss the book
and sign your name! You are indicted for eroto-
mania! . . . Pity me, Cynthia! I will confess
everything if only you will believe that never,
never, NEVER, was this my attitude toward you.
I would have given everything to have been able
to wipe out my entire past. My recollections of
Eunice, and Helen, and Mary gave me nothing
but pain:—and all the countless minor episodes,
of the sort you have been describing, constituted
for me an inferno from which I seemed never
destined to escape. Yes. Horrible. To come
to the gateway in the rain of fire and looking
through it to see the slopes of Purgatory; to
guess, beyond, the Paradise; to see you as the
gracious wisdom who might guide me thither;
and then to know that LAW would not permit, and
that in the Inferno must be my abode for ever!—

Do not think this is merely picturesque or elo-
quent, Cynthia. No. What I am approaching is
a profound psychological truth. It is my own
nature, my character as patiently wrought by my
character, as the snail builds its house, from which
I cannot move. *Why this is hell, nor am I out
of it.* Do you remember what I wrote to you
when you had gone to France? A silly letter, to
be sure. Over-eloquent, over-literary, sobbingly
self-conscious. I told you that I had decided,
finally, to go back to America. I had failed with
you—to tell you that I adored you was out of
the question. But my agile subconscious did the
trick. 'Do not think,' I said, referring to your
description of poppies in Brittany, 'that I don't
know a poppy when I see it!' Fatuous! Could
anything have been in worse taste? Impossible.
My *double entendre,* of course, is quite clear. The
poppy is Europe, and also Cynthia. I was aban-
doning the poppy not because I failed to appre-
ciate it, but because I recognized my own inferiority. It was my Sabachthani . . . *Tin-tin-tin.*
Half-past one. Good God. Try counting again,
shutting my eyes more lightly, breathing through
my nose. Hot in here. *Ten—ten—double ten—
forty-five and fifteen. Um-ber-ella—Cinder-rella*
—Twist. What the devil could that have come
from? A little girl bouncing a red ball as she
said it. Lovely things little girls are—their extraordinary innocence, candour, transparency,
charm. Grace. Something light and beautiful in
women after all, in spite of their boringness and
curious mental and emotional limitations. Toys.
Nice to overhear them talking together and laugh-

ing in a garden. Nuns in a convent garden. Or
singing. How beautiful they are when they sing!
That girl, with scarlet-flushed cheeks, singing
Morgen, waiting for the beautiful melody as given
first by the piano to reach the downward curve,
and then coming in so deeply and sorrowfully
with the slow rich voice. O God, O God that
strange mixture of the soaring melody, so perfect
in its pure algebra, and the sad, persistent meditative voice—there were tears in her eyes when
she finished, and she had to turn away. Then
the piano melody, finishing delicately and ethere-
ally by itself . . . O God, if I could only get
that sort of effect in a play—not melodramatically,
or with stained-glass windows and paper snow,
but naturally and simply by that superb use of
the counterpoint of feeling and thought . . .
Extraordinary sorrow in that song. That queer
feeling that comes over me when something
moves me too much—a kind of ache that seems
to begin in the upper part of the mouth and
throat, and yet it isn't an ache so much as an
unhappy consciousness which seems to be local-
ized there, and then to spread downward through
the whole aching body, a slowly-flowering sort of
echo in a hollow darkness, opening out with painful tentacles . . . MISERY . . . *Now the red rim
of sight discovers* . . . No . . . *Where the red
rim of life discovers* . . . no, sight, is better,
suggesting . . . *Where the red rim of sight discovers* . . . *The void that swarms with shapes
of death* . . . *And the departing spirit hovers
. . . Bat-like above the failing breath* . . . Is it
good or is it bad . . . Impossible to say. Non-

sense. One more of the *'Where the . . . There the'* type of lyric. Give it up NOW . . . Dante would come into the next verse . . . How lovely she was, standing there under the dim lamp, elbows behind her, laughing, saying, *'I'm going to be married'!* . . . Lost. Lost for ever. That afternoon at the concert, if I had only . . . It would have been so simple . . . Or walking back from those absurd dancers; over Waterloo Bridge . . . 'You know, I simply adore you!' . . . But it was too soon—it really *was* too soon . . . It's never too soon . . . But I *thought* it was too soon . . . Is it really gone? that opportunity? Good heavens how often I re-enact all those scenes—impossible to persuade myself that they can be finished! The after-sense is so vivid. I was always expecting to meet her in the street— in the most unlikely places. Always looked at everybody in the street, or bus, or theatre, expecting to see her. I even thought she might be on the ship again,—when I sailed back to America! And on Fifth Avenue, or at Aeolian Hall, or in the Museum—constantly feeling that I was on the point of encountering her, and that she was just round the corner, or behind the Rodin. She would be sure to be standing before the Manet parrot! . . . Why is it? . . . The frightfully vivid experience, with its appalling after-sense, destroys one's reason, one's belief in time and space. Over and over again putting myself into the middle of that concert—the Bach concerto— sitting there in the Wigmore Hall. It was that morning just before lunch, while I was taking off one suit and putting on the other (which

reeked of petrol, just back from the tailor) that
the maid said, 'Two ladies to see you, sir . . .'
'Will you show them up?' . . . Who could it be?
Americans? I was going to tea with Cynthia
that afternoon—therefore it couldn't possibly be
she . . . I hurried dressing . . . It was she,
and that artist's daughter . . . 'What a lovely
room!' she cried, 'and how extraordinary to find
it in *this* street!' . . . The concert suggested . . .
Delighted, but frightened—the complications . . .
this other girl tall, grave, rather lovely. Ought
I to ask them to lunch? No. Perhaps that had
been their idea? Good heavens,—I wonder!
Anyway, I didn't . . . 'Meet in the entrance at . . .'
. . . then they were gone, and I discovered my
awful hasty unkemptness—hair unbrushed, coat
collar kinked up, buttons unbuttoned . . . and at
the concert . . . smelling abominably of petrol,
sitting beside divine Cynthia and listening to the
pure rapture of that music! Cynthia so near me
—her heart within eighteen inches of mine, her
sleeve touching my sleeve,—so that I could feel
the rhythm of her breathing,—her dress once or
twice brushing my foot. O God o God o God o
God o God . . . Squirming. Twisting and
stretching my wrists. The crucified Christ by
Perugino in that chapel in Florence—the wrists
quivering, squirming like a spitted worm, worm-
ing like an earthworm on a hook, the worm that
convulsively embraces the hook, the worm that
squirms, the worm that turns . . . Kwannon,
Goddess of mercy, serene and beneficent idol,
Cathayan peace! Smile down upon me, reach thy
golden hands to me with the golden fingers, touch

my eyes that they may see not, touch my mind that it may remember not, touch my heart and make it holy. Take away from me my gross and mischievous and ailing body, let me lie down before thee and sleep for ever. Let all be forgiven me, who forgive all; let all love me, and have compassion for me, who love all; let all sorrow cease when my sorrow ceases, suffering with my suffering, and life with my life. . . . One three five seven nine eleven thirteen fifteen seventeen nineteen twenty-one twenty-three twenty-five twenty-seven 1 3 5 7 9 11 13 15 17 19 21 23 25 27 29 31 33 35 37 39 41 43 47 49 51 53 55 57. One five nine thirteen seventeen twenty-one twenty-five. Too complicated—keeps me awake. *Child Roland to the dark tower came.* The dead sheep lying under the birch tree, in the wood, with the dead leaves swept away in a neat circle by the last struggle. The dead horse in the cellar of the burnt stable. The cat with one red eye, blood-filled. The old woman lying against the wall, staring, indifferent, breathing slowly, while blood ran slowly from the corner of her mouth. Dying in the street, strangers walking around her in a ring, and she as inattentive as a dying animal. Her pocket-book, muddy, beside her on the sidewalk. B said afterwards he had heard her 'scream like a siren' when the accident occurred . . . *Dying, Egypt, dying* . . . Crowds walking past while she dies, cars and buses honking, taxis ticking, horses clop-clopping, children running and yelling, 'Susie—wait for ME!' the policeman's whistle blowing, the church clock striking, the newsboys running with the EXTRY EXTREE and sliding with nailed boots on the asphalt, ferries hooting on the river, "she's dying, poor Thing-gggg," "Dyingggg." "Susie wait for meeeee . . ." Suuuw-oo-or-nhor-eeeeeee . . . Pax. Pox vobis-cum. Dead. One hundred and thirty-two pounds. Five feet four and three-quarters. Torn flannel showing. The blood had run clear across the sidewalk in four separate rivulets . . . *When the red rim of sight discovers . . . The void that swarms with shapes of death . . . and the departing batsoul hovers . . . Above the fountain's falling breath* . . . Rotten. But there is, off in the void there, an idea, a sort of ghostly fountain, tossing up and dying down again . . . *Green-light* . . . What goes on in the brain just before and just after death? Possible that the brain may live for a time. We may go on thinking, remembering, in a confused sort of way—a jumble of sensations. Or rarefied—a tiny gnat-song of consciousness . . . Dr. Kiernan stated that when called in at 7.13 there was still a spark of life . . . she looked alive but extraordinarily still. Eyes shut. Mouth wide open, fixed in the act of screaming, but silent. TERROR! . . . Perhaps she knew I was there, looking at her, and then walking softly, quickly, away . . . Strange, if that were true—but no stranger than anything else. 'Yes, William, I am dead. But I know you are there. Do you want to know if an accident has occurred? Yes. A dreadful accident has occurred. I am quite all right, now. Run and wake Nanny. Shut the door into the nursery. Wind the clocks on Sunday morning. And say good-bye to this house and world for ever . . .'

MISERY . . . My bonnie has too-bur-kulosis . . .
My bonnie has only one lung . . .My bonnie has
too-bur-culosis . . . HOK HOIK! . . . My bonnie will surely die young . . . Be-ring ba-a-ack.
Be-ring ba-a-ack. Oh, bring back my bonnie to
me . . . I remember how for a long time afterwards I couldn't hear a door squeak on its hinges
without hearing her scream. TERROR! I remember her face vividly. Very like mine, same forehead, same mouth. My bonnie lies over the ocean
—she used to sing it to me, and what was that
other one? that she said used to be sung in the
Civil War . . . *Shine I shine I shine—shine like
the evening star . . . Shoo fly, don't bother me
. . . Shoo fly, don't bother me . . . for I belong
to Company G* . . . I remember her singing and
laughing and singing again: *If you don't wear a
collar and a tie . . . then you won't go to heaven
when you die . . . If you don't wear ruffles on
your drawers . . . then you won't go to heaven
when you die* . . . Negro spirituals. It was
Krehbiel, wasn't it, that wrote that book? *Let
mah—pee-pul—go* . . . And those stories the
negro nurses used to tell us in the mornings while
they dressed us. The crane with the cork. What
a story to tell children. It was Brer Rabbit who
pulled out the cork. At the party, it was—and it
created a scandal . . . Like Smith's story of the
Starcroft Inn. Heavens, how superb—the real
Chaucerian flavour. Pop-eyed Popper Smith
watching eagerly from the door, with all the other
men, while all the women fled from the ball-room
. . . She lying on her back there, laughing hys-
terically, drunk, with her skirt up, fallen down

and unable to stand, screeching with laughter, and the jazz orchestra of niggers going suddenly cuckoo with excitement—drums banged, trombones yelling, saxophones bubbling the Himmelfahrt, the niggers themselves screaming and sobbing . . . Goodness gracious gawdness Agnes. Agnes Day equals Agnus Dei . . . 'No-no!—too many ladies here,' said Smith. Yes, there it is,—that whole side of a man's life that must be concealed. So many things we conceal even from other men . . . We all have our little p-p-p-p-peculiarities which we don't mention; and which nevertheless are of great importance to us. Canyon yodling. Pearl diving. Muff barking. Palpation. The dance of the seven unveils. Arrangements of mirrors. That girl at the casino, when I was with Julian—there was a scuffle in the row ahead of us and the young man was taken out. 'I didn't mind when he give me the leg, but when he give me the'—I wonder if he was arrested or what. . . . That time visiting with Julian for the week-end—at Plymouth it was—the young schoolmarm who was taking her Easter holiday alone at that little deserted hotel. She sat with her knees, oh, so carelessly crossed—black silk stockings. The misty wisty wistful yearning expression in Julian's eyes—he sat on the table-edge and talked to her in a peculiar soft way, gentle, gently laughing, gently suggestive, gently agreeing and gently echoing: turtle-doves, *Cooo—coooo*. A problem: both of us attracted to her, but neither of us admitted it or wanted to say to the other— 'You go on to Plymouth—I'll stay here . . .' At breakfast in the morning I tried to touch her

knee with mine under the table. But I wasn't
bold enough. More wistful conversation, and
then we motored away, both of us sulky for the
rest of the day . . . Wonderful charm such in-
complete adventures have . . . They take on
gradually a special beauty . . . *Abbozzi* . . .
Life is full of them . . . Familiarity breeds contempt. Sometimes they are too painful, though.
C. I. E., on the train, for example. How frightfully unhappy that made me, and still, when I
think about it, makes me . . . I got into the train
and she was sitting opposite me, with her dress-
suitcase on the seat beside her . . . C. I. E. were
the initials on it—a fibre suitcase. In the rack
above her was a violin. Small, she was, in a soft
grey coat; with a mauve or lilac-coloured hat—I
could see white stitches in it. An artificial flower
on her coat lapel. I couldn't decide at first
whether I thought she was pretty or not—but I
couldn't take my eyes off her. She was reading
Tilly of Bloomsbury—I watched her blue eyes,
small and of a sweet roundness, travelling along
the lines. Now and then she smiled. Her mouth
—it seemed to me extraordinary. I can't visualize it, but I thought it like a Michaelangelo mouth
—great richness and subtlety of modelling, voluptuous and yet suggestive of strength and curtness;
the colour rather peculiar, a pale coral. Freckled
a little, with dark golden hair showing in circular
plaits over her ears. Her eyebrows darker than
her hair, and richly curved, softly curved, over
shy eyes . . . She occasionally looked up obliquely at the woman who sat beside me—or looked at
the woman's gay-striped stockings when she put

her feet on the edge of the seat opposite. She avoided my eyes—if she found me looking at her, she slid her eyes rapidly across me and looked out at the fields, and at the bare trees which had been etherealized by a beautiful frost, trees like white smoke. It was cold. The other window open. Had to keep my gloves on. Shy about taking off my gloves to unbutton my grey coat and fish out my handkerchief: she covertly watched me. Then I thought of that theatre programme in my pocket—so I read it to impress her with our similarity in tastes. Sorry I hadn't bought *The Nation* instead of *John o' London.* The cold wind whistling about our feet; she crossed her knees, and then drew them up under her, just touching the floor with the tip of the Cordova slipper, a slipper somewhat worn, but nice. Woollen gloves. Once—half-way, after an hour—she looked at me—O God, what a look. Perplexed, shy, injured, reproachful. 'You shouldn't stare at me like that; I am a nice girl, intelligent and refined, sensitive. Nevertheless I perceive that we have something in common.' Then she turned two pages at once. She read more rapidly, she skipped. A station. Another station. Only an hour more. Clippity clop te clap te clip te clap te cluckle, te WHEEEEEE. Tunnel! Shall I rise and shut the other window? No: too shy. It might lead to a harmless and friendly beginning to talk? No. In the dark (the dusty lamp burning dimly on the ceiling) perhaps our feet would encounter? No. I uncrossed my knees and crossed them the other way, away from the door and pointing towards hers. No . . .

After she looked at me like that, in that desolated way, I turned to the window, sorrowfully, apologetically, suffering, frowning. I'm sorry, I wouldn't offend you for worlds. I too am gentle and refined . . . Then, just that once, her foot slid scraping sharply forward and touched mine. Should I look at her and appear conscious? No. Pay no attention. Out of the corner of my eye observing, I saw that she showed no sign of confusion or self-consciousness. She had withdrawn her foot instantly . . . We were approaching London. She put *Tilly of Bloomsbury* into the suitcase—it was neatly packed, full, covered with a transparent silk. No secrets disclosed. Would she get out at London Bridge? No—but the two old women did. Now! What would happen? Her toe had touched twice, oh so faintly, the cuff of my trouser-leg. Intentional? Probably not. Dare! . . . I dared—I slid the right foot forward, resting a little more palpably in contact. Not enough—it might appear accidental. Dare again! I dared again, as the train started from Waterloo, with only five minutes to go. My right ankle rested firmly and ecstatically against the side of the Cordova slipper. I looked at her— devoured her—stared—but she kept her eyes averted, her face suffused with—what? Unhappiness. Speak to her! But I was shy, hungry, weak, cold, psychically out of joint. I had been desiring her too long and too intensely, and though the words went round and round in my head—Will you lunch with me?—I couldn't speak them. The Thames covered with mist. We were sliding into the station, ankle and toe still praying

to each other. Dare! The last chance! Dare!
Say 'May I help you with your bags?' Hurry!
A porter was at the door, with his red tie. I
stood up, trembling, to take my bag from the
rack. I looked at her beseechingly, still hoping
for a miracle; but as I turned she leaned toward
the opening door and said in a low harassed voice,
her dry lips barely moving, 'Porter!' . . . I got
out and walked along the platform, walking
slowly, so that she might overtake me. How
exquisite, small, graceful she was! The neat, precise, energetic and charmingly girlish gait! She
did not turn toward me—her small chin was lowered humbly into the bright batik scarf. Gone.
She was gone for ever. We were divorced, after
a marriage—how divinely happy—of two hours
. . . MISERY . . . Why hadn't I said, 'Will you
have lunch with me?' Why hadn't I said, 'Need
we separate like this?' Why hadn't I said, 'Do
you like *Tilly?*' Or do you play? I'm passionately fond of music myself. Do you know *Morgen?* by Strauss? or *Wiegenlied?* Do you go to
the Queen's Hall? Wigmore Hall? Have you
heard Coates conduct? Glorious, isn't he? Shall
we lunch at Gatti's—or the Café Royal? . . .
Those side tables at Gatti's, with red plush sofas.
The table-legs so close together that if two people
sit on the sofa their knees must be contiguous.
The music at the far end. That's where Mary
and I went for supper when we came back from
Banstead . . . It would have been so simple to
say, 'Won't you lunch with me? I should so
much like it if you would!' We were so clearly
'made' for each other. And especially now that

Cynthia—it might have prevented that. Lost;
gone into the jungle of London. I advertised
three times in *The Times* Personal Column—there
was no answer. I thought of employing a detective to try and trace her. Yes, I three times proposed in *The Times* that she should meet me at the
platform gate, and each time waited for half an
hour, wondering what we would say when we
met . . . Where are you, C. I. E.? Are you in
London? Am I destined some day to see you
playing in an hotel orchestra, or in a cinema, playing with the spot-light on you, lighting your shyly
downturned small and lovely face? . . . By that
time you will have forgotten me. And as for me
—Cynthia has intervened. I am on a ship in the
Atlantic, passing the Grand Banks, with Cynthia.
I am in love with Cynthia, miserably and humil-
iatingly in love. More intensely than I was with
you? Who can say? Heaven knows I loved you
with a blind intensity that made me unhappy for
weeks after. But then, how much was my misery
due to my feeling of having been so horribly and
unforgivably inadequate? Inferiority complex
. . . And so absurd, that I, who on a score of
other occasions had . . . 'picked up' . . . women
here and there in two continents . . . should have
sat in silence and allowed you to go out of my life
—in spite of your so clearly and so desperately
signalling to me. O God that with divine rightness . . . inestimable lightness . . . O God that
with celestial brightness . . . merciful and benign
Kuan Yin . . . O lamas riding on llamas and
bearded ascetic Arhats hunched meditative on
tigers. O Solomon, O Song of Songs and Singer

of Singers . . . I will never forgive myself, nor
will she ever forgive me . . . She will say, over
and over, 'I met a man once, on a train from
Folkestone' . . . C. I. E. The name—good Lord
—might have been Cynthia . . . Do you hear me,
Cynthia? . . . Hear you, tadpole . . . Forgive
me! Absolve me! Let me bury my infant's face
against you and weep! Like Father Smith, I am
looking, looking everywhere, for my mother. Is
it you, perhaps? I have thought often that it
might be you. You remind me of her. Let me
be your child, Cynthia! Take me to Kensington
Gardens with you in the morning—carry my gol-
liwog in your left hand, and let me clasp your
right. Past the tea gardens. To the banks of the
Serpentine, or the Ornamental Water . . . Who
is it that has that theory of compulsory repetition.
Freud, is it? . . . Orpheus. . . . Sequacious of
the liar . . . I shall go mad some day. Yes.
Aetna will open, flaming and foisting, and I will
be engulfed in my own volcano. I can hear it, on
still days, boiling and muttering. Mephitic vapours
escape through cracks in rock. Red-hot lumps
are flung up and fall back again—I have seen the
livid light of them in my eyes.—And do you
know, Cynthia, what form my dementia will take?
. . . No—tell me, absurd one, poseur! . . . I will
weep. I will do nothing but weep. That is
what I have always wanted to do—to weep.
The sorrow of the world. I will sit and
weep, day after day, remembering nothing save
that the world was created in pain. The syphilitic
family in the cobbled mud of Portobello Road.
Goya. The lost kitten. The crying child. The

dog whose nose had been hurt, bleeding. The old woman dying in the street, far, far from home. Lions weeping in cages and dead men roaring in graves. Our father that weepest in heaven; and angels with whimpering wings. Smith, walking among the stars looking for his wife-mother. The Disciples waiting in vain for the miracle to happen. My father, which art in earth. Billy, who was tied to the bedpost and beaten across his naked back with eight thicknesses of rubber-tubing because his younger brother had told a lie about him. Μακάριοι οἱ πενθοῦντες ὅτι αὐτοὶ παρακληθήσονται The dead sheep under the beech tree by the pond. The numbed bee, crawling for the hundredth time up the window-pane, and falling. The poet, who discovers, aged thirty-five, that he cannot write. The woman who finds that her husband no longer loves her. The child who is mocked at school for her stupidity. I will expiate the sin and sorrow of the world for you, my brothers. You will be happy. I will give up all my selfish ambitions and desires in order that I may help you. I am worthless—I am nobody. Do not think of rewarding me. Anonymous, I will pass everywhere like a spirit, freeing the imprisoned and assuaging the afflicted. The bee I will catch in an empty matchbox and carry to Hymettus, releasing her amid a paradise of heather and wild thyme. I will untie Billy from the white iron bedpost and take him to see the circus. Elephants! Peanuts five a bag! Speedy the high-diver with a gunny-sack over his head! The boxing kangaroo! . . . For the syphilitic family, an immediate cure, money, and a cottage

in the country with a flower garden and a vege-
table patch . . . For the old woman who died in
the street, believing in God and a future life, the
strangers walking round her in a ring will be
cherubim and seraphim, with rainbow wings, and
angelic eyes of love. The throne of God will be
before her; and looking up she will see seated
there,—with Mary star of the sea in a blue mantle
at one side and Jesus in a fair robe of vermilion
at the other,—not Jehovah the terrible, but her
own father, with his watch-chain, his pipe, and
his funny, flashing, spectacles! 'Why, if this isn't
my little Blossom!' he will laugh . . . and she
will cry for joy . . . I will find the lost kitten
and bring it back to a house even more glorious
than that it remembers. Saucers will gleam before every ruddy fire-place: there will be fish-
tails; and there will be cream. Children will dart
to and fro, pulling after them deliciously enticing
strings. Immortal mice of a divine odour will
play puss-in-the-corner, melodiously squeaking and
scurrying. Moths undying will dance with her at
dusk in the corners, and unhurt, sleep all night in
the cups of lilies . . . Smith, star-wandering,
cigar in hand, will find his mother. For the fly
with torn wings, I will make new wings of an even
more dædalian beauty. The clairvoyant I will deliver from his torment of vatic dreams; and Goya,
touched by my hands, will at last close his eyes
. . . The crying child will find his adored blue
shawl . . . Hay-Lawrence will recover the sight
of his left eye, and his wife will no longer sit
alone by the fire reading letters three weeks old
. . . From the whole earth, as it rolls darkly

through space around the sun, will come a sound
of singing . . . MISERY . . . And in order to accomplish this, Cynthia,—how can I accomplish all
this, you ask? Very simple. I will permit myself
to be crucified. My SELF. I will destroy my individuality. Like the destruction of the atom, this
will carry in its train the explosion of all other
selves. I will show them the way. The Messiah.
They will pursue me, mocking and jeering. They
will crowd closer about me, stoning. And at this
moment I will destroy my SELF out of love for
all life,—my personality will cease. I will become
nothing but a consciousness of love, a consciousness without memory or foresight, without necessity or body, and without thought. I will show
mankind the path by which they may return to
God; and I will show God the path by which he
may return to peace . . . Are you listening, Huntress? . . . Listening, madman! . . . Not mad,
not mad,—it is only the well-known doctrine of
sublimation. Suicide of the unconscious. Nothing of it but doth strange into something rich and
change. Recommended by all the best metaphysi-
cians. Miss E. Z. Mark, of No. 8,765,432 Telep-
athy Alley, Chocorua, N.H., writes: 'I suffered
continually from ambitiousness, appetite, and reckless energy, until I tried sublimation . . . Now I
do nothing but beam at the universe' . . . Used
and praised by millions . . . Sublimation rules
the nation . . . One three five seven nine eleven
thirteen fifteen seventeen . . . Is it my heart or is
it the engine? *Te thrum: te thrum.* Seems to me
it's a little rougher. Creaking. Cynthia is asleep
in the First Cabin. I wonder what position she

lies in and how she does her hair. Pigtails—one
or two? Not pigtails? Clothes carefully arranged
on a wicker chair. Pink-white-elastic. Mrs. Battiloro's middle-aged nightgowned body gently
snoring and gulping. A crescendo, and then a
strangling gasp, and the head turned, and silence,
and the crescendo all over again. A Puritan.
What is love to a Puritan? What does he make
of the pleasures of the flesh? Shuts his eyes. A
painful duty. Did you remember to wind the
clock? . . . Oh, dear, I forgot to order the flour
. . . The immaculate conception . . . Sublimation again . . . *Te thrum te thrum*. In my left
ear my heart. Smoking too much. *Sua pipetta
inseparabile*. Pressure on the eye makes a tree,
one-sided, dark tamarack with downward claws,
purpurate and murex. Tamurex. Tamarix. What
was I thinking about, or was it a series of images
simply, or a fragment of dream. Claws hanging
from a tree. Claws paws clods pods. The purple
locust claw. A green bright cataract of leaves.
Tamaract! And a red fish leaps out and up!
Gone. What a lovely thing. Now where did that
come from I wonder. Ah Fsyche from the regions whish. My little trout. Tree-trout, that
swims and sings. Swings. Up from my cabin,
my nightgown scarfed about me . . . fingered her
placket. Coward Shakespeare. Her scarf blew
away along the deck and I ran after it. The squall
blew her skirt up as she went down the ladder.
They laughed. In my left ear my heart *te thrum
te thrum*. The Sea. Sea. Sea. Sea.

V

'IT was Friday the thirteenth. I don't like Friday the thirteenth. We were all scared—every man on the ship. Waves coming right over the old tanker—they're low in the water you know—only about that high out of the water. You hear them going right over. Gosh, it's a terrible sound in the middle of the night when you're lying in your bunk. But no sleep that night. We were on our feet all night . . .'

'—is that so——'

'—is that so——'

'Friday the thirteenth. Who was it, Tom Lawson, wrote that book——'

'But the sound of the water on one of those iron tankers! Gee whiz, man, you think you're going down . . . It was a long trip, a long long trip—all the way from Tampico to New York, wallowing along in the old Gulf Stream day after day. Playing cards all day and half the night, new partners with every change of watch. Good God I got sick of the sight of a bloody card. And no smoking either—on the American tankers they let you, but not on the British, no sir.'

' . . . cock-fighting—Havana . . .'

'Hello there, little Johnny Cagny! You looking for a fight, are you? You want to fight me, do you? Now don't you be climbing up on the back of that seat—you'll be getting a fall . . . There! Now you've been and gone and done it!'

'In Havana, sure. And all those places. Guatemala City, too, I've seen them.'

'Long, you know, knives—little thin steel knives—fastened on to those what-you-call-'ems ——.'

'Spurs——'

'Yes, spurs . . . and one eye only he had, one little red burning eye.'

'Yes, but the food's good on a tanker—better than this is, by God!'

'. . . then she comes into the ring with a fine strapping black son-of-a-gun of a Tom cat. And he had a cock, of course, in his corner, holding it in his hands—and a beauty it was, too! And she says, "I'll fight my puss against your cock," she says, "five dollars to the winner!"'

'. . . ha ha ha ha . . .'

'What the hell's the matter with these hands?'

'It's the jinx.'

'Ah, it's a great sight is a good cock-fight. How they will fight! I saw one once in Mexico City. It was a fight to a finish in every sense of the word. Both of them covered with blood, getting groggier and groggier, falling down and staggering up again for more, finally one of them flopped over, dead. The other one stretched up his neck and gave a little rusty crack of a crow—and keeled over, dead too. That's the fighting spirit for you! You can't beat it . . .'

'I'll fight you! I'll fight you!'

'I'll tell your popper on you.'

No, you won't!'

'I will too! And the policeman, that fellow

with the red face, will get you. He told me he was looking for you.'

'Ah, he was not.'

'They don't like little boys that come into smoking-rooms. Those big fishes will get you—those fishes with great big mouths. They've had four little boys already this morning. They'd have been up again before this, only for the rain.'

'Ah, they wouldn't.'

'Here's the policeman now!'

'Sure—you look out for my badge!'

'No, he isn't either!'

'—a pair of sevens. Good little sevens! Come to mommer.'

'Did you hear about that wild Irishman in the steerage?'

'No, what?'

'He come aboard blind to the world and put away whisky all the first night and all yesterday morning till he begun seein' things. I guess he was seein' every colour of snake there is, from what they said. Then he beat up another feller so bad they had to put him in the ship hospital, at the back. Wild as a cuckoo! Then a couple o' friends of this other chap beat *him* up so bad they had to put *him* in the hospital. And in the middle of the night he leap' out o' bed in a franzy and took all his clothes and tore 'em to smithereens and run out on deck and slung 'em all overboard. Well, now he's sobered up a little, and remembers that all the money he had, and his passport, and everything, was in the clothes he flung overboard . . . Too bad! He's got a wife

and five kids in Brooklyn, and he had all his
savin's with him to buy a farm in Ireland.'

'—is that so!'

'Yeah. Will they let him in, I wonder. I hear
they're passin' the hat fer 'im.'

'For Gosh sake.'

'Old Paddy over there is pretty near as bad.
He's done nothing but souse since he come on.
Whisky and a beer chaser. Them was the days,
boys! Pawin' the rail with a blind foot! . . .'

'Was you speakin' to me?'

'No, sir.'

'Yes you was too! . . . When you get through
with that damn cigarette, come over here, and I'll
fool you.'

'What's that?'

'Come over here and I'll fool you! Write your
name on this paper! I'm the immigration inspec-
tor.'

'He's stewed to the eyeballs.'

'You think I'm drunk? . . . I'll fool you . . .
It's an awful thing to say,—and I don't want to
insult anyone that's present in this room,—but
what I'm telling you is facts and *figures*! There
was an Irishman come to New York, and I knew
him well. He went to stay with a Mrs. McCarty,
who kept a boardin' house. A widow, I think
she was . . . And he was lookin' for a job. So
we got him a job, over on Avenue A I think it was,
where they was buildin' a buildin'. We got him
a job screenin' sand . . . And when he come
home at night, Mrs. McCarty says to him, "Well
Pat, what kind of a job you got?" and Pat says,

"Ah, I been foolin' the public all day! I been throwin' sand through a gate!"'

' . . . ha ha ha ha . . .'

'Who drew number nine, please, in the sweepstakes? Did any gentleman here draw the NINE please in the sweepstakes? There was an error.'

'Hell, I drew the eight.'

'*I wonder—who's kissing—her now . . . I wonder—who's telling—her how——*'

'Did anyone see the sunrise this morning? It had a black mark on it like an arrow.'

'If you saw any sunrise I'll eat my hat. Black mark on it like an arrow! Like a poached egg, you mean. Put up your ante.'

'I *have* antied.'

(How can there be any doubt about it? She looked right at me. 'Do you know that lady?' I said to Purington. 'That's Mrs. Battiloro, sister of A. B. Mandell, the novelist. She has just cut me. Walk round the deck with me again—I want to make sure that it was deliberate . . . And it was. She came coolly towards me, talking with that tall fair girl—she looked at me coolly, still lightly talking—she shot me through with a blue eye. Why? It couldn't have been because of that business this morning, when I pretended not to see Cynthia and her friend? No. I'm sure they didn't guess that I saw them. My damned, absurd, diffidence. Of course it would have been awkward—I was so far away from them, there on the lower deck, and I would have had to shout, or wave a hand, or perform some other such horribly public action, and then go trotting, like a tractable little dog, to the foot of the companionway: to talk with them through the bars of my cage! No—it was a mistake; but I'm sure they didn't guess it. Why, then? Why? . . . I am blushing angrily and hotly at the recollection, while I keep a look out through the open smoking-room window to see if she comes round by the sun-parlour. Is it barely possible that her mother doesn't remember me, didn't get a good look at me last night on the dark deck? No. She cut me. It was a cool and conscious cut if there ever was one. She disapproves of me, and has always disapproved of me. Scheming for a 'good' marriage! Cutting the throats of such outsiders as me! *'I know thee not, old man.'* Was there something I did or said last night? My over-excited greeting? And does it mean that Cynthia too will cut me? Of course. It's all been decided. It was talked over last night, and again this morning, with laughter—gay feminine laughter. My name looked for in vain on the passenger-list—and the white-and-gold breakfast room scanned in vain. No Demarest to be seen. Where is Demarest, the laughing goldfish? He must be in the Second Cabin? But how odd! How funny! Now, Cynthia, take my advice, and *drop him at once*. He is not our sort. Those ridiculous letters he wrote to you last winter—and that awful book——)

'It isn't what you say, it's how you say it.'

'Sure, when you say that, smile!'

'—a club. A little club, more or less. One little club.'

'I don't believe I'll play, but I'll watch you, if you don't mind.'

'What you doin', Susie? Where's Johnny Cagny?'

'I'm writing my name. This isn't as good as I *can* write . . . Say! Don't tear my paper!'

'You shouldn't be in the smoking-room, Susie. It's too rough for you in here. And that little Johnny Cagny, he's too rough for you too.'

'Jesus! Listen to that screw kicking out! *R-r-r-r-r-r!*'

'—and then I got to New York too late for the boat! Though if I hadn't stopped for a bath, and to go to the office for some money, I'd have been all right. But those damned agents told me four o'clock in the afternoon. Hell! And there's my wife, waiting for me all this time in Liverpool . . . Oh well, it's all in the day's work.'

'That's right . . . I've missed plenty of trains, but never a——'

'—*perpendicular*——'

'—sick to death of them. Sixteen days on that damned tanker, and now *this* bloody thing ——'

'—asleep. Are ye asleep, Paddy? Rocked in the bosom of the deep, deep, deep——'

'Ha ha ha.'

'Half seas over. He'll *drink* his way to Ireland. It'll be a dry country by the time he gets there. *Oh Paddy dear and did ye hear the news that's goin' round*—Who's got anything better than a full house? Oh! SHAN*dygaff.*'

'—told me about one trip he had, from Tampico to New Orleans, with some Mexican passengers. Indians, you know, those halfbreeds. They had a *hell* of a time. Every time he turned his

back, those damned Indians would light a fire on
the decks! They're always making little fires,
you know,—just for company, and to warm up a
few old coffee grounds in a can. Well, on a tanker
full of oil! Gee whiz, man! she'd go up so quick
you'd never know what happened. All night
they had to watch them——'

'—is that so——'

'—is that so——'

'Aztecs, I suppose those were. Those Aztecs
were a wonderful people. Wonderful builders—
all just as straight as a die, and according to the
points of the compass, and carvings all over everything. They had a high state of civilization.'

'That's all right, but they were heathen just the
same. They sacrificed human beings to the
sun.'

'They thought Cortez was a reincarnated sun-
god. That's how he got control over them with
so small an army. Damned dirty shame, too.
Still, the world has to be civilized.'

'*Why* has it? . . . I don't believe we're a bit
better than our so-called heathen ancestors.'

'Ah-h-h-h what you talkin' about!'

'Well, look at Ireland, your own country, full
of murders and burnings and treason and God
knows what; and look at the Balkans. and look at
the way we shoot down strikers, or burn niggers,
or the whole bloody world going to war for nothing at all and all lying about it, every man jack of
them, pretending there's something holy about it!
Look at the way in England, when they launch a
battleship, they have a red-faced Bishop there, or
an Archbishop, to *consecrate* the bloody ship in the
name of God for murder! *Civilized!* You make

me sick. The world hasn't changed a hair for four thousand years.'

'That's right, too!'

'Hear hear!'

'That's all very easy to say, but just the same there is some progress. Look at the toothbrush ——'

'Ha ha—make the world safe for toothbrushes!'

'Porter! Bring me the car toothbrush please!'

'Yes sir, and when she come back there was a foot sticking out of every berth——'

'Ante, mister.'

'—and when she whispered *"Sweetheart!"* forty men answered with one voice. *"Come* in, darling! *here's* your icky fing!"'

'Ha ha—that's a good old-timer.'

'*I—can sing—truly rural——*'

'Then I was sent out scouting with a Dodge two-seater and a pocket full of cigars—throwing the bull, you know, you have to do it. Finding out what the other companies were up to. A sort of commercial spy, that's really what it is. I didn't know a thing about it, but I knew enough to bluff, and before they found me out I knew the game. Gee whiz, I had a stroke of luck once! I was up looking over some old wells—gone dry. They didn't say anything about it, but the first thing I noticed, right beside one of these wells, was a couple of dead birds—sparrows or something. Gas! That's what it was. Well, I kept mum, and drove over to a rival company about two miles off, pretending just to drop in for a friendly chat. The first thing I knew, I heard a chap complaining about a gas-well on their place—"It's a funny thing," he said, "the way the pressure's dropped on that well." That gave me an idea! I looked up the geological layout—and sure enough, their gas was leaking through our old *oil*-well. And before they knew it, we had it tapped. A stroke of luck, that was! It gave me a lot of pull with the company.'

'That was pretty good! There's luck in every-thing——'

'It's an awful thing to say; and I'm not insultin' anyone that's present here; but what I'm tellin' you is facts and *figures* . . . There was three Italians come to New York; and they didn't speak no English. They went to stay at a boardin' house—I think it was kept by a Mrs. McCarty. The first night they was there, they woke up hearin' a great noise in the room beneath, and they was scared . . . So one of them went to a little knothole there was in the floor, and listened. Now there was three Irishmen playin' cards in the room beneath, but the Italian couldn't see nothin', and all he heard was a voice sayin'——'

'Major Kendall! Major Kendall! Is Major Kendall here?'

'Outside! Outside!'

'Two scotch? Yes, sir.'

'And a splash.'

'Well, they was so scared they took their bundles and run out of the house; and after a while they come to the Harlem bridge; and when they was half-way across the bridge they come to a dead man lyin' on his back in the middle of the sidewalk with his throat cut and a knife in his hand——'

'I'll bet you've got an ace. Want to bet?'

'—kiddin'——'

'—and while they was standin' there lookin' at the corpse a policeman came up to them—*say! listen* to this! Are you listenin'?'

'Sure we're listening.'

'—and says to them, "Who done this?" "I *drew!*" says the first one, "I *cut!*" says the second one, "I *had a hand*," says the third: so he pinched all the three of them.'

'Ha ha! Some story! Good boy, Paddy!'

'—at the Orpheum, in Boston, two weeks ago, dressed as a woman, with a great big brass padlock hanging down behind, and biting a little Japanese fan—saying he'd been followed right to the stage-door by two sailors and a fireman——'

'Have you a little fairy in your home? Well, we had, but he joined the navy!'

'—and this guy went into a saloon in Chicago, leading a tiger on a leash! A big rattlesnake put his head out of his breast pocket, and he slapped it in again. When the tiger wouldn't lie down, he kicked it on the snout. "Say!" says the bartender. "The town you come from must be pretty tough!" . . . "*Tough!* You said a mouthful, bo. That town's so tough it kicked us fairies out."'

'Ha ha ha . . . You know that one about the lonely fairy in Burlington, Vermont, and the alarm clock? . . . smothered it with kisses! I like that story.'

('*My throte is cut unto the nekke bone,*
  Seyde this child; 'and, as by way of kinde,
  I sholde have deyed, ye, longe tyme agoon . . .' . . .

Of course it was deliberate. That cold blue light
in her eye. She bore down on me like a frigate.
Frigga, the goddess of fertility. Perhaps she and
Cynthia had disagreed about it—and this was her
way of forcing a crisis? She guesses that now I
won't be inclined to approach Cynthia? Damned
clever! *Damned* clever. I take off my hat to her.
It was done so beautifully, too—like an aseptic
operation,—no feelings, no display, no waste of
effort; a miracle of economy. The first time, I
thought—actually!—that it might have been a mistake! I had made ready to bow to her—and I
was so pleased, too, to be discovered walking
there, in broad daylight, like one who 'belongs,'
on the First Cabin deck with Purington—so anxious, also, that I might be seen by Cynthia! I
was positively wagging my tail, as I drew nearer
—discreetly, of course, and to myself; the bow I
had prepared was to be a very refined and quiet
one. Alas! it will never be seen, that clearly pre-
conceived bow on the deck of the *Nordic,* on the
port side, at eleven o'clock in the morning, at latitude such-and-such and longitude so-and-so, with
the sun x degrees above the horizon in a fleece of
cirro-cumulus, and one sea-gull perched on the
foremast like a gilded finial! And now the question is—will Cynthia be told of that encounter?
That depends on whether she is already a party to
the plan. About even chances . . . No—more
than that . . . After all, there was the copy of
Galatea I sent her, and the two silly letters, which
she never acknowledged or answered. She must,
therefore, have been annoyed. In the circumstances, after so brief and casual and superficial

and *unguaranteed* an acquaintance, I had no right
to send them. Of course, I knew that. Just the
same, if she had been as mature, as broad-minded,
as *fine* as I thought——)

'No, you see, I miss boat in New York—got to
take dis one, sure. I lose one week. Torino. I
go Torino. How I go? Liverpool to Lond' is
four hour,' tha's fi' dollar? Lond' to Dover is
t'ree hour? . . . Naw, I don' care, I got plenty
time, sure . . . Torino, I go Torino firs'. My
fader live in Ancona, ol' man, live alone. My
moder, she die six, seven year ago. Look—she
give me——'

'—pretty risky, yes. I saw a man killed on a
derrick once. He was climbing up near the top,
when he slipped. His shoes were worn down, and
the broken sole of one of them—anyway, that's
what we thought—caught on a girder . . . Another time I saw an oil-derrick start to fall—
eighty feet high—with two men on it, right at the
top. They felt it beginning to go—and by gosh
they *jumped*,—first one and then the other,—
eighty feet down to the slush-vat—only a little
thing ten feet square, you know—and both of
them hit it, neither of them hurt! Gosh! The
rest of us felt pretty sick. About five minutes
after it, I began to shake so bad I had to sit down
on a barrel. A thing like that makes you think
. . .'

*Lights of Library and Port Deck. Lights of
Bar and Starboard Deck. Single Stroke. Trembling.*

Sound Signals for Fog and So Forth.

In fog, mist, falling snow, or heavy rainstorms,

whether by day or night, signals shall be given as
follows:

A steam vessel under way, except when towing
other vessels or being towed, shall sound at inter-
vals of not more than one minute, on the whistle
or siren, a prolonged blast.

'Well, Mr. Demarest, why so sad?'

'Sad, do I look sad?'

'You look as if you'd lost your last friend!'

'So I have—I've been crossed in love.'

'No. You don't say so. You're old enough to
know better. Were you on your way to the Library? Do you mind if I join you till dinner-
time?'

'I should be delighted. I've been trying to read
psychology in the smoking-room. But the combination of disappointment in love with the noise
there—was too much for me.'

'Noise! My dear Mr. Demarest, you ought to
be grateful. Up where I come from, if anyone
is so careless as to drop a teaspoon, everybody else
is upset for the rest of the day. I feel like screaming . . . What's the psychology?'

'Well, I'm a little hazy about it. Did you ever
hear of the Bororos?'

'Bororos? Any relation to the Toreadors?'

'No—I believe they're a totemistic tribe in
South America or Australia or is it Madagascar.
Anyway, I know this much about them: their totem is a red caterpillar called the Arara. And
they believe themselves to *be* red Araras. Van
den Stein—of course you've heard of him—asked
them if they meant that after death they would

become Araras? But they were shocked and offended and replied, "Oh no, we *are* Araras!" '

"Is this nonsense you're talking to me? It sounds like *Alice in Wonderland.*'

'Said the Arara to the Bororo——'

'You aren't a psychologist yourself, by any chance, are you?'

'Nothing like that. I sometimes wish I were. Every man his own psycho-analyst?'

'What *do* you do, if you don't mind my asking so personal a question?'

'What *do* I do! That's what a good behaviourist would ask, and what I often ask myself . . . Accurately and dispassionately put, I'm an unsuccessful author.'

'An author! . . . Well. You could knock me down with a toothpick. You don't *look* like an author.'

'No?'

'No. Where's your long hair? your flowing tie? your—pardon me—maternity trousers?'

'Yes, I do lack the secondary sexual characteristics. That's probably why I'm unsuccessful. Or at any rate, the two things go together. If a man takes himself seriously enough to dress the part, and to look like a damned fool, he may perhaps be crazy enough to be some good!'

'Well now, *that's* an interesting point! . . . Wait for me five minutes, will you? I've left my old reekie behind.'

'Sure.'

'—well, that's all *right*. You have *your* opinion; and other people have theirs. Which kills the most—this last war,—or tudercleosis? . . .

So! . . . You would pronounce judgment on it without knowing the facts. That's what women *do* . . . Not all the people that's in the street is *bad*. And not all the people that's in the street is *good*. There's no grand rules by which you can lay down the law,—if you're a good Christian. There's only special cases, that's all; and what you've got to do is to look into each case by itself, and judge it on its own merits . . . Everybody is aimin' for the same place, ain't they? That's the fact to be remembered, and not the fact that they go different ways to get there from what *you* choose. That's the way it is with religion. We all take different routes. But we're all aimin' to get to the same place. So what's the good of quarrellin' about the routes we take, or scorning one man because he goes this way, and another because he goes that . . . as long as they're honestly striving to get to the good place . . . But if there's a place on this earth that's a second Sodom, it's New York.'

'How are you, Mrs. Simpson? Have you got hearts?'

'For fair!'

'Hearts are trumps.'

'—the *dollar,* that's their god, the almighty dollar. You see what they mean by that, don't you?'

'Yes?'

'You remember the Jews in their journey through the desert. You remember how some of them, losing faith, backsliding, went whoring after false gods, and worshipped the golden calf. That is a *symbol*—the golden calf. And the golden calf is to-day the god of America. It's the Al-

mighty Dollar; instead of Almighty God. Mark
my words.'

'Yes, that's true, that's a nice illustration for it.
Everybody *does* worship gold——'

'I made a mistake!'

'That wasn't *fair*!'

'She *reneged*!'

'But what I say is, if they don't want to travel
the same road with me, let them go their own
way.'

'That's what I say to my son, who joined the
Christian Scientists. He's always after me——'

'—*Episcopalian,* they call it in America——'

'Well, that's the reason, you see, why I didn't
want to *play* for anything.'

'*Anything*, that'll keep you in touch with God,
that's the great thing. But they all want to go
their own way, nowadays. You can't prevent it
—it's no use is it? trying to prevent it. But so
long as they keep in touch with God, that's the
great thing.'

'—Christ, I mean.'

'Well, I never played it much, I just started.'

'They don't deny Him. But they say He's not
the Son of God.'

'—*beginning*——'

'They say that Christ was a good *man*. The
only thing they deny is His *Kingship*. But what
do we mean, I ask you, by Christ? Have you
stopped to think about that? That's a point of
very great importance. Is there any reason why
we should reserve the title of Christ only for the
one individual that was known as Jesus? There
have been many Christs since Jesus of Nazareth.

There was Saint Francis. There were some of
the Popes, too, good and holy men. There was
Moody and Sankey. There was Spurgeon. In
what way was Spurgeon not deserving of the name
of Christ? He gave his life to God—look at all
those wonderful words and thoughts of his. And
these are only a few. There have been many
Christs—some of them lowly people that were
never heard of in history. How many have been
put on the rack for their faith in God? No man
can say. There have been many Christs; and
there will be Christs again.'

'We couldn't have made a whole lot, could we?'

'The ace of diamonds was all I had.'

'Nine of trumps——'

'You have to follow suit, you see.'

'What'll you do?'

'One spade.'

'One spade.'

'Ha ha ha! You have to say something *different*
from her! You don't follow suit in the *bidding*!'

'Well, if you've got one spade you'd better hold
on to it!'

'They're playing euchre, is it?'

'Miss Kennedy? No. She wasn't a bigot. She
might see things in a different light from what
you do. But that isn't bigotry. Because you're
Church—and she's Chapel—does that give *her*
the right to call *you* a bigot? No. Miss Kennedy
was a Unitarian, and a God-fearing woman. You
might not agree with her, but that wouldn't make
her a bigot.'

'Well—I try to fathom all these things——'

'It's the way they've been brought up, that's it,

isn't it, Mrs. Covey? They reverence God in their
own way. And it seems good to them, just like
your way seems good to you. It's all in the way
you've been brought up when you're a child.'

'Well—that's true, of course,—and my husband
is right where he says we should all strive to be
tolerant—but just the same there's some things
that's hard to understand or be tolerant of. I've
had a good deal of religious experience, for after
being brought up as a Churchwoman, when I married I became a Wesleyan. And then, singing as
I did,—I used to sing a lot,—I went about a good
deal to different sects and societies, and saw
a good many different points of view. But some
of the Catholic ideas, now, I cannot think they
are good. And this although my best friend, a
woman I've known all my life, died a Catholic.
To my idea, the way they use the crucifix is
wrong, like a kind of idolatry. For them, their
crucifix is just a kind of talisman, to protect you.
Just a talisman. And then the way they worship
the mother of Christ—that's another thing that
seems to me uncalled for. I used to ask Mrs.
Jennings, "Why is it you worship the mother of
Christ as if she was a god? She was only a mortal woman like you or me." And of course, that's
just why it appeals to them. They have her there
to represent all the mothers . . . Lots of my
friends have been Catholics.'

(I could see, watching them out of the corner
of my eye, that Cynthia and the fair-haired girl
were turning, hesitating, there at the top of the
companion-way, as if at a loss. Should they come
down, approach me? Try in some way to catch

my eye? . . . They wavered, Cynthia was biting
her lip—they vacillated, waiting perhaps for some
sign from me—and then, receiving none, departed
slowly forward and did not return. I believe that
Cynthia knew that I had seen her. Yes. She
knew; knew from the stiff unseeing way in which
I stood and stared, staring meaninglessly, with
awkward profile, at the wholly uninteresting sea.
Good God. My folly and weakness are abysmal.
Why must I behave in this extraordinary fashion?
Ask dad, he knows! Ask Clara, the negro nurse!
Ask Mr. Greenbaum, the latin teacher, who
watched me through the crack of the door to see
if I was cribbing! Ask that slattern under the
arc-light, in November, 1909, who carolled at me
"Does your mother know you're out?" Ask the
burly Italian in the Apennine train, who said,
when I had dismally failed to shut that infernal
broken window (and the smoke was pouring in)
"Poco bravo!" Ask that detestable red-faced red-
headed vulgar master (tuberculous, too) who su-
perintended when I was given the water-cure,
aged seventeen! And the God-impersonating
baseball coach who would never trust me with a
chance on the first nine! . . . Ask them all. And
ask my dipsomaniac great-grandfather, my
charming imaginative fibbing mother, my sensual
analytic father, and the delirious wall-paper pattern on my nursery wall. *Behaviour is a function
of environment.* Selah! I wash my hands of it.
But I don't want to behave like this? Or do I?
Is it metaphysically—or physiologically—possible
to will the good and achieve the evil? to desire,
and not to accomplish? and thus to *become* some-

thing which one had not willed? Cynthia's conception of Demarest is not Demarest's conception
⸺)

'Well!'

'Well!'

'Now I should like to ask you a whole lot of questions.'

'Ask, and it shall be given unto you.'

'May I inquire what it is you write?'

'Plays. Also an unfinished novel or two. And a few poems.'

'Have any of them been produced?'

'Published, but not produced. That's the difficulty. Or rather⸺'

'I dare say you're too highbrow. Is that it?'

'No. The trouble is deeper than that. In fact, so deep that it's hard to analyse. I've often made the attempt, never with much satisfaction. Not that it matters very much. Ha ha! I always say that, at this point, and of course it's precisely *that* that matters . . . the fact that I say, and *do* often believe, that it doesn't matter, I mean.'

'Not enough faith in yourself, perhaps.'

'No, not exactly that—though that's a part of it. It's more general—a sneaking feeling that the whole thing is a snare and a delusion.'

'I don't get you. You mean the world in general?'

'No—though I often suspect that too; but that's not just what I mean. No, the sneaking feeling I refer to is a feeling that the arts—and perhaps especially the literary arts—are a childish preoccupation which belongs properly to the infancy of the race, and which, although the race as a whole has not outgrown, the civilized *individual* ought to outgrow.'

'Hm. I see. Or I *don't* see!'

'No reasonable person any longer believes in magic—but many of the ideas and words and fetiches, which we inherit from the age of magic, still survive in debased forms: mascots, lucky pennies, charms, lucky numbers, fortune telling, and so on. Well, when we begin as children to use language, we use it as a form of magic power to produce results. We learn to say 'more' because when pronounced it will actually *get* us more. And, we never wholly lose this early conviction (though it becomes overlaid and unconscious) that some sort of virtue or power resides in language. When we like a passage in a poem or tale we refer to it as "magical." We thus indicate unconsciously the primitive origin and nature of the arts. Art is merely the least primitive form of magic . . . But all this relates chiefly to the *linguistic* side of the literary art. There is also the other side, that part of it which it has in common with the other arts—the psychological content, the affective and emotional necessity out of which it springs. You know Freud's theory that the ordinary dream is a disguised wish-fulfilment or nexus of them? Well, the work of art performs exactly the same function. Some of these æsthetic critics say that *content,* so to speak, doesn't matter at all; they talk of the ideal work of art as one in which everything has become form, and of the ideal critic as one in whom there is no confusion of the emotions aroused in himself (by the work of art) with the work of art itself.

That error seems to me perfectly extraordinary!
And yet it is a very common one. For of course
this pure form, and pure contemplation, are both
chimæras; there ain't no sich animals. What is
the pure form of a potato? The minute you leave
out its potatoishness you leave out everything.
Form is only an aspect of matter, and cannot be
discussed apart from it. You can isolate the feelings and emotions which give rise to a play, but
you cannot entirely isolate its form, for its form
responds to these. Can you conceive of a play
which would be entirely meaningless, one which
was not only unintelligible, but which also aroused
no feelings? Impossible. Language is reference.
And its reference is dual: it refers to facts,—as
the word potato refers to a tuber,—but also it
refers to feelings; for every individual will have,
as the result of his own particular experiences, his
own particular *cluster of feelings* about the potato.
Do I make myself clear?'

'Not at all. But go on, brother. I may catch
up with you at the finish.'

'I'm determined to make you suffer . . . Let's
assume that I like a certain poem. Why do I
like it? The æsthetic critic would say that I like
it because it's beautiful, because, in other words,
it's a "perfect expression of something"; the
something you see, doesn't matter very much, so
long as it has been "æsthetically" experienced!
But this is based on the assumption that all
"somethings," or experiences, are of like value.
We know this isn't true. It would be impossible
to make an Iliad out of the buttering of a potato,
or a Hamlet out of the paring of one's nails.

These experiences are universal,—and could involve no confusion of reference; but they are not of very great interest, or significance, or desirability, *emotionally*. We are all, in a sense, frustrated—we are all of us, each in his particular way, starved for love, or praise, or power, and our entire characters are moulded by these thwarted longings. I won't go into the details of that mechanism, for I don't know too much about it, probably no more than you do; the point I'm making for is this, that art's prime function is the gratification of these longings. We can see this, if we like, as a kind of cowardice. We don't like to grow up; we don't like to face the bare or ugly facts of life, its privations, its miseries, its failures, its uncertainty, its brevity; we don't like to see ourselves as mere automata, whose behaviour is "merely a function of environment"; we don't like to admit our ignorance as to our origin and destiny, or our impotence in the face of the laws that control us; and so we seek refuge and consolation in that form of day dream which we call art. Reading a novel, we become the hero, and assume his importance as the *centre of the action* —if he succeeds, then we too succeed; if he fails, then we can be sure it is against overwhelming odds, against the backdrop of the colossal and unpitying infinite, so that in failure he seems to us a figure of grandeur; and we can see ourselves thus with a profound narcissistic compassion, ourselves godlike in stature and power, going down to a defeat which lends us an added glory . . . Art is therefore functionally exaggerative. When we find our response to things becoming jaded, when the bare bones of reality begin to show, then we clutch at the cobweb of the fairy-tale. Think only of the world of love which literature opens to us! Solomon in all his glory of a thousand wives cannot rival us. We can range from Helen of Troy, or Lesbia, to Imogen with the cinque-spotted mole on her breast; from Isolde to tuberculous Milly Theale; from Cleopatra to Emma Bovary or Raskolnikov's Sonia; or even to the bawdy ballad of sister Mary, who was bilious!'

'Ah—*there* I begin to follow you!'

'Of course! . . . Well now, we jump from that to *another* psychological aspect of this process of wish-fulfilment. And that is this. A work of art is good if it is successful: that is, if it succeeds in giving the auditor or reader an *illusion,* however momentary; if it convinces him, and, in convincing him, adds something to his experience both in range and coherence, both in command of feeling and command of expression. And here we come to the idea which is terribly disquieting to the purely *æsthetic* critic, who likes to believe that there are absolute standards of excellence in art. For if we take a functional view of art, as we must, then everything becomes relative; and the shilling shocker or smutty story, which captivates Bill the sailor, is giving him exactly the escape and aggrandizement, and therefore *beauty,* that Hamlet gives to you or me. The equation is the same. What right have you got, then, to assume that *Hamlet* is "better" than *Deadeye Dick*? On absolute grounds, none whatever. They are intended for different audiences, and each succeeds. Of course, Hamlet is infinitely more complex than the other. And we can and should record that fact and study it carefully, seeing in art, as we see in our so-called civilization, an apparent evolution from simple to complex. Well, all this being true, why be an artist? Or for which audience? . . . That's the horrible problem.'

'I can see you're in a bad fix. But if you feel that way about it, why *not* give it up? And do something really useless like me—selling chewing-gum or lace petticoats to people who don't want them? Why not?'

'Yes, *why* not? The answer is, that though I'm an unsuccessful artist,—pleasing practically nobody but myself,—and though, as a good psychologist, I scorn or at any rate *see through* the whole bloody business, nevertheless I have that particular sort of neurosis, verbal in its outward expression, which will probably keep me an artist till I die or go mad. . . . Suppose I'm a sort of forerunner, a new type. And what then?'

'A new type? Tell it to the marines! You don't look it. You're no more a new type than *I* am.'

'Yes, sir! A type in which there is an artist's neurosis, but also a penetrating intelligence which will not permit, or permit only with contempt, the neurosis to work itself out! If you want a parallel which will make the predicament clear, conceive a Christ, for example, who *understood* the nature of his psychological affliction, foresaw its fatal consequences for himself, foresaw also that to yield to his neurosis would perhaps retard the development of mankind for four thousand years, and nevertheless *had to yield to it*. As a matter of fact, that illustration occurs to me because it is the theme of a play that I've had in mind for some time. *The Man Who Was Greater Than God.'*

'It's a damned good title, I'll say that much for it! But if you ever got it on the stage, you'd be mobbed.'

'Oh, it would be impossible at present. At any rate, it probably would be, if my hero was too palpably modelled on Christ. I could, however, and probably would, represent him as a modern man, an intelligent man, who nevertheless had religious delusions of grandeur. Perhaps an illegitimate child, who compensated for that flaw in his descent by believing himself to be the son of God . . . Or, I've also considered dropping the Messiah idea altogether, and having for my hero an artist, or a writer, or perhaps a social reformer. In that case, I betray *myself*—it's really myself I should be portraying in either character. The Strindberg and Nietzsche and von Kleist type, but with the addition of intellectual poise, or *insight*! However, what good would it do? What's the use of doing it? The predicament of the hero would be too exceptional to be widely interesting—no audience could possibly sympathize with him. The Messiah, on the other hand, would be a figure universally appealing . . . Yes, it would have to be the Messiah, much as I prefer the artist . . . But —why not *act* that play, in my own life, instead of thus taking flight from the problem in one more surrender to my neurosis?'

'Act it? I don't get you. How do you mean act it?'

'Well, in the play the hero would finally decide (perhaps he is pushed, somewhat, to this conclu-

sion by his friend, a psycho-analyst) to abjure his
art, entirely and for ever. To anyone who is an
artist, that scene would be positively *plangent* with
invitations to narcissistic anguish—every artist,
beholding, would weep for himself. Imagine it.
A Shakespeare, for instance, deciding for the
good of humanity, not to write plays! Seeing
them all there,—his Hamlet, his Othello, his
Lear, his Cleopatra, his magnificent Coriolanus
—and dismissing them unborn! Very touching.
And to make it worse, he perhaps pays for this in
a complete mental breakdown, or death . . .
That's the *play*: in which, as you see, I have all
the luxury of this suicidal decision, but also the
luxury of having again, and thus intimately,
adored myself. Now the question is,—why not *do*
it, instead of writing it? Why not give up, in
advance, that play and all my other ambitions?
I think very seriously of it; at the same time sus-
pecting that my whole life would be deranged
by it . . . It's a nice little problem. To write, or
to commit suicide.'

'Don't do either! but have a cocktail!'

'That's not a bad idea, either! a dry Martini
would go nicely.'

'Steward! Can we have two *dry* Martinis,
please?'

'Two *dry* Martinis, yes, sir.'

'Yes, it's very sad and complicated. If you look
at the problem from a purely humanitarian point
of view, and try to solve it solely in the interests
of mankind—even then, it's not too simple. In the
first place, there is always the possibility that the
whole Freudian idea, as thus applied to art, is

wrong. It may be that art will be a permanent necessity for man, a penalty that he pays for having become a social and civilized animal. How can we be sure? If I go on writing plays and novels, may I not at any rate give aid and comfort to a few verbalistic lunatics like myself, and help them to keep their spiritual balance in this melancholy world? And isn't that a good deed? . . . But no, I'm not sure. The intellectual side of me declines to believe in that—or balks at it. I have what my friend Tompkins, the psycho-analyst, calls a Samson-complex.'

'This gets deeper and darker. Have a drink. Here's to the Samson-complex!'

'Your bloody good health!'

'Not bad at all.'

'Shall we repeat?'

'We might!'

'Two more please, steward?'

'Two dry Martinis? Yes, sir.'

'Well, now, Socrates, tell me about the Samson-complex. I hope you don't mind if I just seem to listen, like a sponge.'

'I don't mind, if *you* don't. But I don't want to bore you.'

'Bore me! Great Godfry. I've been dying for something highbrow like this. But don't be surprised if I fall asleep.'

'Well, the name for it was partly a joke, and refers to a dream I had two weeks ago, when I was visiting Tompkins. Tompkins has always been keen to have me drop all this literary folde-rol and become a psychologist, or at any rate a psychological critic of literature. When I was

staying with Tompkins, two weeks ago, he re-
newed his attack on me and once more brought
this schism painfully to the surface. Lately, I
had been backsliding a little. After a year and a
half of pot-boiling, which took the form of book-
reviewing, I suddenly developed a tremendous
resistance to criticism—my destructive speculations, you see, were coming too close to a destruction of *myself,* not only by taking up all my time,
but also by undermining my *amour propre* . . .
How much, please?'

'Two shillings—or fifty cents. Thank you, sir.
Thank you.'

'Here's to your ectoplasm.'

'And yours. May it never grow less. Don't
forget the dream in your excitement.'

'I was just getting to it. It reflects, you see,
this conflict in me between the critic and the artist
. . . The times, I should think, were those of
Euripides: though I'm not positive the place was
Greece. I was a runner, a messenger, and I had
been running since daybreak, bearing some portentous message. What was this great message, this
revelation? I don't know—it was never clearly
formulated in the dream. But at dusk I came to
a great stone-built temple, and entered it. I was
exhausted: I could hardly stand. The temple
chamber, within, was immense, high-roofed, and
ceilinged with blue and gold; and at the far end
of it, before a grim stone altar, a hieratic procession of tall priests was forming. It seemed, however, that they were expecting me, and that whatever it was that they were about to perform must
wait till they had heard what it was that I had to

say. I approached them, spoke, and then, my message delivered, realized that I was going to die, that the long run had killed me. Stumbling, therefore, to a table-shaped tomb of stone, I stretched myself upon it like the effigy of a crusader, my throbbing eyes turned upward toward the ceiling . . . How high it was, how gorgeously azured and gilded, and how massive the masonry of its arch! If it should fall—if it were only to fall— would it not destroy—not only myself, already dying—but also these hateful priests and their mysteries? the temple? And suddenly, then, with a last spastic effort of body and soul, I cried out in terrific command to the ceiling "FALL! FALL! . . ." And it fell.'

'Is that all?'

'That's all.'

'Good gracious Peter . . . I see, yes, where the Samson idea comes in . . . I never dreamt anything like that in my life. All my dreams are in pieces—I'm walking in one place, and then I'm in another. I look into a room and see a *lovely* girl undressing, kiss her—oh boy! notice that she has put too much rouge on her mouth, and looks consumptive,—and the next thing I know I'm watching a crazy play, with that girl, or another one something like her, acting the heroine in *Why Girls Leave Home*. No good at all. Do you always dream dreams like that?'

'Usually.'

'No wonder you've got things to write about . . . Tell me—when you write a novel, for instance, how do you go about it? Do you make up a plot out of whole cloth,—so to speak,—or do you see something in life, simply, and put it down?'

'I don't think it's either method, but a sort of combination. Personally, I find it hard to draw from life. I couldn't, for example, transfer you to a novel, or Hay-Lawrence, and make you real: you would only become real, for my purpose, if I had *invented* you' . . .

'Gosh! Now, suppose we were all of us just ____'

'Characters in a novel? Yes! Every now and then one experiences that sense of a complete dissociation of personality, when one seems to evaporate under the glare of one's own eye. Exactly the way that when you've been lying in bed in one position too long you lose all sense of your body . . . You know, it's something like this, some analagous feeling of unreality and absurdity, a destructive sense of the profound *relativity* of my existence, that makes me a failure. It seems to me—I don't know whether this is idiotic, but thanks to the cocktails I don't hesitate to say it—it seems to me that I can *foresee* everything, exactly the feeling that one has in a hasheesh or mescal trance. Have you ever tried hasheesh?'

'No. Something like opium, isn't it?'

'Something . . . You lose the power to distinguish in time and place. For instance, you remember, as you sit there absorbed in sensory meditation, that you have forgotten to let in the dog. In the course of thinking this, you so sharply visualize the action of descending the stairs, passing the bust of Clytie in the wall-niche,

slipping back the cold brass bolt, feeling the injured screw under the doorknob, hearing the
whimper of the hinge and the threefold scrape of
the dog's nails on the worn door-panel, and then
(the door opened) seeing the mad swarm of
stars above the Baptist church—you experience all
this so profoundly, and the return upstairs, that
you become convinced that you have actually
done it . . . Am I losing my thread, or are these
cocktails making me drunk?'

'I suspect you're drunk!'

'Yes, I have at all times, drunk or sober, a
crippling sense of having foreseen every possible
action or feeling or thought, not only of my own,
but also of every one else. All the alternatives,
too. The whole blooming buzzing cosmic tele-
phone exchange—every connection. This is so
appallingly vivid that in its wake any *real* action
performed by me, or any thought formulated, or
any feeling observed in its progress from belly to
thorax, and from thorax to—possibly—horripilation——'

'Pause there! That word again, please, if you
don't mind, professor.'

'Horripilation—when your hair walks backward on cold feet. Any such *reality* seems to me
in consequence a rather stupid and meaningless
repetition, not worth troubling about. Why write
a book, which one can conceive so much more
sublimely than anyone could possibly write? Why
bother even to *conceive* a new unity in a chosen
gamut of heterogeneity, when one also foresees
disastrously the hour when that unity will have
become merely one item in a larger heterogeneity,

each new system absorbed ·by a larger system?
Why bother to foresee that fatality of decay and
change, of clicking and mechanical and inevitable
death, when one remembers that even oneself, the
foreseer, was foreseen *in the act of foreseeing,*
and that even one's newness is old? . . . This is a
poisonous sophistry from which I find it hard to
escape. I only escape it when the attention of my
senses has been sharply drawn. And even then
the willingness to act or feel is only intermittent.
As in love, for instance.'

'Ah! Thank God! I was beginning to lose all
hope for you. But if you can still fall in love, it's
not so bad.'

'But my God, think how terrible it is to be in
love, and not to be able to believe in it or act on
it!'

'Oh, come come, Mr. Demarest! Do you mean
to ask me to believe that? No . . . No, no!'

'It's true, s'welp me Bob!'

'Well, if you weren't drunk, I'd think you were
crazy.'

'My dear Silberstein, I'm no crazier than you
are.'

'No, sir, you can't tar me with *that* brush. Believe me, when I'm in love—using that as a *very
broad term*—there's plenty of action. I'm no
Hamlet, by God! I either get 'em, or I don't.
And if I don't, I don't cry about it. I look for
another: the woods are full of them. It's as easy
as tripping a cripple.'

'Well, of course, I'm exaggerating slightly——'

'Ah! That's better. You were exaggerating
slightly——'

'—but there's something in it. I don't mean so much as applied to—well, the more fleeting sort of sexual adventure. Though it's apt to be true even of those. But when one's really in love— it's a miserable business. All out of focus. No reasonable centre to one's behaviour. Or *my* behaviour, anyway. I'm always a damned fool when I'm in love.'

'If you're talking about Romeo and Juliet stuff, all I can say is that at your age you ought to know better. The female doesn't exist that can get me in love with her.'

'But I wonder if there's any escaping one's temperament in that regard? Here I am, aged thirty-five, and more horribly in love than I ever was before—in love, mind you, in the most sublimated and sentimental sense imaginable. I actually don't feel the slightest *conscious* sensual attraction to the girl. Not the slightest. Oh, I don't mean that I don't think she's beautiful—I do. But her beauty affects me in a very peculiar way—it seems to me merely a clue to something else, some mental or spiritual quality (though I distrust the word spiritual) which is infinitely more exciting and more worth discovery. Of course, I admit frankly that I've had other affairs in which there was little or nothing of this. Usually, even when I'm mildly *"in love,"* the desire for physical contact is at once uppermost—all my tentacles and palpacles begin to quiver. Why this difference? How can we be sure that one way is any better than the other? You simply take your choice. Both of them have something of value to offer. Perhaps it's the difference between poetry and prose. I always liked Donne's remark on that subject——'

'Donne? Never heard of him. But spring it, if you must.'

> " ' *For they are ours as fruits are ours.*
> *He that but tastes, he that devours,*
> *And he that leaves all, doth as well.*" '

'Well, God deliver me from poetry. You can have it. Take all the lyrics you want, but leave me the legs.'

'I'm afraid I've got to leave you. That was my dinner-horn—quarter of an hour ago. I'm late.'

'Was it! And I haven't changed yet . . . We'll resume this drunken discussion later . . . So long!'

'Yes, so long.'

Lights of Library and Port Deck. Lights of Bar and Starboard Deck. Single Stroke. Trembling.

'Oh! Aren't you ashamed, Mr. Demarest!'

'Ashamed, Mrs. Faubion? What of?'

'Why being so late—we're almost finished! . . . Oh, we know all about *you*.'

'Help, I'm discovered . . . No soup, thanks, steward—hors d'œuvres, and then—let's see.'

'Calf's head in torture is good—I had it. Very good. Good food on this boat.'

'No—roast duckling à l'Anglaise, and vegetables. And ice-cream and coffee . . . So you know all about me. Father's been telling on me.'

'He *has*. He told us all about your swell friend in the First Cabin. When are you going to announce the engagement?'

'Engagement! My God. The family jewels.'

'Is it true, what Mr. Smith told Mrs. Faubion and me, that you first met her on another ship?'

'True as the gospel, Miss Dacey. Believe everything that father tells you and you won't go wrong. But didn't he tell you that we were secretly *married* this morning—at seven bells?'

'Ha ha! Wouldn't you like to, though! Merry laughter.'

'Married, does he say. No, siree Bob. When Demarest marries they won't ring bells, they'll fire cannon and blow up the ship!'

'Why, what do you *mean*?'

'Does he look like a marrying man? Not him. Not much! He's one of these ice-bound bachelors.'

'All right for you, Mr. Demarest—you can't pretend any more that you're a woman-hater. *Now* we know the *real* reason why you avoid us all the time!'

'Avoid you! My dear Mrs. Faubion! What a scandalous and outrageous falsehood! Here I've been pursuing you from morning till night——'

'*Pursuing!*'

'—and I never can get any nearer to you than tenth in the waiting line. And you accuse me of avoiding you! Father, you can testify.'

'Testify nothing! We'll never see *you* again on this ship. No, sir. You're a lost man. Sunk without a bubble.'

'You hear that? And after Miss Dacey and I have been saying such nice things about you, too. Haven't we? Your ears ought to have been burning last night.'

'Last night?'

'Last night after we went to bed.'

'Do tell me! I'm dying to know what it was.'

'Why, did you ever hear of such conceit?' *Actually!*'

'That's right, darling, don't tell him a thing. Tantalize him. That's what gets 'em every time.'

'Don't *darling* me! I'm not your darling, nor *anybody's* darling.'

'She's getting mad again. All pink and mad . . . But didn't you say you had a husband? Ah ha! Look at her blushing!'

'I'm *not* blushing.'

'Oh no, she's not blushing. Not blushing at all. I beg your pardon, Mrs. Faubion.'

'Mr. Barnes! I wish you would teach your passengers better manners!'

'Is Mr. Smith behaving badly to you? I must caution you, Mr. Smith. You must remember that these young ladies are travelling under my protection.'

'I think he's had a cocktail too many, Mr. Barnes.'

'Cocktails! I like your nerve, Mr. Demarest! And you breathing brimstone all over the table. It's a wonder the flowers don't wilt.'

'Where were you at the mock wedding, Mr. Demarest! didn't you see it? I thought you were going to be the wedding-guest.'

'So I was. But I forgot all about it till it was too late. How did the bride look, the pianist?'

'Oh, he was a scream.'

'And you should have heard Mr. Ashcroft doing the marriage service! Oh! I thought I should die!'

'Oh, wasn't he a scream?'

'Yes, he certainly was a scream! What *was* it all about, all that about the man trying to catch the pigeon in the field, and getting it by the tail?'

'What, madam! didn't you understand that? That was the best part of it. Don't you try to let on you're as innocent as all that! *What was all that about the pigeon!* You were the one that was laughing the loudest.'

'Careful, Mr. Smith! Careful!'

'Well, I ask you, Mr. Purser, as man to man ——'

'That will do, father!'

'*Don't* call me *father.* A man is as young as he feels . . . Ha ha!'

'Well . . . what's funny in that?'

'Oh, nothing funny—it's damned serious. Yes indeedy.'

'My little grey home in the west. Don't you *love* that song? I just couldn't *live* without that song. Are we ready to go, Pauline?'

'Yes, are we ready to go, Pauline?'

'*Pauline!* . . . Mr. Smith, your manners are simply *terrible.* Good night, Mr. Barnes—oh are you coming too? Good *night,* Mr. Demarest!'

"Good *night,* Mrs. Faubion!"

'Gosh, that girl gets my goat. Yes, siree, she sure gets my goat.'

'She's damned attractive.

'Attractive! She's a dynamo.'

'Dynamo—dynamas—I loved a lass——'

'Yes, siree. And you know, I've got a damned good idea.'

'What is it?'

'Just between you and me and the bedpost——'

'I must caution you, Mr. Smith. You must remember that these young ladies——'

'No, sir, I'm not swallowing any bunk about those girls. If they aren't—I'll bet they've been in half the staterooms on this boat.'

'I don't believe it. Not Faubion.'

'Oh? You don't think so? Well, maybe not, maybe not. Just the same, I've got a damned good idea.'

'Well?'

'It's simple, and I don't see how it can get me into any trouble . . . It's this. I've got a purse full of gold sovereigns—look! you don't see gold sovereigns every day! Not since the war you don't. They look pretty good, don't they?'

'Very nice.'

'Yes, sir! They look pretty good. And I've got an idea that if I just take them out and kind of flash them at Mrs. Faubion—without saying anything, you know—anything that would give me away too much—what do you think?'

'Gosh, father! You're getting reckless.'

'No! I don't see any harm in it. I'll bet these sovereigns would look pretty good to her. Don't you think so?'

'Suppose not?'

'Well, suppose not. Where's the danger? That's the beauty of it. If she's as innocent as *you* say she is, she won't know what I mean by it. Will she?'

'True.'

'Well, I think I'll try it. If I can get up the nerve. That's where the trouble is! Guess I'll

take a few Guinnesses first . . . And then do it
the last thing before I turn in. I'll bet she'll know
what I mean, all right! Yes, sir, if that girl
doesn't know more than you and me put together,
I miss my guess.'

'Well, I'll put a flower on your grave. A
syringa.'

'You just wait! The old man'll show you something . . . The trouble is with you, you're too
slow. How's your dollar princess?'

'She's dropped me.'

'Dropped you! What do you mean?'

'Her mother cut me this morning. It's all over.'

'You mean to say you're going to *let* them drop
you?'

'Good God, man, you don't suppose I can run
up into the First Cabin forty times a day—where I
don't belong, and where all the officers know me
by sight—in pursuit of people who won't speak to
me when I meet them? Nothing like that. I tried
it twice this afternoon, but the only one I saw
was her uncle, writing letters in the smoking-
room. And he doesn't know me.'

'Well, why didn't you put it up to *him*?'

'Ask him why they were cutting me? Nothing
doing!'

'Well, I guess the trouble is you don't care very
much. Not like me! . . . Coming up? Take a
turn on the deck?'

'As far as the smoking-room. I think I'll get
drunk to-night.'

'Well, I may pop in later . . . What's the singing?'

Single Stroke. Trembling.

Sound Signals for Fog and So Forth.

'*And the next time I met her, she was all dressed
in pink.
The next time I met her, she was all dressed in pink.
All in pink—all in pink—what will her mother
think?
Down in the alley where She followed Me . . .*'

'That's a new one on me.   Well, see you later.
Gosh, look at the smoke in there!'
'—pure as the snow, but she drifted.'
'She was pure as the snow, but she drifted.'

'*And the next time I met her, she was all dressed
in grey.
The next time I met her, she was all dressed in grey.
All in grey—all in grey—what will her father say?
Down in the alley where She followed Me . . .*'

'—two for a nickel poker player like you!   Are
you coming in or are you staying out?'
'*I'll* come in—*I* ain't no piker!'
'*He's* no poker piker!'

'*And the next time I met her, she was all dressed in
green:
The next time I met her, she was all dressed in
green.
All in green—all in green—my, how she did scream,
scream! . . .
Down in the alley where She followed Me . . .*'

'The man said to the girl—"You know what
your personality reminds me of? a handful of wet
sawdust!"   Flap, flap.   And he shook his hand,
as if he was shakin' sawdust off it.   And the girl
said—"Ah, your face would make a false tooth

ache!" . . . "Is *that* so," the man said. "Do you
know what your face is like? It's like an exposed
nerve." And the girl said, "Why, you're so nar-
row-minded you could button your ears at the
back! Ha ha!" . . . And then the man took a
long hard look at her and said, "You want to
know what you remind me of? . . . You remind
me of a neglected grave . . . Where's your
lily?' "

'Ha ha ha!'

*'And the next time I met her, she was all dressed
in red.*
The next time I met her, she was all dressed in red.
All in red—all in red—I stole her maidenhead——
Down in the alley where She followed Me . . .'

'Yes, you hear some funny things there. Another time——'

'ukulele, sure. I was lying right here, behind
the back, and she didn't see me. She was inside
the bar there with the door shut for half an hour.
When she came out and saw me she turned red as
a beet. She tried to laugh it off . . . Well, she's
got a fine pair of shafts, by God!'

'Who can open it. Can *you* open it?'

'Who—? the guy with the long hair—? If he
so much as puts a *finger* on me I'll knock his block
off.'

*'And the last time I met her, she was all dressed in
blue.*
The last time I met her, she was all dressed in blue.
All in blue, baby blue—what will the poor kid do?—
Down in the alley where She followed Me . . .'

'Hooray! Here's old Paddy again.'

'*One—more—drink!*'

'I didn't see you eatin' much, Paddy.'

'Let me tell you somethin' . . . It's an awful thing to say,—and I'm not insultin' anyone that's present here—but what I'm telling you is facts and *figures*. There was an Irishman once and his name, I think, was Mike. And he was living in N'York, at a boardin'-house that was kept by a Mrs. McCarty.'

'She was pure as the snow, but she drifted.'

'Pure as the snow, but she drifted.'

'Prohibition—that's what drove me out of the country. As nice a little saloon as you could want! forty and one-tenth miles from New York. And everything as orderly and nice as it could be. And *now* look at it! *High* school girls goin' out to dances, takin' their own old man's hooch with them, and gettin' so drunk they can't walk! *Paralysed*, that's what they get. *High* school girls!'

'—and the parrot she had,—*ahip!*—he hated it, see? . . . And so one mornin' when he was shavin' he took his razor and cut the back of its neck, and dropped it into the——'

'Ante, God damn you! You can't slip anythink like that over on me!'

'You shut your face! You can't talk like that to me!'

'I can't, eh? Well, tellin' me won't stop me!'

'Sure he antied. It was me that didn't ante.'

'All right, all right, my mistake. No hard feelin's, pardner.'

'—and the parrot said, "By God, if she had that cut, and lived, there's hope for me!'

'Ha ha ha!'

'I'll ask you a question you can't answer, Paddy
. . . Who was it drove the Danes out of Ireland?
Eh?'

'St. Patrick.'

'Ah-h-h-h-h! G'wan with you. It was Brian
Boru . . . And do you know who it was used to
make wine out of the whorts? I'll bet you don't
know that either.'

'I don't know, and I don't *give* a damn . . .
Who was it?'

'Ah, you don't know nothin'. It was the
Danes.'

('*My throte is cut unto the nekke bone! seyde
this child* . . . Bored Silberstein. Deliberately,
in that particular way. Coming the high-brow.
Why did I do it? Some sort of relief—catharsis.
Too bad we had to stop when we did. A good
thing we had to stop when we did. I'd have told
him everything. I'd have told him about——
Why did I lie to him about her physical attraction? But I only recognized the lie as I told it.
So did he. She was pure as the snow, but she
drifted. PURE as the snow, but she drifted. And
the next time I met her she was all dressed in
black. Back. Smack. Crack. Clack. Attack.
Golden engine and silver track. The golden engine on the silver track. I am wounded with
a deep wound. ὀτατοι ποποι δα. He prescribed
whisky—hæmostatic and astringent. Whisky;
and a modest prayer.)

'—Mexico, if a girl is married, and her husban'
find out she is not—what you call? *verges?*—he
take her back to her father and mother. And so,

everybody know; and she have no more chances.
No, sir.'

'Is that so.'

'Is that so.'

> '—plough mus' plough
> And the horse mus' pull,
> The cow mus' cow,
> And the bull mus' bull . . .'

'—and if I was to tell you the Soo Canal flows
uphill—ahip!—you wouldn't believe it, would you,
and you'd think you was smart! . . . but what
I'm tellin' you is facts and figures . . . I was
workin' there for three——'

'And he put his head out and yelled, "Hey!
How do you expect me to find my ring when
there's a guy in here lookin' for his motor-bike!'

'Ha ha ha ha!'

'Such is the life of the Queen of Spain.'

'Three months of leisure, then——'

'A triple whisky, steward.'

'Triple? yes, sir.'

'—and the girl, she said, "But, mama! how you
can be sure this trick will work? How you can be
sure it will fool my fiancé?" . . . And mama, she
say, "Well, I ought to know! It's the same way
I fooled your old man!" Ha ha! And the old
man, he was under the girl's bed all the time,
listening! Ha ha! . . . That was a good one,
eh?'

'Another jackpot. Who can open it?'

'Nobody can open it.'

'Sweeten the pot, then, boys!'

'*Triple* whisky, sir.   Thank you.'

'Thank you.'

'—and all the time she just went on scrubbin' the floor, scrubbin' the floor.   And then she said, without turnin' round her head to see who it was, "Niggerman, Ah ain't seen yo' face,—and Ah don' know yo' name; but lemme tell you, Ah's here every Friday afternoon——'

'Hello! is that the foghorn?'

'Somebody said there was a——'

'Good evening, Major.'

'Good evening, Mr. Demarest.'

'You've been very inconspicuous all day? We're suspicious of you.   How's the Welsh Rarebit?'

'I feared there might be suspicions!   *He he!* That's the worst of attaching oneself to anything so flagrant.   Every one knows, unfortunately, that the attachment can only be——'

'Naturally!'

'Well, believe me, she's a hot one.   And she's all there, too.'

'You aren't suggesting that she's intelligent?'

'Dear me, no!   She hasn't the intelligence of a—barn door.   But she's all there physically.'

'Oh, physically.   So Ashcroft said.'

'Ashcroft?   What does *he* know about it?'

'She went up to his room last night.   He told Hay-Lawrence about it.'

'Did she!   Well, I'll be damned.   Went to his room!'

'Yes, twelve o'clock last night. He told her how to get there—up in the First Cabin, you know—and she carried a book, so as to pretend she was just returning it, in case any question arose.   But

it all went off quite successfully. She's got plenty
of nerve, all right.'

'Well, I'll be—hoodooed! *That's* why she's
been——'

'—what?'

'—stalling.'

'She stalled with Ashcroft. He was mad as a
wet hen. All she would do was fool about with
him. He finally booted her out.'

'Oh! . . . Well, that's just the conclusion *I*
had come to—that's she's a teaser. What they
call a "mugger." '

'You ought to be thankful.'

'Oh, anything to pass the time! . . . Did I tell
you she wants me to take her out to Mespot with
me? . . . Yes, she's begging me to take her, as a
housekeeper. I can see the face of the General's
wife if I turned up with Peggy Davis in tow!
Great Heavens . . . She dropped a pretty broad
hint that there would be more to it than house-
keeping.'

'I don't doubt there would.'

'You know, there's something fascinating about
a woman like that—I suppose there must be something wrong with her. Some sort of twist. I
wish I could make out that husband business. She
showed me pictures of him, all right—but the
whole thing seems a little wanky. She reminds
me of a girl that picked me up in a theatre in
Cincinnati.'

'Oh?'

'Yes. The same type . . . It was a funny
thing. I had an overcoat on my lap, and all of a
sudden I felt something tickling me. At first I

thought it was accidental. I waited a little and it began again. It was quite dark, you know— some scene with a spot-light on the stage, and the rest of the lights turned out. And this girl was, very timidly, exploring under my coat with her hand—trying to find *my* hand . . . *He he!* She approached and retreated several times before she succeeded, and when she did succeed she gave a jump, and withdrew her hand again. Only for a minute, though—back it came. First, just our little fingers kept foolishly tapping each other. It was ridiculous. Then she suddenly became bolder, and slid her hand right over on top of mine—and after that, things became really riotous. And then came the joke. Do you know what she was?'

'No—what?'

'A social service investigator!'

'What! No.'

'Yes, sir, a social service investigator. She was connected with a college hospital out there. Some-one told her there was lots of "picking up" in the vaudeville theatres, so she thought she'd investi-gate. Anyway, that's what she said. So she in-vestigated *me!* . . . It was quite apparent, how-ever, that the investigation wasn't disinterested. She was out for adventure, in her half-scared little way.'

'Well, I'll be hanged.'

'Rum, what? as the English say . . . Well, it's early, but I'm off. Have a night-cap?'

'No, thanks, I'm half tight already. I guess I'll turn in myself. I was just on the point when you came in . . . Good night.'

'Good night.'

Single Stroke.   Trembling.
Follow Red Arrow To Boat Station No. 2.
Gentlemen.
142-156.
Boddy-Finch Lifejacket.
—Is that you, Demarest?
—Yes, this is Demarest.   Who is that speaking, please?
—This is Demarest Two-prime.   How do you do.
—Same to you, and many of them.
—As doctor to patient, I would suggest—ahem —a little sublimation.
—Kindly take the first turn to the left and go straight on till you get to hell.
—Yes.   A little sublimation.   A nice little pair of wings, now?   All God's chilluns' got wings? A pair of gospel shoes?
—Take them back to the pawnshop.   No sublimation!   Inter faeces et urinas nascimur.   So let me live until I die.
—You must be careful not to slip back.   Onward and upward for ever.   To higher things, and more complex: the fatherhood of God, the brotherhood of man, the leadership of Jesus.   This love of yours must be kept pure, precious, and uncontaminated.   A guiding star.   Dante and Beatrice. Art, too.   *Ma tu, perchè ritorni a tanta noia? Perchè non sali il dilettoso monte Ch'è principio e cagion di tutta gioia?* . . . Up, my lad!   Up Helicon once more!   Once more into the breach!
—Thank you kindly, sir, she said.   It isn't sublimation I want, it's a bath of blood.
—Civilization is sublimation . . . Simple to com-

plex. Animalcule to synapse. Synapse to hold-
over. Hold-over to art. Selah.

—It isn't sublimation I want, it's drowning.

—That play, now—the very moment to begin
it. There they are—you see them? On a darkened stage. The hero is lying in bed. He is unconscious, result of mental and spiritual exhaustion. Poor devil. And then, from the shadowy
background, the Chorus comes forward! The tyrant father! The incestuous mother! Narcissus
with a handglass!

—It isn't sublimation I want, it's a bath of
blood.

—Terror, with the dull brow of the idiot! and
the Dark Self Who Wants To Die! You see
them? And they have begun quarrelling! They
are quarrelling for the possession of your poor
body that lies on the bed! The Messiah! You!

—It's a bath of blood. Not evolution: revolu-
tion. Red riot. I'm tired. Tired of clutching
the inviolable shade.

—Nonsense. This is momentary. Or else, en-
during—leads you, by devious ways, through mists
and poisons—you know it perfectly well . . . The
very moment for the play. All this agony can be
projected, and being projected will be healed.
Fixed in immortal shape: turned to stars like Cas-
siopeia. Look! Look! How she shines already!

—Fleshpots!

—You deceive yourself. Granted the fleshly
origin,—but it's too late to turn back. Know your
fate, Demarest! You ARE complex! To return
to the simple is for you impossible! Misery! You
must follow out your neurosis!

—To its bloody roots.   Enough, Two-prime!
Pay attention to your collar-button and leave this
affair to me.   Cursed are they that enjoy their
suffering: for they shall never be healed.

—You may bury his body in the Egyp' garden,
You may bury his body in the Egyp' garden,
You may bury his body in the Egyp' garden,
* O his little soul's goin' to shine.*

VI

THE dew fell softly on the hurricane deck;
stars swung over the heavenward-pointing
mast, swung slightly to and fro, swarmed in an
arc like swarming bees; and the large dew pattered
from the wet shrouds, unevenly, now nearer and
now farther off, on the moist deck and the hollow-
sounding canvas-covered lifeboats. The forestay,
black save for the little golden span under the
yellow mastlight, slid under the Pole Star, and
sliding dipped, as the prow in midnight followed
the Great Circle, yielding with long leisurely pitch
and scend to the persuasion of the sea. A fleece of
cloud passed between Sirius and the ship-boy. It
flew to westward, fluent of shape, and from the
starboard came another, coffin-shaped, and behind
that, from the east, a low irregular cavalry of
others, merging confusedly one with another,
commingling softly and softly disengaging. With
the freshening east wind the sea-sound, from the
darkness under the starboard bow, became louder.
The wash of the short-breaking waves was nearer,
more menacingly frequent. The stars, suddenly
panic-stricken, rushed helter-skelter among the
clouds. An eclipse. One bell: the sound veering
dizzily down to the black water on the port side.
A ship sighted? twelve-thirty? . . . Something
cold touched Demarest's cheek, and was gone as
soon as felt. A snowflake. Another caressed his
lifted hand. There were no more—it was to be
merely a hint, a suggestion: nature employing, for

once, the economy of the artist. St. Elmo protect us! St. Erasmus, patron of the midland sea,
guard your mariners! Castor and Pollux, bless
this ship, and save this ghostly company! . . .
The blue fires alighted softly then on the three
mastheads; three corposants; and then two others,
fainter, perched themselves at either end of the
yard-arm from which hung the wireless antennæ
Was that a footstep? And were those voices?
. . . Sounds almost imperceptible; perhaps only
the whisperings of memory or foresight. It was
perhaps the sound of Smith, giving himself a body
in the darkness; or Faubion, coming up out of the
unfathomable with a short sigh; or Silberstein,
muttering as he clove the cobweb of oblivion in
which he found himself enshrouded; or Cynthia,
waking from granite into starlight. It was perhaps only the little sound of the atom falling in
his mind, the atom falling like a star from one
constellation to another, molecular disaster, infinitesimal tick, which, in its passage, created,
illuminated and then destroyed this night, this
ship, the corposants; Smith, Cynthia, Faubion,
and Silberstein.

He moved a little aft, touching, as he did so,
with his left hand, the damp lashings of lifeboat
No. 14. This was the motor lifeboat, the trial of
which (during boat drill) he had witnessed at
noon. Fourteen is half of twenty-eight. The
Number of the house had been 228—228 Haber-
sham Street. But this too was only the silent falling of a mind-atom. He moved aft, turning his
back on this fatal number, which held his life in
its poisonous coils, turning his back also on that

ghostly company—incorporeal Smith, whose cigar-tip dimmed and glowed; Faubion, on whose lifted fingers little blue corposants danced; Silberstein, who muttered; and Cynthia, whose face was turned to the east. They were already beginning to talk, standing far apart, so that their faces were only faintly discernible; but for the moment he was terrified, and delayed at the after-end of the hurricane deck, looking into the black south-west; hearing the sound of the voices, but not wholly the purport. Smith, he knew, had begun by speaking Italian; then demotic Greek; then Provençal French; then Macaronic Latin. Passing then to ancient Greek, he had quoted Meleager, to which Faubion had replied, soberly, with Plato's epitaph for the drowned sailor: Πλωτῆρες σώζοισθε καὶ εἰν ἁλὶ καὶ κατὰ γαῖαν. Ah! Both by land and sea. Remember him. And remember him that lies by the Icarian Rocks, his soul given to the Aegean; and him too that was lost under the setting of dark Orion, borne helpless in ocean, eaten by fishes,— Callaeschus, whom the sudden squall overtook at night. And him also do not forget, Erasippus, whose bones whiten in a place known only to the seagulls. For everywhere the sea is the sea . . . It was Silberstein who added this last phrase: Silberstein of Sidon, Antipater of Harlem. Yes! It was Silberstein, and Smith repeated the Greek after him, taking his cigar from his mouth to do so: πᾶσα θάλασσα θάλασσα. They were all four silent then for a moment, while Demarest, turning, walked toward them, filling his pipe in the darkness with trembling fingers. And as he took his place a little way off from them, his back against lifeboat No. 14, Cynthia turned again and said:

'They are about us! They go with us where we go. They are our history; and we are their immortality.'

'Yes,' Smith answered sadly. 'It is ourselves whose bones lie unclaimed in the deep water that washes the Icarian Rocks; or beside the Needles; or at the "whuling Cyclades." The sea is the sea —this we know—but also were not our prayers answered? for we had, after all, or we have, our "safe passage home."'

'Yes, we belong to them, and they to us,' said Faubion quietly. Demarest could see that she had lifted her face, and was regarding the blue corposants on the mastheads. 'And they and we, together, belong to the all-gathering memory of the future. Or is it possible that we shall be forgotten? But that question, I can see, is already answered by all of you.'

'Answered already by all of us,' Demarest said.

'Answered already,' laughed Silberstein, 'in the negative-affirmative . . . But who will he be, the last one who remembers us? And where will he stand? In a world perhaps englobed in snow.'

'The one who remembers last,' said Cynthia, 'will remember always. For He will be God . . . That, at any rate, is the affirmative. Of the negative, what can be said? We know it, but we cannot speak of it.'

'But we see it there,' said Smith, 'we see it there! The cold cloud, into which we return, the dark cloud of nescience, the marvellous death of memory!'

All five faces looked in the darkness at one another, as if for the instant almost surprised. At
once, however, they all began laughing together:
lightly, with recognition. Of course, of course!
They had forgotten that for the moment! All except Demarest had forgotten it—Demarest and
Smith.

'Well!' Faubion answered bravely, 'that is of
course what we must see, and what we *do* see.
Nevertheless, can we not remain individual in our
feeling toward this? Choosing, for our *pleasure,* purely (since there can be no other virtue in
the choice) the yes or the no? And I, for one, as
you already see, will choose the yes! I will be
remembered! We will all be remembered! And
never, never forgotten. World without end.
Amen.'

'Amen!' echoed Silberstein. 'But Smith and
Demarest do not feel as you do. Smith is the
dark self who wants to die! Smith represents
clearly—doesn't he?—that little something hidden
in all of us—in the heart, or the brain, or the liver,
or where you will—which all our days is scheming
for oblivion. It's the something that remembers
birth, the horror of birth, and remembers not only
that but also the antecedent death; it remembers
that nothingness which is our real nature, and desires passionately to go back to it. And it *will* go
back to it.'

'Yes, Smith will die and be forgotten,' murmured Cynthia. 'He already knows himself dead
and forgotten; and it is the death in Smith that
gives his brown eyes so benign a beam. Isn't that
so? It is the death in Smith that we love him for.

We respond to it, smiling, with maternal solicitude. Moriturum salutamus . . . There, there!'

Smith tapped his foot on the deck and chuckled.

'No no! Don't be too hard on me. Is that all
I can be liked for? I could be hurt by that
thought! . . . But of course it's perfectly true.'

'But of first and last things,' sighed Faubion,
'there is no beginning and no end.'

The five people stood motionless and silent,
their faces faintly lighted by the corposants. This
is the prelude, thought Demarest. This is merely
the announcement of that perfect communion of
which I have often dreamed. They have lost their
individualities, certainly—but was individuality
necessary to them? Or is it possible that, having
lost their personalities, they have lost that alone
by which harmony or discord was perceptible? Or
is it only that their individualities have been refined by self-awareness, so that the feelings no
longer intrude, nor the passions tyrannize, bringing misery? . . .

'That is true,' said Silberstein. 'Here, at any
rate, we are: poised for an instant, conscious and
delighted, in the midst of the implacable Zero. We
remember—well, what do we remember? We remember that our bones are under the Icarian
Rocks. We remember, too, that we are *only* what
we thus remember and foresee. We foresee our
past, and remember our future. Or so, at all events
to interpose a little ease! And that's saying a
good deal.'

'It means everything,' said Cynthia. 'It means
not only the past and future we have in common,
but the past and future that each of us has sep-

arately. And this, of course, is precisely what
blesses us. It is this diversity in unity that makes
the divine harmony. Think only of the joy of
recognition, or discovery, when Smith tells us—
what indeed we know already, do we not? but in
a sense not so deliciously complete—of his life in
Devon, his opera-tickets in New Orleans, his forgotten yachting-cap and his delightful passion for
Faubion! To know what grass is, does not pre-
clude surprise at the individual grass-blade.'

'How nice of you to compare me to a grass-
blade! It's exactly what I am. But you meant
more than that. Forgive me for parenthesizing.'

'Yes, I did mean more than that. What do I
mean? You say it, please, Mr. Demarest.'

'Consciousness being finite, it can only in *theory*
comprehend, and feel with, all things. Theoreti-
cally, nothing is unknown to us, and nothing can
surprise us or alienate us. But if imagination can
go everywhere, it can only go to one place at a
time. It is therefore that we *have* surprises in
store for each other—we reveal to each other those
aspects of the infinite which we had momentarily
forgotten. Who has not known Smith or Faubion? Cynthia and Silberstein are as old and familiar as God. And this sad facetious Demarest,
who when he laughs looks so astonishingly like a
magnified goldfish, isn't he too as archaic as fire?
Yet you had forgotten that one could be sad and
facetious at the same time, and that in addition
to this one might look like a goldfish seen through
a sphere of water and glass; and the rediscovery
of these qualities, which results when they are
seen in a fresh combination, this is what delights

you and delighting you leads to *my* delight. This
is what Cynthia means, and in fact what we all
mean . . . Yes, and this is what blesses us. For
this,—on the plane of human relationship,—is infinite love, a love which is indistinguishable from
wisdom or knowledge, from memory or foresight.
We accept everything. We deny nothing. We are,
in fact, imagination: not completely, for then we
should be God; but almost completely. Perhaps,
in time, our imagination *will* be complete.'

'You could have put it in another way,' said Silberstein. 'Each of us is a little essay upon a particular corner of the world, an essay which differs
in style and contents from any other; each with
its own peculiar tints and stains transmitted from
environment. A terrific magic is stored in these
little essays! more than the essay itself can possibly feel,—though it can *know.* Of the *power* of
Smith or Faubion to give me a shock of delight
or terror, can they themselves form a complete
idea? No—not in the least. Not, at any rate,
till they have felt the peculiar shock of seeing *me!*
After which, of course, they can begin that most
heavenly of all adventures, the exploration of that
world of feelings and ideas which we then recipro-
cate in creating—seeing at once the warm great
continents, jungles, seas, and snowy mountains,
arctics and Saharas, that we can roam in common;
but guessing also the ultra-violet Paradises which
we shall never be able to enter, and the infra-red
Infernos which ourselves will never be able to
communicate. How can I ever make plain to
Faubion or Cynthia why it is that they cannot as
powerfully organize my feelings as they organize

those of Demarest? There lies the infra-red.
There perhaps, also, whirls the ultra-violet. Dive
into my history, if you like. Look! This deck is
no longer a deck. It is a narrow slum street,
paved with muddy cobbles. Do you see it?'

'It is a narrow slum street paved with muddy
cobbles. On the East Side, New York. There is
a smell of damp straw.'

'The sound of drays, too, and steel-ringing
shovels.'

'Cats, ash-cans, slush, and falling snow!'

'You all see it perfectly. Or almost. You see
it in the abstract—not in the concrete. What you
do not entirely see is the basement which my
father used as his tailor-shop,—dark, damp,
steamy, and incredibly dirty,—where, as he ran
his sewing machine, or peered near-sightedly into
cardboard boxes for the one button which he
couldn't find, he taught me Yiddish, German, and
English. He was always putting down lighted
cigarettes,—on the edges of the tables, on chairs,
on boxes, on the ironing-board; and then forget-
ting them. A smell of burning was always inter-
rupting us, and we would jump up and search
frantically for the cigarette. A good many yards
of cloth must have been ruined, first and last—
and once a customer's raincoat caught on fire and
had to be replaced. There was a terrible scene
about it when the man came in for it . . . We
ate and slept, and did our cooking, in the basement
room behind this, from which yellow brick steps
went up to a yard. My mother was dead—
I don't remember her. When I wasn't at the
public schools, I did the errands—delivered trou-

sers that had been pressed, collected bills, and so forth. Naturally, I learned to cook, sew, and use the gas-iron to press clothes, myself. But I also, at the public schools, and in the course of my running of errands, learned a great deal else. I knew the crowds at every saloon in the district, and the cops, and the buskers, and the leaders of the several "gangs." I knew all the brothels, and all the unattached prostitutes. I knew—as in fact all the boys of my age knew—which of the girls in the district (the girls of our own generation, I mean) had already gone the way of Sara More —the girls who were willing to be enticed into dark basements or unlighted backyards. Beryl Platt, Crystelle Fisher, Millicent Pike, Tunis (so-called, according to romantic legend, because she had been born in Tunis, and had an Arab father) Tunstall—before I was eleven I knew that there was something special about these girls; and when Crystelle one day dared me to come to her back-yard after dark, I knew what was expected, and went. After that it was first one and then another. I had no feelings of sin about it—none whatever. It was natural, delightful, exciting, adventurous—it gave colour to life. But I never fell in love. I liked these girls—I particularly liked the dashing swaggering Crystelle, whose hair was magnificently curled, and whose blue long eyes had an Oolong tilt, and who knew every smutty word in the language—but if they transferred their affections to other boys I didn't mind, or if other boys forcibly ousted me I didn't resent it. What did it matter? Life, I knew, was not exclusively composed of carnal love, and there

was sure to be all of it that one needed. Why
bother about it? Billiards was interesting, too,
and so was tailoring, and I admired my father.
I enjoyed reading with him, playing chess with
him, and going with him to Coney Island or the
Museum. When I was fourteen he took me to
the Yiddish theatre to see *Pillars of Society*. It
made a tremendous impression on me. Why do I
tell you this? Not because it's especially interesting in itself; but because it's exactly the sort of
item which you wouldn't *precisely* guess for your-
selves—isn't that it? Yes. You extract the keen-
est of pleasures from hearing of that, and seeing
me in the gallery of the theatre with my father,
eating buttered popcorn. Just as you enjoy, also,
hearing of Crystelle Fisher. These details enable
you to bring your love of me, and of humanity,
and the world, to a momentary sharp focus.
Can one love in the abstract? No. It is not man
or nature that we love, but the torn primrose, and
young Mrs. Faubion, who is being sued by her
husband for divorce on grounds of infidelity;
Demarest, whose fear of his father has frozen
him in the habit of inaction and immobility, as the
hare freezes to escape attention; and Silberstein,
who was seduced by arc-light under a white lilac
in a Bowery backyard . . . However, it was my
intention, when I began this monologue, to light
for you, if I could, the reasons for the fact that
I cannot, like Demarest, fall in love with Faubion
and Cynthia. Is it now indicated? The only time
I ever came near falling in love was after we had
moved to the country, when Mabel Smith, the
school-teacher, took possession of me. Mabel was

sentimental and maternal.   She did her best,
therefore (as she was also something of a hypo-
crite), to arouse some sort of sentiment in *me*.
And she almost succeeded, by sheer dint of at-
tributing it to me.   She tried to make me believe
that I believed she was my guiding star, and all
that sort of thing.   Pathetic delusion, the delusion
that one needs to be thus deluded!   But this holi-
ness never became real to me.   How could it?
I had been a placid realist since birth, calm as a
Buddha.   One has emotions, certainly; but one is
not deceived by them, nor does one allow them to
guide one's course . . . How, then, can I respond
to all the exquisite romantic Dresden china that
Cynthia keeps—to pursue the figure—on her mental mantel?   No no!   It's not for me; or only,
as you see, intellectually and imaginatively.   It
delights me to recognize this so totally different
mechanism of behaviour—and I love Cynthia,
therefore, exactly as I love that hurried moon,
the snowflakes, or the blue-feathered corposant
who gives us his angelic blessing.   But if it is a
question of *erotic* response, I would sooner respond to Crystelle, who is now a prostitute, and
with whom I've often, since growing to manhood,
had dinner at Coney Island.   Much sooner! . . .
Much sooner! . . .'
    New York.   Spring.   The five people walked
in the darkness along Canal Street.   In Fagan's
Drug Store the red, green, and yellow jars were
brilliantly and poisonously lighted.   Sally Finkel-
man came out, carrying a bottle of Sloan's lini-
ment, and a nickel in change.   Red stains of a
lollypop were round her mouth.   She crossed the

street obliquely, and paused beside Ugo's copper peanut-stand to warm her knuckles in the little whistling plume of steam. Ugo, standing in the garish doorway, held a bag of peanuts, red and green striped, by its two ears, and twirled it, over-and-over, three times. An elevated train went south along the Bowery. The five people crossed the muddy cobbles of the Bowery under the roar of the elevated, and passing Kelly's saloon, and Sam's Shoe Shine Parlour beside it on the sidewalk (where French Louise was having her white slippers cleaned) went slowly toward Essex Place. In the window of Levin's Café were two glass dishes which contained éclairs and Moscovitz; one charlotte russe (dusty); and a sheet of Tanglefoot flypaper, on which heaved a Gravelotte of flies. An electric fan whirled rainbow-coloured paper ribbons over the Moscovitz. Solomon Moses David Menelek Silberstein, aged twelve, came slowly out of Essex Place, with a pair of chequered trousers over his shoulder. At the corner, under the arc-light, he stooped to pick up a long black carbon, discarded from the light. Uccelli, in the alley, was grinding slowly his old-fashioned carpet-covered one-legged organ. Bubble and squeak. The monkey took off his red velvet cap. Crystelle Fisher had given him a sticky penny, which he had put into his little green velvet pocket. Winking, he took off his cap again. The organ's wooden leg had a brass ferrule, worn down on the inner side: a leather strap, attached to the two outer corners, passed round Uccelli's neck. Bubble bubble squeak and bubble. *Ta-ra-ra-ra-boom-de-ayy*. Crystelle danced a cakewalk, knees flinging her dimity high, a huge hole showing in the knee of her right stocking, a coarse lace petticoat flouncing. She snapped her fingers, jerking backward her shapely head of golden curls, her oolong eyes half-shut. *Coon—coon—coon—I wish that colour was mine.* Beryl Platt put her head out of a fourth-story window, between two black geraniums, and yodled. I can't come out, she sang. I've got to wash the dishes. And mind the baby . . . At the corner, overtaking Silberstein, Crystelle touched his trousered shoulder—Would you like to know a secret, she said—I can turn a Catherine wheel—would you like to see me. Ha ha! Pork chops and gravy—I wish I was a baby . . . Are you coming round to the yard to-night? . . . Bubble bubble whine and bubble. Yes, I'll be there, said Solomon, and sauntered toward the Bowery. Twenty-six Mott Street. A warm smell of benzine rose from the damp trousers. With the carbon he drew a black line along Kelly's wall, just as French Louise was getting down from the high brass-studded shoe-shine throne. She gave Sam a nickel, and said—Where is that mutt. He said he'd only take five minutes . . . A train rattled north on the elevated: empty: a conductor reading a paper on the rear platform, his knees crossed . . . The five people, drifting slowly in the evening light under the few pale stars of New York, paused before a battered ash-can on which the name Fisher had been red-leaded. Passing then through a door, which was ajar, they saw the white lilac in blossom under the arc-light. Below it, on the hard bare ground, lay the bright

skeleton of a fish, picked clean by the cat. There
was also the sodden remains of a black stocking
. . . Crystelle came running up the yellow brick
stairs from the basement, and at the same moment Solomon reappeared at the door. Look!
she said. She turned a series of swift Catherine
wheels, hands to the ground, feet in the air, skirts
falling about her head, her flushed face up again.
Solomon, pulling a spike of lilac-whiteness toward his nose, surveyed her without expression.
Pork chops and gravy, he said. You've got a
big hole—in your stocking. I have not, she
answered. You have too, he said. Where! she
answered. O Jesus, how the hell did I do that.
Have you ever kissed Tunis? . . . Sure I have
. . . Where? . . . In her cellar . . . Was it
dark? . . . No, not very . . . Well, why don't
you kiss *me*? . . .

'Πᾶσα θάλασσα θάλασσα,' said Smith absent-
mindedly. ' "Rich happiness, that such a son is
drowned." '

'Well!' cried Cynthia into the sea-darkness.
'Why not? We must all, in that sense, drown
some day. Is Silberstein's drowning at twelve
any worse than ours at twenty?'

'I like it,' said Faubion. 'Isn't it really better,
a good deal, than all the refined hypocrisy of the
honeymoon? . . . Always supposing that the
honeymoon is the first!'

'Was it—with you?' Smith's voice had a
chuckle in it.

'Of course not! I didn't live in a village for
nothing . . .'

Her voice trailed away like the dying sound of

a wave. A seagull, floating astern, and crying, with turning head, *Klio*. Where do the seagulls go at night? The seagulls in mid-Atlantic? Do they sit on the waters? . . . *Klio klio.* The five blue corposants preened their blue phosphor-feathers. Demarest, leaving lifeboat No. 14, walked aft again, sucking at his cold pipe. The five people moving eastward with the ship. Five corposants. Five seagulls. *Klio, klio.* Interchangeable. If one thinks in terms of quality-complexes, then a very slight dislocation of affects will give one a world in which no identities are permanent. An alarm clock rises in the east. A sky swarming with stars, at two in the morning, is merely the sensation of *formication*—ants crawling, as when one's foot is asleep. Faubion, uttering a short word quickly, with averted head, is a seagull going down wind, crying, with turning head, *klio* . . . The corposants are five celestial voices, singing in the tops of the trees. They ululate softly in chorus, while the tree-tops thresh in the wind, as the mad nymphs ululated when Dido and Aeneas fled into the cave from the thunder. *Angels follow her—gravely, slowly— with silver and vermilion and rainbow wings— One, more luminous: lost in his own light: sits on a cherry-tree bough, and sings—Blest be the marriage of earth and heaven! Now, in the round blue room of space, The mortal son and the daughter immortal . . . make of the world their resting-place* . . . The marriage hymn, prothalamium, for my wedding with Cynthia, the stained-glass widow. Stained-glass window.

'Poor Demarest!' Cynthia was laughing, in the darkness. 'Poor darling Demarest!'

'Am I so much to be pitied?'
'Is he so much to be pitied?'
'Much to be pitied?'
'Pitied? Pitied?'
'Pitied?'

The bird voices echoed one another, *klio klio,* wheeling and screaming. The sea-claws and sea-beaks pitied him, and the waves too, coming louder from the south-east, their surfy voices the voices of destroyed universes of bubbles, sea-froth, evanescent as human pity.

'Of course he is to be pitied. And loved too, in his fashion—as Silberstein said we love the hurrying moon and the angelic corposant. Loved, therefore, and pitied, as we love and pity our-selves. Who is this William Demarest? this forked radish? this carrier of germs and digester of food? momentary host of the dying seed of man? . . . He came to me to play chess, a copy of *The Spoils of Poynton* under his shiny coat-sleeve.'

'Ha ha. Demarest, the goldfish chess-player.'

'Fool's mate. Watchman, what of the knight? The psychiatrist beat him in ten moves. The man-doline player gave him his queen, and then drew the game. Nevertheless, he considers himself a very talented chess-player. Poor Demarest.'

'Treasure him, nevertheless, for he is a mirror of the world.'

'We cherish him as we cherish ourselves. Is he not an epitome of universal history? Here he stands, on the deck of a dark ship, which is moving eastward at fifteen knots an hour. The steersman shifts the wheel, his eyes on the bright binnacle. The stokers stoke. The second engineer carries a long-beaked oil-can up a clammy iron ladder. The first engineer lies in his stuffy bunk, reading *His Wife's Secret*. Under the ship are two miles of sea, and under the sea the half-cold planet, which rushes through freezing space to destruction, carrying with it continents of worthless history, the sea, this ship, Demarest . . . Who is this little, this pathetic, this ridiculous Demarest? We laugh at him, and also we weep for him; for he is ourselves, he is humanity, he is God. He makes mistakes. He is an egoist. He is imperfect—physically, morally, and mentally. Coffee disagrees with him; angostura causes him anguish; borborigmi interrupts his sleep, causing in his dreams falls of cliff and the all-dreaded thunderstone; his ears ache; his nostrils, œdematous; frontal headaches . . . Nevertheless, like ourselves, whose disabilities differ from his only in details, he struggles—why? to avoid the making of mistakes, to escape the tyrant solipsism, and to know himself; like us, he endeavours to return to God. Let him cry out as he will, let him protest his scepticism ever so loudly, he is at heart, like every other, a believer in perfection! . . .'

Klio klio! Cynthia's was the harsh melancholy voice of the seagulls. The five seagulls wheeled and screamed over the brown mud-flat, at the edge of the eel-grass, where the obscene fiddler-crabs scuttled in and out of oozy holes. Brown viscous froth, left by the receding tide. Cape Cod. What is that dark object that attracts them? A dead man. The corpse of Charlie Riehl, the hardware man, the suicide. The bluefish have picked at his head and hands these six days, since he jumped from the bridge; and now the sea-gulls flap over him, crying, and the fiddler-crabs advance with buzzing fiddles, crepitant army of mandibles.

'A believer in perfection.'

'A believer.'

'Perfection.'

'Rich happiness, that such a son is drowned.'

The five people crossed the meadow, stepping carefully among the fishing-nets which Mr. Riley had spread out to dry. The hot sun drew a salt smell out of them, marshy and rich, fish-scaly. Passing under the arrowy-leaved ailanthus tree, and then rounding the sand-banked corner opposite Mr. Black's forge (Mr. Black was shoeing a horse) they stepped upon the wooden bridge, tripartite, the first and third sections of which crossed the two branches of the forked river, the intermediate section being merely a built-up road-bed on the tongue of marsh. The telegraph wires were singing multitudinously in the wind, a threnody. A metal windmill clanked. They crossed the first section of bridge, looking into the deep and rapid water, and seeing the red sponges that wavered deep-down on the pediments of bar-nacled stone; and then paused on the squeaking path of trodden and splintered scallop-shells, which was bordered with starry St. John's Wort, coarse sappy honeysweet goldenrod, and scarlet-blistered poison-ivy. Leaning then on the red wooden railing, they watched the two Rileys and Mr. Ezra Pope, the town constable, rowing the dirty dory toward a point at the farther end of the marsh. Low water. Seagulls rose in a screaming cloud as they approached. The younger Riley, in red rubber boots, jumped out and pulled the dory up into the eel-grass. The two others got out, and all three moved slowly into the marsh, lifting high their knees. They were stooping over. Then they rose again, carrying something. It was Charlie Riehl, who had drowned himself rather than appear as a witness at the trial. *Klio klio!* At five in the morning it was: there among those red sponges. Feet first; with his pockets full of lead. *Klio!*

'Those are holes that were his eyes,' murmured Smith. 'Nothing of him but hath fed——'

'Narcissus! He sees himself drowned, like this Charlie Riehl. And pities himself. Well, why not? *That's* normal enough . . .'

Faubion held up her hands, on which the blue corposants were beginning to fade.

'Scavengers!' she cried. 'That's what we are. Devourers of the dead: devourers of ourselves. Prometheus and the vulture are one and the same. Well! I *will* not countenance it. Any more than Demarest does.'

She gave a little laugh, and the others laughed also, lightly and bitterly. Something had gone wrong with the scene. Disruption. Dislocation of affects. Quarrel of ghosts. Foecal colouring of imagery. The night falling over like a basket, spilling miscellaneous filth. No! Only the atom in the brain! falling infinitesimally, but by accident wrecking some central constellation. The five ghosts quarrelling on the deck with harsh voices were the five seagulls in Trout River.

Charlie Riehl was himself. Drowning was consummation. It was all very simple—you turned a screw, and everything at once changed its meaning. *Klio*, said Cynthia. *Klio, klio,* sang the mad nymphs for Dido, ululating; and the vulture, tearing with sadistic beak at the liver of Prometheus—*klio, klio!* it cried, turning the Semitic profile of Silberstein . . . But this was disturbing! One must pull oneself together—set the basket of stars on end again. What was it that had caused this trouble, this quick slipping brain-slide, vertigo, that sent everything skirling and screaming raucously down the abyss? Whirlpool. Cloaca. Groping for trout in a peculiar river. Plaster of warm guts. Clyster. Death, with your eyes wide open. *Christ!* . . . He leaned hard on lifeboat No. 14 (the motor lifeboat—they took off the canvas cover to test the engine, and stepped a little wireless pole in the bow thwart) and shut his eyes. Think. Project. Sublimate. Everything depends on it. In the sweat of your brow, the ventricle contracted, the dew dripping——

'Is it not possible, then'—he cried—'this perfection of understanding and interchange? Cynthia?'

'Oh, as for that——' Cynthia's voice seemed to come from farther off, floatingly.

'As for that!' jeered Silberstein.

'That!' quacked Smith.

He opened his eyes. The four figures, in the now almost total darkness, were scarcely perceptible—mere clots in the night. The stars had been engulfed.

'He came to me with a shabby chess-board under his arm! And he had forgotten to button——'

'Please adjust your dress before leaving . . .'

'He permitted me to pay his fare in the bus! Yes, he did! You may not believe it, but he did!'

'Rear seat reserved for smokers . . . Lovers with umbrellas at the top——'

'And do you know what he said when I asked him if he would like to come one afternoon to hear my brother William play Bach on the piano? Do you know what he said, delicious provincial little Yankee that he is and always will be? . . . *"You bet!"* '

'Ho ho! Ha ha! He he!'

'Suppress that stage laughter, please. Silence! His impurial highness——'

'I beg you,' said Faubion, 'I beg you not to go on with this!'

'Silence! His impurial highness, greatest failure as a dramatist that the world has ever known, supreme self-devouring egotist, incomparable coward, sadist and froterer, voyeur and onanist, exploiter of women—William Demarest, late of New York, and heir of all the ages——'

'*Stop!*'

'What's the matter with Faubion? Is she in love with the idiot?'

'Perhaps she's right. We ought to be sorry for him. More to be pitied than blamed. After all, he's an idealist: a subjective idealist.'

'Who said so? An automaton like the rest of us. Nigger, blow yo' nose on yo' sleeve, and let dis show pro-ceed!'

'You must remember that we are only figments of his——'

Klio! klio! klio!

The gulls, the waves, the corposants, all screamed at once. The wave in Caligula's dream. The sea-ghost, seaweed-bearded, with arms of green water and dripping fingers of foam. *Oo——wash—oo—wallop*—are you awake—King Buskin? . . . And he never said a mumbalin' word. The blood came twinklin' down. And he never said a mumbalin' word . . . Tired, tortured, twisted; thirsty, abandoned, betrayed.

'—Silence! The transfiguration scene will now begin. Dress rehearsal. Special benefit performance for Mr. Demarest. At the first stroke of the bell, Miss Battiloro, arch snob and philanderer, several times engaged, virgin in fact but not in thought, she who stood on a June day perspiring and admiring, adoring and caloring, before the unfinished Titian, will take her place beneath the mainmast, on the port side, facing the stern. Her head will be bowed forward meekly, and in her hands she will clasp lightly, with exquisite Rossetti unlikelihood, a waxen lily. At the second stroke of the bell, the five angelic corposants will unite in the air above her, singing softly, as they tread the wind, the verses written by Mr. Demarest for the occasion—*King Caligula*. No weeping, by request. Listening to this heavenly music, with its message of healing for all mankind, Miss Battiloro will lift her eyes, in the attitude of one who sees, at long last, the light that never was on land or sea. While she is in this attitude, the third stroke of the bell will be given by the shipboy;

and on the instant Miss Battiloro will be trans-
formed, for all time, into a stained-glass widow.
Beg pardon, I mean window. Now is everything
in readiness, please? Shipboy, are you there?
. . . He says he is there. Is Miss Battiloro ready
to make this noble and beautiful sacrifice?'

'Ay ay, sir.'

'Miss Battiloro says she is ready to make this
noble and beautiful sacrifice. And Mr. William
Demarest—is Mr. William Demarest present?
Mr. Demarest, please?'

'Oh yes, *he's* here, all right!'

'Very well, then, we will proceed . . . Ship-
boy, the first bell, if you will be so kind!'

It was painfully true, every word of it. The
bell-note fell down from aloft, a golden ingot of
sound, and Cynthia was standing under the tall
tree as announced; like a charade for purity and
resignation; clad in white samite; and clasping
a tall lily with unimaginable delicacy. Wasn't it
perhaps, however, more Burne-Jones than Rossetti? It was a little dark, and therefore difficult
to see; but Demarest thought so. Yes. And at
the second bell-note,—three minutes having
elapsed, silent save for the hushing sound of the
waves,—Cynthia lifted her meltingly beautiful
eyes, and the five blue seraphim, treading the
night air above her, began softly, sighingly, to
sing. This was very affecting. In spite of the
warning, it was difficult to refrain from tears.
Smith, in fact, gave an audible sob, like a hic-
cough. At the words *'resting-place,'* the five
seraphs disbanded, two deploying to starboard,
two to port, and the fifth catapulting straight up

toward the zenith. At this moment, Demarest
experienced acutely a remarkable temptation. He
desired to rush forward, kneel, bury his face
passionately in the white samite, and cry out—
γύναι, ἴδε ὁ υἱός σου! Before he could do more
than visualize this action, however, the third
stroke of the bell was given. The whole night had
become a Cathedral. And above Demarest,
faintly luminous in the cold starlight that came
from beyond, was a tall Gothic window, where
motionless, in frozen sentimentalites of pink,
white, and blue, Cynthia was turned to glass.

VII

*TO his Lady, his Mother, his Wife, his Sister:
her Servant, her Child, her Lover, her
Brother, and to express all that is humble, respect-
ful, and loving, to his Cynthia, W. D. writes this.*

I

You are not ill-educated, Cynthia—if for the
first and last time you will permit me so to address you—and you will therefore recognize this
clumsy paraphrase of the salutation with which
Heloise began the first of her letters to Peter
Abelard. It is not by accident that I choose this
method of opening what will no doubt be the
last letter I address to you. For what, under the
peculiar circumstances—I refer to the fact that,
for reasons into which I forbear to inquire, your
mother and yourself have decided to drop me
from your acquaintance—what could be more likely than this beautiful exordium to persuade your
eye to read further? And that, for me, is all-im-
portant. The reasons for this you will readily
understand. Suppose this letter is delivered to
you by your stewardess. I shall be careful to
address the envelope in a style which you will not
recognize, so that you will at least not destroy it
unopened; but having opened it, is there not a
great likelihood that you will then tear it to pieces
as soon as you see from whom it comes? Yes.
And for that reason I have—let me confess at
once my iniquity, calculated iniquity!—employed

this striking method of greeting you.   It will
perhaps—that frail pontoon 'perhaps,' on which
so many desperate armies have crossed—amuse
you, perhaps even a little excite your curiosity.
You might retort, derisively, that it is odd of
me to model my salutation on that of Heloise
rather than on that of Abelard?   But unfortunately, Abelard is altogether too blunt for my purpose. He plunges in with a directness quite dis-
concertingly up-to-date; beginning with a mere
'could I have known that a letter not addressed
to you would fall into your hands.' Would this be
more likely to tempt you on, Cynthia?   Or could
I have the heart to begin, as Abelard began his
fourth epistle, 'Write no more to me, Heloise,
write no more'? . . . This would be both melancholy and absurd.

And the impulse to write to you, by way of
leave-taking, is imperious. It seems to me that I
have an infinitude of things that I must say to
you. You know how one feels on a dock, when
one sees one's friend sail away, perhaps for ever?
the regret, almost the agony, with which one remembers a few of the things one has forgotten to
say, or hadn't the courage to say? One never,
after all, told him how much one loved him. Not
even a hint. One never, after all, showed one's
simple joy in the fact that one, at least partially,
possessed him. One never so much as breathed
the suggestion that one would feel his absence.
And then, there is all the good advice that one
has forgotten to give, all the solicitude for his
future that one has somehow failed to express!
You are going to a tropical climate? Do not for-

get your cork helmet and your parasol! Remember, when you get up in the morning, to empty the scorpions out of your boots! . . . You are going to the North Pole? Be sure, then, to take a thermos flask filled with hot rum and coffee, and plenty of almond chocolate, and your goloshes, and your heaviest woollens! . . . Nor do I mean this facetiously. The advice is usually just as stupid as this, just as useless. But it serves its purpose: no matter how clumsily administered, it serves to express the aching concern with which one sees the departure; and its expression is at once accepted as just that and nothing else. And so it is with me, Cynthia. I have never told you in so many words that I love you—partly because there was no time for it, our acquaintance being so brief and so scattered; and partly for psychological reasons: my profound sense of inferiority, my sense of filthiness, and my fear of all decisive action, all being partially responsible. And now it is too late, for I find you (again in mid-Atlantic! surely one of the most remarkable coincidences that ever befell two human creatures!) engaged to be married; and no sooner am I informed of this fact than I am 'dropped' by you—given, in fact, the 'cut direct' by your mother. Well! This has one saving grace, this magnificent disaster,—for I *can* now say, once and for all, that I love you.

Having said this much, however, I find myself oddly at a loss as to how to continue. The truth is, my imagination has dealt with you so continuously, and so strenuously, and so richly, that I have no longer any definite sense as to where, exactly, between us, the psychological boundary lies. Two

nights ago, for example, after our encounter on
the deck (where, of course, as I am in the Second
Cabin, I had no right to be) I lay awake all night,
re-enacting every scrap of our little history, and
improvising a good deal besides. In this you were
—as indeed you are in *all* my reflections—'Cynthia'; and you were admitted to an intimacy with
me (this may surprise you!) which I have vouch-
safed to no one else. As I look back on that long
orgy of self-communion, which had you as its
chief but not as its only theme, I find in its *naïveté*
a good deal that amuses me. It is a curious and
instructive fact, for example, that in that moment
of *Sturm und Drang* I should have experienced
so powerfully a desire to talk to you about my
childhood. I found myself constantly reverting to
that—babbling to you my absurd infantine confidences and secrets, as if you were—ah!—my
mother. Exactly! And isn't that the secret of
your quite extraordinary influence upon me? For
some reason which I cannot possibly analyse, you
strike to more numerous and deeper responses in
me than any other woman has done. It must be
that you correspond, in ways that only my unconscious memory identifies, to my mother, who died
when I was very small. Can it be that? . . .
Anyway, there it is; and as I sit here in my
beloved smoking-room, waited on by Malvolio,
(do you remember how, on the nice old *Silurian,*
you reproached me for sitting in the smoking-
room so much? do you remember how, one evening, we listened, standing just outside the door,
on the dark deck, to the men singing there?)—
well, as I sit here, hearing the slap of rubber quoits

on the deck above, it is again a desire to talk to
you of my childhood that comes uppermost.
Strange! It really seems to me that there is something exquisitely appropriate in this: it seems to
me that in this there might be some hope of really
touching you. I do not mean that I harbour any
hope that you will break off your engagement and
engage yourself to me. (For one thing, I am not
at all sure that I would want to marry.) Nor do
I mean anything quite so obvious as that you
should be touched *sentimentally*. No. What *do*
I mean, then? Well, I mean that this would be
the most direct, simple, and really effective mode
of establishing the right communion between us.
I don't think this is merely a circumlocution or
clumsy evasion. What I am trying to say, perhaps, is that to talk to you of my childhood—to
tell you of some one particular episode—would be
for us what the good advice regarding goloshes
was for the departing traveller: a profound symbol of intimacy. Even that is not the whole story.
For also—and here, I admit, I *do* plunge reck-
lessly into the treacherous underworld of affects
—I feel with a divine confidence that is tantamount to clairvoyance that to tell you of some
such episode would be to do you an *exquisite violence*. Why? Because I am perfectly certain that
whatever is true—I mean *idiosyncratically* true—
of me, is also deeply true of you; and my confession would therefore be your—accusation! An
impeachment which you would be the first (but
with a delighted shock) to admit.

But no—— This *is* an evasion, an attempt to
rationalize a mere feeling, *ex post facto*. The

truth is, I am confused, and scarcely for the moment know what I *do* think or feel. Unhappy? Oh, yes! as the negro spiritual says. What else could be expected? Yet I blame no one but myself for my unhappiness, and I hope I am too intelligent to suppose that my unhappiness is of any importance. Confused. My imagination darts in fifty directions, checked in each. I desire you— I hate you—I want to talk intimately with you— I want to say something horribly injurious to you . . . At one moment, it is of the purely trivial that I should like to talk to you. I should like to tell you of the amusing affair of old Smith (who was with me when I met you) and Mrs. Faubion, who sits opposite us at table; of how, last night, having made himself mildly tipsy with Guinness, he attempted to get into Mrs. Faubion's room, just as she and her room-mate (an incredible young woman!) were going to bed; how he put his foot inside her stateroom door (and such funny shoes he wears! horned like the rhino!) and tried to engage her in banter, meanwhile displaying, as if guilelessly, a purse full of gold sovereigns! At dinner, last night, he had told me of this project, and I had tried to dissuade him from it. No use. He was convinced that Mrs. Faubion was *'that sort'* . . . And this morning at breakfast, when Mrs. Faubion and I were alone, it all came out, the whole wretched story. 'What was the matter with Mr. Smith last night?' 'Matter? Was something the matter?' 'Yes! He came to our room, and got his foot inside the door, and *wouldn't* go away—all the time trying to show some gold money he had in a pocketbook! We

had to shut the door in his face! . . . Actually!
. . . And *then* he tried to come back again! I
had to threaten to ring for the steward . . .' She
looked at me, while she said this, with an air of
profound wonder and mystification, perhaps just
faintly tinged with suspicion. It puzzled her.
What could have been the matter with the old
man? And was *I* involved? . . . I suggested,
of course, that he was just a little tipsy, and urged
her to pay no attention to it. She remained, however, puzzled, and a little unconvinced . . . And
Smith! When I walked round the deck with him
later in the morning, did he say anything to me
about this tragic—for him, I assure you, tragic
—adventure? Not a word. Not a single word.
But he was unhappy, and quiet—I could see the
misery in him turning and turning round that
dreadful and brief little disaster; while he revolved in his mouth one of the 'expensive' cigars which his employer had given him as a part-
ing present . . . Well, a horrible little episode,
you will say, and why should I want to describe
it to you? Again, because I am sure it will touch
in you certain obscure chords which it touched in
me, and set us to vibrating in subconscious harmony. Pity? Horror? Wonder? A sense of
the disordered splendour and unexpectedness and
tragedy of life? All these things, Cynthia; but
chiefly the desire that we might again, as last year
at the Bach concert, *listen together*.

And of course my childhood recollection is even
better than that; for, narrated by me to you, it
constitutes the playing upon us both of a chord
unimaginably rich in stimuli. Consider some of

these. The fact that I tell you this story—(as a 'story' it is nothing,—merely, say, the description of the sailing of a whaleship from New Bedford) —puts you in the position of the mother, and me in the position of the child; but it also makes our relation that of father and daughter. Again, it makes us both *children*—brother and sister, perhaps. Or, once more, it takes the colour of a dual conspiracy, the delicious conspiracy of two adults to *become* children. Sentimental? No doubt. But the device, if anything so entirely spontaneous can be called a device, is universal. Baby talk! My baby doll! Icky fing! . . . Revolting when we detect others in this singular regression, but just the same the instinct is powerful in all of us, and given the right circumstances will betray itself without the least compunction . . . Very well, then—the right circumstances have arisen *chez moi,* and I must report to you this tiny episode taken from my childhood. Like the flowers that bloom in the spring, tra la, it seems to have no connection; but, tangential though its pertinence may be, its pertinence is none the less profound.

When my mother and father died, the children were distributed, for temporary shelter, among various relatives; and it was my good fortune to be sent for a winter to the house of my father's cousin, Stanley Bragg, in New Bedford, who had come forward with an offer to look after 'one male child.' Of course, I was at first bewildered by the abrupt change, the removal from tropics to New England, the separation from my brother and sister; but on the other hand I had always been fond of Cousin

Stanley; and his house, which I had several times visited, had always seemed to me quite the most beautiful and romantic in the world. It stood well back from County Street, concealed by elms and huge horse-chestnuts, on a high grassy terrace. On the lower lawn (and this had, to begin with, particularly fascinated me!) stood a life-sized figure of a stag, cast in dark metal. It looked very lifelike, especially when it had been wetted (as frequently in summer) by the garden-sprinkler. The garden, behind the house, was divided formally into squares by high box hedges which were full of spiderwebs and superb spiders—the latter I used to tempt out of their deep funnels of silk by twitching a strand of web with a twig: and I had the feeling that they used positively to *growl* at me. Here there was an old-fashioned chain well, like a little latticed house, overgrown with honeysuckle, which worked with a crank; and which kept up a gentle clinking while from the revolving cups on the chain it gushed forth the most delicious water. There were also fruit trees, flower-beds, a wilderness of nasturtiums round the pump, and at the end of all, before you got to the barn, grape-arbours all across the back wall,—so thickly grown that on a not *too* rainy day you could crawl in under the vines and eat grapes in shelter. In the stable, of which John was the benevolent king, were the two horses which Cousin Stanley kept; a solemn black closed coach; a light buggy, for country driving; and, in the cellar, a pig. On one wall, where the whips and harnesses were hung, was nailed a wood-carving of a large heart-shaped leaf.

The house itself was a comfortable mansard-

roofed affair, with a wide 'piazza' (on which stood
tubs of hydrangeas) and lofty rooms in which one got
impression of a good deal of white marble. Among
its wonders, for me, were the wooden shutters,
which slid magically out of the walls beside the
windows, and a great number of small carved ob-
jects of jade and soapstone and ivory, brought
from China and Japan by Cousin Stanley's father.
Best of all, however, was the attic, and its cupola.
Cupola! I remember how strange the word
sounded when I first heard it pronounced by Miss
Bendall, the housekeeper, who smelt of camphor.
It struck me as 'foreign'—a *Northern* word, surely!
—and I hadn't the remotest idea in the world how
one would go about spelling it. But from the
moment when Cousin Stanley, stooping a little (as
he was very tall) led us up the dark stairs to the
warm wooden-smelling attic, and then, with triumph (this was several years before) showed us
the cupola itself, I entertained no doubts as to its
fascinations. Miserable child, who has no cupola
for his rainy mornings! It was in itself a perfect
little house, glassed on all sides, with a window-
seat all around, so that one could sit on whatever
side one liked and look out to the uttermost ends
of the earth. Over the slate roofs of houses, one
looked steeply downhill to the harbour, the bright
masts, the blue water, the Fairhaven ferry, and
Fairhaven itself beyond. Further to the right one
saw the long red brick buildings of the cotton mills
(not so numerous as now) and then the Point,
and the Bug lighthouse, and the old fort, and the
wide blue of Buzzard's Bay. With a good glass,
one might have made out the Islands; or observe

the slow progress of a Lackawanna or Lehigh Valley tug and its string of black coal barges all the way from Fort Rodman to Cuttyhunk; or pick up the old *Gay Head* sidewheeling back from Wood's Holl, with its absurdly laborious walking-beam.

You can imagine, Cynthia, how enthralled I was with all this, and how quickly, in my absorption in such wonders, I forgot the separation from my brother and sister, and the tragedy—now far off, tiny, and soundless—which had brought it all about. It soon seemed as if I had always lived in New Bedford, with Miss Bendall and Cousin Stanley and old John (a perfect stage coachman!) and Mabel, the Irish cook, who churned the butter in the pantry. I knew every flower and spider in the garden, every branch of every tree, and whether it would hold my weight or not; and every picture in every one of the forty-odd bound volumes of Harpers which I used to take up with me to the cupola. The great black cistern, which concealed somewhere a sinister little tinkle of water, was my ocean, where I sailed a flotilla of small blue-painted boats provided by Cousin Stanley. In the evenings, there was often a game of cribbage with Cousin Stanley or Miss Bendall, or else Cousin Stanley would talk to me about ships and shipping —he was a ship-owner—and the voyages he had made as a young man. Smoking a crackling great calabash pipe, he talked rapidly and vividly; so much so that I sometimes found it difficult, afterwards, to get to sleep: my senses stimulated, my imagination full of sights and sounds. It was a result of these talks that I began, in the afternoons and on Saturdays, exploring the wharves for my-

self. With what a thrill I used to start down
Union Street, seeing, at the bottom of the mile-
long cobbled hill, the bright golden eagle of a
pilot-house! Or how entrancing to discover in
the morning, when I looked down from the cupola
before breakfast, a new four-master coming up
the harbour, with its dark sails just being dropped!

The magnificent climax to all this, however,
came early one Saturday morning—when Cousin
Stanley woke me and told me to get dressed quickly:
he 'had a surprise for me.' The big bell in the
Catholic steeple, a block away, by which I always
went to bed and got up, was striking five, and it
was just beginning to be light. What could the
surprise be? I had no idea, but I knew better
than to spoil Cousin Stanley's delight in it by asking. When I went down the stairs, he was waiting
for me in the darkness by the door, holding one
finger to his lips as a sign to me to be quiet. We
stole out, tiptoed across the piazza, and down the
flagged path to the gate, where John was waiting
for us with the buggy. 'To the Union Street
Wharf, John!' said Cousin Stanley—and instantly
I was lost in a chaos of intoxicating speculations.
Were we going to sea? but how could we, without
luggage, without even our coats or sweaters? . . .
The sky was beginning to turn pink as we turned
from North Street; the city was profoundly still;
not a sound, except for Betsy's *clip-clop* on the
asphalt and the twittering of sparrows and robins
in the elms, where a deeper darkness seemed still
to linger. But when we turned again, into the
foot of Union Street, what a difference! For there
before us, on the long confused wharf, was a scene

of the most intense activity—a whale-ship was
being made ready for the sea.

Dismounting, we plunged into the midst of this
chaos.   The ship, in which Cousin Stanley owned
a share, was the *Sylvia Lee:* she was, he told me,
pointing to her crossed spars, a brig, and one of
the last sailing vessels in the whaling trade.   Two
gangways led aboard her; and along these shuffled
a steady stream of men, carrying boxes, bundles,
small kegs, and coils of rope.   Cousin Stanley
moved away to talk with someone he knew, leaving me beside a pile of fresh wooden boxes, the
very boxes which were rapidly being shouldered
aboard.   Shouts, cries, commands, a fracas of
voices—how did they manage to hear one another?
A man with a brown megaphone was leaning over
the bow rail of the brig (the white bowsprit pointed
up Union Street) and shouting 'Mr. Pierce! Mr.
Pierce!' . . . Where was Mr. Pierce? and what
was he wanted for? and who was the man with
the megaphone?   The tops of the masts were now
struck by the sun, and became surprisingly brilliant, orange-coloured, in contrast with the still-
sombre wharf and the dark hulk of the vessel herself.   Seagulls fluttered and swooped, quarrelling,
around the stern, where a man in a white jacket
had emptied a pail of garbage.   These too, when
they rose aloft, entered the sunlight and became
flamingo-coloured.   'Mr. Pierce! . . . Mr. Pierce!
Is Mr. Pierce there?' I became anxious about
Mr. Pierce.   What if he should arrive too late?
It might be something terribly important.   'Jones!
send one of your men up to the office, will you, and
see if Mr. Pierce is there.   If he is, tell him I

haven't got my papers yet. At once!' Where
was Jones? I heard no reply from him, but there
must have been one, lost in the general hubbub,
for the megaphone seemed to be appeased. Only
for a moment, however: it reappeared immediately
on the high deck of the stern, before the deck-
house. 'Now then men, make it lively. I want
those gangways cleared in five minutes . . . Mr.
Jones, will you see that the slack in that cable
is taken in.' . . . A block began a rhythmic chirping in the bow,—two men, leaning backward,
pulled in short, hard pulls at a rope. The pile of
boxes beside me was diminishing—a dozen, ten,
eight, six—condensed soup.

'Well, Billy! Shall we go aboard?'

This was the moment of Cousin Stanley's delight, and in reply I could do nothing but grin.
Was he serious? I didn't like to commit myself,
one way or the other.

'Come along, then!' he added, and led the way
to the bow gangway, which was now clear. It
consisted merely of two great planks lashed together at the ends, and it swayed, when we reached
the middle, with a shortening rhythm which
seemed disquietingly to come up to meet one's
foot in mid-air. In the dirty water between wharf
and ship a lot of straw, bottles, and some lemon-
peels rose and fell, suckingly. I felt dizzy. I was
glad to jump down from the broad black bulwark
to the weatherworn deck. We walked aft, and
climbed up the short companionway to the poop.

'Good morning, Captain! Just about ready,
eh?'

'Mornin', Stanley. Yep—tug should be here

now. . . . There she is, too. You haven't seen
Pierce, have you?'

'Pierce? No. Why?'

'He hasn't brought my—'

The little tug *Wamsutta* (old friend of mine)
floundered astern of us with ringing bells and a
sudden up-boiling of foam over her reversed pro-
pellers. The pilot was leaning out of his little
window, shouting, a corn cob in his fist. The
Sylvia Lee began swaying a little, agitatedly, with
creaking hawsers. The Captain turned his megaphone toward the *Wansutta* and spoke quietly—

'I'll be ready in five minutes, Peter . . . Mr.
Jones, get your men aboard. Has Mr. Pierce
been found?'

'Yes, sir. He's just goin' aboard.'

'All right. When he's off, throw out your gangways, and be ready to give Peter a hand. And
have some men standing by to cast off.'

'Yes sir.'

The wharf had suddenly become perfectly silent.
A dozen men stood motionless, in a group, watching us with an air of profound wonder, as if already
we had passed out of their lives and become something remote, unexplained, transcendental. One of
the last of the whale-ships! But we were something more than that—we were a departing world,
the moon taking its first flight from the earth. And
I felt myself that I belonged to the *Sylvia Lee*, and
was at last taking leave of everything familiar, setting forth at daybreak toward the unimaginable,
the obscure, the unattainable. *Islands* somewhere!
the Islands of the Blest! or wherever it was that
old Ulysses went, beyond the Pillars of Hercules—

those same islands that I still dream about periodically, lying in mid-Atlantic, two fair green isles
divided by a deep strait, and inhabited by a tall
race of surpassing beauty! Was it something like
this I thought of? The *Wamsutta* had come puffing
alongside, its bell ringing twice and then once and
then three times; the hawsers were cast off and fell
swashing into the dirty water; and the *Sylvia Lee*,
trembling, began to glide stern-foremost into the
breezy harbour. The men waved their caps and
shouted farewells. 'So long, Mike! Don't lose
your false teeth!' 'Don't forget to tell Jim what
I told you!' 'So long, boys! We'll be back for
the next election!' ' So long! So long!' . . .
Phrases were replaced by shouts, and then the
shouts by wavings; and as the *Wamsutta* turned
us handily about in midstream, and then strode
ahead of us with easier puffs and lengthening tow-
rope, a pandemonium of bells and whistles gave us
a wild salute. Good-bye, New Bedford! Good-
bye, Acushnet River! We're rolling down to Rio,
rolling down to the Horn, racing north to the Pole,
where the icebergs grind screaming together and
the right whale breaches through a sheet of ice and
snow! . . . The lighthouse-keeper in the 'Bug' ran
out on his lowest circular balcony and blew his
little tin foghorn three times as we passed, and then,
waving his arm, shouted something unintelligible.
He looked very small, and his dinghy, bowing on
the end of its painter under the balcony, seemed
no bigger than a peasepod. I felt that I was leaving this too forever; and the gaunt scarred rocks
of Fairhaven, which smelt so deliciously of kelp
at low tide, where I had so often explored the salt

pools; and Fort Rodman, where the tiny blue sentry crept back and forth by the barracks like a toy. Good-bye, good-bye! William Demarest is going away on the *Sylvia Lee;* you will never again see him driving on the Point Road, or gathering scallop shells on the salt beach that looks westward toward Padanaram. Never again, Never again.

Away on the *Sylvia Lee!* We had cleared the Point already, and now we could glance up the deep inlet that led to Padanaram and Dartmouth. Further off, on our starboard bow, lay the low green brightening shore of Nonquitt, with its Elephant Rock, its Spindle, its rickety little wharf, its mosquitoes, and its bog full of red lilies and orchis. I tried to make out the Spindle, with its little keg on top of the iron pole, but it was too far away. Farewell, Nonquitt! We are whalers sailing away to perils and wonders in uncharted seas! . . . Cousin Stanley suddenly lifted me up so that I could see into one of the whaleboats, with its rusty harpoons and tub of coiled rope. Mr. Jones and the Captain were beside us; and Mr. Pierce, who had not gone ashore after all.

'She doesn't look very smart, does she?' said the Captain. He rubbed a harsh finger on the blistered gunwale. 'But there'll be plenty of time for paintin' and polishin' between here and Valparaiso . . . I think if you're goin' to get some breakfast, Stanley——'

'Yes. I suppose we'd better have it. Like some breakfast, Billy?'

Breakfast! a deep qualm opened within me like a kind of marsh-flower. I sudddnly became conscious of the fact that I was on a *ship*. We went

down a steep stairway into the officers' saloon,
gloomy and evil-smelling, where a red and pink
tablecloth covered a long table. At the forward
end, the table abutted on a slant mast-root which
was beautifully encased in varnished and inlaid
wood, and around which ran a little mahogany
tumbler-rack, like a verandah. But the smell was
appalling! The smell of whale-oil, perhaps, which,
after years of whale-voyaging, had saturated the
ship. My gorge rose, and I was terrified lest, on
a calm day, with no excuse whatever, I should disgrace myself by being sick. I sat down gingerly.
The idea of eating food became abhorrent to me;
the bread looked dusty and hard, the corned-beef a
thousand years old; the dishes, too, were thick and
greyish, somehow oppressive. And then, to have
corned-beef, and boiled potatoes, with their skins
imperfectly removed, for breakfast! In a state of
passive weakness, not daring to move or speak lest
the paroxysm should seize me, I allowed Mr. Jones
to give me corned-beef and potatoes. Reluctantly,
I raised my fork to begin, when the cook (the man
in the white jacket whom I had seen emptying the
pail of garbage!) put down before me a thick china
bowl, full of *melted butter*. Into this he dropped a
dull leaden spoon. 'Help yourself, sonny!' he said.
'Whale-oil.' Incontinently, I raised my hand to
my mouth, and felt myself on the point of giving
that horrible little crow which is the prelude to
disaster. My mouth drew itself together—I felt
my tongue cold against my cold palate—and then
I rose and fled. Disgraced! The laughter that
followed me up the steep stairway was kindly,
however, and as I stood again by the bulwark in

the fresh wind I forgot that momentary discomfort in the sheer romanticism of the voyage. Valparaiso! Was it really possible? These sails, which the men were now breaking out one by one, and which now gently filled with the following wind, and shifted a little with a settling creak of spars long unused, these sails would carry the *Sylvia Lee* all the way to Tierra del Fuego, and round the Horn to Valparaiso. What would Union Street seem like then, with its little green streetcars? Would the men remember Buttonwood Park, and the bears, and the motor-paced bicycle races at the bicycle track? Would they talk about these things, or long for them, these things which were now so commonplace and real? Would these things then seem as distant and incredible as Valparaiso seemed now? . . .

Well, Cynthia—I draw to the end of this simple narrative. I find myself losing heart or losing impetus. What if, after all, the impulse to tell of it should seem to you rather silly? . . . Yet, at the last minute, it had its thrill of terror, which perhaps more than anything else served to make it memorable. For when the sails had all been spread, and the tow-rope had been cast off, and the *Wamsutta* drew away to starboard and stopped, her nose pointing toward Cuttyhunk, it was then that the greatest moment came. One of the whaleboats was manned and lowered into the sea; into this we clambered, Mr. Pierce and Cousin Stanley and I; and the men pulled away toward the waiting tug. The *Sylvia Lee* hung enormous above us, her sails flapping, as we drew out from her shadow; but I now paid little attention to the beautiful tall ship, for I had discovered that the whale-boat was leaking, leaking fast! In a moment I had to draw up my feet. Before we had gone half the distance to the *Wamsutta* we had taken in about four inches of water. Were we sinking? Would we get there before we sank? What astonished me was the indifference of the men at the oars— they sat with their feet in the swashing water and hauled stolidly away as if nothing whatever were occurring. I felt, therefore, that it would be a breach of etiquette to comment, or show anxiety, and I scarcely knew *what* attitude to take toward Mr. Pierce's humorous observation that it looked 'as if they were trying to drown us.' It hardly seemed a subject for joking. I was measuring the water, measuring the gap between us and the *Wamsutta;* and seldom have I experienced such an acute sensation of relief as when we drew along-side and climbed aboard in a smell of oil and hot-breathing engines. More remarkable still, how-ever, was the fact that the men in the whaleboat did not pause to bail out the water—which was now half-way up their legs—but at once turned the heavy boat about and started back again. How slowly, how laboriously, she seemed to creep! By the time they had come up once more with the *Sylvia Lee* her gunwales were only a foot out of water. They were safe, however—we saw them climb briskly aboard. And then we saw the boat being hauled up, while one man bailed with a pail, flinging great scoops of hollow silver over the side; and at once, majestically, with filling sails, the *Sylvia Lee* bore away. The men waved to us and shouted—the *Wamsutta* blew three vibrating blasts

of her whistle—and while the ship moved statelily southward, we turned and chug-chugged back toward New Bedford.   Good-bye, *Sylvia Lee!* . . . Good-bye indeed.   For the *Sylvia Lee* was destined to be one of the tragedies of the sea.   None of the men who sailed away with her ever returned.   No one ever knew how she was wrecked.   All that was found of her, two years later, west of the Horn, was the fragment of sternplate that bore her name.
(Not sent.)

II

MY DEAR MISS BATTILORO:
    You will be surprised to learn that this is the second letter which I have written to you to-day —and that to the writing of the first (which I have decided not to send to you, and which I am not sure I *ever* intended to send) I devoted several hours.   This behaviour must seem to you very peculiar.   Indeed, it seems peculiar to me, though I am (if anybody is!) in a position to understand it.   Why should I be writing you letters at all? Why on earth?   It is easy for me to put myself in your place (bad dramatist though I am) and I can therefore without the least difficulty imagine the mixture of bewilderment, curiosity, contempt, and annoyance, or even *shame*, shame for me, with which you will receive this last of my underbred antics.   Why in God's name should this upstart young man (not so young either), this mere ship's acquaintance, this New Englander with intermittent manners, presume to write to *you*? you who so habitually and unquestioningly regard yourself as one of the world's chosen few?   And how en-

tirely characteristic of him that instead of coming
to see you he should *write*,—send you, merely from
one end of a ship to another, a morbidly and mawk-
ishly self-conscious letter! . . . All of which is
perfectly just, as far as it goes; and I doubt whether
I can find any very adequate defence. You have,
of course, an entire right to drop me without advancing reasons. Who among us has not exercised
that privilege of selection? If the manner in
which you have administered the 'cut' seems to me
extraordinarily ill-bred and uncharitable, who am
I that I should rebuke you for a want of courtesy?
I have been rude myself. I have even, occasionally, to rid myself of a bore, been inexcusably cruel.
One must, at times, defend oneself at all costs,
and I recognize perfectly that this has seemed to
you an occasion for the exercise of that right.
Ah! (you will say) but if you admit all this, why
talk about it? Why not take your medicine in
silence, like a gentleman? . . . Well, I could reply that as I seem to have lost in your eyes the
privileges of a gentleman, I have therefore lost
also the gentleman's obligations; and as you have
put me in the position of an outcast, I might as
well make a virtue of necessity, and, as a final
gesture of pride, haul up the Jolly Roger.

But no—that's not exactly what I mean. Why
is it that I seem always, in trying to say the sim-
plest things, to embroil myself in complications
and side-issues, in references and tangents, in qualifications and relativities? It is my weakness as
an author (so the critics have always said) that I
appear incapable of presenting a theme energeti-
cally and simply. I must always wrap it up in

tissue upon tissue of proviso and aspect; see it from a hundred angles; turn laboriously each side to the light; producing in the end not so much a unitary work of art as a melancholy *cauchemar* of ghosts and voices, a phantasmagoric world of disordered colours and sounds; a world without design or purpose; and perceptible only in terms of the prolix and the fragmentary. The criticism is deserved, of course: but I have often wished that the critics would do me the justice to perceive that I have deliberately aimed at this effect, in the belief that the old unities and simplicities will no longer serve. No longer serve, I mean, if one is trying to translate, in any form of literary art, the consciousness of modern man. And this is what I *have* tried to do. I am no longer foolish enough to think that I have succeeded—I am in process of adjustment to the certainty that I am going to be a failure. I take what refuge I can in a strictly psychological scrutiny of my failure, and endeavour to make out how much this is due to (1) a simple lack of literary power, or genius, or the neurosis that we give that name, and how much to (2) a mistaken assumption as to the necessity for this new literary method. What if—for example—in choosing this literary method, this deliberate indulgence in the prolix and fragmentary, I merely show myself at the mercy of a personal weakness which is not universal, or ever likely to be, but highly idiosyncratic? That is perfectly possible; and it brings me back to my starting-point. I *am* like that—I do think and feel in this confused and fluctuating way—I frequently suspect that I am nothing on earth but a case of *dementia praecox, manqué*, or

arrested. Isn't all this passion for aspects and
qualifications and relativities a clear enough symp-
tom of schizophrenia? It is as a result of my uncertain and divided attitude toward you that you
now finally wash your hands of me; the conflict in
me between the declared and the undeclared produced that callow and caddish ambiguity of behaviour which offended you. And now, in this
letter, I continue the offence! I mumble and murmur and beat round the bush—and succeed in
saying nothing. Why is it that I don't simply say
that the whole trouble has been that, from the
moment when I first saw you coming up the gangway to the *Silurian*, last year, I adored you and
was terrified by you? Yes, you terrified me. But
what use is there in analysing this? None. The
important thing is merely to say that I have loved
you, that I love you, and that I must, now that
you have dropped me, take any available way of
telling you this, no matter how much the method
may offend you.

Alas! all this is beside the point. Why is it
that I cannot, in some perfectly simple and com-
prehensive manner, tell you exactly how I feel
about you, and exactly what sort of creature I
am? One wouldn't suppose that this would present inordinate difficulties. Yet, when I set myself the task this morning, do you know what form
my unfinished letter was going to take? A long,
sentimental reminiscence of my childhood! Yes,
I actually believed for a moment that by some
such circumferential snare as that I might trap
you, bring you within my range, sting, and poison
you with the subtle-sweet poison of a shared ex-

perience and consciousness. That again is highly
characteristic of me. It is precisely the sort of
thing I am always trying to do in my writing—to
present my unhappy reader with a wide-ranged
chaos,—of actions and reactions, thoughts, mem-
ories and feelings,—in the vain hope that at the
end he will see that the whole thing represents only
one moment, one feeling, one person. A raging,
trumpeting jungle of associations, and then I announce at the end of it, with a gesture of despair,
'This is I!' . . . Is it any wonder that I am considered half mad, a charlatan, or, worse still, one
who has failed to perceive the most elementary
truth about art, namely, that its first principle is
selection? . . . And here I struggle in the same
absurd roundabout way to give you some inkling
of the springs of my behaviour, in a vain hope
that you will think better of my failure to—what?
To attract you? But I did attract you. To capture you? To avoid disgusting you? Perhaps it
is that. 'Here I am' (I might say), 'this queer
psychopathic complicated creature: honeycombed
with hypocrisies and subtleties, cowardices and
valours, cupidities and disgusts; on the whole,
harmless . . .'

But let me make a new start. Am I not, at
bottom, simply trying to *impress* you? behaving
exactly like the typical male in spring? And the
behaviour exasperated, in my case, by the fact that
I must, if possible, overcome a judgment which
has already declared itself to be adverse. However, I can see no possible escape from that predicament. *Any* behaviour, if calculated (whether
consciously or unconsciously) to attract, is in its

origin sexual. Why, then, be ashamed of it? You, yourself—since we last encountered—have been embraced by the male of your species; the sexual instinct has finally flowered in you and taken possession of you. Is there anything repugnant in this surrender? . . . To tell the truth I think there is. Whether this is a mere outcropping of Puritanism, I cannot say. It may be. Anyway, I find something essentially horrible in this complete abandonment of oneself to an instinct. Mind you, I do not for one moment deny the appalling beauty and desirability of the experience. I have known it several times, and never without ecstasy. But there is something in me which insists that this ought not to be made the centre or foundation of one's life; that it is a tyranny of the gross over the subtle; and that like every other attack on the liberty of one's spirit it ought to be met with all the forces at one's command. Must we be slaves to our passions? 'For the poor benefit of a bewitching minute,' must we give up our freedom for ever? No—and it was with all these perplexities smouldering in my eyes and heart that I first approached you, Cynthia. And more than this, I approached you with a definite and peculiar hope in my mind. Will this hope seem to you a kind of madness? Perhaps it will. What I hoped was that at last I had found a love which somehow *transcended the flesh*. Yes—I actually persuaded myself that I had captured the chimæra; and that in Cynthia and poor William the phœnix and the turtle were met anew. A beautiful, a divine illusion! One of those heavenly beliefs which, in intensity of being, makes the solidest of our realities seem insubstantial as a shade. I am not a believer in souls, nor in immortality; I have no sentimental conception of God, no religion from which to extract, for my daily needs, colour and light; yet in encountering you I felt that I could only explain what was happening to me by assuming at least a *symbolic* meaning and rightness in the treacherous word 'soul.' For was I not at once treading a brighter star? And was I not—gross Caliban that I was—endeavouring, all of a sudden, to become an Ariel? And were we not, you and I, already partaking of a direct and profound communion from the moment that we looked at each other and spoke the first casual words of greeting? This communion was so perfect, so without barriers, and so independent of our bodies, our hands, our eyes, our speech even, that for the first time since I had become a man I found myself looking, startled, into the eyes of God—the God whom I knew as a child. Of course, the habit of criticism was too deeply engrained in me to permit any such illusion to go long unchallenged. I suppose, to tell the truth, that I never really wavered at all—unless my frequent visits to Westminster Cathedral (where, however, there was the additional motive that I hoped to encounter you) can be considered a wavering. Yet, if my mind was steadfast in its refusal to abdicate, it was also wise enough, or weak enough, to allow the soul a holiday. It observed, it recorded, it even despised, but it didn't feel called upon to interfere. And in the end—this is what astonishes me!—it has come very near to believing that in this extraordinary holiday of the affections it might discover some sublime first principle of things by which the whole melancholy world might be explained and justified. This miraculous communion between us, Cynthia—was this perhaps an earnest of what was to come? I do not mean simply for us, for you and me, but for all mankind! Was it possible to guess, from this beautiful experience, that ultimately man would know and love his brother; that the barriers of idiosyncrasy and solipsism, the dull walls of sense, would go down before the wand of Prospero? This possibility seemed to me not merely a thing to be desired, but a necessity! And what obstacles lay between us and this divine understanding? Only one—the Will. When we sufficiently *desired* this communion, when at last we realized the weakness and barrenness of the self, we could be sure that we would have sufficient wisdom to accomplish the great surrender.

To what pitch of intensity this illusion, this belief, this doctrine of sublimation, was brought in me by my loss of you—if truly it can be said that I have lost you!—may be suggested to you when I tell you of a very peculiar experience which I had last night. I do not deny that I had taken a drink or two. Whisky is a useful anodyne. And after a whole day of concentrated misery it became pressingly necessary to break the continuity of my thought. I had sat too long in one place in the smoking-room, keeping a watch through the half-opened window for a glimpse of your striped and diamonded Hindu jersey—and what a pang I suffered when at last I saw it, worn by your friend! Was that an intentional twist of the knife? No, of course not—it was an accident. But I had sat

thus too long, and for too long I had blown round
and round in one fixed vortex of thoughts and feelings.   The only relief I had known all day was
a talk with Silberstein, a Jew, and a fellow-passen-
ger of yours—a rather remarkable man: a seller of
'chewing-sweets' and a chess-player.   But, though
I (to some extent consciously) sought release by
talking of myself with reckless freedom to Silberstein, I had found no real comfort in it, nor had I
found any more, at dinner, in the company of
Smith and Mrs. Faubion.   It is perfectly true—I
may as well confess it—that Mrs. Faubion (vulgar
little strumpet that she is) attracts me; and I discovered last night at dinner, with a gleam of delight which not even my prevailing misery could
extinguish, that Mrs. Faubion is attracted by *me*.
An extraordinary reflection on the deep pluralism
of things, life's contrapuntal and insoluble richness!   Here, in the very crisis of a passion, a passion which is as nearly all-absorbing as a passion
can be, I pause for a moment's delicious flirtation
with *another* woman!   Nor is it so simple a thing
as flirtation, either—it is darker and stronger than
that, a deep current of mutual delight, which
might easily, and might well, sweep us off our feet.
We know this as we look at each other—we tacitly
admit it.   Between meals we always avoid each
other, just as we always avoid any but the dullest
banter, because we both know that to take any
step whatever would be to be lost.   Well! last
night I was in no mood to be lost—lost in this
sense.   And when Mrs. Faubion—who *was* in a
mood to be lost—touched my foot with hers under
the table, I made no response, pretended that I

thought it was an accident. Of course, it *may* have been an accident—but I sincerely doubt it. No, it was unmistakable . . . I rejected, then, this gay little overture from the pluralistic universe, not because it was in itself unattractive, but because—well, why, exactly? A psychologist might say that it was because my nervous system was at the moment too acutely in the state known as a 'motor set'—a motor set which was directed to a woman named Cynthia. That is one way of putting it. My mandibles were poised, and pointed and ready to spring, but only in that one direction, and on receipt of that one stimulus. Mrs. Faubion, it is true, *might* have sprung the trap. I quite seriously entertained the thought. But I foresaw, or thought I foresaw, a more than usually swift disillusionment, followed by a horrible agony of self-reproach. She would satisfy, for the fleetingest of instants, the blind animal maw; but the mind, or soul, or whatever you like to call it, would be cheated, and being cheated would be even wretcheder than before. I do not pretend that I thought this out at the time as clearly as I think it out now for you. I merely felt the thing in an image or warm coalition of images, in a pang or an inkling of a pang, as I talked with Mrs. Faubion, withdrew my foot reluctantly, and met her sombre eyes in a gaze a little too protracted. And I was saddened by it, and further and still more deeply saddened, when old father Smith confessed to me once more his amorous desire for her, and outlined for me the ugly little scheme by which he hoped to gain possession of her. A sinister and sorry little tangle! Demarest in hopeless pursuit

of Cynthia, whose eyes were fixed on—whom? a
captain in the Belgian army? while Smith desired
Faubion, and Faubion (*pour mieux s'amuser*) rested
her dark gaze on the absent-hearted Demarest.
Why must things be like this? Why, Cynthia?
I returned after a while to the smoking-room, where
men were singing smutty songs and telling smutty
stories—where, in fact, as invariably occurs, the
whole world was being reduced to its lowest common denominator—and drank whisky, meditating
on these things. If only—I thought—we had some
subtler medium than language, and if only we
weren't, all of us, little walled fortresses self-centred
and over-sensitive and so perpetually on the defen-
sive! If only we could more freely *give* ourselves,
more generously, without shame or stint! . . .
And it was out of these confused reflections, which
were not so much reflections as feelings, that my
peculiar experience developed, the peculiar little
experience which I have approached in so roundabout a way, and of which in the end I shall have
so absurdly little to tell you. For what did it
amount to? Only this—that I had a kind of
waking dream, one so vivid that it was almost a
hallucination. A cynic would say of it that it was
simply the result of whisky. But it was more
than that, though I freely admit that whisky had
broken down certain inhibitions and permitted to
my unconscious a greater freedom. I was on the
point of going to bed, when I decided to take a
sniff of fresh air—up to the hurricane deck I went,
therefore, disregarding once more the barriers;
and there, as I stood in the marvellous darkness,
alone in the world, alone with my ridiculous tran-

sitory little unhappiness, I indulged myself in a
phantasy. I was then, suddenly, no longer alone.
You were there, Cynthia, and so was Faubion, and
so too were Smith and Silberstein. We were all
there: but we were all *changed*. For when I first
moved toward you, among the lifeboats, under the
autumnal stars which seemed to gyrate slowly
above us, I heard you—astonishing!—exchanging
quotations from the Greek Anthology. Could it
be true? It was true—all four of you had achieved
a divine intimacy, a divine swiftness and beauty
of mutual understanding and love, so that your
four spirits swayed and chimed together in a
unison, unhurried and calm, which made of the
whole nocturnal universe a manifest wisdom and
delight. I too participated in this gentle diapason,
this tranquil sounding of the familiar notes, but
my part was a timid one, less practised, and I felt
that I had not yet sufficiently passed out of myself to move as freely as you others among dark-
nesses become luminous and uncertainties become
certain. I still loved myself too much to love the
world; too desperately struggled, still, to understand my own coils, and therefore, found the world
obscure. But I did participate, a little, and I
listened with joy. It was a miracle. These four
utterly dissimilar beings, these four beings whose
desires were in conflict, nevertheless understood
each other perfectly, loved each other angelically,
uttered one another's thoughts and faintest feelings as readily as their own, and laughed together,
gently, over their own profoundest griefs! What
could I do but worship that vision? For the vision
was indeed so vivid that for an instant I wholly

forgot that all this excellence had come out of my
own heart, and I could joyfully give myself to a
pure worship. Only for an instant, alas! for
abruptly the phantasy began to go wrong. A jar-
ring note was sounded, a note of jeering corruption and hatred, then the clashing of individual
will with will. As sometimes in a dream one is
aware that one is dreaming, so I began to feel my
own ugly idiosyncrasies which underlay each of
these four beings, and to see that they were only
projections of myself; and though I could continue
the phantasy, and indeed was compelled to do so,
I could no longer direct it; darker powers in my
heart had taken command of it. The beautiful
harmony which love and wisdom had achieved,
and of which it seemed to me that they were about
to make something final and perfect, became a
nightmare in which my own lusts and hatreds
shaped events swiftly toward a nauseating climax.
The scene was a parody of the Crucifixion—and of
a good deal else. I find it impossible to analyse
completely, for a great deal of its meaning, at the
end, was in the insupportable ugliness of its *tone*.
In this horrible scene, I beheld you transfigured,
Cynthia — turned into a stained-glass widow!
What can have been the significance of that?
Does it represent simply an effort to sublimate my
love of you? Or was it—as I suspect—intended
to show that this attempt at a sentimental sublimation could only partially succeed? Certainly, it
presented you, or my conception of you, in a very
unattractive light. Perhaps that is tantamount
to saying that it presented *me* in a very unattractive light. I was pillorying myself for hypocrisy.

Perhaps I was—or certain darker forces in me, a
profounder and truer animal honesty—perhaps
these were taking their revenge by wrecking this
pretty dream of a 'perfect communion.' Anyway,
it is true that shortly before this waking dream I
had been pondering the question of sublimation
versus immersion. How can we possibly decide
which is the better course to pursue? Shall we
take the way of art, and lie, and try to make life
as like the lie as we can—remould it nearer to the
child's desire—or shall we take the way of nature,
and *love?* Love, I mean, savagely with the body!
. . . You can call that a quibble, if you like, replying that it is not really a question as between
art and nature, but between two aspects of nature
—the more primitive and the less primitive. But
it makes no difference how you phrase it: the problem is there, and is insoluble. At one end savagery
—at the other hypocrisy? Hypocrisy fine-branch-
ing and beautiful as coral, hypocrisy become an infinitely resourceful art? Either extreme is for us
unreachable, or untenable if reached. We must
struggle and fluctuate in the Limbo between—saving ourselves now and then from an art of life too
fine-drawn by a bath of blood; or from an awareness and control too meagre by a deliberate sup-
pressing of our lusts, a canalization of those ener-
gies . . . And never, at any time, knowing exactly
where we stand, what we believe in, or who we are.

It is to this awful dilemma that my failure with
you has brought me. Of this schism in my nature,
which has always been known to me, I have now
become acutely and horribly and unintermittently
conscious . . . What shall I do? Shall I go on,

half-civilized liar that I am, and add a few more
reefs of flowery coral to my already disgracefully
massive production, and thus help deluded mankind to add delusion to delusion?   Or shall I turn
back, and do my best to destroy this terrible struc-
ture of hypocrisy? . . . I think, Cynthia, I will
turn back.   I think I must turn my back on you.
I think I must decide, once and for all, that though
you are beautiful, and though I have fixed my
heart on you as on nothing and no one else, you
are a sham, a fraud, an exquisite but baseless, or
nearly baseless, work of art.   A living lie.   A beautiful betrayal of nature.   A delicious fake . . . I
remember that you refused to have tea with me,
at a Lyons or A.B.C., because they were 'such
grubby little places' . . . But as for me, I like
them; and the grubbier the better.

(Not sent.)

III

DEAR MISS BATTILORO:
    To say that I am astonished by what has oc-
curred is to put it mildly.   What have I done which
could so offend you that you must 'cut' me?
Heaven knows I have enough 'inferiority complex'
to enable me to supply my own explanations—as
far as *that* is concerned, I could find sufficient excuse for it were the whole world to conspire against
me.   But that is not the same thing.   I should
prefer to know—if you could bring yourself to tell
me—what it is that has moved *you* to this sudden
action.   Do I, in asking this, expect too much?
Perhaps I do.   I remember only too well—as I remember every episode of our brief acquaintance—

how, as we left the Wigmore Hall, after the concert,
you made me run with you, positively *run*, so that
you could avoid someone by whom you didn't wish
to be seen. This, at the time, rather disconcerted
me. It brought pretty sharply before my eyes
a feature in your character which alternately
frightened, attracted, and repelled me, and which
I had taken some care not to examine too closely.
This was—is—your snobbishness. Well—now *I*
am to be sacrificed on this exquisite altar, in this
exquisite pre-Raphælite boudoir-chapel of yours! Is
that it? Perhaps you think I have been remiss in
not coming to see you, or in failing to salute you
yesterday morning? But I *have* tried, several times,
to find you, in vain. I am in the Second Cabin,
and therefore I cannot too freely wander about in
your precincts. As for the other matter, I am
simply too shy.

I mention these points in the very faint hope
that the whole thing may have been an unfortunate misunderstanding. If that is the case, I
am heartily sorry. But I know, at the bottom of
my heart, that it is something more than that.
It may even be—why in Heaven's name not?—
that you have taken a dislike to me. But if you
consider—no, there is no use in considering. I
was on the point of advancing our delightful acquaintance of last summer as a kind of claim upon
you, and suggesting that, these things being so,
it would be only decent of you to give me some
hint of an explanation. But, as I abruptly see,
one does not, when one decides to cut a friend,
hand him a nice little note of explanation. One
just cuts him; with a hard eye. Exactly as you,

and your estimable mother, have done to me.
And if he presume to *ask* for an explanation—as
I am doing—why that only makes it more appar-
ent that the cut was required.

But it occurs to me, belatedly, that in such a
situation as this I ought to show myself possessed
of a certain amount of pride. And so I am. I
am not lacking in *amour-propre*. I suffer from
that form of egotism which vacillates between an
excessive vanity and a humility equally excessive.
And as a matter of fact, the injury you have done
me is so deep that even should the whole affair
now turn out to be a mistake, even were you to
apologize, I could never forgive you and never
again quite respect you. I may not cease to love
you—why need I any longer conceal this, which
may have been the point from which your action
has sprung—but already a profound hatred has
joined itself to my love. I shall hate you, loathe
you, despise you, as I have never hated before.
Pride! If we encounter again, you will see that
I have plenty of it. It will be Satanic. And if
any smallest opportunity ever occurs, I will revenge myself upon you, 'after no common action,'
with the deftest psychological cruelty: for I am
a master of that art, I am by nature cruel. That
I will still be in love with you will not in the least
prevent this. You have behaved like a char-
woman. And if only once I may have the chance
to treat you as such, to cut you face to face, to
turn my back on you, it may be that I shall thus
be able to rid myself of you for ever, and recover
my lost self-esteem. It may be that I——

(NOT FINISHED).

IV

I am extremely sorry that things should have turned out like this. I am sorry for any sins of omission, on my part, which may have brought it about; though I am at a loss to know what they may be. I am sorriest, however, that you should have felt it necessary to *cut* me, as if I were the most ordinary of ill-bred nuisances. Good Heavens! That is a new and illuminating experience, and one from which I hope greatly to profit. You need not have feared that I would ever become trouble-some—I am sufficiently sensitive to know when others want to be rid of me, and I usually know it long before they know it themselves. To be misprised in *that* sense is an extreme surprise to me. But not so surprising, perhaps, as the find-ing how deeply I have misprised *you*.

(*Not sent.*)

V

Sick transit!

(NOT SENT.)

VI

. . . . . .

(NOT WRITTEN.)

VIII

DEMAREST sat alone in the dim-lighted
smoking-room. A calf-bound octavo lay on
the green table before him, opened at page 544.
On the black skylight, a heavy rain rattled: drumming dripping pattering whimpering. It was not
loud enough, however, to drown out the gusts of
music that came upstairs fitfully from below, where
the masquerade ball was in progress. In fact, he
could hear Hay-Lawrence's voice—Hay-Lawrence
was now a *chef*—in shrill imitation of broken Gallic
English, followed by a spate of expostulatory
French. Demarest smiled. How admirable, to
be able to throw oneself into a thing like that!
With so little self-consciousness! He could see,
in his mind's eye, the absurd actions with which
Hay-Lawrence must be accompanying that fury
of sound—the shrugged shoulders, the palms lifted
and narrowed, the eyebrows extravagantly arched.
'*Mais oui!*' Hay-Lawrence positively squealed
the *oui*; and then was heard no more, lost in a
combined outrage of rain and ragtime. Of course,
he must be delighted at the chance to show off his
excellent French . . . What was that tune. *An
Old-Fashioned Garden*. Modern Bach. Drumming dripping pattering whimpering. Running
whipping spattering scampering. 'First, for the
scene' (he read), 'a *landtschap* consisting of small
woods, and here and there a void place filled with

huntings: which falling, an artificial sea was seen
to shoot forth, as if it flowed to the land, raised
with waves which seemed to move, and in some
places the billows to break, as imitating the orderly
disorder which is common in nature. In front of
this sea were placed six tritons, in moving and
sprightly actions, their upper parts human, save
that their hairs were blue, as partaking of the
sea-colour: their desinent parts fish, mounted above
their heads, and all varied in dispositions. From
their backs were borne out certain light pieces of
taffeta, as if carried by the wind, and their music
made out of wreathed shells. Behind these, a pair
of sea-maids, for song, were as conspicuously seated;
between which, two great sea-horses, as big as the
life, put forth themselves; the one mounting aloft,
and writhing his head from the other, which seemed
to sink forward; so intended for variation, and that
the figure behind might come off better: upon their
backs, Oceanus and Niger were advanced.' An admirable descriptive prose! And what impudence
to assert that there was no prose before Dryden!
Great sea-horses as big as the life. And the orderly disorder which is common in nature . . .

Silberstein, in a dinner-jacket, entered laconically; with a cigar, on which the red-and-gold band
was intact. In a dinner-jacket, with plump shirt,
he looked more than ever batrachian. Brek-ek-
ek-ek. He sauntered, he rolled, he twinkled, he
trolled. Drumming dripping pattering whimpering. In an old-fashioned garden.

'I don't blame you,' he said. 'I never saw such
a lousy collection in my life. Hay-Lawrence is
pretty good, though.'

'He looks the part to a T.'

'I don't speak French myself, but I guess he slings it about as well as the froggies do?'

'It sounds all right to me. Have you been dancing?'

'No. I gave them the up-and-down—there's nobody there worth looking at, except that little Irish kid and Mrs. Faubion. And, of course, your friend the Welsh Rarebit. By Godfry, she's got up fit to kill!'

Drip drop drip drop. An old-fashioned garden in the rain.

'Have you seen her? . . . Hello—there she is. Mrs. Davis! *Mrs. Davis!*'

Mrs. Davis, a Hawaiian clad in swishing grass, with a white rose in her black hair and a purple Japanese lantern in each hand, leaned coyly through the doorway, one leg lifted behind her. Scarlet slippers. Then she was gone again.

The glass-eyed poker-player came in, looking angrily about the room, and four others. Also Smith, soft-stepping in the rear, drawing back a little to avoid getting mixed with the game. He had been out in the rain—he had on his tweed hat and a rain-splashed raincoat. After him came a trampling troup of others, refugees from the dance. The thirsty hour was beginning to summon them.

'Didn't see you at the dance,' said Smith, dropping off his coat.

'No, I'm not a dancing man.'

'The little girl was asking me where you were—says she's mad at you.'

'Mrs. Faubion?'

'Sure. Who'd you think? Looks nice too.

Got on one of those blue embroidered mandarin cloaks, and nice little white silk pantaloons.'

'She's the best-looking thing there,' said Silberstein, 'which isn't saying much.'

'She's all right! Yes, sir, she's all right. And she can dance, too. I wish I could dance—I'm too old to learn these new-fangled things. But I'd sure like to dance with her.'

'Well, gentlemen, I think I'll slide for home. I'll see you in the morning, if the rain doesn't sink us. Good night.'

'Good night!'

'Good night.'

Silberstein departed in a rattle of rain: the *Long, Long Trail* came mournfully up the stairs: a cork popped.

'Have a game?' said Smith. 'He makes me tired, swelling in here with his dress suit.'

'No, not to-night, thanks. I haven't got the energy. Lazy as a nigger.'

'Lazy as a nigger! Ever seen niggers work in the gangs down south?'

'Yes, I have.'

'They sure can work—when they want to.'

'Oh, I have the greatest respect for the nigger. I'm all for him.'

'He's all right in the fields and the servants' quarters. Yes, siree!'

'The negro has genuis—give him a chance and he'll prove it.'

'Genius! I never noticed it. Give him a chance, and he gets too uppish.'

'Oh, I don't agree with you. When he's uppish, it's only because he imitates the bad manners with which he's been treated.'

Smith looked astonished.

'You don't know what you're talking about!
You ought to live down south.'

'I *have* lived down south.'

'Well then, you ought to know better. Give
him an inch and he'll take an ell.'

'Why shouldn't he?'

'Why shouldn't he! . . . Do you think he's
the equal of the white man?'

'Potentially, certainly! Good Lord, he's only
had a generation or two of freedom, scarcely any
schooling, and look what he's done already! His
folk songs are the only American music, practically,
that's worth a toot.'

'Just plain savagery, that's what it is, and I'm
surprised you fall for it. You come down and
live with them and look for their genius! Genius
my hat! They're black, and don't you forget
it.'

'What difference does *that* make?'

'A whole lot! You can't let them mix. Got to
keep them in their place.'

'Nonsense. They're human beings, like any
others. You can't condemn a whole race because
of their colour! Good Lord, I never heard anything so childish!'

'Childish! Would you sit down to dinner with
a nigger?'

'Certainly! I not only would, but I *have*.'

Smith stared.

'What! Well, no self-respecting man would.
No sir.'

'I suppose you're one of these people who feel
the same way about the Chinese and Japanese.'

'Sure. To hell with them. They're yellow—
they're not white . . . Good God, sitting down to
dinner with a nigger! Will you listen to that!'

Smith turned his head, showing a disposition to
draw in, as witnesses, the men at the next table.
His voice had become louder. Demarest felt himself flushing.

'Certainly. The negro I sat down to dinner
with was a human being, and as civilized and intellectual a man as you could find. And a man
very widely known.'

'Every man to his own taste, as the farmer said
when he kissed the pig! I suppose next you'll
say it was an honour to sit down with him!'

'So it was.'

'You'll have to excuse me. That's hot air. You
just fool yourself. Now look here. Suppose you
had a sister——'

'I *have* a sister.'

'All right—you have a sister. Suppose she
wanted to marry a coon, would you let her? . . .
You know you wouldn't.'

'I admit I've got strong enough primitive racial
feelings in me to make me feel that any crossing
of species is a mistake. And I'd certainly do my
best to make HER feel this, and to make her see
the social consequences of such a marriage. But
if she realized all that, I don't see that I would have
any further business to interfere. No. She's an
adult, and can manage her own life. I should regret the step, for various reasons, but among them
would not be any feeling that the negro is something sub-human. Not at all!'

'Oh, good Lord deliver me! Did you hear that,

you people? This man says he wouldn't mind if
his sister married a nigger!'

There was a mild, embarrassed laugh at the next
table, and Demarest felt himself flushing under
the scrutiny of amusedly hostile eyes. Loss of
caste—this was what the smiling eyes said, but
almost as if apologetically. He was made to feel,
for a flash, the isolation with which a race punishes
its individuals for excessive individualism, for dis-
obeying totem and taboo. Outcast. Pariah . . .
How idiotic of him, to discuss such a thing, with
such a man, in such a place! Served him right.
Drip drop. Drop drip. Better fill and light his
pipe with ostentatious calm and care, and let them
see his large new splendid tobacco-pouch! the un-
hurrying fingers manipulating the sea-damp tobacco, with percipient care for every shred!

Smith, guessing that he had gone a little too far,
watched, unseeing, the fingers working in the
pouch. But the scene was now beyond mitiga-
tion. He rose, flushed, with angry evasive eyes.

'Funny ideas some people have,' he said. He
picked up his coat.

'*De gustibus*—as you remarked,' said Demarest.
His voice was cool, and he directed at Smith a
glance which he intended to be penetrating.

'What? . . .' Smith wavered, hoping for a
friendlier note on which to take his departure.
'Well, I guess I'll take a look at the dance before it
stops. Getting toward the end.'

He moved off sadly, sedately, as if in padded
slippers: quiet upholder of the conventions; modest efficient tool of society. *My Little Grey Home
in the West.* And now he was on his way to watch

Faubion—Faubion, who was wearing a blue mandarin cloak and nice little white silk pantaloons.
Delicious! Smith watching hungrily, brown eye
among the potted palm trees, wistfully, waiting.
Misery. Misery is creation. Misery is love. Misery is——

He opened the fat octavo again. A book so
massive, in a ship smoking-room, smacked of affec-
tation. Page 568. 'The spurging of a dead man's
eyes. And all since the evening star did rise . . .
A storm of rain, another of hail. We all must
home in the egg-shell sail' . . . The cokwold's
daunce would be more appropriate? *The cokwolds
lokyd yche on other*—how did it go. Gone. *My
Little Grey Home in the West.* His little grey head
on her breast. Blue mandarin breast . . . 'The
mast is made of a great pin, the tackle of cobweb,
the sail as thin——' Oh, I've got a pin and it
must go in . . . 'And if we go through, and not
fall in——' Imitating Middleton and Shakespeare: but he did it supremely well. And then
there were the moon-calves. Nymphs that smell
of ambergris. And the Epicoenes, that laugh and
lie down in moonshine. Where was that . . .
Page 616 . . . 'and stab with their poniards; you
do not know the delights of the Epicoenes in moonshine.'

Dripping dropping. Not raining so hard now.
The ship, in a gentle rain, on a rain-dark sea. The
dance had come to an end. Gooooood-night,
Ladies—— A Bass, two Basses, and a John
Collins . . . 'And when they have tasted the
springs of pleasure enough, and bill'd, and kist,
and are ready to come away; the shees only lay

certain eggs (for they are never with child there)
and of these eggs are disclosed a race of creatures
like men, but are indeed a sort of fowl, in part
covered with feathers (they call them VOLATEES)
that hop from island to island; you shall see a
covey of them presently . . .' Happy Epicoenes!
Too happy, happy Epicoenes! And what an exquisite solution of the problem! And what a light
it let in upon the dark soreness of that soul! The
same troubles then as now. The same troubles
always, world without end, Amen. Horror becomes poetry. Horror becomes—he must go and
say something friendly to old Smith. Yes. By
this time he was probably in his room. Nothing
about the quarrel, no reference, just a friendly remark. Ask him if he had anything to read? But
no! Was it necessary? It was Smith who had
transgressed. *Did you hear that, you people?*

They were still conscious of him, he could feel,
as he passed them—they were noting the peculiar
shape of his head, and the fat calf-bound octavo
awkward under his arm. Yahoos! Dabblers in
filth! He would show them! . . . But what
would he show them? . . . Nothing. Nothing at
all. They were foolish people, simple people, helpless people, like himself; in an analogous position,
as one of a homogeneous group, he too would join
in the throwing of stones. 'Have you read X's
last book? . . . The man's gone completely to
pot. I *never* read such tripe!' . . . All of us mur-
derers. *Single Stroke. Trembling.* Forgot, in the
excitement, to say good night to Malvolio . . .
The stewards in the dining-saloon were dragging
the long tables back to their places and screwing

them down. The pianist (pimply!) was lunging away forward, with his sheaf of dirty music. Cigarette ends in the palm-tree pots. The blade of a fan. A smell of face-powder. After the ball was over.

Smith, on the point of turning down his alley, waited for him, mournfully scratching his moustache.

'Well!' he said. 'You turning in too?'

'Yes, that damned poker-gang makes too much of a row.'

'They do, don't they. They say the fellow with the glass eye is a professional.'

'So I've heard.'

'Good man to keep away from, I guess. He looks like a tough customer . . . Hello! *Here* she comes!'

Mrs. Faubion bore down upon them, threateningly, with a tooth-brush in her hand. In the blue mandarin cloak. The ship, the long red carpet, pitched slowly downward toward the bow, and, laughing, she advanced with a little exaggerated run, stopping short with her face impudently close to Demarest's face, the tooth-brush flourishing in her lifted hand.

'Well!' she cried. 'Mr. Man! What would *you* like!'

He deliberated, diving delightedly into her delighted eyes.

'I'd like to bite you!' he said.

'Oh *would* you!' she said.

'Yes, and if you don't look out I will!'

She gave a little shriek of laughter, and darted down the alley that led to her stateroom. With one hand on the doorknob, she paused, put the tooth-brush to her lips, and blew him a kiss, extravagant and mocking.

'The same to you!' he cried, suiting the action to the word. They smiled at each other, for a moment, with fixed eyes. Then she vanished into her room, the door shutting softly.

'Good Lord!' moaned Smith. 'Why does she do that to *you?*'

'Yes, why?' laughed Demarest. 'Good night!'

'Good *night.*' His tone was brusque, and he turned on his heel almost angrily. This was the death of Smith! A triumph! . . . *Yes, why?* 142–156.

Yes, why? and again, yes, why? How delight-ful she had looked, the impudent little strumpet. Nothing epicene about Faubion. They call them VOLATEES. A little rougher again to-night. Creak-ing woodwork. That charging run of hers—a skilful improvisation. And holding her charming savage mouth so close, so startlingly close, to his! . . . He unhooked and lowered the tin wash-basin. A tepid trickle of water for the tooth-brush. She had been brushing her teeth: as now he brushed his, with lips quaintly arched and an overflow of blood-streaked foam. Round, and round, and round, in front. Back and forth, back and forth, at the sides. Scooping downward at the nicotine-strained tartar on the backs of the lower front ones. Over the grinding-surfaces of the molars—*ouch.* That cursèd ice-cream tooth. Must be a little crack in the filling . . . Nymphs that smell of ambergris; and the wholesome dew called rosmarine. He looked once again, once again, once again, with a

profound amused wonderment, with blank black
pupils, into his mirrored eyes. What an extraordinary-looking object he was, with pink ears,
animal hairs in his nose, and a blue mole on his
cheek! And was this monstrous object making
itself miserable for a—*female?* 'But Socrates, you
say these monsters are sometimes unhappy. Tell
me, will you, what it is that you mean by unhappiness? For, if I can believe you, these creatures
are endowed with reason; and as you will agree, a
truly reasonable being cannot know unhappiness
save as an attribute of the foolish . . .' *Te-thrum
te-thrum: te-thrum te-thrum.* Delightful, this hour
when the passengers were all gone to bed, and most
of the crew, and the whole ship became quiet,
absorbed, as if at last concentrated singly and solely
on the business of crossing an ocean! One became
aware of it—one heard the engines: the beating of
its lonely heart. One felt the frame quiver, saw
it change its shape even, became startlingly conscious of the fact that one was at sea; alone with
the infinite; alone with God. These rows of white
marshmallows on the ceiling—these little painted
bolts that held the ship together—these were one's
faith! But it all seemed ridiculous, unreal. What
was a ship? . . . What were human beings? . . .
What was a world? . . . Cynthia and himself were
a world . . . Misery. The whole thing was somebody's dream. The whole thing was a tiny twinkle,
a bursting bubble——

He turned out the electric light and crawled into
the bunk, sighing. Not a sound from the Irish
girl—she must be asleep. Cynthia—was she too
asleep? *Te-thrum te-thrum: te-thrum te-thrum.*

Yes, she was probably asleep. Or was she lying awake, anguished over the affair? Miserable over what she had done? really in love with him all the time? staring into the atomy darkness with eyes wide as the world? thinking of that time when—that time when—with a pongee dress—and a wide soft straw hat—with a floppy brim—English——

There was a soft footstep outside the door—it passed, then came back again—and then on the panel of the door something that sounded like a tiny knock, a knock as of one small knuckle. He lifted himself on straining elbows, the blood beating painfully in the side of his throat. Had he only imagined it—was it only the nocturnal creaking and knocking of the ship? *te-thrum te-thrum; te-thrum te-thrum.* He held his breath, concentrating all his attention, staring in the dark toward the suspected door, listening for the slightest sound. Suppose it was! Eagerly, softly, he withdrew himself from the pocket of ship-folded bed-clothes. And as his foot touched the coarse carpet, the knock was repeated, the turning knob gave a little creak, and the door began softly to open. Faubion.